THE I TATTI
RENAISSANCE LIBRARY

James Hankins, General Editor

ALBERTI

MOMUS

ITRL 8

LEON BATTISTA
ALBERTI
◆ ◆ ◆
MOMUS

ENGLISH TRANSLATION BY
SARAH KNIGHT

LATIN TEXT EDITED BY
VIRGINIA BROWN

AND

SARAH KNIGHT

THE I TATTI RENAISSANCE LIBRARY
HARVARD UNIVERSITY PRESS
CAMBRIDGE, MASSACHUSETTS
LONDON, ENGLAND
2003

Series design by Dean Bornstein

Library of Congress Cataloging-in-Publication Data

Alberti, Leon Battista, 1404–1472.
[Momus. English & Latin]
Momus / Leon Battista Alberti ; English translation by Sarah Knight ;
Latin text edited by Virginia Brown and Sarah Knight.
p. cm — (The I Tatti Renaissance library ; 8)
Includes bibliographical references (p.) and index.
ISBN 0-674-00754-9 (alk. paper)
1. State, The—Early works to 1800.   2. Political science—Early works to 1800.
I. Knight, Sarah.   II. Brown, Virginia, 1940–   III. Title.   IV. Series.
JC143.A5 M613 2003
320.1'01—dc21   2002038837

Contents

꿿꿿꿿

Introduction

꽃⟩꽃

Leon Battista Alberti's *Momus* is one of the great comic master-pieces of the Italian Renaissance. A complex narrative that charts the tumultuous career of Momus, god of fault-finding and the personification of embittered mockery, it has been variously read as an allegorical attack on the fifteenth century papacy, as a satire on Florentine humanists and statesmen, and as disguised auto-biography. It has been seen as foreshadowing the work of Ma-chiavelli, Erasmus, Rabelais, Cervantes and Swift. Yet it never achieved wide popularity, whether because of its unorthodox Latin style, its evidently unpolished state, or its cynicism it is difficult to say. Alberti wrote *Momus* between 1443 and 1450, after returning to Rome with the papal curia following the Council of Florence. For more than seventy years it circulated only in a handful of manuscript copies before being published in 1520 by two different editors. In the later sixteenth century it was translated into Italian and Spanish and in the eighteenth century into German. Al-though most of the printed editions and translations bear the subtitle *De Principe* ("On the Prince"), there is no evidence that this title goes back to Alberti himself.[1] Indeed, *Momus* subverts the conventions of the *speculum principis* ("mirror for princes") tra-dition. Rather than writing within one identifiable genre, Alberti causes mythology, literary fiction, political theory, philosophical dialectic and broad farce to jostle for primacy within this highly unusual work.

Momus is divided into four books, introduced by a preface. In the preface, addressing an anonymous dedicatee,[2] Alberti introduces the work's subject and briefly outlines his literary methods. His stated aim is to show how the prince must be elevated above other

men and unique. Alberti then defends his use of humor and irony, arguing that he wants to entertain as well as instruct. As the book opens, Jupiter has just created the world. He gives the Olympian gods a commission to create objects for use on earth. The other gods produce practical and pleasant designs, such as cows and houses, but we first meet Momus plotting to cause trouble with his offering. Momus criticizes the efforts of the other deities, and unleashes a plague of biting insects upon the world. Momus' duplicitous lover, the goddess Mischief, plots to have him exiled from Olympus, and tricks him into making treacherous statements about Jupiter's regime. Jupiter discovers Momus's disloyalty, and the other gods demand that he be punished. Fleeing from Olympus, Momus only narrowly escapes their wrath. He falls though a hole in the sky and lands in Italy. In revenge, he tells humans of the gods' immorality and wickedness. Aiming to infiltrate human society, he poses first as a poet, then as a philosopher to spread slanders against the gods and foment atheism.

Momus' successful attacks cause human worship of the gods to dwindle, and so the goddess Virtue is dispatched to appease him. Virtue arrives on earth, attended by her children Praise, Trophy and Triumph. She sets up headquarters in the temple of justice, where princes and heroes queue up to render homage to Virtue and her family. She meets Momus and assures him of her help, but he cannot stay out of mischief. His next two actions have catastrophic results. First, he changes into the sister of Thersites, a notoriously ugly girl but now suddenly beautified, and tells mortal women that his metamorphosis is the result of prayer. Momus wants humans to overwhelm the gods with prayers, forcing them to work, making them cantankerous, and causing trouble. Second, Momus breaks into the temple of justice, and rapes Praise, Virtue's daughter. The union of Praise and Blame instantly begets Rumor. Virtue's rival, Fortune, urges Hercules, Praise's suitor and Momus' enemy, to capture Rumor. Rumor flies up to heaven,

dragging Hercules with her and depositing him in the house of Mars. A group of humans invade Virtue's temple and cause the goddess and her offspring to scatter. Momus looks on enraged.

Book II opens with a description of how the practice of prayer is increasing on earth, and how warmly the Olympians welcome this renewed attention. Jupiter realizes how instrumental Momus has been in promoting prayer. He sends Pallas and Minerva to earth to recall him from exile and disgrace. When the increasingly paranoid Momus meets the embassy, both sides are equally suspicious, but Momus nonetheless agrees to return to heaven. He decides that he will dissemble there, feigning simplicity and kindness to insinuate himself into Jupiter's favor. Restored to heaven, he prostrates himself before Jupiter. Momus tells the story of his trials on earth, causing great merriment among the gods. Then Juno bursts into Jupiter's house. She laments the votive offerings that clutter up her palace, and warns Jupiter of Momus' duplicity. Momus asks Mercury why the gods are so bothered by human prayer, and Mercury replies that mortals have started to pray selfishly and wickedly. The physical manifestation of these prayers on Olympus is a filthy blockage, which prevents the gods from moving freely around their homes. Meanwhile, Jupiter and Juno establish an uneasy truce. Jupiter asks the other gods, particularly Momus, to dine with him.

Momus continues to recount his terrestrial adventures. Listing the different mortal jobs he tried—craftsman, soldier, king—he explains that nothing satisfied him until he discovered the career of the beggar. Momus argues that beggars have no business concerns, no troublesome political or social affiliations, and no need for possessions; they lack all responsibility and can travel freely. Momus' ironic wit earns Jupiter's favor, and as a result the other gods also start to cultivate Momus' friendship. Hercules invites all the gods to a banquet. Momus starts to tire of being treated like a mere entertainer, and only grudgingly continues his stories. He

scares the Olympians with tales of widespread atheism, and tells of how certain unscrupulous individuals manipulate popular religious sentiment. Hercules springs to the defense of his fellow humans, urging the gods to regard Momus' stories with skepticism. Momus and Hercules are about to fight when a loud crash interrupts their squabble. Juno has built a bronze arch loaded with all of the golden offerings she has received, but because of its shoddy construction the arch buckles immediately under its own weight. Jupiter lambastes the folly of women, and laments the burden of kingship. He criticises the gods for their squabbling and humans for their demands and greed. He decides to destroy the flawed world and rebuild it. Momus congratulates himself on the success of his plan to sow discord, but his delight does not last long, for Mischief hints that she has transferred her affections to Hercules. Mischief and Momus fence in a match of guile and insinuation, and eventually Momus storms off.

At the start of Book III, the gods debate whether or not a new world should be constructed. Juno, Hercules, Bacchus, Venus, Folly and Mars support the survival of humans, since Juno and Mars in particular are relying on human offerings to support their various building projects. Momus decides to become Jupiter's political advisor, and plans to give him the notebooks he compiled while among the philosophers on earth. The notebooks are full of advice for kings and insight into politics. The gods advise Jupiter to consult human philosophers about his new enterprise. Jupiter takes the books from Momus, throws them down unread, and travels to earth. First, he enters the Platonic Academy, but Plato himself is absent. Jupiter's paranoia causes him to fear that humans have discovered his true identity, and so he runs away. Next, he meets the Cynic philosopher Diogenes, whose hostility causes Jupiter to boast defensively. Realizing his interlocutor's identity, Diogenes yells that other humans should demand sunshine from the king of the gods. Jupiter escapes, and comes across Demo-

critus, another philosopher, who sits in a ditch dissecting animals. He too offends Jupiter, who decides to return to heaven. Before he can escape, Jupiter overhears still more people within an enclosed garden arguing about the existence of the gods.

Back in heaven, Jupiter still desires to hear philosophical opinions, but he does not risk his kingly self again. Instead, he sends Mercury to earth. Mercury meets Socrates and Diogenes: Socratic dialectic forces Mercury to reveal Jupiter's plans, and then Diogenes beats the unfortunate god with a club. Mercury returns to heaven violently cursing philosophers. The different factions on Olympus start to argue more bitterly. In despair, Jupiter sends for Apollo, who, like everyone else, suggests consulting human philosophers for advice. Jupiter encourages him to travel to earth. He consults Apollo's oracle, but its answers are inconclusive, and Apollo's exegetical sophistry does not clarify the oracle's pronouncements. Apollo departs for earth, but promises to return by the Kalends of the month, when Jupiter has convened the divine assembly.

The Kalends come, and Apollo is still absent. Jupiter panics and hides. Finally, facing the assembly he plays for time with an elaborate speech of vague statements. Momus enters the assembly, eager to advocate universal renewal. He faces the other Olympians' hostility, for they are impatient with Jupiter's lack of resolution, and resent Momus as Jupiter's representative. Several gods address the assembly in turn, but the speeches of Saturn, Cybele, Neptune, Mars, Pluto, Hercules, and Venus contribute little apart from rhetorical bombast and blatant self-interest. Previously, Pallas and Juno have conspired to overthrow Momus. In her speech, Pallas deliberately provokes chaos in the assembly. Momus attempts to quell the tumult, but his oration contains both misguided misogyny and a comparison of the noble Olympians to a debauched rabble of drunks, and unsurprisingly provokes outrage. Mischief flies to Juno, tells her what Momus has said, and urges

her to subdue him. Calling the Olympian matrons and Hercules to arms, Juno persuades them to drag Momus out of the assembly. They castrate him and throw his genitals into the sea.

Fearing the mob's frenzy, Jupiter overlooks the assault. Meanwhile, Apollo returns from earth. While he speaks to the other gods, the goddess Night secretly steals his purse of oracular sayings. Apollo endures Jupiter's reproaches for his lateness, and then describes his encounters with Democritus and Socrates, praising them fulsomely. However, when he discovers his purse has been stolen, Apollo immediately blames Socrates. Jupiter's admiration for the philosophers is undiminished, and he calms the furious Apollo. In the meantime, Heat, Hunger, Fever and other blights have heard of Jupiter's plans to destroy and rebuild the world. They decide to get a head start on their task of mass destruction, and so humankind responds to their attacks by increasing its votive offerings. Mortals decide to hold games and spectacles in honor of the gods, and decorate the city most sumptuously. Dazzled by this show of veneration, the Olympians decide not to wreck creation after all, and humans become their favorites. Jupiter decrees that because of his plots against humanity, Momus should be chained forever to a rock jutting out of the sea.

At the start of the fourth book, the gods search for the best seats in heaven so as to watch humans prepare for the games on earth. The minor deities of the sea comfort Momus. He sighs in despair, and his sigh becomes a thick black cloud. He asks the sea nymphs to stretch this cloud over the sky, to prevent the gods from gloating over his fate. The nymphs obey, and the cloud prevents the gods from watching activities on earth, which was Momus' real intention. Thwarted, the gods long to view the spectacle more closely, and so they descend to earth and enter the theater. The god Stupor suggests that they take the place of their own effigies that decorate the theater. Stupor hides his statue in a

wood, and the other deities rush to hide their statues in appropriate places. While the gods position themselves in the theater, some bandits kidnap a philosopher-actor named Oenops, who was on his way to the games, and keep him prisoner in the wood. They prepare to torture him, so Oenops, hitherto an atheist, prays desperately. One of the bandits sees the statue of Stupor, which terrifies him, and all of the bandits flee. Oenops instantly becomes a religious convert. He returns to his fellow actors and praises the gods. The actors clamor to know which god caused Oenops's conversion, and when he prostrates himself at the feet of Stupor in the theater, they laugh.

While all of this is taking place on earth, in the underworld Charon, ferryman of the dead, contemplates a trip to earth before its destruction. As his guide, he enlists Gelastus, a dead philosopher who cannot afford the fare to cross the River Styx. Charon and Gelastus set out for earth. They arrive in a flower-filled meadow, and the beauty of nature overwhelms Charon. On their journey, the two companions discuss many subjects, including human vanity, folly, and expertise. Gelastus tries to explain various philosophical doctrines to Charon, but ends up confusing himself and bewildering the skeptical ferryman. Charon tells him that when mankind was first created, deceitful people quickly learned to wear masks to conceal their true personalities. As they talk, Charon and Gelastus arrive at the theater. Oenops and the actors hide from view, but shout abuse from their hiding places. Charon and Gelastus flee in fright. Disguised as their own statues, the gods look on and laugh at the sight. This divine laughter unsettles Gelastus and Charon further, and so they decide to return to the underworld.

Setting out on the high seas, they see a ship, but realize that it belongs to pirates. They make for dry land, and hide. The pirates follow, not in pursuit but rather to carouse and visit the local

baths. As Charon and Gelastus watch, a mutiny is staged to kill the pirate king and replace him with a camp-follower. The pirates soon depart, and Charon and Gelastus continue their voyage. A storm blows up, and again the two sailors are forced to find land. They espy the rock to which Momus is chained, and sail towards it. The storm is the direct result of the laughter of the gods in the theater. The laughter causes Aeolus, god of the winds, to leave his cave to investigate. The winds, incited by the wild narrative of Rumor, also break out of their prison cave, eager to know what is happening. They rush to the theater and wreck it, causing consternation among the gods still hiding there. Jupiter, Cupid, Hope, Pluto and Night are damaged as the winds toss their statues all over the place. Apollo discovers that Night has stolen his bag of fortunes, and swears revenge. A gang of pimps blind and rob Pluto. The winds leave the scene of their crime, and make for the sea. Their bickering provokes the storm that drives Charon and Gelastus to Momus' rock. Gelastus and Momus recognize one another from philosophical discussions they held when Momus first fell to earth. They exchange accounts of their misfortunes. Neptune descends from Olympus, and calms the sea, explaining what has befallen the Olympians. Charon and Gelastus set out once again for the underworld. While floating in an underground cave, Charon relates a debate between King Megalophos and his herald Peniplusius, in which the latter argues that he is happier in his humble role than the king with his royal power.

Back on Olympus, Jupiter laments his troubles and berates himself for the recent catastrophe the gods faced in the theater. While tidying up his palace, he stumbles upon the notebooks Momus once gave to him. Jupiter regretfully realizes that he should have read them much earlier, for the books are full of valuable advice on government. The final section recommends how the prince should distribute good, evil, and the morally neutral to his subjects. He should distribute good and evil to those who actively

seek them, but place Fortune in charge of neutral things such as riches and honors.

Battista Alberti was born in Genoa in 1404, the illegitimate son of a banker father. Alberti only took the forename Leone later in life. His family had been exiled from their native Florence at the end of the fourteenth century. He studied at Padua from 1415 to 1418 under the humanist Gasparino Barzizza, learning both Latin and Greek. Alberti went on to study canon law at Bologna until 1428, and at university he wrote his first Latin work, the comedy *Philodoxeos* (1424). Over the next few years, he wrote the treatise *De commodis litterarum atque incommodis* ("On the Utility and Disadvantages of the Study of Letters," 1428–29). He also wrote his first Italian works, including the two prose dialogues *Deiphira* and *Ecatonfilea*, which dramatise the vicissitudes of love. Around 1430, he wrote the first of the *Intercenales* or "Dinner Pieces," a collection of satirical and philosophical dialogues which he would go on to augment and embellish over the next two decades.

In 1428, Pope Martin V revoked the exile of the Alberti family from Florence, and Leon Battista embarked on an ecclesiastical career. He entered the papal curia in 1431 as Latin secretary to Biagio Molin, patriarch of Grado. Alberti took holy orders, and in 1432 Pope Eugenius IV gave him the living of San Martino a Gangalandi, near to Florence. Biagio Molin commissioned a hagiographical work from him, the *Vita S. Potiti* ("Life of St. Potitus"), the story of a boy martyr, which Alberti wrote in 1433. Between 1432 to 1434, he also composed three books of his first major vernacular work, *Della famiglia* ("On the Family"). Book I deals with education, Book II with creating and maintaining a happy family, and Book III with domestic economy. During the same period, Alberti developed his interests in architecture and optics. In 1434, he left Rome to travel to Florence with the Curia and attended the ecumenical council convened in Ferrara by

Eugenius IV in 1437. It was in Ferrara that he first became acquainted with members of the ruling Este dynasty, later to be his patrons. The council, which in 1438 transferred to Florence, proved an important venue for the transmission of Greek culture to the Latin West.

In Florence, alongside his ecclesiastical and administrative duties, Alberti associated with many of the important artists of the day. He numbered Brunelleschi, Ghiberti, Donatello and Masaccio among his acquaintance. The artistic milieu in which Alberti moved during these years partially inspired *De pictura* ("On Painting"), perhaps his best-known work, written in Latin in 1435. Alberti translated the treatise into Italian in 1436. The *De pictura* was dedicated to Giovanni Francesco Gonzaga, Duke of Mantua, and the *Della pittura* to Brunelleschi. *De pictura*, a humanistic program for pictorial art rather than a strictly technical treatise, nonetheless gives insight into contemporary artistic practice, describing, for example, recent experiments in perspective. During the early 1440s in Florence, Alberti wrote copiously in Latin and the vernacular on diverse subjects. In Italian, he added a fourth book, on friendship, to *Della famiglia*, and wrote two moral dialogues, the *Teogenio*, dedicated to Leonello d'Este, and the *Profugiorum ab aerumnis liber* ("Escapes from Hardship"). In Latin, in 1437 alone, he produced a treatise *De iure* ("On Right"), a work on the episcopacy *(Pontifex)*, a short autobiography, and one hundred *Apologi*, modelled on the fables of Aesop. He also wrote two works on love and marriage, *Sofrona* and *Uxoria*.

In 1441, with the help of Piero de'Medici, Alberti organized a poetry competition, the so-called *Certame coronario*. Contestants had to write a vernacular poem on the subject of friendship, and Alberti himself composed Italian verse in honor of the occasion. During the same year, he wrote a treatise on horse-training, *De equo animante* ("On Horse-Training"), which he also dedicated to Leonello d'Este. During these last years in Florence, Alberti wrote

books hastens his political failure. Throughout the satire, Alberti depicts human and divine government as hazardous, confused and arbitrary, and frequently bungled as a result of greed, vanity and inept diplomacy.

Alongside Alberti's political analyses, *Momus* is also underpinned by its author's lifelong interest in the function and value of architecture and the visual arts. *Momus* is a story of creation, and when this creation proves flawed, Jupiter the ultimate architect undertakes the ultimate design project of universal renewal. Aesthetics and architecture, the function of design and its decorative appeals are constantly debated both on earth and in heaven. In Book I, we first encounter the Olympian gods engaged in a design contest, competitively crafting objects to impress Jupiter, so that he can place them in his doll's house, the earth. In Book II, the gods delight in using the gold from votive offerings to decorate their palaces, and in the third book, they gaze in rapture at the grand architecture of the theater in which they will suffer bitter humiliation at the end of *Momus*. One architectural historian has suggested that Alberti's involvement with Nicholas' building projects prompted him to write an extended mockery of architectural grandeur.[6] Certainly the pitfalls of constructing *grands projets* are illustrated throughout *Momus*.

Alberti's discussion of artifice dovetails with his exploration of spectacle and performance. Acting and illusion are central to a work in which everyone continually dissimulates. Alberti's characters play roles and conceal their purposes beneath façades of misleading rhetoric and deceit. Momus himself performs as a Mittyesque sequence of characters. Within the main narrative and also through his own boastful accounts, the reader watches Momus assume a series of roles: poet, philosopher, courtier, soldier, jester, ivy on a temple wall, beggar, and, perhaps most memorably, sister of Thersites, Homer's brutish malcontent. Alberti repeatedly uses the word *persona* ("mask" or "personality") to un-

derline the false, theatrical behavior of his characters. Theater and masking are central to Alberti's satire of political and social behavior.[7] In Book IV, the extended climax of *Momus* occurs in an urban theater where the gods act as their own effigies. The infernal ferryman Charon's cynical attitude towards humans rests on his observation that many people literally wear masks to deceive and beguile others, and that only the rivers of the underworld can remove these masks.

Critics have attempted to read *Momus* biographically as a humanist *roman-à-clef*, wishing to peel the masks away from Alberti's human and divine characters. Detective efforts have centered on the two main characters of the satire, Jupiter and Momus. Jupiter has been interpreted as a symbol of the mid-Quattrocento papal administration Alberti knew so intimately, and the policies and personalities of two popes in particular have been mapped onto the satire. Jupiter's crowd-pleasing tendencies and courting of popular approval have been read as a mockery of the ecumenical ambitions of Eugenius IV (1431–1447). The doomed arch Juno constructs and the elaborate palaces built on Olympus, as well as a zeal for public architecture such as theatres and temples, have led other scholars to see Jupiter as Nicholas V (1447–55). As well as seeking possible historical equivalents for Alberti's Jupiter, scholars have also tried to pinpoint the origins of Momus himself.

Two of Alberti's contemporaries have been suggested as prototypes for the irascible god, Bartolomeo Fazio (1400–57) and Francesco Filelfo (1398–1481). On the title-page of one of the manuscripts collated for this edition, an anonymous exegete went as far as to write *Bartholomaei Facii Historia* ("The Story of Bartolomeo Fazio") as a subtitle. Fazio was a pupil of Guarino of Verona, on whose translation of Lucian Alberti's *Musca* was based. Filelfo studied under Barzizza at Padua at the same time as Alberti. A particular episode early in Alberti's satire prompted Filelfo to write to his former classmate to ask whether Momus represented

him: Filelfo once had his beard torn by assailants, just as Momus does in the first book. A wit, political advisor, chameleonic actor, and malcontent, Alberti's anti-hero is both energetically conceived and multi-layered, yet ultimately he remains an enigmatic and elusive figure.

However intriguing it may be to map its characters and situations onto Alberti's social and intellectual milieu, such an enterprise remains conjectural. Whether or not historical characters and situations lie beneath the work, in his preface Alberti states that his foremost wish was to entertain and divert. He expansively urges his reader to "read on, above all to enjoy yourself." Despite this exhortation, however, the harshness of Alberti's satire has prompted recent scholars to interpret *Momus* as the dark and mordant work of a cynical man. Read thus, *Momus* might be seen to add a pessimistic dimension to Burckhardt's famous portrait of Alberti as model polymath humanist and *uomo universale*.[8] Even if the darkness of the satire stems from literary ancestors and satirical purpose rather than from personal circumstances, one cannot deny that as fiction *Momus* is both sardonic and detached.

Perhaps we can most fully appreciate *Momus* by taking its author's advice and reading the work *quasi per ironiam*. Ironic enjoyment, in Alberti as in Lucian, is satirical rather than jolly, provoked by frailty, incompetence and pretension. This sharp, mocking enjoyment prompted some of the finest satire of the Renaissance. A keen sense of irony pervades Erasmus' *Praise of Folly*, More's *Utopia*, the irreverent brilliance of Rabelais, the wry musings of Montaigne, the humorous observations of Robert Burton, and the mock-heroic wit of Cervantes. Alberti wrote *Momus* in the century before the earliest of these satires were published, heralding one of the dominant literary trends of the sixteenth century. We might read *Momus* as political allegory, witty fable, variation on a theme found in classical mythology, cluster of humanist in-jokes, or serious philosophical exploration, but ultimately and per-

haps most importantly the satire illustrates its author's avowed wish to produce a "new and unexpected sort of writing."

Sarah Knight would like to thank Professor David Quint for his suggestion that she undertake the project, and for his ongoing encouragement and valuable criticism. Work on *Momus* benefitted greatly from the intellectual generosity and meticulous advice of Professor George Hunter and Professor Lawrence Manley. Early discussions with Professor Robert Babcock, Dr. Jill Kraye and Professor David Marsh also proved most constructive. Expertise and help of various kinds were unstintingly provided by Lindsay Allen, Katy Cawkwell, Clay Dean, Sasha Dugdale, the Knight family, Kate Lancaster and Marc Lempérière, Tamsin and Ian Miller, Shanna Perkins, Susan Rogers and Sarah Wall.

NOTES

1. In one of the two early manuscripts corrected by Alberti (P: see "Note on the Text," below) a hand of the later Quattrocento (not the scribe) has written "Liber qui de regno dicitur Momus, compositus a domino Battista de Albertis", i.e. "The Book on Kingship called the Momus, composed by Lord Battista degli Alberti." But there is no independent evidence that this subtitle was intended by Alberti himself. See Michel Paoli, "À propos des manuscrits parisiens du *Momus* et de la *Cena familiaris* signalés par Mazzuchelli," *Albertiana* 2 (1999), pp. 280–283 at p. 282. The subtitle "De principe," "On the Prince," found in all modern editions of the *Momus*, first appears in the late fifteenth-century Vatican manuscript (O) and in the Guillery edition of 1520.

2. The dedicatee of *Momus* is anonymous. Leonello d'Este, ruler of Ferrara from 1440 to 1450, has been suggested as a possible dedicatee. Alberti also dedicated to Leonello his comedy *Philodoxeos* (written in 1424, revised 1437), the Italian dialogue *Theogenius* (1441) and a treatise on the horse, *De equo animante* (ca. 1444).

3. See Marsh, "Alberti's *Momus*" and *Lucian and the Latins* for discussions of Lucian's influence on *Momus* and the *Intercenales*.

4. John F. D'Amico has written a panoramic account of archaism and Apuleianism in late fifteenth- and early sixteenth-century Latin, "The Progress of Renaissance Latin Prose: The Case of Apuleianism," *Renaissance Quarterly* 37 (1984), pp. 351–392. For Alberti's specific debts to Apuleius, see David Marsh's "Alberti and Apuleius: Comic Violence and Vehemence in the *Intercenales* and *Momus*," in Furlan, *Leon Battista Alberti*, pp. 405–427. Plautus and Terence were also archaising influences on Alberti's style; see Lucia Cesarini Martinelli's edition of the *Philodoxeos fabula* in *Rinascimento*, ser. 2, 17 (1977), pp. 111–234.

5. See Alberto Borghini, "Un'altra probabile fonte del *Momo* di L. B. Alberti: Esopo," *Rivista di letteratura italiana* 5 (1987), pp. 455–466.

6. See Tafuri, "Cives esse non licere." Tafuri argues (p. 69) that it is "possible — as has often been stated — that the Jove in *Momus* represents Pope Eugene IV (though there is no reason to think that he could not have come to represent Nicholas V over the course of the writing)."

7. See Cesarini Martinelli, "Metafore teatrali," for Alberti's use of theater.

8. See, for example, Eugenio Garin, "Studi su L. B. Alberti."

MOMUS

Prooemium

❧❦❧

1 Principem opificemque rerum, Optimum et Maximum Deum, cum pleraque omnia admiratione dignissima ita distribuisset rebus a oe procreatis ut singulis quota aliqua praestantissimarum divinarumque laudum obveniret, illud praesertim sibi servasse palam et in promptu est, ut voluerit unicus admodum solusque plena et integra esse divinitate accumulatissimus. Nam cum vim astris, nitorem caelo, orbi terrarum pulchritudinem, rationem vero atque immortalitatem animis et huiusmodi mirifica omnia rebus singulis quasi viritim impertiens adegisset, voluit ipse esse unus tota et integra confertus counitusque[1] virtute, cui penitus parem non invenias. Quae res quidem omnium esse prima in divinitate, ni fallimur, censenda est, ut sit unice unus, unice solus.

2 Hinc fit ut rara omnia, quae a ceterorum similitudine segregentur, quasi divina esse vetere hominum opinione existimentur. Namque et monstra, portenta ostentave et huiusmodi, quod rara evenerint, deorum religioni apud veteres adiudicabantur. Tum et natura rerum maxima et invisa quaeque ita cum raritate coniunxisse a vetere hominum memoria in hanc usque diem observatum est, ut elegans grandeque nihil effingere, nisi id quoque sit rarum, novisse videatur. Hinc fortassis illud est quod si quos praestare ingenio et prae ceteris eo a multitudine deflectere animadvertimus, ut sint illi quidem suo in laudis genere singulares ac perinde rari, hos divinos nuncupemus proximeque ad deos admiratione et honoribus prosequamur natura edocti. Qua nimirum intellegimus rara eo sapere omnia divinitatem, quo illuc tendant, ut unica atque egregie sola a ceterorumque coetu et numero segregata habeantur.

Preface

The prince and maker of creation, Best and Greatest God, has   1
distributed all things most worthy of admiration to his creatures
in such a way that each one might be allotted some portion of the
praises due to divine excellence. Yet it is perfectly obvious that he
wanted to keep uniquely for himself alone the fullest abundance of
undiminished divinity. He bestowed power on the stars, radiance
on the sky, beauty on the world, reason and immortality on souls,
allotting marvellous gifts individually to each being, but he wanted
to be the only one possessed of an undimished, perfect and con-
centrated virtue whose equal you may never find. This uniqueness,
unless I am mistaken, must be deemed the primary characteristic
of divinity. Only God is uniquely one and uniquely set apart from
all else.

Hence it was that all things rare and unique were regarded by   2
the ancients as practically divine. Antiquity attributed freakish
events, omens, portents and the like to the agency of gods simply because they occurred rarely. From the beginnings of human
memory down to the present day people have noticed that Nature
seems always to have marked the greatest and the strangest things
with this same rarity. She seems not to know how to form things
elegantly and on a grand scale without their also being rare. Hence
too, perhaps, our tendency to label some people as divine when we
notice them excelling the rest in genius and turning aside from the
crowd, becoming exceptional and thus rare. Nature teaches us to
hold such persons in honor and admire them as nearly godlike.
The same Nature makes us understand that all things rare have a
taste of divinity insofar as they incline towards the godlike, and so
may be considered unique and truly exceptional, worth separating
off from numbering and association with other things.

3   Possem et multa repetere nullam ob gratiam habita in pretio, nisi quod unica sint. Quid, ut cetera omittam, quam multa sunt apud veteres scriptores quae probentur, si esse vulgata et trita videantur? Aut quid erit illud quod non maxima cum voluptate admirationeque legatur, si erit eiusmodi ut a ceteris non dico neglectum et explosum, sed parum praevisum parumque perceptum intellegatur, ut scriptoris officium deputem nihil sibi ad scribendum desumere quod ipsum non sit his qui legerint incognitum atque incogitatum?

4   Quae cum ita sint, non me tamen fugit quam difficillimum ac prope impossibile sit aliquid adducere in medium quod ipsum non a plerisque ex tam infinito scriptorum numero tractatum deprehensumque exstiterit. Vetus proverbium: nihil dictum quin prius dictum. Quare sic statuo, fore ut ex raro hominum genere putandus sit, quisquis ille fuerit, qui res novas, inauditas et praeter omnium opinionem et spem in medium attulerit. Proximus huic erit is qui cognitas et communes fortassis res novo quodam et insperato scribendi genere tractarit. Itaque sic deputo, nam si dabitur quispiam olim qui cum legentes ad frugem vitae melioris instruat atque instituat dictorum gravitate rerumque dignitate varia et eleganti, idemque una risu illectet, iocis delectet, voluptate detineat, quod apud Latinos qui adhuc fecerint nondum satis exstitere, hunc profecto[2] inter plebeios minime censendum esse.

5   Cuperem in me tantum esset ingenii, quantum in hac una re, procul dubio difficili assequenda, adhibui studii et diligentiae. Nam fortassis essem assecutus ut apertius intellegeres versari me in quodam philosophandi genere minime aspernando. Et didici quidem ipsa ex re quantum industriae debeatur ubi te studeas esse

I could enumerate many things that have been thought valuable   3
simply because they were unique. To put other cases aside, how
many works by ancient writers, do you suppose, would win approval if they left an impression of banality and the commonplace?
On the other hand, what will not be read with the greatest pleasure and admiration if it is understood to belong to the class of
things that are unpredictable and difficult, not to say neglected
and jeered at by the rest? So I think it is the duty of the writer to
undertake to write nothing that his prospective readers will find
familiar and obvious.

This being so, it still does not escape me just how difficult and   4
almost impossible it is to introduce an idea that has not already
been discovered and handled by a good many out of so infinite a
swarm of writers. Think of the old proverb: nothing is said which
has not previously been said.[1] For this reason it is my considered
opinion that the man who introduces new, unheard-of, and unorthodox material, whoever he happens to be, should be considered
a member of this rare genus of humankind. Next to this sort of
writer will rank the one who uses an original and surprising literary genre to treat known and common ideas. So I would lay it
down that, if we shall ever be granted someone who equips his
readers to enjoy a better life, instructing them with weighty sayings and varied and choice material, while at the same time charming them with laughter, pleasing them with jokes, and diverting
them with pleasure — a thing which among Latin authors has not
hitherto happened often enough — then I think this author should
certainly not be ranked with common, ordinary writers.

I wish I had enough wit to apply my zeal and effort to this one   5
objective, which is beyond doubt a difficult one to achieve. Possibly I should then succeed in making you understand more clearly
that I am turning my hand to a philosophical genre of a sort, and
one by no means to be despised. Indeed I have learned from this
same endeavor how much effort it requires when you take pains to

quovis pacto dissimilem ceteris dignitate et gravitate servata. Sin vero ad te susceperis ita scribere, ut in rebus gravissimis tractandis nusquam a risu iocoque discedas, cum insueto tum et digno et liberali, profecto illic plus laboris et difficultatis invenies quam inexperti opinentur. Etenim sunt qui dum huic uni, de qua loquimur, raritati intendunt, etsi ea dicant quae admodum vulgata et plebeia sunt, eadem tamen quadam severitatis sumpta persona ita proferunt ut dignissimi laude habeantur. Nos contra elaboravimus ut qui nos legant rideant, aliaque ex parte sentiant se versari in rerum pervestigatione atque explicatione utili et minime aspernanda. Id quantum assecuti simus tuum erit iudicium ubi nos legeris. Quod si senseris nostra hac scribendi comitate et festivitate maximarum rerum severitatem quasi condimento aliquo redditam esse lepidiorem et suaviorem, leges, ni fallor, maiore cum voluptate.

6   Sed non erit ab re instituti nostri rationem eo explicare, quo cum operis comprehensio fiat clarior, tum me purgem cur deos introduxerim et quasi poetarum licentia in scribenda historia abusus sim. Nam veteres quidem scriptores ita philosophari solitos animadverti ut deorum nominibus eas animi vires intellegi voluerint, quibus in hanc aut in alteram institutorum partem agimur.[3] Ea de re Plutonem, Venerem, Martem et caecum Cupidinem, et contra Palladem, Iovem, Herculem huiusmodique deos introduxere: quorum hi cupiditatum voluptatumque illecebras atque labem, concitatosque impetus ac furores, hi vero mentis robur consiliique vim significant, quibus animi aut virtute imbuuntur rationeque morantur,[4] aut interea de se male merentur, prava inconsiderataque agendo et meditando. Itaque cum sit in hominum animis perassi-

be different from the rest, by whatever means, while maintaining dignity and seriousness. But if you take it upon yourself to write in this way, that is, to preserve a humorous tone even when you're dealing with high and serious matters — to be original besides being well bred — you will surely find that this involves more labor and difficulty than the uninitiated might imagine. And indeed there are those who, while aiming at this unique rarity of which I speak, say things that are rather banal and commonplace, presenting them, however, behind a mask of high seriousness, in order to be thought praiseworthy. I, on the other hand, have worked hard to make my readers laugh, but also to make them feel they are involved in a thorough inquiry into, and a worthwhile explication of, real life. How far I have achieved my aim is yours to decide when you read my work. If you feel that serious and important subjects have been rendered more amusing and pleasant when seasoned with this elegant and playful style of mine, then you will read it with greater pleasure, if I mistake not.

But it will not lead us astray to explain the rationale behind my 6 undertaking, so as to make the work clearer and more comprehensible. Let me justify, too, my reasons for introducing gods and why I have taken advantage of poetic license while writing a story in prose. I noticed that the ancient writers used to philosophize this way: by the names of gods they wished their readers to understand those mental qualities which compel us towards one or another course of action. For this purpose they used Pluto, Venus, Mars, and blind Cupid, and on the other side Pallas, Jove, Hercules, and gods like that. The former group represents the attractions and defects of desires and pleasures, arousal and frenzy, while the latter represents the strength of mind and power of deliberation by which our rational souls are steeped in virtue or checked by reason — or at times behave unworthily, scheming and doing corrupt, heedless things.[2] Consequently, since there is usually a relentless and arduous conflict between these qualities in the

dua difficilisque istorum concertatio, nimirum sunt dii quales esse et Homerus et Pindarus[5] et Sophocles et optimi poetarum introduxere in scaenam. Sed de his alius erit tractandi locus, si quando de sacris et diis conscribemus.

7   Hos[6] igitur poetas imitati, cum de principe, qui veluti mens et animus universum reipublicae corpus moderatur, scribere adoriremur, deos suscepimus, quibus et cupidos et iracundos et voluptuosos, indoctos, leves suspiciososque, contra item graves, maturos, constantes, agentes, sollertes, studiosos ac frugi notarem, quasi per ironiam, quales futuri sint in vitae cursu et rerum successu, dum aut hanc aut alteram vitam inierint, quid laudis aut vituperii, quid gloriae aut ignominiae, quid firmitatis in republica aut eversionis fortunae, dignitatis maiestatisque subsequatur; ut his quatuor libris, ni[7] me laboris mei amor decipit, cum nonnulla comperias quae ad optimum principem formandum spectent, tum etiam non paucissima sese offerant quae ad dinoscendos mores pertinent eorum qui principem sectantur: ni forte illud desit, quod assentatorem, quo principum aulae refertae sunt, praetermiserim consulto. Nam illum quidem veteres poetae, praesertim comici, abunde explicarunt.

8   Tum a me[8] tantum abest ut possim quae assentatoris sunt ut interdum me redarguendum praebeam, quod meritas[9] et locis debitas dignissimorum laudes omittam, ne mihi ipse videar id genus hominum voluisse ulla ex parte imitari, quos penitus oderim. Qui error nunc mihi habetur tecum. Nam quis est qui in[10] prooemiis scribendis non blandiatur, non applaudere gestiat his ad quos scribat, ut fictis etiam collaudationibus vetere et praescripta[11] prooemiorum lege rem ornare ad decus ducant? Ego nudum prooe-

souls of men, it is no surprise that Homer, Pindar, Sophocles and the best poets ushered them onto the stage as if they were gods. But there will be another opportunity for discussing these matters, if ever I come to write of sacred matters and gods.

As I am undertaking to write of the prince, who governs the 7 entire body politic like a mind and rational soul,[3] I have employed the gods, therefore, in imitation of the poets. Using the names of gods, I have designated (as it were ironically) characters that are grasping and wrathful, pleasure-seeking, uneducated, frivolous and suspicious; and on the other hand characters that are serious, mature, steadfast, active, clever, painstaking and thrifty. I have shown what sort of men they will become on their life's journey and in the course of their affairs, depending on whether they enter upon one or another kind of life, and [by extension], what praise or blame, glory or notoriety, what political stability or overturning of fortune, rank and authority follows [upon their choice of life]. Unless love for my own work deceives me, in these four books you will find not only a number of ideas which have in view the shaping of the best sort of prince. I also include not a few things which pertain to analyzing the behavior of the prince's entourage. Perhaps you will miss the flatterers who crowd the palaces of princes, but I deliberately left them out, since the ancient poets, especially the comedians, describe them copiously.

I am so unable myself to act like a flatterer that occasionally I 8 will lay myself open to criticism for having left out worthy and apposite opportunities for praise of deserving persons. I do this to avoid the appearance of imitating in any way the kind of man I thoroughly detest. Whether this is a mistake on my part I leave to you to decide. For who does not pay compliments when writing a preface? Who does not try to applaud his dedicatees, so that in accordance with the ancient and prescribed law of prefaces, they induce him to embellish decorously his theme with fictional blandishments? I have presented you with a bare preface, and I have

mium attuli, tuisque tantis tamque maximis ex virtutibus nullam recensui, et feci quod qui te meque norunt non vituperabunt. Nam et tu ex te id agis ut tua sese virtus, fama et celebritate, per omnium aures et ora mirifice efferat posteritatisque fructum accumulatissime consequatur: ergo aliorum ope in ea re non indiges. Ego vero, quoad in me sit, tua et dicta et facta observans et colligens malo te totis voluminibus amplecti atque cupidis litterarum commendare, ut habeant quem egregie imitentur, quam levi (ut ita loquar) congratulatione permulcere.

9   Sed de his hactenus. Ceterum cum tu[12] nos per otium legeris et tibi inter legendum res ex desiderio meo, tua pro expectatione, successerit, totiens congratulabimur quotiens incideris ut rideas. Et utinam tam saepe eveniat ut sales et inventorum formas admireris, quam non interraro dabitur ut rideas iocos et comitatem quibus tota haec historia refertissima est. Ergo lege vel maxime ut ipsum te recrees, proxime ut faveas et studiis et lucubrationibus nostris volens ac libens. Sis felix.

enumerated none of your very considerable, indeed great virtues, and I have done what those who know both you and me will not criticize. In any case, you yourself do everything possible to ensure that your virtue, thanks to rumor and reputation, is carried marvellously in every ear and mouth, to earn its fruit abundantly with posterity. You do not need the help of others in this matter. But by noting and collecting your words and deeds, I prefer (as far as I can) to appropriate you in all my volumes and to commend you to lovers of literature. Thus they will possess a man whom they would distinguish themselves to imitate, rather than — if I may put it this way — complimenting him with inconsequential flattery.

But enough of this. For the rest, when you read me at your leisure, should your reading proceed according to my wish and your expectation, I will be flattered every time you pause to laugh. I hope too that you will admire the wit and arrangement of my fictions whenever you laugh — not infrequently, I trust! — at the jokes and elegance that fill this whole story. And so read on, above all to enjoy yourself, and secondarily so that you may willingly and with pleasure show favor both to my zeal and my nocturnal labors. Be happy.

LIBER PRIMUS

1 Mirabar si quando apud nos humiles mortales in vita degenda pugnantem aliquam et inconstantem rationum iudiciorumque vigere opinionem intellegebam. Sed cum superos ipsos maximos, quibus omnis sapientiae laus attributa est, coepi animo accuratius repetere, destiti hominum ineptias admirari. Nam apud eos repperi varia et prope incredibilia esse ingenia et mores. Alios enim sese habere graves et severos, alios contra exstare leves et ridiculos, aliosque deinceps ita esse a ceteris dissimiles ut vix esse ex caelicolarum numero possis credere.

2 Qui tamen cum ita sint, cum longe moribus inter se dissideant, neminem tamen seu apud homines seu apud superos reperias ita singulari et perversa imbutum natura, cui non alium quempiam multa ex parte comperias similem praeter unum deorum, cui nomen Momo. Hunc enim ferunt ingenio esse praeditum praepostero et mirum in modum contumaci, naturaque esse obversatorem[1] infestum, acrem, molestum, et didicisse quosque etiam familiares lacessere atque irritare dictisque factisque. Et consuesse omne studium consumere ut ab[2] se discedat nemo fronte non tristi et animo non penitus pleno indignatione. Denique omnium unus est Momus qui cum singulos odisse, tum et nullis non esse odio mirum in modum gaudeat.

3 Hunc memoriae proditum est ob eius immodestam linguae procacitatem ab vetere deorum superum coetu et consilio omnium conspiratione et consensu deiectum exclusumque fuisse, sed inaudita pravitate ingenii et pessimis artibus tantum valuisse, ut potuerit superos omnes deos omneque caelum et universam denique

BOOK I

I used to be surprised whenever I noticed the contradictory and   1
inconsistent judgements and reasonings that abound amongst us
mortals in the conduct of our lives. But when I began to reflect
more carefully on the greatest gods themselves, who are given
praise for universal wisdom, I stopped wondering at the foolishness of men. I discovered that the natural inclinations and mores
of the gods are varied and almost incredible. Some of them conduct themselves with austere gravity, while others, on the contrary,
stand out for their frivolity and silliness, and some are so different
from the others that you could hardly believe that they number
among the sky-dwellers.

Be this as it may, and despite the wide differences in behavior   2
among them, you would still not find amongst either men or gods
anyone *so* extraordinary, *so* naturally perverse, *so* multifariously unlike anyone else as one of the gods whose name is Momus. People
say that he is possessed of an incredible bloody-mindedness; that
by nature he is an aggressive obstructionist, hostile and annoying;
and that he has learned how to provoke even his friends and to be
irritating both in word and deed. He habitually does his best to
see that no one leaves him without a miserable face and a soul
brimming with indignation. In sum, Momus is unique among all
beings as someone who takes amazing delight both in hating and
being hated by everyone.

Tradition has it that because of the outrageous insolence of his   3
tongue, he was, by universal agreement and consent, expelled and
barred from the ancient councils and assemblies of the gods above,
yet, through the unheard-of wickedness of his disposition and the
worst kinds of trickery, he was strong enough to drag all the gods,
all heaven and finally the whole machinery of the world to the

orbis machinam in ultimum discrimen adducere. Hanc nos historiam, quod ad vitam cum ratione degendam faciat, litteris mandare instituimus. Id ut commodius fiat, repetenda prius est quaenam causa et modus extrudendi in exilium Momi fuerit; post id reliquam historiam omnium variam et non minus rerum dignarum maiestate quam iocorum venustate refertissimam subsequemur.

4 Nam cum Iuppiter optimus maximus suum hoc mirificum opus, mundum, coaedificasset et eum quidem esse quam ornatissimum omni ex parte cuperet, diis edixerat ut sua pro virili quisque in eam ipsam rem aliquid elegans dignumque conferret. Iovis dicto certatim paruere superi. Idcirco alii alias res, alii hominem, alii bovem, alii domum, singulique praeter Momum aliquid muneris Iovi non ingratum in medium produxere. Solus Momus, innata contumacia insolescens, nihil ab se fore editum gloriabatur. Et in tanto aliorum tamque communi producendarum rerum studio sua in pervicacia summa cum voluptate perseverabat.

5 Tandem cum plurimi maximopere ex eo expostulassent ut Iovis gratiam et auctoritatem modestius consultiusque coleret, non quod[3] illorum suasionibus aut monitis moveretur, sed quod assiduas monitiones, hortationes precesque multorum nequiret sine stomacho diutius ferre, aspero, ut semper, supercilio, 'Vincite' inquit 'molesti: abunde quidem vobis satisfaciam.' Inde igitur rem se dignam excogitavit. Universum enim terrarum orbem cimice, tinea, fuconibus, crabronibus, scaraveonibus[4] et eiusmodi obscenis et sui similibus bestiolis refertissimum reddidit.

6 Ea res primum apud caelicolas ridiculo haberi, ioco ludoque accipi. Ille indigne ferre quod non exsecrarentur, verum gloriari suo secum facto et passim aliorum munera improbare, munerum auctores vituperare. Denique universorum odia dictis factisque in

point of ultimate catastrophe. I have decided to write this story down so that it might cause us to lead a rational life. In order to do this more conveniently, I must first of all trace the cause and manner of Momus' banishment. Then I will lay out the rest of this motley history, which is as packed with grand and worthy affairs as it is with delightful humor.

When Best and Greatest Jupiter[1] had just built this amazing cre- 4 ation of his, the world, he wanted it to be exquisitely wrought in every way, and so decreed that each god should contribute something as elegant and worthy as he or she could to achieve this end.[2] The gods competed to obey the command of Jupiter. They all produced different things: some made a man, some a cow, some a house; and one by one, apart from Momus, they brought forth gifts that did not displease Jupiter. Only Momus, overbearing and congenitally obstinate, boasted that he would give nothing. Amid such great communal zeal for producing gifts, he persisted in his obstinacy with the greatest possible relish.

Numerous gods urged him in the strongest terms to behave 5 more humbly and more advisedly, and to do homage to the benevolence and authority of Jupiter. Finally — not because he was moved by their persuasion and warnings, but because he could not endure any longer the entreaties and prayers of so many without irritation — he cried (raising a prickly eyebrow, as always): "You've won, you vexatious lot! I'll more than satisfy you!" So he devised a gift worthy of himself. He filled the world with bugs, moths, wasps, hornets, cockroaches and other nasty little creatures, similar to himself.

At first the gods found this funny, and took it as a joke and a 6 prank. But Momus could not bear that they were not cursing him. He began to boast about his deed and to find fault with the gifts of the others, heaping abuse on their givers. Each day, by word and deed, he increasingly incurred the hatred of all. Amongst the

dies magis atque magis subire. Erat inter ceteros celebres opifices deos magna in admiratione suorum ab se conditorum munerum Pallas quod bovem, Minerva quod domum, Prometheus quod hominem effecissent. Proxime ad hos accedebat ut belle dea Fraus fecisse videretur quod mulieribus mortalium adiecisset delicias artesque fingendi risumque lacrimasque.

7 Etenim hos praesertim cum ceteri dii[5] laudibus extollerent, solus Momus vituperabat. Aiebat enim utilem quidem esse bovem et ad fortitudinem aeque atque ad laborem satis comparatum, sed non suo decentique loco fronti fore oculos adactos, quo fiat ut cum pronis cornibus oppeteret, oculis ad terram destitutis, non destinato et praefinito loco liceat ferire hostem; et ineptam procul dubio fuisse artificem, quae non summa ad cornua vel unum saltem oculum imposuisset. Domum itidem asserebat nequiquam esse tantopere approbandam uti ab imperitis diis approbabatur, quandoquidem nullos currus subegisset quo malo a vicino in pacatius solum posset trahi.[6] At hominem quidem affirmabat quippiam esse prope divinum; sed, si qua in eo spectaretur formae dignitas, id non auctoris inventum, sed ab deorum esse ductum facie. In eoque opere illud tamen stulta videri commissum ratione, quod intra pectus mediisque in praecordiis homini mentem obdidisset, quam unam suprema ad supercilia propatulaque in sede vultus locasse oportuit.

8 Ceterum apud se nullius probari[7] aeque atque Fraudis deae ingenium. Eam enim adinvenisse quo pacto, pulchra Iunone abdicata, sese pellicem deorum regi subigat; amatorem esse Iovem et facile delicatam ornatamque virginem appetiturum. Futurum hinc ut irata ob eam iniuriam coniuge et thoros iugales dedignante, doli

gifts that the other celebrated artisan-gods had created, the gods particularly admired the cow that Pallas had made, the house made by Minerva,[3] and Prometheus' man. Next to these ranked the achievement of goddess Mischief,[4] who seemed to have done wonderfully by adding charms to mortal women, giving them smiles and tears and the arts of insincerity.

Momus alone found fault with these gifts, particularly when 7 the other gods sang their praises. He said repeatedly that the cow was certainly useful and had been fashioned both for tests of strength and for toil, but its eyes were not placed in the most sensible place on its brow. When it charged, he remarked, with its horns pointing forwards and its eyes fixed on the ground, it would not then be able to gore its enemy in its intended target. No doubt it must have been a singularly inept artisan who had not placed at least one eye on top of each horn. In the case of the house, Momus maintained that it certainly did not deserve such lavish approbation from the uninformed gods. For it had not been placed upon wheels and so could not be drawn from rough neighborhoods onto more tranquil soil. As for man, he agreed that this creation was almost divine. Yet if any nobility of form could be seen in him, it was not the invention of his maker, but was drawn from the appearance of the gods. Still, said Momus, the job had been carried out stupidly in one respect, for man's mind had been hidden in his chest, among his internal organs, whereas it ought to have been placed upon his lofty brow, in the open space of his face.[5]

But Momus praised nothing as much as the cleverness of the 8 goddess Mischief. For she had found a way (Momus said) to push the lovely Juno aside and seduce the king of the gods herself. Jupiter was known as a great lover, and would easily go for a tender, pretty maiden. And what then? His wife would be angered by the insult and would spurn their marriage-bed, then the goddess who had thought up the trick would snare the favor of that woman-

17

artifex dea mulierosi principis gratiam aucupetur. Quod si sapiat
Iuno, si suos amores integros perennesque velit, ex deorum coetu
deam Fraudem sibi ducet exterminandam. Haec Momus dicere
adversus Fraudem usurparat, tametsi deam ipsam amabat perdite:
sed quod suspicionibus amoris per id temporis[8] dissidebat, crimi-
nose iracundeque magis iactabat quam esset par, ut iam tum hinc
acerba istiusmodi lacessita iniuria dea suas omnes decreverit curas
et cogitationes ad sui vindictam prosequendam exercere.

9   Itaque, ut pulcherrime ingrato amanti pro meritis referret, suis
freta artibus, in gratiam volens ac libens cum Momo redisse simu-
lat. Frequens ideo una esse, crebros cum illo trahere sermones,
dicenti ultro omnia assentiri, petenti obsequi; subindeque credulo
amanti futilia quaedam commentitiaque secreta aperire consi-
liumque suis in agendis rebus ficta fide poscere, ac modo unis
atque item alteris diis inflexo diductoque sermone obtrectare[9] ut
procacem ad obloquendum illiceret. Postremo nihil praetermittere
quo illi esse in tempore nocua egregio aliquo malo posset.

10   His artibus multa ab inconsulto et incaute confabellanti extor-
serat, quae quidem ad eos ipsos quos id gravate ferre arbitrabatur
detulerat, ea spe ut, multorum in unum Momum invidia odiisque
excitatis, ad hostem obruendum impetu et manu firmiori attemperate irrumperet.[10] Dederat praeterea operam Fraus dea ut
per varios interpretes crebre in dies multorum adversus Momum
querimoniae[11] exporgerentur Iovi, et quo omnem ab se istius
malivolentiae suspicionem amoveret, si quando de Momi nequitia
se coram sermo habebatur, quasi pro amoris officio patrocinium

crazy king. If Juno understood this and wanted her love to remain unharmed and enduring, she would resolve to drive Mischief from the council of the gods. Momus repeated all of these charges against Mischief over and over, even though he himself loved the goddess to distraction, but because his jealousy made him fractious for the time being, he angrily kept throwing out unfair criminal accusations. Eventually the goddess, wounded by bitter charges like these, decided that she would devote all her thoughts and efforts to wreaking vengeance on him.

To pay back her ungrateful lover as beautifully as he deserved, 9 she relied on her wiles and pretended she was ready and willing to be reconciled with Momus. She was always by his side, talking to him constantly, freely agreeing to everything he said, ready to do what he asked. She often confided unreliable gossip and imaginary secrets to her gullible lover, and with feigned trust asked for his advice on how to conduct her business. Now truthfully, now falsely, she criticized first one, then another god with insinuating and divisive remarks, hoping to entice the insolent Momus to slander. She overlooked nothing that could cause him serious harm and trouble when the time was ripe.

Through her skilful tricks Mischief drew out many compromis- 10 ing words from the indiscreet and careless Momus, which she then related to the very gods whom she thought would be most offended. She hoped that if she stirred up the hatred and ill-will of many gods against an isolated Momus, then at the right moment she might strike suddenly and with a stronger hand to destroy her foe. Moreover, Mischief did her utmost to ensure that through various intermediaries constant complaints about Momus from numerous gods would reach Jupiter's ears on a daily basis. To distance herself from all suspicion of malevolence, if there was ever any talk in her presence about Momus' wickedness, she pretended to extend her protection to him, as though discharging her duty as a lover. With long speeches (however cool in tone) she defended

praestare se assimulabat, et pluribus verbis, sed frigidula oratione Momum omnibus accusantibus et omnium sententiis damnatum defendebat, inquiens Momum quidem esse mente alioquin non pessima, sed animo fortassis immoderate libero, eaque re videri lingua esse dicaciori et intemperantiori quam sit.

11 Interea totis oculis et auribus evigilanti deae accommodatissima laedendi occasio oblata est. Nam aegre ferentibus diis novum alterum deorum genus, homines, procreatum esse et eos quidem aura, fontibus, domo, floribus, vino, bove et huiusmodi deliciis multo ferme quam superos esse beatiores, Iuppiter optimus maximus, quod caelicolarum benivolentia suum sibi regnum vellet communire, quae suae fuere partes, huic se rei probe provisurum pollicitus est, et daturum se operam asseruit ut superum nullus posthac sit quin se deum malit esse quam hominem. Ergo in hominum animos curas metumque iniecit, morbosque et mortem atque dolorem adegit. Quibus aerumnis cum iam adeo essent homines longe deteriori in sorte quam bruta animantia constituti, non modo deorum erga se invidiam exstinxere, verum et sui misericordiam excitavere.

12 Accessit ut gratificandi studio Iuppiter caelum ornare lautissime aggressus sit. Caeli enim domicilia constituit eaque multis variisque signis, auro et[12] gemmis, omnique denique copia deliciarum pulcherrime distinxit. Demum haec diis Phoebo, Marti, Saturno patri, Mercurio, Veneri, Dianaeque ultro elargitus est. Et quo laetam dehinc et omnibus caelicolis gratam acceptissimamque suam tyrannidem curis vacuus ageret, munia, magistratus[13] imperiaque in quos visum est impertitus distribuit. Et inprimis Fato deo, ad res curandas agendasque omnium sollertissimo, semper agenti, numquam otioso, nihil per ignaviam, per inertiam prae-

Momus, who had been condemned by all his accusers and by common opinion. She said again and again that his heart was in the right place, but that perhaps he was too much of a free spirit, and for that reason his tongue seemed more cutting and out of control than it really was.

Keeping her eyes and ears open, the goddess was eventually 11 offered the ideal opportunity to do him harm. The gods were not taking it very well that a new race of gods, that is, mankind, had been created. They could hardly bear it that these men were much more blessed, practically, than they were, enjoying as they did breezes, fountains, homes, flowers, wine, cattle, and all sorts of delights. So Best and Greatest Jupiter, who wanted the heaven-dwellers' good will in order to fortify his kingdom, promised that he would take it upon himself to attend to the situation in a fitting way. He assured them that he would take pains to ensure that, from that moment onwards, no god would ever prefer to be human. Thus he injected anxiety and fear into the minds of men, and introduced disease and death and pain. Since men, owing to these hardships, were now placed in a far worse situation than the brute animals, they not only put an end to the gods' envy of them, but even excited their pity.[6]

Next, to please the gods, Jupiter started to decorate the heavens 12 with great luxury. He built celestial dwellings and embellished them exquisitely with many different devices, gold and jewels, and all manner of delights. He donated them voluntarily to Apollo, Mars, his father Saturn, Mercury, Venus and Diana. And so that he might henceforth reign free from care and make his tyranny a happy one, popular and well-liked by all the heaven-dwellers, he distributed official duties, magistracies, and commands to whom he saw fit. First of all, Jupiter granted the task of revolving the heavenly spheres to the god Fate, and gave him ultimate authority over the stars. Fate was most assiduous in looking after things and getting them done; he was always busy, never at rest; he never ne-

tereunti, nihil precibus aut praemiis a vetere more, a legitimisque
institutis deflectenti, volvendorum orbium curam summamque
ignium potestatem legavit.

13　　Contione habita, qua in contione illud iterum atque iterum
affirmavit, sese otii esse cupidissimum, ac rerum quidem regni
aliud nihil sibi esse relictum velle quam ut una cum reliquis diis
integra voluptate ex animi libidine frueretur. Suorum vero erga
deos meritorum hoc sibi satis videri praemium, si per eorum mansuetudinem dabitur ut possit vitam degere curis vacuam atque li-
beram.

14　　Hic locus admonet ut quando summam ignium potestatem
Fato datam diximus, quinam ipsi ignes et quaenam ea sit potestas
referam. Est apud superos sacer aeterno ab aevo ductus focus, cui
quidem cum cetera, tum illud insit admirabile, ut nulla substituta
materia nullove liquore subfuso sese confovens perpetuis lucescat
flammis. Quin et eiusmodi est, ut quibus adhaeserit rebus, eas
quoad una constiterit immortales incorruptibilesque reddat. Sed si
ex eo foco sumptas flammas crassis liquentibusque rebus terrenis
adegeris, sponte sua diffluent ad pristinamque sedem, ni assiduis
flatibus celerique motu exagitentur, dilabentur.[14] Accedit quod solis in villis mapparum quas dea Virtus contexuit sacer ipsus ignis
viget.

15　　Istoc sacro ex foco hausta flammula ad summum frontis verticem quibusque deorum illucet, atque ea quidem in diis hanc habet
vim, ut ea conspicui in quas velint rerum formas sese queant ex arbitrio vertere, quod ipsum plerique maximorum deorum effecere,
alii in aureum imbrem cygnumve, alii aliud in animal[15] sese prout
sua tulit libido convertentes. Hoc ex foco cum Prometheus radium
subripuisset, ob perpetratum sacrilegium ad Caucasum montem
fixum relegarunt. Quae cum ita sese res haberet, cum is focus[16]
ad tantas res agendas esset commodus, cavere superi, magistratu

glected anything through sloth or laziness; and neither prayers nor bribery would ever divert him from ancient custom or established practice.

Jupiter held a council, and in this council he repeatedly affirmed 13 that he wanted free time above all else. He said that the only kingly prerogative he wanted was to be able to enjoy unadulterated pleasure together with the other gods, following his heart's desire. He saw this as sufficient reward for what the gods owed him: that they should be so kind as to allow him to live independently and free from cares.

At this point I must digress. I mentioned above that Fate was 14 given supreme power over the stars, and I should explain what those stars and that power actually is. From all eternity a sacred altar has existed among the divinities, which as well as other properties has this most extraordinary one: the altar is bright with perpetual flame, tending itself even though no material is laid under it and no liquid poured over it. Better still, it has the property of making whatever it touches instantly immortal and incorruptible. But if you take flames from this altar and set them on earthly matter, whether solid or liquid, the flames will disappear and return to their original place in heaven, unless they are kept burning by constant and rapid ventilation. Moreover, the sacred fire flourishes only in threads of cloth woven by the goddess Virtue.

A little flame taken from the sacred hearth burns on the fore- 15 head of every god. It gives the gods the power to turn themselves at will into whatever remarkable form they want. The majority of the most important gods do this: some turn themselves into a golden rain or a swan, others turn themselves into another animal, wherever their fancy takes them.[7] When Prometheus took a spark from this fire, he was banished and bound to Mount Caucasus because of his sacrilege.[8] So since this fire could easily be used to compass such important ends, the gods created the special office of

ignium creato, ne huiusmodi furta posthac ullius audacia temerita-
teve possent perpetrari.

16   Haec de ignibus hactenus dicta sint, ad rem redeo. Itaque tantis
ab Iove exhibitis donis caelicolae, pro insigni suscepta munificen-
tia, ordinibus confluebant iamque universa immortalium multitudo incredibilem prae se alacritatem ferens ad regiam convenerat
habitura gratias Iovi. Eoque loci quisque certatim maximis laudibus rem prosequi aggrediebatur. Recte enim pieque optimum
principem Iovem pro sua prudentia caelicolarum ordini providisse
uno ore affirmabant. Solus Momus, vultu tristi, gestu moroso alte-
roque sublato supercilio, hunc atque hunc ad congratulandum properantem torvo obliquoque lumine despectabat. Sensit illico perfidia[17] dea, unicum erga inimicum intenta, Momum esse animo in
Iovem subinfenso. Idcirco suas ad artes conversa, quae opus facto
sint parat.

17   Temporis enim dei filiam Verinam,[18] Iovisque pellicem Profluam, quam eandem nympharum esse alumnam praedicant,
proximam post ad convivalem aram, ad quam fortassis adhaerebat
Momus, collocat iubetque uti assideant humo et aliud inter se dis-
simulantes latitent. Iovis enim causa parari quae sic parentur.
Proinde rem sedulo exsequantur et tacite quae illic dicentur auscultent atque adnotent.

18   Compositis insidiis, dea vultu hilari ad amantem propius accedit. Salutant mutuo sese. Post id, cum paululum Fraus obticuisset,
mox contracto supercilio 'Et quidnam' inquit 'mi Mome? Num et
tu, ut videor videre, de Iovis in superos merito secus atque vulgus
hoc imperitum sentis? Ne vero eadem una mecum de hisce rebus
statues? Non ausim ea cuiquam profiteri quae sentio, ni forte uni
tibi, quem aeque atque hosce oculos meos diligo. Verum quid me
celem apud te, a quo me intellegam in amore ita accipi prope ut
merita sum mea simplicitate[19] et fide? Hei nos infelices, qui qui-

supervising the fire to insure that no such theft could ever be perpetrated again through anyone's reckless audacity.

So much for the fire; now back to the story. After Jupiter had 16 given them such amazing gifts, the gods, in response to his lavish generosity, came together in their ordered ranks; and now the whole throng of immortals, showing incredible promptness, gathered at the palace, ready to give thanks to Jupiter. There they began to compete in heaping praise upon him. They declared with one voice that their great ruler Jupiter in his wisdom had taken just and pious care to provide for the order of the gods. Momus alone, with a surly attitude and one upraised eyebrow, gave a fierce, sidelong look as the gods, one after another, rushed to thank Jupiter. At this, Mischief, intent on her matchless enemy, perceived that Momus was angry with Jupiter, and so the treacherous goddess looked to her arts and made ready the ones she needed for her deed.

During a banquet, she placed the daughter of the god Time, 17 Verina,[9] and the mistress of Jupiter, Proflua (whom people say was the nurseling of the nymphs) just behind an altar against which Momus happened to be leaning. She told them to sit on the ground and hide and pretend to be doing something else. She said that she was doing all this in the interest of Jupiter, so they should accordingly be sure to do what they had been told: listen silently and pay attention to what was said there.

Having set her trap, the goddess approached her lover wearing 18 a cheerful expression. They greeted one another. Then, after a moment's silence, Mischief arched her eyebrows and said, "Well, my dear Momus, what's up? It seems to me that you have views about Jupiter and what he's done for the gods that differ from those of this ignorant crowd. Don't you agree with me? I wouldn't dare tell anyone but you how I feel—you, whom I cherish as much as my eyes. But why should I hide my thoughts from you, since I know that it is my very simplicity and trust that have earned your love?

dem huic—sed de his alias. At pulchra esse Iovis opera non infi-
tior, tametsi meminisse deceat quaeque princeps maximorum deorum aggrediatur ea esse omnia oportere ita, ut nihil supra et[20] nihil
aeque. Rectius pro tua prudentia tu quae dixisse velim intellegis
quam a me explicentur.' Haec dea.

19   Tum Momus 'Profecto' inquit 'sentis uti res est. Sed nondum
satis apud me constat stultine ea sint principis opera magis an ambitiosi.' Hic dea subridens 'Et quid tum' inquit 'utrumque, illi forte
si adsit non vitium, inquam, sed consilium?' Tum Momus 'Consi-
liumne' inquit 'tu id quod meram sapiat stultitiam nuncupas? En
bene constitutam rerum agendarum rationem! Loquar quae me
decere arbitrer. O quam commodius cum deorum republica ageretur, si maturius consilia pensitarentur! Neque enim sat est principem praesenti libidini prospexisse, ni et quae futura sint ita
utramque in partem perpenderit atque adduxerit, ut non aliena
posthac, sed sua praesertim sibi vivendum sit (uti aiunt) quadra.

20   'Vel quid hoc dementiae in deorum regem[21] incessit? Scilicet
tum primum maiorem in modum gaudebat Iuppiter optimus maximus homines factos esse, ut haberet quos nobis superis, seu iure
seu iniuria succensens, aemulos ad invidiam obiectaret. Post ubi
antiquius duxit veteribus incolis quam adventiciae mortalium deorum multitudini superas patere sedes, illic[22] homines habere sibi
voluit, in quos suos irarum aestus ex animo profunderet, in quosve[23] immani saevitia grassaretur. Hinc fulgura, hinc tonitrua, hinc
pestes et quod durius intolerabiliusque est miseris hominum animis, curas metusque[24] et quaecumque[25] excogitari fingique possint
mala, ingessit atque in unum accumulavit.

21   'Alia ex parte, si certare adversus mala pigeat, miseris reliquit,
quo se ex crudeli hoste munitissima tutissimaque recipiant in ca-

Alas! How unlucky we are that he . . . but no, another time. I don't deny that Jupiter's works are lovely, though it should be remembered that everything the prince of the greatest gods undertakes should be neither surpassed nor equalled. But in your wisdom you understand what I wish to say better than I can explain it."

Momus said, "You've certainly seen things as they are. But I haven't yet decided whether these works are those of a stupid prince or an ambitious one." The goddess, smiling, said, "What then?[10] How can he be either, if he does not possess any faults, but only wisdom?" Momus replied, "Do you call unadulterated stupidity wisdom? Look at his well-considered method of conducting business! I'll tell you how I think it should be done. How much more suitably the state of the gods could have been governed if his plans had been pondered with greater care! A prince cannot just think of the pleasure of the moment; he should also bring forward and weigh the pros and cons of things that may happen in the future, so that he won't some day have to live off someone else's table, as they say.

"Perhaps the king of the gods has even been seized by a bit of madness? At first, of course, Best and Greatest Jupiter was overjoyed that he had created men: if he became angry, rightly or wrongly, with us gods, he could push them forward as our rivals to excite our envy. But when he realized it would be better for heavenly homes to be occupied by their old inhabitants rather than by an upstart crowd of mortal gods, he decided to keep men down there, to pour out his raging floods of anger on their heads, and to run riot against them with his bestial savagery. Hence he heaped up lightning, thunder, pestilence and everything wretched human souls find harsh and unbearable, also anxiety and fear and every evil that can be devised and fashioned, and inflicted them all upon mankind at once.

"On the one hand, if fighting these evils irks them, he has left the poor wretches one way of escape from their cruel enemy into

19

20

21

stra, mortem. Sin vero certare iuvat, o inconsulte Iuppiter, qua te
et iratum et armatum deorum principem superent, homunculis
non ademisti patientiam! De orbium igniumque provincia quid est
quod sine commiseratione iam iam nostrorum impendentium malorum referam? Quis tam vecors, tam obtusi exstat ingenii quin istuc mentem adhibens intellegat non defuturum ut nullis magis
quam te auctore,[26] o Iuppiter, tuique ipsius proditore pereas? Tune
Fato tantam vim et potestatem agendarum rerum tanta cum volu-
bilitate coniunctam dedisti? Quod si semper, ut coepere, novas res
cupere et posse astrorum orbiumque ductores non desistent, quis
hoc non perspicit futurum, ut olim quempiam alium superis daturi[27] sint regem?'

22   'Hen' inquit hic Fraus 'regemne?' 'Quidni?' inquit Momus. 'An
tu Iovem alium esse quam deum reris, quod deorum sit rex?' 'Mihi
quod autumas' inquit Fraus 'fit non iniuria verisimile. Verum et
quisnam tanto imperio dignum se, etiam iubentibus Fatis, deputet?' 'O te ridiculam!' inquit Momus. 'Tamne esse deos omnes animis modicos et pusillos censes ut non aliquem inveniri credas, qui
imperandi oblatam sortem non recuset?' 'Te quidem' inquit Fraus
'etsi maxima quaeque mereri deputem, tamen est aliquid tanta in
re, quo[28] te quoque posse commoveri arbitrer. Sed quidnam tum?
Nos vero quanti voles esse apud te, si forte dabitur ut imperes?'
'Mihi tu' inquit Momus 'altera eris Iuno.'

23   Hic Fraus coepit collacrimari. 'Atqui nimirum' inquit 'cui prae
libidine quae velit liceant, huic nihil diutius cordi est. Aliam tibi
reperies amatam, Mome; tibi Fraus, quae te misere amet, erit fastidio.' His et plerisque huiusmodi ultro citroque dictis, coegit Fraus
iurare amantem, ipsa in ara, sese cum factus forte deorum fuerit

that strongest and safest of forts, namely death. But if, on the other hand, it avails them to fight, O heedless Jupiter, you have not refused these little men the patience to beat you, the angry and heavily armed prince of the gods! As for the governorship of the planets and stars, what could I say without lamenting the evils that threaten us at this very minute? Who is so demented, so thick-witted as not to realize on reflection that you, O Jupiter, shall inevitably perish, not by another's hand but by your own agency, betrayed by yourself alone? Weren't you the one to give Fate such great strength and power to act, coupled with such great instability? What if those who command the starry spheres, having begun to desire and to enable revolution, should never stop? Who could not foretell that at some point they will give the gods another king?"

"A king?" Mischief interjected. — "Why not?" said Momus. 22 "Do you think that Jupiter is different from the gods, just because he is king of the gods?" — "What you're telling me seems highly credible. But who would think himself worthy of such a great empire, even if the Fates ordained it?" — "Oh, how silly you are!" said Momus. "Do you really think the gods are all so mediocre and low-spirited that you couldn't find a single one who wouldn't refuse that power if it was offered to him?" — "Indeed, I imagine that even you — though I do think you worthy of the highest honors — even *you* could be shaken by such an offer," said Mischief. "But what then? How much would you value me, if you were chosen to rule?" — "You will be another Juno to me," said Momus.

At this point Mischief started to cry. "But no one who can sat- 23 isfy his every desire remains constant in his heart for very long. You will find another lover, Momus, and you will spurn Mischief, who loves you desperately." After exchanging these and many similar words, Mischief forced her lover to swear, on that very altar, that if he should be made king of the gods, he would put Mischief in Juno's place. Then, returning victorious to where the goddesses

rex Fraudem Iunonis loco habiturum.[29] Post haec ad dearum coetum victrix rediens, Verinam et Profluam arbitras bene et docte subornat quibus verbis, quo gestu, qua hora ad Iovem quicquid ad aram ex insidiis audissent referant.

24   Fiunt omnia ex sententia. Atroci ergo ad se delata amittendi regni suspicione commotus Iuppiter, quod iam pridem aliorum causa esset, erga Momum occulte factus iratior. Nunc suis rationibus quantum coniectura prospiceret paratum adversarium intuens, sese acerbum iniuriarum vindicem exhibuit. Irato Iove omnia atque omnia contremuere. Obstupuere superi. Cogitur frequens deorum senatus: iubentur Proflua dea, nympharum alumna, et Verina, Temporis filia, testificari quae a Momo dicta nuper ad aram subaudissent. Instituebat deum pater et hominum rex Iuppiter sollemni more diem reo dici, constitutisque iudicibus audiri causam, legitimoque iudicio litem percenseri.

25   Sed totis ab subselliis una omnium eademque repente oborta vox publicum odium Momum maiestatis teneri acclamavit: 'Io, prehendendum sceleris obnoxium! Io, et Promethei loco vinciendum!' Tanta inimicorum conspiratione tantisque in se unum insurgentibus irarum procellis Momus animis prostratus et trepidans fuga sibi consulendum statuit. Eridanum caeli fluvium citato gradu fugiens petebat, quo inde sumpto navigio secundis aquis ad nostras hominum regiones applicaret. Sed, dum ab insequentium strepitu sibi cavisse properat, in voraginem multo hiatu praeruptam, quae quidem caeli puteus dicitur, incautus corruit.

26   Illinc, amisso flamine deorum insigni, in solum Etruscum quasi alter Tages irrupit. Eam gentem religioni maiorem in modum deditam offendit. Suas idcirco primas suscepit partes idque sibi

were gathered, she skilfully tutored Verina and Proflua in their roles as eye-witnesses, instructing them about the words, demeanors and timing to use when telling Jupiter everything they had heard by the altar.

Everything happened as she had expected. Terrified by the awful suspicion relayed to him that he might lose his kingdom, Jupiter secretly became even angrier with Momus than he already was for other reasons. Having now solid grounds to add to his suspicions, he saw an enemy prepared to stand against him, and he showed himself to be a bitter avenger of wrongs. When Jupiter was angry everything—everything!—trembled. The gods were stunned into silence. A senate of the gods assembled; it was packed. The goddess Proflua, nurseling of the nymphs, and Verina, the daughter of Time, were commanded to testify as to what they had recently overheard Momus saying at the altar. Jupiter, the father of the gods and king of men, solemnly ordained a day to be set for the trial, and appointed judges to hear the case and render judgement in accordance with the law.

But then from all the seats a unanimous cry suddenly arose denouncing Momus as a public enemy, guilty of treason: "Hey, catch the criminal! Hey, chain him to the spot that held Prometheus!" So great a combination of enemies and such a storm of hatred and animosity dashing against him alone floored Momus. Trembling, he decided to escape. Running as fast as he could, he made for Eridanus, the heavenly river,[11] hoping to catch a ship and use favorable currents to head for our lands, those of mankind. But while he sped along, avoiding the hue and cry of his pursuers, he carelessly fell into the steep, gaping chasm known as the pit of heaven.

Losing the sacred flame that identifies all gods, he forced his way onto Etruscan soil, like a second Tages.[12] There he encountered a race wholly devoted to religion. He took up his usual role and declared that it would be his sole task, and his revenge, to lead

24

25

26

unum indixit fore negotium, vindictae gratia Etruriam ab deorum cultu ad se observandum[30] imitandumque abducere. Itaque nullum erat uspiam deorum commissum flagitium in eam diem, cuius Momus diligentissimus exquisitor non meminisset codicibusque adnotasset. Ergo obscenas quasque superum fabulas, desumpta poetarum persona, seriove iocove ad multitudinem decantabat. Iovis audiebantur in scholis, in theatris, in triviis adulteria, stupra turpiaque amoris furta. Tum et Phoebi et Martis et horum et item horum superum nefanda facinora vulgo asseverabantur. Denique veris falsa miscebantur et vulgatorum in dies scelerum numerus et fama multo excrescebat, ut iam deorum dearumque caput nullum non incestum flagitiisque perditum haberetur.

27 Post id, philosophantis persona sumpta, ut erat barba promissa, torvo aspectu, hispido supercilio, truci nutu et gestu, ut ita loquar, fastuoso, per gymnasia non sine multorum corona contionabundus disceptabat deorum vim aliud nequiquam esse quam irritum et penitus frivolum superstitiosarum mentium commentum. Nullos inveniri deos, praesertim qui hominum res curasse velint; vel tandem unum esse omnium animantium communem deum, Naturam, cuius quidem sint opus et opera non homines modo regere, verum et iumenta et alites et pisces et eiusmodi animantia, quae quidem consimili quadam et communi facta ratione ad motum, ad sensum, ad seseque tuendum atque curandum consimili oporteat via et modo regere atque gubernare. Neque tam malum comperiri Naturae opus, cui non sit in tanto productarum rerum cumulo ad reliquorum usum et utilitatem accommodatissimus locus. Fungi idcirco quaecumque[31] a Natura procreata sint certo praescriptoque officio, seu bona illa quidem, seu mala pensentur ab hominibus, quandoquidem invita repugnanteque Natura eadem ipsa per[32] se nihil possint. Multa pensari peccata opinione, quae peccata non sint. Ludum esse Naturae hominum vitam.

the Etruscans away from worshipping the gods and get them to follow and imitate him instead. There was no outrage committed anywhere by the gods up to that very day that Momus, a most careful observer, had not remembered and noted down in a book. Disguised as a poet, he recited to the crowd every scandalous tale of the gods, both seriously and in jest. In the schools, in the theaters, and on streetcorners tales were told of Jupiter's rapes, his disgraceful behavior and his amorous abductions. Next the wicked crimes of Phoebus and Mars and many other gods were retailed everywhere. Truth became mixed with falsehood, and the number and infamy of these crimes grew daily in the telling, so that the person of every god and goddess was considered unclean and lost to debauchery.

After that, having assumed the persona of a philosopher, with 27 a long beard, sidelong look, shaggy eyebrows, and a truculent, haughty demeanor, he demagogued his way through the gymnasia, surrounded by large groups, arguing that the gods' power was nothing other than a vain, useless, and trifling fabrication of superstitious minds. He said that the gods were not to be found, especially gods who took any interest in human affairs. Or maybe, in the end, there was only one deity common to all living things, Nature, whose calling and labor it was not only to govern mankind, but also flocks, birds, fish and similar creatures. In the same way and manner she must rule and govern all animate beings, who were made with a common instinct driving them to move, to perceive, and to care for and protect themselves. No work of Nature was so bad that it did not find a most fitting place in the great abundance of things she had produced, that it did not make a contribution to the general utility. Whatever Nature fashioned had a proper and pre-ordained function, whether men thought this good or bad, and they could do nothing on their own behalf if Nature was unwilling and opposed them. Many things were believed to be bad which were not bad. Human life was a sport of Nature.

28   Itaque his dicendi rationibus plerosque mortalium moverat
Momus ut iam intermitti sacrificia et sollemnes antiquari ceri-
moniae deorumque cultus passim apud mortales deseri occiperent.
Id ubi a superis cognitum est, fit ad Iovis regiam concursus.
Actum de rebus suis queruntur, opem auxiliumque mutuo (ut fit
in perditis rebus) alter ab altero exposcunt, iamque se prospicere
affirmant, sublata apud homines opinione deorum et metu, nequiquam esse quod se amplius deos deputent.

29   Interea Momus vindictas acrius prosequi et omnium philosophantium scholas disputando incessere non desistebat. Disputanti
deo iam tum seu invidia seu garriendi cupiditate catervae occurre-
bant philosophorum. Etenim comminus[33] eminusve circum astabant, interpellabant, vexabant. Momus vero acer, durus, omnium
impetum magis pervicacia quam iustis viribus solus sustinebat.

30   Alii praesidem moderatoremque rerum unum esse aliquem arguebant; alii paria paribus, et immortalium numerum mortalium
numero respondere suadebant; alii mentem quandam omni terrae
crassitudine, omni corruptibilium mortaliumque rerum conta-
gione et commercio vacuam liberamque, divinarum et humanarum
esse rerum alumnam principemque demonstrabant;[34] alii vim
quandam infusam rebus, qua universa moveantur, cuiusve quasi
radii quidam sint hominum animi, Deum putandum asserebant.

31   Neque magis inter se varietate sententiarum philosophi ipsi dis-
crepabant quam uno instituto omnes una adversus Momum sese
infestos variis modis obiciebant. Ille, ut erat in omni suscepta con-
troversia pervicax, suam durius tueri sententiam, negare deos, ac
demum falli homines, qui quidem ob istum, quem caelo spectent,

Through such arguments Momus persuaded many mortals to   28
stop making sacrifices and to reject solemn rituals, and mankind
now began to abandon the worship of the gods everywhere. When
the gods realized this, they rushed to Jupiter's palace. They lamented the state of their affairs, and begged one another for help,
as people will do when all seems lost. They declared that they
foresaw the day, should humans lose their belief in and fear of the
gods, when it would be vain to think of themselves any longer as
divine.

Meanwhile Momus relentlessly pursued his revenge and did not   29
stop attacking all of the philosophical schools with his arguments.
Prompted by jealousy or by the desire to chatter, troops of philosophers now hurried to meet the contentious god. They surrounded him, some standing close by, others at a distance, inter-
rupting him, harrying him. But Momus, keen and hard, bore up
alone under all their attacks, more out of stubbornness than true
fortitude.

Some argued that there was only one ruler and governor of   30
things.[13] Some urged that all things were in proportion, and that
the number of gods corresponded to the number of mortals. Others offered demonstrations that a mind empty and free from all
earthly grossness, from all contagion and commerce with corrupt-
ible and mortal matter, was the original nurse of every divine and
human thing.[14] Still others maintained that the force infusing everything, which moved the universe and whose rays, as it were,
were human souls, must be thought of as God.[15]

The philosophers disagreed among themselves in the variety of   31
their opinions, but their common aim, to unite from various directions in bitter opposition to Momus, was still stronger. He, stubborn in the midst of all the controversy that had arisen, clung the
more doggedly to his own opinion, denying the gods' existence,
and finally claiming that men were deceived when they believed
there were tutelary gods in addition to Nature, just because they

conversionum ambitum moti, praesides deos ullos praeter Naturam putent. Naturam quidem ultro ac sponte suesse erga genus hominum innato et suo uti officio, eamque haud usquam egere nostris rebus, sed ne eam quidem nostris moveri precibus. Ac demum frustra eos metui deos qui aut nulli sint, aut si sunt, nimirum suapte natura benefici sunt.

32   Disceptantium philosophorum tumultu perciti superi, unde a caelo exaudiri voces possent ad rem spectandam accursitarant[35] suspensique animis disputationis eventum exspectabant, nunc Momi responsis tristes, nunc philosophorum vocibus laeti. Etenim[36] philosophi adversus Momum concitati, natura ambitiosi, mente arrogantes, usu vehementes (uti erant) altercatores, pertinacius instabant, urgebant, neque interdum conviciis parcebant. Hinc ad maledicta utrimque prorumpere. Postremo ardescente rixa pugnis, unguibus dentibusve obstinatum garrientis Momi os obtundere lacerareque prosecuti sunt.

33   Tumultum supervenientes nonnulli proceres sedavere. At Momus horum ipsorum[37] fidem opemque implorans dimidia deperdita barba foedatos vultus ostentabat. Eam enim, dum circum hostium manibus obvallatus oppressusque fugam meditaretur et cubito et umbone validus hunc atque hunc deturbasset, pusillus quidam cynicus trepidantis Momi ab collo pendens morsu barbam decerpserat. Proceres tantam barbato homini illatam iniuriam prae se moleste ferre, sceleris auctores quaeritare, sed circumstrepentium philosophorum vocibus Momum accusantium satis explicite exaudiri homo nemo narrans poterat. Tandem, tota intellecta historia, ubi pusillum eum cynicum demorsorem adductum reum conspicati sunt, et hominem accepto pugno commaceratis oculis obscenum et inter conandum loqui maximis screatibus demorsae vorataeque barbae pilos exspuentem intuentur, mutuo risere atque re neglecta despectaque abiere.

saw orbits altering their motion in the sky.[16] Nature freely and spontaneously carried out her customary, inborn offices with regard to the human race, but she did not need our services at all, and could not be moved by our prayers. Finally, it was pointless to fear the gods, since either they did not exist, or if they did, they were surely benevolent by their very nature.

The gods were aroused by the uproar of the disputing philosophers, and so they rushed to a part of the sky where they could hear the voices and watch what was happening. On tenterhooks, they awaited the outcome of the dispute. Now Momus' answers saddened them, now the words of the philosophers made them happy. And indeed the philosophers opposed to Momus, being ambitious by nature, arrogant by inclination, and forceful disputants by habit, pressed him ever more insistently, bore down on him, and did not spare him their mockery. Next, both sides broke into taunts and insults. Finally, as the altercation grew more heated, they began to hit and tear at the obstinate face of the garrulous Momus with their fists, nails and teeth.[17] 32

Several officials intervened and quelled the fight. Momus, imploring their trust and help, showed them his half-torn beard and bloody face. Surrounded and beset by enemy fists, he planned his escape, and had managed to elbow a few of them out of the way. But then a little Cynic philosopher, hanging from the neck of the terrified Momus, bit off his beard. The officials, unable to countenance so great an injury to a bearded man, sought out those responsible for the crime. But no witness could be clearly heard above the clamor of philosophers screaming on all sides, accusing Momus. At last, when they had taken in the whole story, and saw that the offender brought to them was a little Cynic biter,[18] with black eyes where he had been punched, who coughed hard while trying to speak so as to spit out the beard hairs he had chewed up and swallowed, they had a good laugh together and went away, overlooking the incident. 33

34   Superis id ad maiestatem deorum conducere nequiquam visum
est, ut discant homunculi in quemquam divorum tametsi consceleratissimum atque penitus incognitum inferre manus. Alia ex parte
prospiciebant non defuturum quin propediem, Momo (ut coeperat) vindictam prosequente plebeque ignara et credula assentiente,
prisci gentium ritus et iusta diis sacra collabefactata obliterarentur.
Coacto ea de re senatu deorum, duae proferebantur sententiae.
Una erat, in quam quidem pedibus ibant cuncti, ut ad superum
auctoritatem dignitatemque revocandam grati aliqui acceptique
hominibus mitterentur, qui apud mortalium animos quovis argumento in integrum veteres[38] cerimonias ac deorum venerationem
restituerent atque refirmarent.

35   Altera erat sententia, in qua variabatur sed primarios habebat
auctores, ut Momus, cuius iam tum mores caelicolis omnibus essent cogniti, revocaretur: plus enim detrimenti ex illius exilio divorum ordini redundaturum quam si garrulum blatteronem, cui nulli
amplius credituri sint, domi continuerint. Quod si Momi poena
delectentur, esse quidem genus exilii deterrimum ita inter suos
versari ut omnibus invisus atque infensus sit.

36   Tandem ex Iovis senatusque decreto Virtus dea, quod et aspectus maiestate et apud mortales auctoritate plurimum valeret, ad
terrarum incolas, veluti in provinciam, summa cum imperii pote-
state demittitur mandaturque ut provideat ne quid deorum respublica detrimenti patiatur.

37   Dea proficiscente universi ordines comitandi gratia frequentes
adfuere. Tum et singuli senatores caelicolae, prout necessitudine
aut familiaritate apud proficiscentem valebant, solliciti admonere,
hortari rogareque ut quibusque possit artibus communi in peri-

The gods thought that divine majesty was not exactly upheld   34
by the fact that mere mortals had learned to hit a god, even if the
god was utterly wicked and virtually unknown. On the other hand
they foresaw that if Momus pursued his vendetta, and if ignorant
and credulous plebeians went along with him, then very soon the
ancient rituals of the nations and the sacrifices justly due to the
gods would slide into oblivion. The senate of the gods assembled
to deal with the matter, and two proposals were made. One, which
most of them favored, was that some popular gods should be sent
down to earth to re-establish divine dignity and authority. These
gods, with various arguments directed to mortal minds, would
fully confirm and restore the ancient ceremonies and veneration of
the gods.

The other proposal, on which they were divided, but which had   35
powerful backers, was that Momus should be recalled from exile,
since all of the sky-dwellers knew his character. He would cause
more damage to the divine order in exile than he would if the talk-
ative windbag were kept at home, where no one believed him any
more. If they would really like to punish him, it would be the
worst form of exile to live among his own kind where he was a
universal object of scorn and hatred.

Finally, by decree of Jupiter and the council, the goddess Virtue,   36
whose majestic appearance and authority among mortals would
prove highly effective, was dispatched to the inhabitants of the
earth like a provincial governor.[19] She was entrusted with the
highest imperial authority, with a mandate to ensure that the commonwealth of the gods did not suffer damage.

As the goddess set out, all the divine orders turned out en   37
masse to accompany her. Then, as necessity or familiarity with the
departing goddess gave them leave, individual members of the divine Senate advised her of their concerns and encouraged her.
They asked her to maintain public security by whatever arts she
could in this time of communal danger. They also asked her to

culo publicam ad salutem advigilet detque operam ut cuius ope[39] deorum flamines exstarent, eius cura et diligentia sacrosancta immortalium maiestas tueretur. Illa, optimam de se spem in tanto deorum discrimine pollicita, quantum ex tempore captari afflictis rebus consilii potuit, mature inivit.

38   Quattuor deae Virtutis filii aderant adulescentes, formae venustate indolisque gratia ac vultus proceritate morumque praestantia facile principes caelicolarum iuventutis. Hos laute ornatos secum dea proficiscens[40] ducit, per quos, sin aliter nequeat, deorum veteres hospites, proceres mortalium heroasque, quos esse pulchrorum amatores meminerat, moveat: tanti erat Momi conatus velle evertere!

39   Eccam[41] igitur deam quadrato reptantem[42] agmine: hinc Triumphus, hinc Trophaeus: duo Virtutis mares liberi praetextati praeibant; Virtus mater subinde media subsequitur; matrem deam binae item puellae filiae Laus atque Posteritas consequebantur. Deorum numerus ad septimum usque lapidem longo ordine conferti deam egredientem comitati sunt. At legati illic nubem candidissimam omnium conscenderunt, qua quidem per aethera proclive labentes ad terras delati devenerunt. Hac Virtutis profectione dii plurimum recreari toto caelo professi sunt: neque defuturum arguebant quin, tam praeclaris fulta coadiutoribus, dea violatam caelicolarum maiestatem ab impuri facinorosissimique Momi iniuriis esset vendicatura.

40   Dea ut primum appulit ad terras, mirabile dictu quantum universa terrarum facies plausu laetitiaque[43] gestiret! Sino quid aurae, quid fontes, quid flumina, quid colles adventu deae exhilarati[44]

take pains that she, by whose aid the priests of the gods were kept in existence, would protect the holy majesty of the gods through her care and diligence. Virtue gave every assurance that their affairs were in good hands during this divine crisis, and speedily took in, on the spur of the moment, as much advice as she could given the imminence of the threat before hastening on her way.

The goddess Virtue had four adolescent children, easily the 38 flower of heavenly youth for their physical beauty, their charm, their princely demeanor and their outstanding character. Splendidly dressed, they escorted the goddess as she set forth. If nothing else worked, she would use her children to influence the old hosts of the gods, the leaders and heroes of the mortals, whom she remembered to be lovers of the beautiful: yes, destroying the machinations of Momus was that important!

Behold the goddess slinking along in a squared-off battle array! 39 Here is Triumph, there is Trophy: Virtue's two male children are in the van, dressed in the *toga praetexta*.[20] Then Virtue their mother follows in the middle. Praise and Posterity, her two daughters, bring up the rear behind the goddess their mother. A number of the gods accompany the departing goddess together in a long line as far as the seventh milestone. Then the ambassadors climb onto the very whitest cloud in the sky, which slips through the empyrean and bears them down to the earth. Throughout the whole of heaven the gods declare themselves much relieved by Virtue's mission. They stress that the goddess, bolstered by such illustrious supporters, will not fail to rescue the damaged majesty of the sky-dwellers from the injuries inflicted by the impure and abominably wicked Momus.

It is truly marvellous to relate how the whole surface of the 40 earth exulted with joy and praise when the goddess first set foot on land. Never mind how exhilarated the breezes, the springs, the streams and the hills became at the approach of the goddess! You could see flowers bursting out of even the toughest flint, smiling

sint. Videbas flores vel ipso praeduro ex silice erumpere praeter-
euntique deae late arridere et venerando acclinare, omnesque sua-
vitatum delicias, ut odoratissimum id iter redderent, expromere.
Vidisses et canoras alites propter advolitantes circum applaudere
pictis alis, modoque[45] vocis deos hospites consalutare.

41   Quid multa? Omnium mortalium oculi divinos ipsos ad vultus
contuendos intenti haerebant. Multi spretis officinis tantum ad-
ventantium specimen diutius contemplaturi iterum atque iterum
sectabantur; nonnulli inter sectandum prae admiratione obstupe-
scebant, quoad prope attoniti redditi haerebant. Undique confluebant ex vicis, ex angiportibus et matres et nurus et senes et omnis
aetas, et quinam hospites et quid sibi velint inscii mutuo ab insciis
sciscitando fatigabantur. At dea, composito gradu[46] et vultu, multam prae se ferens admixtam cum dignitate facilitatem, lento motu[47] laetoque supercilio salutatrix per militarem viam ad gymnasium, inde ad theatrum, postremo in aedes Publici Iuris hominum
subingressa constitit.

42   Senserat Momus advenisse deas, sed partim odio deorum tae-
dioque rerum suarum e conspectu diffugiebat, partim quod procul[48] visam Laudem Virtutis filiam, omnium pulcherrimam, ardere
incepisset, seductus sectabatur. Atque, ut erat ingenio suspiciosis-
simo, sua fuisse deas causa demissas interpretabatur, et curis plenus varia intimo pectore consilia volvebat. Veniebat in mentem
quid sibi esset cum iratis divis causae. Senserat apud quos divertisset mortales multo quidem[49] quam possis credere truces et trucu-
lentos; deos alia ex parte meminerat solere flecti precibus. At deorum legatum congredi haud putabat fore utile exuli, ni forte id

far and wide at the goddess as she went by, bending down to do her homage, and breathing out every fragrance to fill her path with sweet odors. You would have seen melodious birds flying around her, applauding with painted wings, and greeting the visiting gods with their song.[21]

In short, the eyes of all mortals were riveted, staring intently at the very faces of the gods. Many people abandoned their shops and followed them, just to gaze longer, again and again, on the outward form of the newcomers. Not a few of them were struck dumb with awe while following the gods, transfixed almost as though they'd been struck by lightning. Matrons, young women, old men, people of every age, rushed together from their neighborhoods and alleyways. Again and again they importuned those just as ignorant as themselves as to who the visitors were and what they wanted. But the goddess Virtue, with serene face and step, demonstrated to all a fine mixture of dignity and ease, greeting everyone with a glad expression in her measured progress. She made her way along the military road leading to the gymnasium, went thence to the theatre, and finally stopped at the courthouse.

Momus had realized that the goddesses were approaching, and while part of him was ready to flee from their sight owing to his hatred of the gods and to his own parlous situation, another part was ready to follow them. For he had seen from afar Praise, the daughter of Virtue, and had been smitten by her unique beauty. Being naturally paranoid, he surmised that the goddesses had been sent down because of him. Plagued with anxiety, he turned over various plans in the depths of his heart. It came into his mind why the gods were angry with him. He realized that the mortals he had led astray[22] were now much more savage and fierce than you could believe. On the other hand he remembered that the gods used to be softened by prayers. He thought that a meeting with the ambassadors of the gods would hardly be useful for an exile, unless he put on an attitude of complete submission and defeat. Momus

41

42

multa fiat cum significatione animi penitus deiecti atque demissi,[50] et supplicem praebere se Momus omnino ab suo instituto esse alienum statuebat. Neque inveniebat quo pacto sibi ipse imperaret ut acris, austeri semperque infesti improperatoris personam poneret, quam quidem dudum susceptam aeterna pervicacia servasset. Alia ex parte metuebat ne deam ipsam, alioquin facilem et mitem, sibi exasperatam redderet sua contumacia, et convenire suis rationibus intellegebat hanc ab se fore non alienam, a qua aliquid opis consiliique sua in causa esset impetraturus. Accedebat eo novissimus erga Laudem initus amor. Tandem in hoc irrupit consilii, ut deam sibi conveniendam duceret.

43   Itaque sese dictis castigans 'Ponendi nimirum' inquit 'sunt miseris, o Mome, fastus, servandaque rebus felicioribus gravitas; satis pro decore fiet, Mome, ubi te, quoquo id queas pacto, ex infimo abiectoque loco in pristinam dignitatem vindices. Neque tu hoc putato dedecere, cum agas ut quae agas deceant. Nam est quidem sapientis parere tempori, quin et assentando supplicandove conferet ad res maiores capessendas aditum parasse Momo. Dices: "Nequeo esse non Momus; nequeo non esse qui semper fuerim, liber et constans." Esto sane: ipsum te intus in animo habeto quem voles, dum vultu, fronte verbisque eum te simules atque dissimules[51] quem usus poscat. Et tuam, qui tam belle id possis, et illius, qui id non recuset, rideto ineptias!'

44   Huiusmodi secum versans Momus, cum propius accessisset ad templum, tam repente tantam illuc accursitasse multitudinem tamque varios illic ludorum conari apparatus dedignatur.[52] Namque inter divas[53] puellas ingenio erat Laus levissimo et oculorum flagrantia propemodum immodesta, iamque ut se appete-

considered that offering himself as a supplicant would be utterly alien to his purpose. Nor could he find a way to make himself set aside the mask of a caustic, severe, and ever-hostile scold, which he had put on so long ago and which his eternal obstinacy had made him keep. On the other hand, he feared that his own defiance would make the goddess exasperated with him, even though she seemed easy-going and gentle. He worked out that alienating her would not suit his plans, since he was hoping to obtain help and advice from her in his cause. His new-born love for Praise further complicated matters. In the end, he pitched on the plan of winning the goddess over to his side.

So he started to chasten himself thus: "Momus, the wretched 43 must lay aside their pride; save your dignity for more fortunate circumstances. You can satisfy your honor, Momus, when you've rescued yourself from this lowly and abject place and reclaimed your former glory in whatever way you can. Don't think it dishonorable to do what honor requires you to do. A wise man adapts to the times he's living in. If conforming and acting as a supplicant will lead to bigger and better things, then Momus is prepared to adapt. Now you will say: I cannot *not* be Momus, and I cannot *not* be who I have always been without sacrificing my freedom and my consistency. Well, let it be so: keep the real you, the man you want to be, deep inside your heart, while using your appearance, expression and words to pretend and feign that you are the person whom the occasion demands. Laugh at the absurdity of it all—at your own absurdity, because you can pretend so beautifully, and at the absurdity of the man who doesn't gainsay it!"

Momus was turning these matters over in his mind when he ar- 44 rived just outside the temple. That such a great crowd had hastened there so quickly, and that they were arranging so many different kinds of celebrations, filled him with contempt. Now among all the girl-goddesses, Praise had the most frivolous disposition and a fire in her eyes that was almost wanton. She had al-

rent[54] illexerat complurimos, quorum catervis circum adventanti-
bus divae paene obsidebantur. Enim alii fidibus, cantu saltuve, alii
palaestra, alii opum divitiarumque ostentatione, denique quisque
qua plurimum posset polleretque re placere Laudi puellae adorie-
batur. Lasciva Laus omnibus, ac praesertim his qui lauta praesta-
rent veste, amoenam offerre se quantis poterat artibus, matre non
recusante, elaborabat.

45   Tantos Momus offendisse rivales aegre ferebat. Sed, qua de re
advenisset sollicitus, quendam ex proxima taberna mittit, qui Virtuti deae nuntiet esse[55] aliquem suae gentis, Momum, qui se non
invitas percupiat adire. Metuebat enim ne, si non tentata et cognita deae in se gratia adivisset, exclusus multitudini ludibrio haberetur. At Virtus dea 'Utinam' inquit 'satis meminisset is quidem
nostra se habitum esse ex gente! Non profecto sibi tantas commi-
sisset rerum perturbationes. Verum accedat ut libet.'

46   His verbis Momus renuntiatis quam in partem acciperet non
tenebat: oculis, vultu animisque se in omnes partes versabat. Tandem curarum plenus ad templi vestibulum adstitit, quo loci vix
unum aut alterum prae sui conscientia verbum poterat proferre.
Sed ab dea perbenigne susceptus, ipsum se colligens, plura est orsus dicere. Etenim veterem coepit familiaritatem, mutua officia,
summam erga deam benivolentiam commemorare, suas calamitates deplorare, opem orare, seque modis omnibus commendatum
facere. Dea ut fractum exulis animum recrearet, quae ad rem per-
tinere arbitrabatur, mature et graviter pro loci temporisque ratione
respondit.

47   Inter quae non defuit illud, ut admoneret commodius cum pro-
fligato agi si desineret olim non usque se omnibus praebere infen-

ready lured numerous men into desiring her, and troops of them were coming from all directions, practically laying siege to the goddess. Some played lyres, sang and danced, while others showed off their athletic ability or their resources and money, and each man strove to please the girl Praise by excelling in whatever activity he did best. Frisky young Praise worked hard — with no objections from her mother — to make herself pleasant to all of them, especially the best-dressed ones, using all the skills as her disposal.

Momus found it unbearable to come into contact with such rivals. But, remembering his reasons for coming, he sent a man from the nearest tavern to apprise the goddess Virtue that one of her own kind, Momus, desired greatly to wait upon her, if she were willing. He was afraid that if he approached the goddess without having tested and verified her goodwill towards him, he might be shut out and mocked by the crowd. But Virtue said, "If only he had remembered to behave like one of the divine race! Surely then he would not have caused such great upheaval. But he may approach me if he likes."   45

Momus did not know how to interpret these words when they were relayed to him. His eyes, face and mind whirled in every direction. Finally, his heart heavy with cares, he stood in the vestibule of the temple, where he could barely utter a word or two from acute self-consciousness. But the goddess received him graciously, so he gathered his wits and attempted to say a few things. He began to talk about their long-standing friendship, their shared concerns, and his great goodwill towards the goddess. He lamented his misfortunes, asked for help, and recommended himself in every way he knew. Virtue thought it important for the sake of the matter in hand to rebuild the shattered confidence of the exile, so she replied swiftly and seriously, as befitted the time and place.   46

Among other things, she did not refrain from advising him that he would encounter less trouble if he stopped behaving so aggres-   47

sum atque invisum. Obesse rebus agendis nimium properam et
proclivem ad detrectandum loquacitatem. Rogare ut poneret animos concitatos, temperaret iracundiae: abhorrere quidem a suis
temporibus ut iniuriarum tam obstinate meminerit. Eo mentem
intendat, ut spectet quam quaeque in superos astruat, facilius ea
quidem in sui caput sint ruitura quam superos affectura. Repetat
ipse secum quid assecutus sit suis artibus et vetere vivendi more:
dolendum quidem ad id paene redactas esse Momi rationes, ut qui
velit opitulari nequeat. Se tamen pro vetere gratia non defuisse
cum publice, tum private Momi causae curasse ut superi Momi
salutem non neglegerent,[56] curaturamque ut benemerenti accumulatissime referant, modo suas esse partes Momus sentiat ut in animis hominum suis verbis labefactatam et paene convulsam deorum opinionem religionemque restituat. Momus insperato gaudio
excitus cuncta polliceri, nihil non spondere, omnia ab se deberi
diis magnifice de se meritis deierando insistit.

48   Interea proceres primariaeque matronae, inter quas[57] sunt qui
opinentur adfuisse Herculem, Liberumque patrem natum Semele,
Medium Fidium fratresque Tyndaridas[58] atque item Matutam
Cadmi filiam, Carmentam Cereremque et istiusmodi, hi, plebe
abacta et una protruso Momo, in templum deam consalutatum ingressi sunt. Cumque coepissent poscere ut bona venia liceret nosse
essentne, quales aspectu et corporis habitu viderentur, ortae ex
deorum genere, cumque rogare obtestarique perseverarent ut privatim apud se hospitio diverterent, Momus, spe admodum plenus
et dearum praesentia fretus, sese elatius agitare coeperat quam

sively and showing everyone how he hated them. She said that a tongue so quick and inclined to criticize prevented anything getting done. She asked him to lay aside his angry intentions and to govern his rage. She reminded him that he would be unwise in his present circumstances to remember his injuries so stubbornly. He should also bear in mind that if he were plotting against the gods, then this would probably rebound on his own head rather than affect them. She asked him what he had ever gained from his old tricks and his former way of living. It was truly sad that Momus' methods had reduced him nearly to the point where even someone who wanted to help him could not. Because of her long-standing goodwill, she had not failed to take an interest in Momus' cause, publicly as well as privately, so that the gods should not neglect his well being. She would ensure that his good deeds were amply rewarded, so long as he felt his obligation to restore in the minds of men belief and reverence towards the gods, which his words had weakened and nearly destroyed. Momus, struck by unexpected joy, promised all of these things, offered every guarantee, and swore that he owed the gods everything, as they had dealt so generously with him.

Meanwhile the leading gentlemen and the most important matrons entered the temple to greet the goddess. Some believed that these included Hercules, Father Liber son of Semele, Medius Fidius,[23] the twin sons of Tyndareus,[24] Matuta the daughter of Cadmus,[25] Carmenta,[26] Ceres,[27] and others like this. The lower classes were held back while Momus pushed himself forward. These people started to ask — if graciously they might be allowed to know — if the newcomers were of divine birth, as their appearance and garments seemed to suggest. With great insistence they asked and besought the deities to accept their private hospitality. Momus, full of hope and supported by the presence of the goddesses, began to get above himself and act overbearingly. Indeed he incessantly ordered people about, got in people's way, and made

48

esset par. Enim imperitare, obversari detrectareque[59] non cessabat. At multitudo, insolentissimi huius unius arrogantiam contuma- ciamque fastiditi, e templo extrusere.

49   Insperata iniuria commotus Momus, mediam inter plebem sese ingerens, huiusmodi dictis excandescebat: 'Ne vero tantis lacessiti iniuriis, o cives, horum istorum procerum dementiam aeternum perferemus?[60] Sint illi quidem, malam suam in rem, malumque in cruciatum, opum affluentia et praedarum[61] cumulis nobis humilio- ribus, quoad eorum fata velint, superiores, nosque innocentes, quod eorum flagitia non probemus, oderint. Fulgeant auro et gem- mis, stent unguentis illibuti, dum et omnium libidinum sordibus delibuti et immersi degant. Nos trita veste, sudore obsiti, sem- perne pessundabimur istorum impudentia? Semper intolerabilem istorum insolentiam perferemus? Non ergo licebit fortibus viris, quod pauperes simus,[62] nostrae gentis necessitudineque coniunctos hospites, istis ipsis invitis, congredi? O nefandam et perniciosam nostrae communis libertatis labem atque excidium! Arroganti im- perio dispellunt, superbo impetu deturbant.

50   'Nos vero nostram dignitatem, tam atroci iniuria lacessiti, virtute non tuebimur? Nos insignem paucorum audaciam tam multi uno consensu et conspiratione numquam refellemus? Pu- deat foedae servitutis! Huc cives liberos esse nos ostendite! Adeste viri fortes, tyrannos nequire diutius perferre ostendite! Ius vestrum tueri, libertatem defendere ac denique vitam servituti postponere olim posse ostendite! Adeste cives, vi temeritas coercenda![63] Se- quatur libertatis vindicem qui se civem libertateque dignum putat! Arma, arma, viri!'

51   Haec Momus. At cives qui aderant, ut est vulgi vitium et na- tura sponte quosque rerum novarum auctores sequi et praecipites in ostentatos seditionum fluctus ruere, iam tum irritatis animis

abusive remarks. At last the crowd, disgusted by the arrogance and stubbornness of this single, highly obnoxious individual, expelled him from the temple.

Furious at this unexpected injury, Momus worked his way into the middle of the mob, and spat out these words:[28] "O citizens, are we going to put up forever with the madness of these important gentlemen who have harassed you with such great injustices? Granted, they *are* superior to us humble folk—in their evil ends, their evil torments, their rivers of wealth and the piles of plunder their fates have allowed them. They hate us who are innocent, because we do not approve of their wickedness. They glitter with gold and jewels, they stand there smeared in scent, while living lives stained with filthy lusts. Shall we, in our ragged clothes, covered in sweat, be always downtrodden by their arrogance? Shall we always endure their unbearable insolence? Will brave men be barred—just because we are poor—from meeting guests of our race, with whom we are linked by ties of obligation, even if they themselves are unwilling? O the sacrilege, the ruin, that attends the corruption and collapse of our common liberty! Their arrogant power divides us, their overweening force drives us before them.

"But shall we not bravely protect our position, harassed though we are by foul injustice? Shall we, who are so many in number, never oppose with one accord the outrageous boldness of a few? Shame on this foul servitude! Here, show us that you are free citizens! Come forth, brave men, show that you cannot bear tyrants for one minute longer! Show that you can preserve your rights and defend your freedom; show that hereafter death is preferable to slavery! Come forth, citizens, let your force check their insolence! Let anyone who thinks of himself as a citizen and worthy of liberty follow this protector of liberty! To arms, men, to arms!"

Momus finished. The citizens present showed the vicious tendencies of a mob to follow spontaneously any and all rabble-rous-

49

50

51

fremebant et passim indignum facinus procerum accusantes undique ad tumultum insurgebant.

52   Id cum animadvertisset dea, ad templi vestibulum se conferens, perturbationum auctore Momo accito, facile surgentem tumultum circumstrepentis plebis sedavit frontis et manus gestu, regia quadam cum maiestate innuens. Et ad Momum conversa 'Num tu hoc' inquit 'pacto, Mome, quae modo apud me pollicebare incohabas? Sicine indomitam multitudinem ad immanem audaciam concitabas[64] ut me et hasce puellas medias inter pericula facium, ferri armorumque constitueres? ut mutilatorum cadentiumque nostra inter gremia cruore aspersae divae ad superos rediremus? Saniore esse Momum posthac mente optamus.'

53   'Ego vero' inquit Momus 'desperatus[65] meis in rebus, tantis laesus incommodorum et horum istorum mortalium iniuriis, possum ipsum me non cohibere quin mea mala sentiens paululum cedam dolori. Tuum erit, Virtus, hoc providere: utrum iniuria nobis sempiterne magis quam beneficiis certandum siet?'

54   'Adsis,' inquit dea 'hoc velim de me tibi persuadeas, tuis me commodis curandis minime defuturam; et quo firmiori spe atque exspectatione quae tuae sunt[66] partes exsequare, da manum. Hoc tibi spondeo: tu quidem, si quid, uti mea de te fert opinio, bene de genere deorum apud mortales fueris promeritus, profecto efficiam ut nulla ex parte officii tui paeniteat. Atqui est quidem ut de te omnia mihi pollicear. Novi ingenium tuum, Mome, et de te sic statuo, dum ita instituas aliquid et tibi salutare et diis gratum velle experiri, profecto ex sententia perficies. Tu modo id para et te pri-

ers, and to rush headlong into the waves of sedition that had been pointed out to them.[29] Their spirits now aflame, they set up a clamor, everywhere accusing their rulers of shameless wickedness, and rose up in riot.

When Virtue realized this, she betook herself to the temple 52 vestibule and summoned Momus, the instigator of the commotion. With ease she quelled the rising tumult of the ravening plebs, motioning to them majestically with royal gestures of head and hand. Turning to Momus, she said "Is this how you enter on the promises you made to me only a short while ago? So you've been inciting this ungovernable mob to bestial audacity, placing myself and my daughters here in the midst of perils, fire, sword and arms? Shall we goddesses return to the gods above, our bosoms bespattered with the blood of mutilated corpses? We hope that Momus will be more reasonable in the future."

"But in my situation I was desperate!" said Momus. "I was up- 53 set by the great injustice of my misfortunes and the injuries done me by these mortal men. I couldn't stop myself from feeling my woes and giving in a bit to my grief. It's up to you to deal with this, Virtue: must I always struggle with injury rather than reap rewards?"

"Come here," said the goddess, "I want you to be convinced 54 that I will not fail you in looking after your interests. Give me your hand, so that you will carry out your responsibilities with firmer trust and hope. I guarantee you this: if your behavior towards mortals is able to benefit the race of the gods, as I think it is, I shall certainly see to it that you will not repent of any part of your duty. Indeed, I have reasons for promising all this to you. I know your ability, Momus, and I have decided that, so long as you undertake to accomplish something which is both in your own interest and pleasing to the gods, you will certainly carry it out satisfactorily. Now get ready, and show yourself worthy of the divine

stina deorum gratia dignum praesta: maiora longe a nobis repen-
dentur quam promiserimus.'

55   Momus ad haec quid aut de se statueret, aut benigne admo-
nenti referret praeter lacrimas non habebat. Illud commovit deam,
quod vetula quaedam incurva cum senio, tum et metu praesen-
tium rerum paene confecta, properans, tremitans, anhelitans, voce
summissa 'I Iue, homo, hoe,' inquit 'ne tu quantis in periculis ver-
sere non intellegis! Fuge hinc, miser, teque ab paratis adversum te
insidiis eripe. Acinacem vidi servo ab latere procerem tradere, ac
iubere uti quam primum te rerum omnium perturbatorem confoderet.'

56   Dea ne quid coram immite huiusmodi et nefarium perpetrare-
tur verita, velum quo esset accincta, instar apicis quod e caelo in
puteum corruens amisisset, ad Momi caput advolvit. 'Ac tu' inquit
'quas voles varias in facies versus infestam in te insidiarum manum
effugies. Quod si pro tuo officio quae ad deorum rem pertineant
exsequere, id mihi assumo de te ut benemerito benefactum con-
gratuleris.' Post haec ad proceres conversa dea sese nisi in templo
alibi pernoctare instituisse negat, sed postridie mane, si redierint,
habere quippiam quod cum illis sit maximis de rebus actura. Demum, ubi salutatores missos fecerat, e vestigio aeneas graves valvas
obducit templo, quo ab impurissimorum audaciumque contumeliis sit obclusis foribus tutior.

57   Momus, postquam quae nequam et improbe tentasset tam
praeter spem atque exspectationem bene vertere animadvertit, suis
ab successibus animos atque spiritus pristinos resumens, omnes
curas cogitationesque suas ut aliquod se dignum facinus aggrede-

favor you once enjoyed. I shall recompense you with far greater things than I promised."

In response to this speech, Momus either had nothing to say 55 for himself or nothing except tears to repay her who had given him such kind counsel. Then something else touched the goddess' heart. A little old woman, bent almost double with age, nearly dead from fear of what was happening, rushed towards them, trembling and gasping, and said in a humble voice, "Oh, oh, fellow, you don't know the danger you're in! Get out of here, you poor man, and escape the traps that have been laid for you! I saw one of the rulers hand a spear to a slave at his side. He ordered him to stab you, the instigator of all this tumult, as quickly as possible!"

The goddess, fearing that something horrible and wicked like 56 this would be committed in her presence, wound the veil she was wearing around the head of Momus, to take the place of the coronet he had lost when falling from heaven into the pit. "Now change your appearance however you want," she said, "and flee the hostile gang plotting against you. If you carry out your duty in that matter concerning the gods, I shall take it upon myself to see you rewarded for your good deeds, just as you deserve." Then turning to the rulers, the goddess said she had no plans to spend the night anywhere other than in the temple. If they returned the next morning, however, she had some important matters to discuss with them. At last, when she had seen the last of her wellwishers depart, she quickly shut the heavy bronze doors of the temple. With its doors closed, she would be more secure from the attacks of profane and reckless persons.

Momus realized that his worthless and wicked undertaking had 57 turned out much better than he could have hoped or anticipated. As a result of his success, he regained his old spirit and intentions. He set his mind to thinking about how he might accomplish a crime worthy of him. Thus he devised a new and unheard-of way

retur intenderat. Ergo novam atque inauditam laedendi rationem adinvenit, qua ubi nefarie misceret omnia, illic pie et probe fecisse videretur, et pro malo invento ab his qui iniuriam accepissent gratiae haberentur.

58   Puellarum enim una erat, Thersitis soror, inprimis ob egregiam deformitatem urbe tota cognita. Haec, quod regio langueret morbo, rus valitudinis gratia petierat. In hanc conversus Momus se[67] ceteras inter puellas, quae tunc forte in triviis atque angiportibus congruerant, immiscet vultusque suos non ut antea pallentes et squalidos, sed novo quasi miraculo factos roseos et miro venustatis splendore amoenos ostentans, manuque sibi insuetos aureos capillos demulcens, bellissime inflectebat.

59   Invidentibus[68] puellis atque poscentibus unde una haec Thersitea omnium incuriosissima puella tam repente connituerit, Momus, composito ad delicias vultu, 'Ehodum' inquit 'adeste[69] meae cupidines, meae puellae, animoque, si id vacat, advertite quae vobis utillima[70] et gratissima dictura sum. Discetis enim a me quo pacto et vos huiusmodi vultu ornatissimo prodeatis. Atqui eritis quidem tanto quam ipsa sim ornatiores quanto prae me vestrarum quaeque ex se est longe formosior atque decentior. Quod ni ita ut facerem tam mirifici doni largitores dii imperassent — meum apud vos sit fas profiteri peccatum — fortassis poteram tacendo meo cum animo mecum hoc nostro solo potiri gaudio, proprioque hoc inter puellas triumpho gloriari. Sed superis diis sponte ac libens pareo. Tu Venus, tu Bacche, tuque aurea Aurora adeste faveteque, dum sancto pioque vestro pro imperio tanti tamque divini muneris meas hasce amantissimas carissimasque puellas participes facio.'

60   His Momi dictis puellae non facile dici potest quam sese audiendi discendique avidas praestiterint. Tum Momus commenti-

of doing harm, so that while he was embroiling everything in wickedness, he would appear to be acting piously and righteously. He would receive favors in recompense for his wicked device from the very persons he had injured.

There was a girl, the sister of Thersites,[30] who was known all over the city, chiefly for her remarkable ugliness. Because she was suffering from jaundice, she had gone to the countryside to improve her health. Momus, transforming himself into her likeness, mingled with the other girls who gathered on streetcorners and in alleyways. She showed off her face, which was not pale and dirty as it had been formerly, but almost miraculously rosy and attractive owing to its wonderful radiant beauty; she stroked her newly golden hair with her hands. She was most beautifully altered.

The other girls, deeply jealous, asked why only Thersites' sister (who had been, of them all, the most careless about her appearance) had suddenly become so elegant. Momus, putting on a charming expression, said, "Gather round, my darlings, my dear girls, and pay attention, if you can, to what I'm about to tell you — you'll find it highly useful and gratifying. Find out how you, too, can get a face as gorgeous as this. Indeed, you'll be much lovelier than I am to the degree that every one of you is naturally more pretty and attractive than I am. But it's right that I confess a sin to you. If the gods, the donors of this miraculous gift, had not ordered me to tell you about it, I might have kept it to myself. I alone might have revelled in this delight, and I alone might have gloried in this triumph of mine over you other girls. But I freely and happily obey the will of the gods. Thou Venus, thou Bacchus and thou golden Aurora, be near me and bless me while, in conformity with your holy and pious command, I share your fabulous divine gift with these dearest, darling girlfriends of mine."

One can barely do justice to how greedily the girls pressed forward to listen and learn from the words of Momus. Momus then began to recount "her" false tale with fine verbal embellishments,

58

59

60

ciam fabulam ordiri grandi verborum apparatu coepit in hanc fermc sententiam. Nocturna se quidem vigilia fessam curisque animi fractam atque defatigatam ruri mane diluculo obdormivisse et in somniis visam sibi curas easdem sua cum defuncta nutrice repetere. Id erat suam se vehementer sortem accusare quod alioquin non omnino repudiandam ob ingenii dotes puellam videret se nullis fore non ingratam atque una praesertim re, coloris obscenitate, haberi a cunctis mortalibus spretam atque reiectam. At vetulam nutricem visam dicere: 'Desine, anime mi, te hisce fletibus commacerare, dabo quo pacto fias formosissima. Ito, voveto[71] superis et Veneri et Baccho atque Aurorae diis te coronas tua manu illibatis floribus consertas ad aram illorum simulacris admoturam, modo aliquid dent ad te honestandam opis. Namque obsequii memores et gratissimi dii quaeque petieris praestabunt.'

61   Hac nutricis oratione recitanda, Momus iam tum animos puellarum spe atque cupiditate maiorem in modum oppleverat. Quas cum ita affectas intueretur, unam atque alteram spectans, perquam bellulo gestu coeptos sermones prosecuta[72] 'Haec mea' inquit 'dixerat nutrix. At ego experrecta pronis manibus quanta dabatur animi fide ex insomnio vovi. Credin? Illico me bona spe factam firmiorem sensi. Quid multa? Iterato consopitam me Aurora dea per somnum qua arte resina cerusaque pingerem et pumice fingerem et croco nitroque crinem tingerem edocuit. Qua ex re nos puellas bis felices arbitror, et quod divinos Aurorae vultus his artibus, quoad libeat, liceat imitari, et quod nostris in curis et laboribus patefactam ad superos deos immortales consulendos placandosque viam habeamus. Hac pacem opemque poscere superum, hac, diis volentibus et annuentibus, quasi quodam rerum agendarum com-

more or less as follows. "She" said that she had been exhausted by a sleepless night, her spirit crushed by care and weary with country life, when finally, near dawn, she had fallen asleep. In her dreams, it seemed to her that she was recounting her cares to her long-dead childhood nurse. She complained bitterly of her lot in life. Though she ought to have been valued for her talents, she saw that she would always be undesirable, and all mortals would spurn and neglect her for one reason in particular, namely, her horrible complexion. Then her little old nurse seemed to say, "My dear, stop blotching your face with these tears. I'll tell you how you can become beautiful. Go! Make a vow to the gods that you will gather garlands of fresh flowers with your own hands, that you will go to the altars and arrange flowers on the statues of Venus, Bacchus and Aurora, provided they help you to improve your looks. For the gods will take notice of your offering and it will please them, so they'll give you whatever you seek."

Momus, recounting this speech of the nurse, had by now filled 61 the girls' hearts with immense hope and longing. When she saw that they had been so deeply affected, looking from one to another, Momus resumed her speech, accompanying her words with pretty little gestures. "This is what my nurse told me. So when I woke up, I stretched out my arms and prayed with all the fervor that my dream had given me. Do you believe it? I perceived immediately that my faith had made me more resolute. In short, when I fell asleep again, in my dream the goddess Aurora taught me the art of painting my face with resin and white lead. She showed me how to rub myself with a pumice-stone and tint my hair with saffron and nitre. That's why I think we girls are doubly lucky! Using these techniques, we can copy the divine looks of Aurora as much as we like, and when we get into any trouble, we have a ready way to serve and placate the holy immortal gods. In this way, we can ask for sanction and help from the gods; in this way, if they're willing to approve our requests, we can bind ourselves to

mercio iungi superis facili levique negotio possumus. Ite ea de re
posthac puellae, atque a diis audete votis quaeque collibuerint petere.'

62   His fabulis recitatis, Momus puellam unam atque alteram bellissime adornavit atque sese qua pingerent arte instructas plerasque omnes reddidit. Verum petiit in abdito facere id consuesce-
rent, ne viri quoque sibi una tantas[73] delicias usurparent, neve
morosae domi et causatrices novercae rescirent.[74] Haec Momus,
atque abiit ita secum acta sua reputans ut prae laetitia prope insaniret.

63   'Enim' aiebat 'profecto, uti aiunt, rerum omnium vicissitudo est.
Quis tantam tamque variam temporum meorum commutationem
conversionemque factam uspiam potuisset suspicari? Nuper exul,
miseriis obtritus diisque atque hominibus odio et ludibrio qui fueram, nunc repente ex afflictis perditisque rebus in tanta haec mea
tractus gaudia nimirum exsulto laetitia.

64   'Sed nondum[75] apud me constat inprimis ne congratuler quod
ab exilio restitutus pristinam dignitatem recuperaturus sim,[76] an
quod haec mihi vindicandi mei ratio in mentem inciderit, qua inveniri nulla possit festivior. Et profecto hic apud homines versari
oportet, si quid ad dolum et fraudem velis astu perfidiaque callere.
Hui quale bipedum genus homines! Apage! Atqui hoc mihi ex
acerbo exilio obtigisse voluptati est, quod vafre et gnaviter versipel-
lem atque tergiversatorem praebere me simulando ac dissimulando
perdoctus peritissimusque evaserim. Quas profecto artes commo-
das et usui pernecessarias in illo apud superos otio et luxuriae illecebris constitutus numquam fuissem assecutus. Nunc his meis
vexatus exagitatusque casibus, quid est quod te, Fraus, verear? O

the gods, as it were commercially, through this simple and smooth exchange. So get on with it now, girls, and don't be shy about petitioning the gods in prayer for whatever they will grant."

After telling this tale, Momus made up one girl after another 62 with great elegance, and instructed them all in the cosmetic arts. But she asked them to practice these arts in secret, as a rule, so that men would not appropriate such delightful techniques for themselves, and so that their peevish and nagging stepmothers at home would not find out. Having completed his task, Momus went away, self-satisfied with his actions to the point where he nearly went mad with glee.

"Yes indeed," he said, "all things certainly *are* changeable, just as 63 people say.[31] Who would ever have suspected that such a radical change and reversal of my fortunes would take place? Just now I was an exile, buried amongst wretches, an object of hatred to both gods and men, a laughing stock! Now I've suddenly been pulled out of my stricken and doomed state, and amid such happiness it's no wonder I'm skipping with delight.

"But I've not yet decided whether I should first congratulate 64 myself because I've been restored from exile and am about to recover my former dignity, or because I've thought of a way of avenging myself. Nothing could be more entertaining than that. The fellow who wants to master the arts of trickery and deceit and cunning treachery really needs to spend time with men! Whew! what a race of animals these two-footed creatures are! Get out of here! But if there's one agreeable thing I've learnt from bitter exile it's this: I've come out of the experience a clever and careful skin-changer and dodger; I've become an expert at simulation and dissimulation. I would certainly never have acquired these handy and indispensable skills when I lounged at ease in besotted luxury among the gods. Now that I have been harassed and buffeted by these misfortunes of mine, why should I fear *you*, Mischief? O, how happy I would have been, if during my former life of privilege

me felicem, si pristina illa in rerum affluentia quid possent in dies
nova incommoda tenuissem! Non me, fedifraga Fraus, tuis prodi-
toriis artibus exterminasses! Quod si ad superos rediero. . .

65   'Sed de his alias. Hoc scio, Momum fallet nemo, quandoquidem omnes fore improbos pridem perdidicit Momus. Ad rem redeo. Sic se res habet: hic apud homines, hic ferendo tolerandoque
dura et adversa, ad grandes praeclarasque res prospere agendas ratio et modus comparatur. Vel quis meum hoc, uti par est, satis
laudarit vindicandi commentum? Ne vero non me architectum
elegantem omnis malitiae praebui? Hoc nimirum meo facto id
venturum sentio: superos discet mortalis voto incessere; novi eius
petulantiam, novi procacitatem, arrogantiam, temeritatem. Nihil
sibi rerum optimarum atque divinarum non deberi deputat. Quid
erit quod votis non aggrediatur? Stulte appetet, temere affectabit,
proterve exposcet; nihil sibi negandum, nihil non ultro conferen-
dum ducet.

66   'Denique quivis unus homunculorum cunctos deos sua insolentia expostulando defatigabit. Illi vero deliciosi, qui quidem lauta
inter caeli domicilia omne aevum per otium et incuriam ducere
instituere, si quid has res votorum curarint, conferant ad res agendas manum animumque oportet, ac desinent quidem suo cum Ganymede, sua cum Venere et Cupidine desipiscere voluptatibus.
Adde quod, si de mortalibus benemereri occeperint, in dies excre-
scet desidiosis inertibusque labor. Sin haec neglegent desidia et fastidio, actum est, nulli sunt. Tolle qui pareant, frustra imperes.
Non habeant dii qui ad sui numinis venerationem animos subi-
gant, quanti tu putes esse te superum? Accedit huc, quod sunt
quidem dii ipsi plus satis ambitiosi et popularis submissionis as-
sentationisque maiorem in modum avidi; sunt alia ex parte supini,

I had known what new discomforts would here befall me daily!
You would not have been able to crush *me* with your treacherous
arts, faith-breaking Mischief! When I get back to heaven . . .

"But enough of this. I know this now, that no one can deceive   65
Momus, since Momus has learned through long, hard experience
that everyone will behave badly. I'll get back to the point. And this
is the point: here on earth, humans have worked out ways and
means of achieving great things by putting up with hardship and
adversity. Will anyone give me my fair share of praise for my
scheme of revenge? Have I not shown myself to be an elegant architect of all kinds of mischief? I realize, of course, what will come
from my deed in the end. Humans will learn to pummel the gods
with prayers; I know well their impudence, their audacity, their arrogance and temerity. Humans all think they deserve the best possessions, divine possessions. What is there that they will not seek
to acquire through prayer? They will covet stupidly, aspire rashly,
demand shamelessly; they will think that nothing must be denied
them, that everything should be given to them freely.

"In due course, one or another of these homunculi will wear   66
out all the gods with the insolence of his demands. Those plea-
sure-loving gods, who have spent an eternity in the luxurious halls
of heaven at ease and free from care, will have to put their hands
and minds to work, if they are at all concerned with this matter of
prayer. They will have to stop fooling around with Ganymede, Venus and Cupid. Besides, if they start to satisfy the mortals, the
work for these lazy slackers will increase daily, but if they neglect
their duties through apathy and pride, that's it, they're finished. If
you lose your subjects, you rule in vain. If you gods do not have
subjects who worship your divine power, how great a god do you
think that makes you? Moreover, though the gods are indeed ex-
cessively ambitious and incredibly greedy for popular submission
and adulation, by the same token they are also passive, lazy, and
indolent. Yet, besotted though they are with nectar and ambrosia,

ignavi, desides, quo fiet ut, nectare atque ambrosia immersi et obruti, nova et insperata huiusmodi re quasi a somno exciti, quid quisque sibi privatim consiliorum captet non habeat et communi in re quid statuisse conferat non inveniat. Disputabunt altercationibus magis quam sententiis.

67   'Illic nostrae aderit operae pretium non mediocre. Nam, me ni eorum mores et consuetudo fallit, futurum profecto video, ut contentionis studiis aliquid irarum et odii inter eos excitetur. Neque dubito quin in me multa ex parte illarum perturbationum aestus redundet, sed quo me purgem atque ab inita invidia revocem illud semper patebit, ut dicam me bona fide illorum maiestati contulisse quantum ingenio et simplici prudentia valui, et bene; mihi quidem, quoad in me fuit merito, insperatum rei eventum ad culpam esse non detorquendum. Postremo et quid illud? Numnam qui incultas agrestesque potuit puellas deperisse, Iuppiter factas per me venustiores non ardebit? Vale, Iuno!'

68   Dum haec secum commentaretur Momus, incidit in mentem ut taetrum aliud adoriretur facinus, diis superis et diis inferis et hominum generi invisum, infestum et detestabile. Digna res memoratu levi re, si id ita licet dicere, tam exitiosum exsecrabileque malum esse exortum. Tum et ipsum flagitium ob inventi novitatem habet in se quippiam quod quidem legentibus voluptatem[77] afferat. Momum diximus Laudem, unam Virtutis filiam, coepisse adamare. Laude igitur ut potiretur animo destinarat nihil rerum omnium praetermittere. Ea de re ad obclusum templum circum astabat, lustrans omnes aditus, undique repetens omnia atque pertentans; sed cum omnes eius haberi frustra conatus obiectis firmatisque templi portis intellegeret, pedem animumque inde

this new, unexpected state of affairs will shake them out of their torpor. They'll have no idea what advice to take in their private interest and they won't find a way to confer together and make decisions about the common good. Their debates will be squabbles, not a rational exchange of views.

"Here, the considerable value of my efforts will become evident. 67 For unless I am mistaken about their customs and habits, I see quite clearly what is going to happen. Their fervent disagreements will stir up anger and hatred among them. I don't doubt that much of the tide of their wrath will fall upon my head. But to exonerate myself and prevent their getting angry with me I can always say that I have always consulted the interests of their majesty in good faith, so far as my wit and simple wisdom allow, and consulted it well. The unexpected outcome of the affair, insofar as it was my fault, should not be distorted so as to blame me. And what will happen after that? Maybe, once I've made them better looking, Jupiter will get hot for these raw country girls, whom he might otherwise miss. Good-bye, Juno!"

While Momus was thinking about these matters, it occurred to 68 him to start in on another dreadful deed, one which would be hateful, hostile and odious to the gods of heaven, the gods of the underworld and to the human race. It is worth mentioning how such a pernicious and lamentable evil sprang from so trivial a source, if one may call lust trivial. Moreover, the crime itself, because of its novelty, also has a certain entertainment value for the reader. We have said that Momus had started to fall in love with Praise, one of the daughters of Virtue. He resolved to stop at nothing to have his way with the girl. With that end in view, he was hanging about the closed temple, lurking in all of its entrances, reconnoitering and testing out all the possibilities. But when all his exertions had failed, and he realized that the temple doors were shut and fastened securely, he turned away, changing his purpose, as though already lifting the siege he had started.

quasi iam tum coeptam obsidionem dissolvens averterat. Sed cum inter discedendum iterato ad templum versus constitisset et suspirans rursus huc atque illuc suspexisset, forte neglectam posticam fenestram animadvertit; per ipsam hanc, seu furtim seu vi, suos sibi fore petendos amores instituit.

69   Scalas eo admovere loco et publico et hominum frequentia circumsesso[78] cum difficile atque arduum, tum et pro re agenda erat haudquaquam tutissimum. Ergo istic oculis ab fenestra ipsa pendens, hinc vero animum in omnes partes concitans plura deliberabat, multa audebat, cuncta metuebat, furoreque libidinis agitatus inter spem atque metum aestuabat. At cum sese collegisset et memoria repetisset quid velo ab dea Virtute suscepto posset, illico sese hortatus ad murum templi vetustate asperum adhaerescere et brachia multo sursum versus tendere, unguesque barbamque inter lapidum iuncturas infigere totis manibus totisque contendit pedibus, quoad in hederam versus ipsam per fenestram arduus irrepsit.

70   Illinc ubi aspexit solam fortassis Laudem, matre fratribusque consopitis, in suis concinnandis capillis ad tersum templi lapidem quasi ad speculum advigilare, prae amoris furore male sui compos et animo in omnem audaciam percitus, quo se vertat,[79] quid captet consilii non invenit praeter id, ut pronus tacitusque amatorii furti occasionem praestoletur. Idcirco muro sensim diffluens, intensis brachiis animo suspensus dependebat; quo in statu atque exspectatione positus difficile dictu est quam et morae et sui esset impatiens. Ad puellam enim factus propior acrius flagrabat amoris facibus; alia ex parte, multa veritus, refrigescebat atque contremiscebat.[80] Rursus omnia poterat aggredi, rursus item sese levissima quavis oborta suspicione revocabat atque continebat; iterato ad temeritatem excitabatur, iterato inter audendum haesitabat ac ad

However, when he had just started to walk away, he turned towards the temple again and, sighing, gave the place one last inspection. By chance he noticed that he had overlooked one of the rear windows, and decided that he would pursue his love-affair through this, either stealthily or by force.

To bring a ladder up to the place, which was crowded and 69 public, was a difficult proposition and hardly risk-free, given his agenda. So he fastened his eyes on the window, and worked through all of the possibilities in his mind. He thought up a number of daring ideas, but was afraid to carry any of them out. Raging with passion, buffeted by hope and fear, he pulled himself together and remembered the power of the veil the goddess Virtue had given him. He urged himself on to take hold of the weathered old wall of the temple, and stretched his arms far upwards, pushing his nails and beard into the fissures between the stones. Struggling with his hands and feet he snaked his way upwards and through the window as he turned himself into a vine of ivy.[32]

From this vantage, he could see that Praise happened to be 70 alone. Her mother and brothers had gone to sleep, but she was awake, arranging her hair, using as a mirror a polished stone of the temple. Momus could barely control himself owing to the frenzy of his love, and though his spirit was ready for any audacious action, he didn't know where to turn or what course of action to take, except to wait, still and silent, for an opportunity to abduct his beloved. And so he clung cautiously to the wall, his arms spread out and rigid, his mind uncertain. Placed in such a state, with such hopes, it is hard to say how impatient he was both with the delay and with himself. On the one hand, the torches of love burned the more fiercely because of his proximity to the girl; on the other hand, he was terribly afraid, he was freezing, and he was starting to shake. Now he would feel ready for anything, now he would withdraw and hold himself back at the lightest suspicion of trouble; again he would be incited to boldness, and again he would

omnes animi[81] in tanto facinore concitatos metus[82] nequibat totis frondibus non titubare.

71   Puella dea, commotarum frondium levi tum primum illecta[83] sonitu, oculos eo deflexerat. Mox ubi pendentis ramos hederae et quasi plausu gestientes frondes conspicata paululum a crinibus innodandis destitisset, suae non oblita levitatis viridanti ex palmite sibi coronam facere aggrediebatur. Quid hic Momi audaciam referam? Enim sese[84] attrectantem puellam totis lacertis complexus oppressit, atque omnem in partem, ne diis[85] a somno excitis male quod tentasset verteret, oculos atque aures intentas atque arrectas porrigens pervicit. Mox se in fenestrae limitem retraxit et illic paululum suos inde amores victor securusque spectans constitit.

72   Sed vide quid faciat improbitas. Plebei aliqui vilissimi scurrae, quod nullos neque deos neque homines vereri, id demum in vita optimum commodissimumque deputent, per hederam istam ipsam conscendebant stuprandi[86] profanandique templi gratia, prehensisque hinc atque illinc ramusculis multa vi innixi in fenestram evadere elaborabant. Qua ex re effectum est ut Momus, non secus atque per capillos distractus, cum parte putrentis vetustate muri corruere coactus sit. Eam iniuriam Momus aegre tulit. Idcirco in torrentem versus impudentes ipsos scurras foetidam per cloacam traxit atque submersit.

73   At Virtus dea, primo reluctantis filiae strepitu excita, ut erat ingenio acutissimo et consilio praesenti, optimum opportunissimumque ex tempore consilium inivit, quod quidem doctissimi prudentissimique rerum agendarum in hanc usque diem cuncti comprobavere. Quam enim rem ne facta esset poterat ope nulla consequi,[87] eam noluit ad praesentem suam suorumque notam et ignominiam promulgare atque committere fortassis clamitando, ut ad unius filiae acceptam contumeliam novae etiam inimicitiae[88] in

hesitate in the midst of his daring. Every time he worked himself up to commit the crime, he couldn't help shaking like a leaf.

The girl goddess, alerted now for the first time by the gentle 71 sound of the shaking leaves, looked over at them. When she saw the boughs of hanging ivy and leaves that moved as though applauding, she stopped fixing her hair for a moment. With her usual frivolity, she started to make a crown for herself out of the leafy vines. How can I describe Momus' daring at this point? When the girl touched him he embraced her with all his strength and overpowered her. Stretching his eyes and ears in every direction—lest the gods wake up and ruin his plan—he completed his conquest. Then, pulling himself back onto the window-sill, he paused a little while, gazing at his beloved, secure in his victory.

But observe the consequences of wickedness. Some layabouts of 72 the lowest sort, who thought that to fear neither gods nor men was the best and most convenient way to live, set about climbing that very ivy for the pleasure of defiling and profaning the temple. Grabbing here and there at the vines and struggling violently, they worked their way up towards the window. The result was that Momus, exactly as though his hair had been pulled, was compelled to come tumbling down, together with a part of the wall that was crumbling with age. Momus did not take the injury well. Turning himself into a stream, he swept those impudent layabouts into a stinking sewer and drowned them.

Roused for the first time by the screams of her struggling 73 daughter, the goddess Virtue, having an extremely sharp and ready mind, immediately formed an excellent and highly serviceable plan, one which all the wisest and most experienced men of action have commended up to this very day. She could not undo something that had already been done, and did not want immediately to publicize and expose her ignominy and that of her family by raising an outcry, so that new animosities redounding upon the heads of those dear to her would be added to the shame of one of

suos redundaturae accumularentur. Itaque praesentis pro temporis
iniquitate commodius ducit quasi per somnum dissimulando et
obaudiendo, quoad tempus ferat rei atrocitatem levare. Ergo prona
despectat, tacitaque exspectat qualem sibi res ipsa exitum adducat.

74   Puella vero, insperato Momi scelere exterrita, vixdum animos
crinesque collegerat, cum se factam compressu gravidam et partui
maturam sentit. Eodemque ferme temporis momento (mirum
dictu) sponte sua foetum erupisse animadvertit; post id, quod ex
se natum esset colligens, monstrum horrendum teterrimumque
demirans stupuit atque vehementer indoluit. Monstro praeter cetera foeda et obscena illud aderat longe incredibile, quod totidem
oculis, totidem auribus, totidem micabat linguis quot et ipse modo
parens hedera[89] confertus fuerat foliis. Accedebat quod prae se
eam ipsam animi ferebat sollicitudinem et curiositatem circum-
spectandi omnesque motus excipiendi qua inter vitiandum parens
agitabatur. Illudque vehementius perturbabat, quod mira et nimium intempestiva esset loquacitate praeditum: namque vel na-
scendo quidem conari verba coeperat.

75   Tantum ex se natum malum puella non odisse non poterat: ea
de re id opprimere omnibus aggressa est modis, sed frustra. Deo
enim deaque progenitum animans, morti nequiquam obnoxium,
vigebat, sed hinc, huc, illac e matris manibus resultitare, suffugi-
tare, rursus repere per sinus per vestesque interlabi non cessabat:
quin et plagis ictibusque collisum voce, corpore ac viribus excrescebat. Aderat illic propter ex Leuconicis plumis pulvinar, quo sol-
licita puella volutabile inquietissimumque id monstrum suppres-
sans opprimere innitebatur.[90] At monstrum miris modis reluctans
unguibus dentibusque ita pulvinar collaceravit ut medias inter plumas inserperet. Enim tum istic puella intrudere monstrum iterum
atque iterum innitebatur, quo saltem, si minus posset necare, a

her daughters. So she thought it would be better, in regard to the
evil of the present moment, to feign sleep and listen until time had
lessened the horror of the event. Thus she lay silent and watched,
waiting to see how the incident would turn out.

But the girl, terrified by Momus' unexpected attack, had barely   74
put her thoughts and her hair in order when she felt herself becoming heavy in the loins and ready to give birth.[33] Amazingly, at
almost exactly the same moment, she noticed the foetus spontaneously bursting out of her body. She soon gathered that she had
given birth to a horrible, revolting monster, and dumbfounded,
she fell into a profound state of depression. In addition to its other
foul and horrible features, the monster possessed one truly incredible characteristic: it was as thick with eyes, ears and darting
tongues as its ivy parent had been with leaves.[34] Moreover, the
monster showed the same mental anxiety, the same curiosity to see
all around and notice every movement as its father had shown
while committing his crime. But even more disturbing was the fact
that it had been overly endowed with untimely loquacity; indeed,
even while it was being born it had tried to speak.

The girl could not but hate this great evil which she herself had   75
spawned, and she tried in every way to put it down, but in vain.
The creature born of a god and a goddess was alive, unkillable and
flourishing. Here, there and everywhere it kept recoiling from its
mother's hands, eluding her, and again snaking through her bosom
and slipping in among her garments. In fact, every time Praise
slapped or hit it, its voice, body and strength grew. Nearby was a
cushioned couch stuffed with Leuconian down with which the
distraught girl was trying to hold down and smother the restless,
coiling monster. But the monster fought back in amazing ways,
tearing up the couch with its nails and teeth so it could snake its
way through the feathers. The girl struggled again and again to get
the monster under the couch, so that if she couldn't actually kill it,
she might at least hide it from her family and expose it.[35] But

suorum oculis abderet atque exponeret. In eo exsequendo opere
iam tum animis nervisque defecerat.

76 Tantis igitur casibus confectam puellam dea mater dudum
conspicata ingemuit. Ergo ut puellae tanto in discrimine opem
afferret, quasi tum primum a somno expergefacta astitit, ac 'Desine' inquit 'ipsa expediam', graduque citato properans dextero
pede volutantis monstri colla compressit. Monstrum vero, etsi
quasi irretitum nequiquam hisceret, verborum tamen petulantia
insolescebat. Quaeque enim illic conspicarentur decantare minime
intermittebat, quin et quae audisset vidissetque, nonnumquam[91]
vera falsis miscens,[92] referebat. Trophaeum enim Triumphumque
non Virtute natos, sed Casus Fortunaeque filios, et eorum alterum
esse stolidum, alterum dementem adiurabat, hosque irridens
'Io Trophaee, io Triumphe!' vociferabat. 'Tuque heus, Trophaee,
quidni, uti assoles, in triviis ad pueros fessosque vectores tete ostentans signis, mutorum more ganniens,[93] restitas?' Addebat et
Laudem oculo esse indecenter lippam, tum et Posteritatem pedibus retroversis aegre pergere affirmabat. Et ad Virtutem deam versum[94] 'Cum tibi' inquit 'Laus capillum pectit ad frontem, pectus
gremiumque tuum multo[95] conspergitur sordium foeditate.'

77 Monstri istiusmodi commota procacitate Virtus dea animo repetebat quam ferme omnium dicacissimorum sit natura et ingenium ut facile queant vetera neglegere, modo nova ad obloquendum suppeditent. Et eosdem meminerat recentibus in horas
undevis captis rumoribus gaudere, spretisque vulgatis historiis
semper aliquid recentis fabulae captare. Quae cum ita essent, bene
consulta[96] dea 'Abi tu' inquit 'malam in rem, Fama, quandoquidem
fari non desinas, aliasque tibi quas recites fabulas alibi comperito!'
Atque haec dicens, per quam fecisset Momus fenestram furtum,
per hanc monstrum eiecit.

then, in the midst of carrying out her plan, all her strength and resolution failed her.

Thus, seeing the misfortune that had overcome her daughter, 76 the mother goddess groaned. To help her daughter in such a crisis, she stood up as if newly shaken from sleep, and said, "Stop! I shall help you!" Hastening with swift steps, she crushed the throat of the wriggling monster beneath her right foot. The monster, though it could barely open its mouth, trapped as it was, nevertheless grew overbearingly offensive in its language. It wouldn't stop reeling off everything that had gone on there, but it often mixed falsehoods with truth even when describing what it had seen and heard. It swore that Triumph and Trophy were not the sons of Virtue, but of Chance and Fortune, and that one of them was stupid, the other mad. Mocking them, it shouted again and again, "Hi there, Trophy! Ho, Triumph! Hey Trophy, why aren't you hanging around on the streetcorners as usual, showing off your flag to boys and tired porters, whimpering like an animal?" It added that Praise was unbecomingly blind in one eye, then declared that Posterity could scarcely walk with her splayed feet. Turning to the goddess Virtue it said, "When Praise combs her hair in front of you, your breast and lap get spattered a lot with disgusting filth."

Virtue, upset by the monster's foul mouth, reflected how the 77 character and disposition of nearly all those with ready, abusive tongues leads them to ignore old stories with ease, so long as they can supply new ones for obloquy. She recalled that the same sort of person enjoyed hearing the latest rumors, no matter where they came from, and in the incessant search for the freshest gossip spurned stories that were commonly known. So, having considered this well, she said, "Go to hell, Rumor! Since you won't stop chattering, learn some other stories and tell them somewhere else!" With this, she threw the monster through the same window that Momus had used to carry out his abduction.

78   Fama idcirco, quo primum solutis membris licuit, eo repente la-
certos intentans se agitare ac perinde sublimi pendere aere voli-
tando institit, quoad e vestigio didicit evolare tanta pernicitate ut
non radius et umbra, non oculi acies, non animi ulla vis ulla ex
parte ad istius unius celeritatem possit comparari. Ferunt hanc
unico temporis momento[97] campos Marathonios Leuctricosque et
Salaminas et Thermopylas et Cannas et Trasimenum et Furculas
et Scyllaeos scopulos et Cyclopia saxa Idaliasque silvas et Hercu-
leas Gades et Byrsen et Thalas et Atlantis axem et ubi niveos Aurora Phoebo frenat equos et ubi glaciali strident oceano immersus
Sol, omnia, inquam, haec et pleraque omnia quaevis alia istiusmodi momento lustrasse Famam. Accessit quod visendi,[98] auscul-
tandi referendique aviditate ac studio flagrans, nihil uspiam tam
seclusum, abditum obinvolutumque latitabat, quod ipsum Fama
dea non continuo scrutari, renoscitare vulgoque propalare summa
industria, incredibili vigilantia intolerabilique labore inniteretur.

79   Tam exsecrabile ex se progenitum malum intuens Momus
primo coeperat suspicari fore ut pessime secum ab diis ageretur.
Redibat in mentem quale ab se foret in templo, praeter deum hominumque ius fasque, commissum facinus. Illud etiam perturbabat, quod suorum apud divos commodorum interpretem deam
alienasset ab se audaci temerarioque libidinis scelere, et verebatur
ne maximo istius unius Famae praeconio magnorum deorum apud
homines vis et maiestas innotesceret, atque inde et metuere et venerari[99] deos credulum vulgus multo assuesceret. Sed alia ex parte
erat ut se recrearet quod intellegebat Famam non quae approbes
modo, verum et inprimis quae improbes aliorum gaudere facta re-

Thus Rumor, as soon as her body was free, suddenly flapped   78
her arms energetically and forced herself to fly, hovering high in
the air. In an instant, she had learnt how to fly at such high speed
that neither a sunbeam nor a shadow, neither the keenest eye nor
any mental power could in any way compare with her unique
swiftness. It is said that in a single moment of time Rumor travelled through the battlefields of Marathon, Leuctria, Salamis,
Thermopylae, Cannae, Trasimeno, and the Caudine Forks,[36] as
well as the rocks of Scylla, the crags of the Cyclopes, the Idalian
glades, Herculean Gades, Byrsa, Thala, the pole of Atlas, the place
where Aurora curbs the white horses of Phoebus, and where Sun
hisses as he sinks into the freezing ocean.[37] Rumor traversed all of
these places, I tell you, and many others in the same instant!
Moreover, there is nothing so private, hidden and wrapped in
shadow that the goddess Rumor, burning with lust to see, hear,
and tell, does not incessantly try to search out, identify, and divulge to common view, with the utmost diligence, astounding
watchfulness and unbearable toil.

Momus, observing the unspeakable evil to which he had given   79
birth, now began to suspect that he was going to be in big trouble
with the gods. In his mind he revisited the crime he had committed in the temple, a crime which violated the laws of gods and
men. He was deeply worried because, thanks to his villainous and
rash act of lust, he had alienated the goddess who was to negotiate
in his own interest among the gods. Momus also was afraid that
humans would come to know the strength and majesty of the
gods, thanks to the enormous publicity that Rumor, all by herself,
was giving them, and that the gullible crowd would get used to
fearing and worshipping the gods. On the other hand, he comforted himself with the knowledge that Rumor enjoyed gossiping
not only about the meritorious deeds of others, but also—especially—about their disgraceful ones. He had noticed the tendency
of human beings to be less moved by just and pious deeds than

censere. Et adnotarat mortalium mores, qui quidem non tam recte pieque cuiusquam factis moveantur quam ut ex his quae pro officio minus facta appareant graviter offendantur, esseque hominum ingenium huiusmodi meminerat, ut graves etiam laudatores atque maturos habeat suspectos, levissimis vero obtrectatoribus ultro credat, et optimorum egregie facta minori cum voluptate audiat quam perditissimorum calumnias; calumniasque ipsas pro cognitis exploratissimisque referat, veris vero laudibus aliquid semper detrahat atque imminuat. Adde his quod totam hominis mirificam divinamque animi, ingenii, morumque pulchritudinem et laudis decus unico suspecto vitii naevo despiciunt atque fastidiunt.

80   Quae cum ita essent, de re ipsa sic statuebat Momus fore ut, quo superum ferme invenias neminem cui non insint domesticae aliquae insignes illustresque maculae turpitudinis, eo non defuturum quin Famae rumoribus apud mortales deorum opinioni vehementer officiatur. Ceterum, pro vitiata ab se in templo puella, non difficilem habere se apud Iovem causam rebatur, eum qui, amore captum, se non neget quippiam fecisse, in quo patris hominum deorumque regis facta imitatus videatur. Haec tum secum Momus.

81   At alia ex parte dea Fortuna, Virtuti eam ob rem infensa quod iam pridem constituendarum rerum apud mortales provinciam affectasset quodve in ea re sibi deam Virtutem praelatum iri dedignaretur, totam se ad aemulam deturbandam apparabat. Ea de re, dum quaeque apud mortales agerentur observat, sensit quale interea esset terris obortum immane monstrum, cumque visendis monstris maiorem in modum delectaretur, et instituisset suas esse partes Virtutis deae coepta, quoad in se esset, dirimere,[100] laeta ad terras applicuit[101] conveniendi Famam cupiditate captandaeque ad laedendum occasionis gratia. Sed illico in rem sibi ingratissimam incidit: namque Herculem quidem, acrem assiduumque adversus monstra perduellionem, clavam manu librantem totoque innixu[102]

scandalized by those deeds that seemed to fall short of correct behavior. He remembered that human nature is suspicious of pane-
gyrists, even when they are serious and mature, while it freely
credits the most irresponsible of critics. People hear about the
great deeds of eminent men with less pleasure than they listen to
the calumnies of the utterly wicked. They speak of these calumnies as though they were well-established and known facts,
whereas they always temper and lessen true praise. Furthermore,
they will criticize and despise all the amazing and godlike beauty
of mankind's soul, intelligence, moral character and achievements
because of one suspected flaw.

This being so, Momus came to the conclusion that, since   80
scarcely any god could be found whose household had not been
tainted by some famous scandal, it was inevitable that Rumor's
gossip would prove a serious obstacle to the reputation of the gods
among men. Besides, it wouldn't be difficult to plead his cause before Jupiter in the case of the girl he had defiled in the temple.
Momus would simply affirm that, in the throes of love, he had
done something that imitated in appearance the deeds of the father of men and king of the gods. Such were Momus' thoughts.

Now the goddess Fortune, furious at Virtue because the latter   81
had earlier taken the responsibility for restoring human affairs as
her province, and scornful that the goddess Virtue had been preferred to herself in this regard, prepared for the complete overthrow of her rival.[38] To this end, while observing what the humans
were up to, she noticed the horrible monster that had appeared on
earth. Fortune took tremendous delight in looking at monsters
and decided to take it on herself to break up Virtue's enterprises,
insofar as she could. Gleefully, she traveled to earth, full of the desire to meet with Rumor and on the lookout for a chance to do
mischief. Then something most unpleasant happened to her. She
ran into Hercules, that eager and untiring battler of monsters,
brandishing his club in his hand and pursuing Rumor with all his

Famam petentem offendit. Ea de re substitit, secum ipsa quidnam consilii caperet pensitans. Multa offerebantur quae se perturbarent, inter quae illud inprimis animo versabatur, quod audiebat coram bacchantem Famam et deorum facta consiliaque toto aethere explicantem.

82   Quas inter fabulas illud erat, adventasse Fortunam deam ut Virtutis deae coepta interturbaret[103] et Virtutem instituisse in ara apud mortales focum succendere divorum flamma, quo mortalibus in astra pateret via. Huiusmodi vocibus tametsi commoveretur, Fortuna dea tamen quod totis terrarum montibus atque convallibus festivissime resonarent delectabatur; accedebatque ad voluptatem monstri ipsius species informis, omnique corporis facie longe praeter exspectationem opinionemque ostentuosa, ex quo fiebat ut cum monstri futilitatem odisset, tum et cuperet salvum esse atque illaesum.

83   At vero ubi perpendit ipsum Herculem nonnulla ex parte monstri esse persimilem, non se continuit quin hominem accursitans amplexaretur. 'Et quidnam hoc rei est' inquit 'quod denso[104] gravique roboris trunco fretus, tete fatigans, dura et difficilia pro! meditaris[105] in deorum genus? Num tu adeo ignarum te rerum existimatorem habes ut quam oratione rationeque pollentem levi pendere aere sentias non eandem ex deorum progenitam genere intellegas? Hoc moneo, facilius quidem efficies ut quod ipsum mortale sit immortalitatem assequatur, quam ut quod immortale siet a mortali quoquam opprimatur.

84   'Tu proinde quae tuam in rem futura sint dum et tua et mea causa refero, auscultato ipsa: quo argumento te in deorum ordinem facile irripias edocebo, neque erit ut foco[106] quem posuerit in ara Virtus tibi opus deputes. Hoc age: clavae istius corticem deli-

might. Fortune stopped to consider the matter and to decide what plan she should adopt. She was encountering much that disturbed her, but what principally gave her pause was hearing Rumor raving like a bacchante in her presence and exposing the deeds and plans of the gods to the whole world.

One of these stories was that the goddess Fortune had arrived to interfere with the goddess Virtue's plans, and that Virtue had set up among humankind an altar on which she had lit the flame of the gods, thus opening for mortals a pathway to the stars. Although Fortune was shaken by these reports, she was nonetheless delighted that all the mountains and valleys of the world were reverberating joyously with them. Her pleasure was increased by the deformed shape of the monster itself, which was far more striking in every way than she had hoped or believed. As a result, although she hated the deceitfulness of the monster, she also wanted it to be safe and unharmed.

However, when she realized that Hercules himself was quite similar to a monster in some ways, she couldn't stop herself accosting him and flinging her arms about him. "Why is it," she asked him, "that you wear yourself out lugging that thick heavy trunk of oak, planning harsh and difficult deeds against the race of the gods? Are you so inexperienced in sizing up situations that you haven't figured out that this creature, so effective in word and thought and able to hover in thin air, was begotten from divine seed? Let me remind you that you'll find it much easier for a mortal to attain immortality than for an immortal to be beaten by a mortal, whoever he may be.

"Listen: I'll tell you something that might turn out to our mutual advantage. I'll teach you how you can easily break into the divine hierarchy, and you won't need that fire Virtue placed on her altar. Do this: strip the bark from that club of yours — it will make you lighter and faster — and hide yourself in the shade among the soft grasses. There shake the bark, brandish it, whistle, groan, and

82

83

84

brato, quo levigato sis onere expeditior, teque inter molles istas
herbas obdito in umbra, illinc corticem agitans ostentato et insibi-
lato et immugito, vocesque crepitusque varios personato. Dea, ut
est rerum omnium noscendarum curiosa, confestim ad te propera-
bit: illam tu saltu prehendito atque rapito. Ego, ne semel ea facta
manceps te discusso diffugiat, aureum hunc crinem tuum ad capillum innecto: hic robur nervis et pectori firmitatem adhibebit.
Unum cave manu corticem mittas, ne te fortassis foedato, expetita
cum praeda advolet dea.'

85   Enim[107] successit res Herculi ex sententia. At complicitum ad
monstri collum toto amplexu haerentem Momus efferri in altum
Herculem ut vidit, non facile dici potest quantis utramque in partem commotus animi perturbationibus exstiterit. Principio, non
posse hominem ratus tam immane pondus clavae suique una corporis molem diutius sustinere, coepit hortari filiam deam ut hostem audacem et temerarium quam alte sublimem tolleret, quo
collapsus casu gravius confringeretur. Sublatum vero ut vidit, iterum atque iterum coepit efflagitare ut ab se discuteret atque dimit-
teret.

86   Ut demum perpendit Herculem ipsum ad Martis usque regiam
advectum in caelum atque illic in area Martis seu fessitudine seu
consulto elapsum restitisse, coepit prae dolore capillum vellere, ge-
nas unguibus lacerare pectusque contundere et magno cum eiulatu
sese miserum vociferare, 'Actum est, Mome' inquiens 'de te; actum
est! Ne vero non mihi erat apud superos inimicorum satis, ni et is
ex numero eorum[108] qui quidem servo acinacem ut me confoderet
praebuerant,[109] in caelum me auctore asportaretur? Ac videre quidem iam videor hunc artibus istis, quibus apud mortales assuevere, assentando, blandiendo et sese iactando, apud minime ma-

shout with as many different voices and noises as you can. The
goddess, eager as she is to find out everything, will immediately
rush towards you: you'll then leap out, grab her, and carry her off.
I'll bind this golden lock in your hair, so that once she's been taken
prisoner she won't shake you off and escape. This thread will give
strength to your sinews and resolution to your heart. Be careful
not to drop the bark from your hand: otherwise, you'll disgrace
yourself and the goddess will fly off with the prey that she was
hunting."

Hercules' attack went according to plan. But when Momus saw   85
Hercules being carried into the sky, clinging to the monster's neck,
it is not easy to describe how wracked he was with anguish and in-
decision. At first, since he could not imagine how the man could
sustain for so long the enormous burden of his club together with
the weight of his own body, he started to urge his daughter the
goddess to lift their bold and rash enemy as high as she could, so
that when he fell he would be crushed under the greater weight.
Then, when he saw them going higher, he began to implore her to
shake him off and let him drop.

Finally, when he figured that Hercules had been carried up into   86
heaven as far as the palace of Mars and was staying put there in
Mars' province—either through exhaustion or design—Momus
began to tear his hair with grief.[39] He scratched his cheeks with
his fingernails, beat his breast, and with a great wail lamented his
wretchedness over and over again. "You're finished, Momus, finished! Haven't you got enough enemies among the gods already,
without one of those humans—one of the very men who gave a
sword to a slave to kill me—being carried up to heaven? And it's
my own fault! But I predict that this man, by employing the very
arts he has practiced among mortals—toadying, flattery, and self-
promotion—will be able to match that third-rate sinner, King Jupiter, inside of three days. So the man who here used to dance at-

lum illum principem Iovem triduo assecuturum ut qui hic
mulierculae servierit illic regnum inter deorum principes ineat.

87 'Vel ego, omnium stultissimus, quid insanivi? Quid alienas
iniurias ad me recepi? Quid mei[110] capitis periculo, nullis munitus
copiis, exul, invisus, male acceptus, sponte graves aliorum inimici-
tias subivi? Quid mea intererat? Num tacitus poteram mortalem
Herculem immortali cum filia Fama luctantem[111] spectare? Tu,
Mome, tu mortalibus in caelum patefecisti viam tua irarum impa-
tientia, tu hostem in caelum sustulisti. Et profecto in vita ita
convenit, sapientem nullum habere stomachum. Vorandae quidem
sunt hominum iniuriae, sed nostra intolerantia fit ut quae fortassis
levia ferendo essent, ea gravem molestamque in aerumnam cre-
scant male ferentibus. Itaque nunc sapis, Mome, nunc gratis philo-
sophabere. En mortales caelum petunt, tu exulas, Mome, tu eie-
ctus, exclusus exulas. Et quanti est me esse non mortalem, cui
novis in dies molestiis congemiscendum sit? O dulcem laborum
requiem, mortalibus dono a diis deditam, mortem!

88 'Sed quid? Ego itane sum demens? Non perpendo quam
pulchre quae putabam incommoda ea sint meam futura in rem?
Est ergo uti aiunt, sub metu voluptas latitat. Quid igitur? Tene fu-
giunt hominum mores, Mome, quam sint illi quidem ambitiosi,
procaces, audaces? Quotus erit quisque istorum heroum, qui non
et se quoque caelo dignum deputet? Hinc fiet ut tanto ex numero
non paucissimi qua[112] valebunt quidem fraude, quo poterunt dolo,
quo licere sibi omnia putabunt, eo[113] novis excogitatis insidiarum
artibus Herculem imitati consequantur. Da forte ut sint illi quidem, vel duo, in eas recepti regiones caelicolarum: pro quantos
discordiarum turbines conflabunt! Videre videor plenos caelicola-

tendance on his little wife will there be numbered among the principal gods of the realm![40]

"But am I completely stupid, have I lost my mind? Why have I   87
taken on myself the injuries of others? Why, with my life in danger, without resources, an exile, hated, ostracized—why did I voluntarily incur the grave hostility of others? How did that help
me? Why couldn't I shut up and watch the mortal Hercules fighting with the immortal Rumor, my daughter? You, Momus, *you*
have laid open for mortals the way to the heavens, because you
couldn't control your own anger. *You* have lifted up an enemy into
the heavens. The rule that says 'the wise man never gets angry'[41] is
certainly a good one. Mankind's injuries should be swallowed, but
our lack of self-control ensures that things which might be easy to
bear grow into hard and painful trials for those who bear them
ill. So you're a wise man now, Momus; now you can philosophize
free of charge. Look at the mortals making for heaven, Momus,
while you're an exile—you're a cast-out, locked-out exile! What's it
worth that I'm immortal, if every day I have to groan at new
woes? O sweet respite from toil, O divine gift to mortals, Death!

"But what am I talking about? Am I *that* insane? Can't I figure   88
out how beautifully the things that I thought were bad for me
might work to my future advantage? So it's true what they say,
that pleasure lurks under fear. What then? Have the ways of men
escaped you, Momus, how ambitious, overreaching and bold they
are? How many of these heroes are not going to think that they,
too, are worthy of heaven? The logical result will be that among so
many men a goodly number are bound to rely on deceit, to prevail
through trickery, and to think that they have free license to do
anything. Imitating Hercules, they will act in accordance with unheard-of new arts of treachery. Just let this lot—even two of
them—get into the domain of the sky-dwellers! Oh, what storms
of dissent will blow up! I can see the councils of the gods full of
sedition, thanks to their evil tricks and those of their informers

rum coetus seditione malis istorum et delatorum et calumniato-
rum artibus. Hic demum apud mortales quantas clades, quantas
urbium eversiones, quanta gentium excidia futura intueor! Dum
Herculem imitari inter se studiis contentionis inflammati arde-
scent, dum hi per ambitionem Famam occupasse, hi contra per invidiam occupantes interpellasse, ferro, igni, vitaque certabunt.
Nunc me iuvat esse immortalem, nunc non est ut pigeat exilii,
quandoquidem unam hanc ob rem refertum cadaveribus mare,
cruentatas provincias, foedata astra flagrantium urbium fuligine vi-
surus sum. Gaude, Mome!'

89   Itaque haec Momus, atque ut horum inter homines malorum
quasi seminaria iniceret, in Herculis speciem versus ad proceres,
qui de summis rebus consulturi[114] convenerant, composita oratione[115] multa quae ad rem faciant, tum et qua sit ratione et via factus
deus refert seque ut imitentur persuadet. Mox ut eos ad rem exsequendam animis iam et armis accinctos vidit, in auram conversus
evanuit, filiaeque edixit ut hunc sibi ludum usurparet, mutuo sese
his atque his proceribus ostentando.

90   Interea Fortuna dea, quod usui futurum arbitrabatur ne quis
vacuas Iovis aures ad invidiam sui ob Herculis factum praeoccupa-
ret, docta quam in animum cuiusque primas inscripsisse formas
intersit, confestim ad Iovem institit, suadens hunc Herculis insperatum eventum optimam fore in partem accipiendum. Non enim
alio illustriori potuisse argumento deorum maiestas ad venerationem et metum deorum mortalibus monstrari, quam ut discerent
olim se fieri posse deos.

91   Dum haec aguntur Fama dea, ab Hercule excedens, studio visendi propinquas Iovis sedes petierat. Huius taetro truculentoque
aspectu territi dii toto caelo tumultuavere, et qui modo Herculem
ad se delatum aegre tulerant, ii non modo percommode hospitem

and slanderers. And here below, among mortals, what disasters, what sackings of cities, what slaughter of nations do I foresee! As long as they're eager to imitate Hercules, inflamed with zeal to contend among themselves, as long as some from ambition try to seize Rumor, while others from envy try to stop them, they will struggle with fire and sword and with their very lives. Now it does me good to be an immortal; now I don't mind being an exile for this one reason alone: I'll get to see the ocean full of their corpses, their provinces soaked with blood, and the stars blackened with the smoke of their burning cities! Rejoice, Momus!"

Momus finished speaking, and in order to sow the seeds of these evils among humanity, he assumed the guise of Hercules. He addressed the leading men, who had gathered to discuss high affairs of state, and in a set speech told them a number of relevant details; then, describing why and how he had become a god, he persuaded them to imitate him. Presently, when he saw them girding on their weapons and their resolution to execute the plan, he transformed himself into a breeze and vanished, instructing his daughter to take over the game, and pointing out first one, then another of these distinguished gentlemen. 89

Meanwhile the goddess Fortune thought it vital that no one get there first and fill Jupiter's empty ears with envious complaints about Hercules' deed. She knew how important it was to make the right first impressions in anyone's mind. She immediately went to Jupiter and urged him to accept favorably the unexpected arrival of Hercules. She said that the gods' majesty could make no better case for why mortals should venerate and fear the gods than for them to learn that they might one day become gods themselves. 90

While this was going on, the goddess Rumor abandoned Hercules and made for Jupiter's residence, consumed with a desire to see him. Through the whole of heaven the gods, terrified by her foul and truculent appearance, fell into disarray. Those who had only recently been displeased about Hercules' apotheosis to their 91

appulisse, verum et ab inferis arcessendum ni adesset arbitrabantur, ac permaximi quidem interesse asserebant quo duce contra in-
sueta et immania monstra dimicarent.

92 Datur idcirco Herculi ferrea Iovis clava, Vulcani arte facta, qua
monstrum Famam penetralia omnia deorum lustrantem abigat.
Hac fretus Hercules duellum adversus congreditur. Fama, armatum acerrimumque perduellionem nequiquam sibi exspectandum
statuens, caelo a summo se praecipitem dedit, atque inter veniendum[116] magno cum eiulatu vociferabat: 'Nos, diis genitae, prius
reiectae caelo quam conspectae ad infimas mortalium terras insontes pellimur; facinorosissimi mortalium armis deorum ornantur, et
pro tantis iniuriis illud rependitur, ut qui nos laeserint in deorum
numerum ascribantur!'

93 Haec dicendo Fama pervolans nova nefandaque mortalium
coepta offendit; ea de re ad matrem,[117] ceteris omissis[118] rebus,
quasi temulenta, ingenti alarum stridore advolat, magna voce referens quod viderat ac vociferans: 'Fugite hinc, deae,[119] heu fugite,
namque proci amatoresque mortales, vim inferre parati, ad templum adventant! Adsunt armati ut vi de caeli possessionibus paci-
scantur!'

94 His concussae vocibus deae, armatorumque strepitu subaudito
furentium, istiusmodi motibus insuetae, quo se vertant non reperiunt. Itaque intus trepidatur, at foris circum ad templi portas tu-
multuatur; ipsa Fama dea fremitu virum attunditur. Enim[120] fit
hinc refractis vectibus armatorum irruptio in templum, hinc per-

level, now not only greeted him warmly as a guest, but also opined that they would have summoned him from the lower world themselves if he had not arrived on the scene of his own accord. A very large number of them insisted that it made a great difference to have him as their leader in the fight against this unfamiliar and horrible monster.

Thus Hercules was given the iron club of Jupiter, skillfully manufactured by Vulcan, to drive away the monster Rumor, who was roaming through the homes of the gods. Wielding this club, Hercules went out spoiling for a fight. Rumor decided that by no means should she face so well-armed and skillful an opponent, and flung herself down from heaven. As she left, she set up a great wail, howling, "I, the offspring of gods, have been cast out of heaven before even seeing it, and have been driven, though innocent, to the lowest lands of the mortals. The most criminally wicked of mortals are arrayed in the arms of the gods, and the reward I get in return for so many injuries is that those who have harmed me are enrolled in the ranks of the gods!"

With these words, Rumor flew off and discovered some new and wicked schemes among mankind. Forgetting everything else, like a drunken woman, she flew to her mother with a great flapping of wings, and recounted in a loud voice what she had seen, shouting, "Flee from here, goddesses, flee! Some amorous mortal suitors, who are prepared to use force, are nearing the temple! They're armed so as to enjoy violently the property of heaven!"

The goddesses were alarmed by her words. They heard the clatter of savage armed men, and being unused to such behavior, they didn't know where to turn. So inside they shook in fear, whilst outside there was an uproar by the temple doors. Even the goddess Rumor was stunned by the roar they made. The door bolts were smashed in and the armed men burst into the temple. The terrified young divinities wailed with fear in the bosom of their

territorum deorum adulescentulorum ad matris gremium eiulatus. Mater Virtus ne se ita vestibus comprehensam detentent admonet, seque una inde quam ocissime in quippiam rerum versi proripiant sollicitat. Illi cum hebetes tardique natura, tum armatorum aspectu animis consternati haesitabant. Dea vero Virtus, et mortalium audacia et suorum ignavia irritata, maximo deorum voto imprecata est ne desidibus posthac in caelum uspiam aditus pateat, atque ignavis diis nisi unam[121] liceat in formam verti. His peractis exsecrationibus, in fulgur versa emicans evolavit. Laus Virtutis filia, pallio amisso, levem in fumum versa hos atque hos sui prehensatores occaecatos reliquit.

95   Momus, nefastum taetrumque mortalium scelus conspicatus, nequivit non facere quin, suorum temporum similitudine commotus, trium relictorum in templo deorum vicem ingemisceret. Ergo, ut erat in auram versus, in templum ad divos confestim pervadit, rogatque se vertant in quampiam rem, quo se in libertatem vindicent. Consulentibus diis[122] in hominemne, quo, raptis insultantium armis, strage et occidione infestos occiderent, 'Etsi opto' inquit Momus 'ut quo acinace ipsum me petierint eodem cadant, vos tamen quidvis fieri malim[123] quam homines, namque in terris nihil est homine quod vivat durius. Quin et animantis cuiusquam personam ne induatis admoneo: namque mortale qui iniverit corpus cum multa offendet incommoda, tum illud grave atque iniquum urgebit, quod sui ferre carcerem oportebit.'

96   Haec Momus. At negavit Triumphus admodum se absque corporis commercio, quo voluptatibus perfrueretur, velle degere. Idcirco in papilionem se vertens attrectantium admirantiumque e manibus lubricis alis delapsus evolavit. Trophaeus vero, ut erat corpore vasto, immane in saxum versus, aliquot eorum qui manum ad se attulissent suppressit. Puella dea Posteritas pro dignitate et

mother. Mother Virtue told them to let go of her clothes, and advised them to turn themselves as quickly as possible into something else and get out of there. Being slow and sluggish by nature and also alarmed by the sight of armed men, they hesitated. But the goddess Virtue, angered both by the audacity of the mortals and by the cowardice of her offspring, prayed, with the gods' strongest vow, that hereafter slackers should be always denied entry to heaven, and that cowardly gods should only be allowed to transform into one shape. Having finished her execrations, she turned into lightning, flashed, and disappeared. Praise, the daughter of Virtue, who had lost her outer garment, turned into a puff of smoke, leaving various of her attackers blinded.

Momus, having witnessing the mortals' foul and wicked crime, 95 could not help lamenting the fate of the three gods left in the temple, as it was so similar to his own misfortunes. So he transformed himself into a breeze, and blew quickly towards the gods in the temple. He implored them to turn themselves into something else to secure their liberty. The gods debated whether to turn into a man, so that they could seize the weapons of those who had outraged them and exterminate their enemies with slaughter and carnage. Momus said, "Although I wish they might die by the same sword they pointed at me, I'd prefer you to become something other than human, because on earth nothing has a harder life than man. Furthermore, I'd advise you not to assume the appearance of any animate being. Anyone who enters a mortal body will encounter many troubles, and he will be oppressed by this grave and evil fact: that he has to endure the prison of his own body."

Thus Momus. Triumph said that he did not want to live with- 96 out a body he could use to enjoy pleasures. He turned himself into a butterfly, and on slippery wings he flew from the hands of his amazed attackers. Trophy, who had an enormous body, turned himself into an immense rock, and crushed several of those who had laid hands on him. The young goddess Posterity very properly

temporis necessitate rectius consuluit: in eam enim se vertit deam, quam quidem Echo nuncuparunt. Quae cum ita essent, frustrati mortales non sine rixa ereptum Laudi pallium horsum istorsumque carpendo collacerarunt et minutissimas in particulas, ut casus tulit, conscissum diripuerunt.

took thought for her dignity and the need of the moment: she turned herself into the goddess they call Echo. Thus the frustrated mortals fought noisily over the dress they had snatched from Praise, and by pulling and tearing it this way and that, they reduced it to tiny pieces which they carried off as chance directed.

LIBER SECUNDUS

1 Quas perturbationes Momi exilium apud mortales excitaverit hactenus recensuimus; nunc dicendum qua ratione ab exilio in Iovis gratiam restitutus et quam novis inauditisque perturbandarum rerum artibus paene ultimum in discrimen deos et homines et universam orbis machinam adduxerit. Atqui erit quidem operae pretium legisse quam varia incertaque consilia insperati inauditique rerum eventus quamque frequentes et digni memoratu sint casus subsecuti, ut nesciam ipsane me rerum dignarum et magnitudo et copia plus ab scribendo, dum ingenio diffidimus, absterreat, quam historiae amoenitas ad scribendum voluptate illectet atque invitet. Dices de Momo quicquid hucusque legeris fore nulla ex parte comparandum cum his quae deinceps consequentur.

2 Nam cum auctore Momo coepissent puellae ab superis diis levia primum et pusilla poscere, quod solent amantissimi patres blaesis puerulis et delicatis filiolis poma et similia poscentibus tradere cum voluptate et risu, ita et diis iucunda erant puellarum vota illa ridicula. Dum aliae quod pingulentae essent, aliae quod nimia macritudine non placerent, aliae quod aliud quippiam ad speciem liberalis formae desiderarent,[1] id simplici quadam animi puritate deprecarentur, et quo erat facile obsequi, eo et[2] dii benigne conferebant, hinc desumentes quod huic alterae puellae contribuerent. Ac manavit quidem res pari deorum facilitate usque dum patres maioresque natu facere et ipsi vota accessere, sed primo iusta atque ea quidem eiusmodi ut facere palam medio in foro amicis (ut aiunt) inimicisque probantibus deceret: ergo ab diis sponte ac vo-

BOOK II

So far, we have recounted the upheavals caused by Momus' exile 1
among the mortals. Now I must tell how he was restored from exile to the favor of Jupiter, and how, using new and hitherto unknown arts of agitation, he nearly drew men, gods, and the whole
machinery of the world into utter calamity. It will be worth while
indeed to read about the various fluctuating plans, the unexpected
and unprecedented outcomes, and the numerous and memorable
incidents that took place. I hardly know whether the greatness and
abundance of memorable events should deter me from writing,
diffident as I am of my talent, or whether the delightfulness of the
tale should rather beguile and attract me to the pleasure of writing
it. You will have to admit that what you have read of Momus so
far cannot at all be compared with what happened to him next.

At Momus' instigation, girls first began to demand trifling and 2
petty things from the gods. Just as doting fathers, smiling with
pleasure, are wont to give their lisping little boys and spoiled little girls apples and things like that when asked, so too were the
gods pleased with the girls' ridiculous prayers. Some prayed, with
touching simplicity of heart, because they were too chubby; others
because they didn't like being so skinny; and others because they
wanted to add something else to their already ample good looks. It
was as easy for them to ask as it was for the gods benevolently to
grant their requests, taking from one girl what they bestowed
upon another. The practice spread, thanks to the even-handed
kindness of the gods, until fathers and adults began to say prayers,
too. Initially their prayers were righteous and of the sort that
could be made openly in public, with the approval of friends and
enemies alike, and so the gods heard their prayers freely and with

lentibus audiebantur. Accessit item ut reges ditissimaeque respublicae votis deos poscere assuescerent.

3 Principio hominum haec adversus deos et[3] veneratio et cultus adeo fuit accepta superis, inventi novitatem probantibus,[4] ut nulla in re libentius versarentur quam in votis mortalium benigne suscipiendis. Perquisitoque idcirco atque cognito huius tam gratae rei auctore, cunctorum animi ab eo quo erant erga Momum praediti odio ad misericordiam fuere atque ad benivolentiam conversi. Hinc summo omnium consensu et sententiis fit amplissimis verbis de revocando Momo lex, constituunturque legati Pallas dea atque altera Minerva, quae quidem optime de deorum genere promeritum Momum quam honorificentissime suas in pristinas sedes ad caelicolarum ordinem reducant atque restituant, et datur inclusus gemma sacer ignis deorum, quo divinitatis insigne apicem inflammet ad verticemque adigant reduci.

4 Recusarat Pallas velle ad mortales accedere, nam eos quidem armis posse et animis valere audierat: tandem, imperio Iovis et amicorum suasionibus victa, sumptis thorace et armis, parere instituit. Vixdum rogata erat apud superos lex: eccam Famam stridentibus alis properantem ad Momum anxiam! Atqui, uti est eius natura veris falsa immiscere et omnia tametsi pusilla dicendo reddere grandiora, parenti nuntiat tumultuari apud superos, maximos parari motus, iam coepisse delabi caelo armatos deos. Quam rem audiens Momus, flagitiorum suorum conscientia exagitatus atque aestuans, procidit. Vexabat animum quod violatos ab se fore optimi et maximi deorum immortalium regis legatos meminisset, quo suo detestabili scelere omne caelum in se infestum iraque in-

good will. Then it transpired that even kings and wealthy repub-
lics grew used to making demands on the gods in prayer.[1]

At first mankind's worship and veneration of the gods was so 3
welcome to the higher beings that they applauded the novel invention and enjoyed nothing more than graciously answering the
prayers of mortals. Thus, having sought out and identified the inventor of this welcome practice, they all experienced a change of
heart. Once filled with hatred for Momus, they now regarded him
with compassion and good will. Hence they unanimously and in
gracious language passed a law recalling Momus, and appointed as
their ambassadors two goddesses, Pallas and Minerva, to escort
Momus home in the most honorable fashion and restore him, as
one well deserving of the race of gods, to his former place in the
divine hierarchy. They were given the holy flame of the gods, en-
cased in a jewel, so that this sign of divinity might glow in the coronet which they were to place on the head of the returning god.

Pallas protested this expressed desire that she visit the mortals, 4
for she had heard that they were resolute and strong in arms, but
finally, overcome by Jupiter's command and the persuasion of her
friends, she took up her breastplate and weapons and decided to
obey. Scarcely had the law been passed by the gods when look!
Rumor, in distress, is rushing off to Momus with a whirr of wings.
And as it is her nature to mix the false with the true and, by talking about it, to magnify every little thing into a big one, she tells
her father of uproars among the gods, that great changes are afoot,
that armed gods have already started to slip down from heaven.
Hearing the news, Momus collapsed, seething and disturbed by
the consciousness of the crimes he had committed. He was tormented when he remembered how he had outraged the ambassadors of the best and greatest king of the immortal gods. Reckoning that all of heaven would be angry and hostile towards him
because of his hateful crime, he doubted that he could survive so
great an onslaught of anger. And so with urgent entreaties he pres-

censum arbitrabatur, et tantos irarum impetus perferre diffidebat. Ea de re maximis precibus agit apud filiam uti, quoad in se sit, deos ipsos adventantes interpellet atque frustretur, quo sibi et capiendi consilii interea et delitescendi locus detur, si forte liceat fallere subterfugiis. Fama ut parenti obtemperet advolat.

5   Momus vero difficile dictu est quam omnes in animi perturbationes iactarit se atque agitarit. Multa incohabat consilia, cuncta displicebant; omnia tentabat, nihil non aggrediebatur quod ad opem atque salutem suam facere suspicaretur. Alia[5] ex parte singulis diffidebat locisque rebusque, quicquid inierat consiliorum repudiabat; nihil fuit formae in quod[6] vertere se non affectarit. Tantis curis confectum Momum Fama rediens recreavit. Nam 'Bonis commodisque usurum te diis, Mome, annuntio' inquit 'et, quod minime reris, pacem gratiamque afferunt, et una sacrum deorum igniculum ad te dono deferunt.'

6   Id cum intellexisset, etsi veteris cum dea Fraude inimicitiae memor verebatur ne quid doli ad se intercipiendum importaretur, tamen, quod abscondendi sui nullus aut locus aut facultas dabatur diis superis omnia spectantibus, quodve taedium sui ferre diutius dedignaretur, in quoscumque sibi essent parati casus praecipitem obicere se admodum festinabat. Ergo ultro progredi animumque alioquin labefactatum atque prostratum erecto vultu fictaque hilaritate integere[7] et de seipso quid sentiat habere alta reconditum dissimulatione instituit.

7   Factus inde obviam, cum se mutuo salutassent atque ex legatorum vultu verbisque plane atque aperte intellexisset praeter spem se ex omnium rerum difficultate ad superum delicias evocari exque diuturnis tenebris miseriarum suarum in summum illustremque pristinae dignitatis gradum assumi, amens factus repentino gau-

sured his daughter to waylay and harass the approaching gods as much as she could, to give him an opportunity in the meantime to formulate a plan and find a place to hide, to see whether he might deceive them by trickery. Rumor flew off in obedience to her father.

It is difficult to describe the many anxieties that tossed and rat- 5 tled in Momus' mind. He outlined numerous plans, but they all displeased him. He tried everything, but nothing occurred to him that he guessed would help him or would keep him safe. On the other hand he despaired of every thing and every place, and whatever plan he had begun, he would reject. There was no shape into which he did not want to transform himself. Just when he had exhausted himself with such anxieties, Rumor flew back and revived him. "I tell you that the gods want to heap you with good things and benefits, Momus! It's the last thing you thought would happen—they are offering peace and thanks, and they're also bearing with them the holy flamelet of the gods as a gift for you!"

When he heard this, Momus, remembering the inveterate hos- 6 tility of the goddess Mischief, was afraid that some device was being brought to trap him. However, either because he had neither place nor opportunity for hiding himself, as the gods saw everything, or because he scorned to put up with his loathsome condition any longer, he rushed to throw himself headlong into the arms of those who had prepared his fate. He decided to approach them voluntarily, covering up his corrupt and defeated spirit with a confident attitude and false merriment, and hiding deep inside his real feelings about himself.

So having met and exchanged formal greetings with them, 7 Momus saw clearly from the ambassadors' expressions and words that, beyond all hope, he was being recalled from endless problems to the delights of divinity, and from the shadow of chronic wretchedness he was being assumed into the high and illustrious rank he had previously held. Delirious with sudden delight, he could not

dio, quibus verbis pro animi libidine congratularetur non habebat,
sed prae laetitia prope delirans multa dicebat inconsiderate, inter
quae illud ex ore inconsultum excidit, ut diceret: 'Sicine, Mome,
quod apud mortales aiunt, omnes ab exilio ad imperium veniunt?'

8   Quod Momi dictum Pallas (ut sunt mulieres ad suspicandum
pronae, ad perversa interpretandum faciles, ad nocendum paratae
et proclives) altiori discursu pensitavit quam ut id ulla vultus fron-
tisve significatione indicaret. Sed tacita profundo pectore Momi
naturam atque improbitatem versans, statuebat neque Iovis neque
superum rationibus convenire ut huic nequissimo veteris iniuriae
procul dubio memori et innata consuetudine improbitatis ad omne
genus audaciae promptissimo id conferatur, quod magnas gravesque res agendi potestatem et facultatem praestet.

9   Repetebat item cum ceteras, tum has rationes Pallas, ut suo
cum animo diceret: 'Nos quidem debilitatum exilio et fractum aerumnis hunc monstrorum procreatorem aegre sustinuimus. Quid
tum? Utrumne superum donis confirmatum et integrum nullo
cum periculo sustinebimus? Quid illud aut quanti intererit, divini
muneris spe et exspectatione Momum a furore cohibere an porri-
gere quod promptum et in flagitium accinctum excitatumque impellat? Vel quis erit iniuriis atque inprimis exilio lacessitus, qui
non vindicandi sui praestari occasionem cupiat? Et quis erit vindicandi sui cupidus, qui non perficiendi facinoris proposita spe et facultate omnia aggrediatur?'

10   His rationibus mota Pallas, ut commodius rem totam cum collega[8] definiret, edicit Momo uti sese interea ad fontem Helicona
comparet[9] atque ornet, quo posito squalore honestior ad consalutandum superos redeat. Misso Momo, cum satis deliberassent in-

find words to express his pleasure, but almost gibbering with happiness, he said many things thoughtlessly. Among these, he let this ill-advised remark slip from his lips: "So it's really true, Momus, just as mortals say, that everyone comes to power from exile?"

When Momus said this, Pallas — since women are inclined to 8 be suspicious and to take things in perverse ways, and are both ready and willing to do harm — mulled it over more searchingly than either her expression or her appearance belied. Silently, deep in her heart, she ruminated on Momus' character and lack of principle. She decided that neither Jove's purposes nor those of the gods would be served by giving this nefarious individual the power and opportunity to undertake large and weighty enterprises. He no doubt remembered his old grievance, and thanks to his congenitally unscrupulous way of behaving he would be all too ready for every kind of roguery.

Pallas ran through first these, then other reasons, debating thus 9 with herself: "We have hardly been able to check this father of monsters while he was weakened by exile and shattered by hardship. What then? Will we be able to control him without danger once he has been made whole and is fortified by the gifts of the gods? Isn't there a big difference between checking Momus' rage when he still has hope and expectation of a heavenly reward, and offering something that will make him active, ready and motivated to do harm? Who would not long to be given the opportunity for revenge, if he had been struck down by injuries and especially by banishment? And what man who wants to avenge himself will not make every effort to do so, especially if the hope and the opportunity are set in front of him?"

Pallas was moved by these arguments, and wanting to settle the 10 whole matter more easily with her colleague, she packed Momus off to the spring of Helicon in the meantime to wash off the grime and smarten himself up, so he would be more respectable when he returned to greet the gods. Once Momus had left, the goddesses

ter se, decernunt deae fore id Iovis consilium ut mature videat quam e republica deorum deputet Momum versari insignem inter caelicolas atque munitum sacro deorum igniculo, ni prius perversi indomitique animi rationes perspectas et cognitas habeat.

11   Momus ubi solus lavat haec secum animo coepit deputare: 'Olim quod tristem personam gererem illam et[10] severam, taetrico incessu, truculento et torribili aspectu, vestitu aspero, barba et capillo subhorrido atque inculto, superstitiosa quadam severitate,[11] multo supercilio nimiaque frontis contractione gestiebam, quodve me aut contumaci quadam taciturnitate aut odiosa obiurgandi mordendique acrimonia publicum terrorem omnibus offerebam, merito nullis eram non invisus atque infensus. Nunc vero aliam nostris temporibus accommodatiorem personam imbuendam sentio. Et quaenam ea erit persona, Mome? Nempe ut comem, lenem affabilemque me exhibeam. Item oportet discam praesto esse omnibus, benigne obsequi, per hilaritatem excipere, grate detinere, laetos mittere. Ne tu haec, Mome, ab tua natura penitus aliena poteris? Potero quidem, dum velim. Et erit ut velis? Quidni? Spe illectus, necessitate actus propositisque praemiis, ipsum me potero fingere atque accommodare his quae usui futura sint. Sequere, Mome: namque de te quicquid abs te voles impetrabis et quae tute tibi non negabis, ea tu quidem omnia perquam pulcherrime poteris.

12   'Quid tum? Igiturne vero nos insitum et penitus innatum lacessendi morem obliviscemur? Minime; verum id quidem moderabimur taciturnitate, pristinumque erga inimicos studium nova quadam captandi laedendique via et ratione servabimus. Demum sic statuo oportere his quibus intra multitudinem atque in negotio vi-

discussed the situation and decided that it was up to Jupiter to weigh carefully how it would benefit the heavenly commonwealth for Momus to hold a distinguished position among the sky-dwellers, fortified by the holy flame of the gods, without the intentions of this perverse and ungovernable individual being first investigated and ascertained.

Momus, washing all alone, began to muse thus: "Before, when I wore that grim and forbidding mask, that foul attitude, that quarrelsome and frightening look, when my beard and hair were bristling and ungroomed, when I used to affect a kind of humorless fanaticism, raising my eyebrow and wrinkling my forehead, or when I presented myself to everyone as a public menace, with my contemptuous silences and my odious keenness to scold and criticise, everyone had good reason to hate and despise me. But now I realize that I must adopt another mask, one more suitable to my circumstances. What will that mask be, Momus? I must show myself to be a friendly fellow, of course, easygoing and affable. I must learn how to be useful to everyone, how to humor people indulgently, receive them with good cheer, entertain them graciously, and send them away happy. Can you do something so completely against your own nature, Momus? Yes, I can, as long as I want to. And will you want to? Why not? Enticed by hope, driven by necessity and proffered rewards, I *shall* be able to pretend and to adapt myself to situations I can benefit from. Go for it, Momus: when it comes to getting things from yourself, there's no one to say you nay, so you can make a brilliant success of it.

"What next? Shall I then forget my deep-rooted and almost congenital habit of doing harm? No; but I will control it silently, and I shall preserve my old zeal against my enemies, using, however, another way, a new method for entrapping and hurting them. I have come to the conclusion that men who have to live and do business among the multitude must never in their heart of hearts blot out the memory of an injury they have sustained, but they

vendum sit, ut ex intimis praecordiis numquam susceptae iniuriae memoriam obliterent, offensae vero livorem nusquam propalent, sed inserviant temporibus, simulando atque dissimulando. In eo tamen opere sibi nequiquam desint, sed quasi in speculis pervigilent, captantes quid quisque sentiat, quibus moveatur studiis, quid cogitet, quid tentet, quid aggrediatur, quid quemque expediat, quid necesse sit, quos quisque diligat, quos oderit, quae cuiusque causa et voluntas, quae cuique in agendis rebus facultas et ratio sit. Alia ex parte sua ipsi studia et cupiditates callida semper confingendi arte integant; vigilantes, sollertes, accincti paratique occasiones[12] praestolentur vindicandi sui, praestitam ne deserant; sempiterne sui sint memores; numquam adversariis parcant nisi cum velint gravius laedere, arietum more, qui quidem abscedendo impetum concitant, quo vehementius impetant.

13   'Multandoque inimico re quam verbis, facto quam ostentatione insistent; frontis familiaritate et blanditiis iram animi operient; omnium sermones aeque esse insidiosos deputent; credent nemini, sed credere omnibus ostentabunt. Nullos vereantur, sed coram quibusque applaudere atque assentari omnibus condocefiant. Qui se sic instructum paratumque exhibuerit vulgo habebitur frugi, servabitur apud doctos; metuent omnes, observabunt,[13] idque praesertim cum te viderint quasi ex commentariis omnem eorum vitam tenere ad unguem. Alioquin si ipsum te neglexeris, si cesseris petulantibus, si pertuleris irritantes, fiet ut immodesti in te in dies insolentiores reddantur tua patientia; fiet item ut procaces temulentique quodammodo ad te unum vexandum illectentur.

must never make public their anger at this offence. Instead, they must be time-servers, practicing simulation and dissimulation.[2] Nevertheless, they should always stick to their plan, remaining on guard, as in a watchtower, finding out what each man thinks, where his loyalties lie, what his dreams are, what he tries to do, what he undertakes, what is profitable to him, what he needs, whom he likes, whom he hates, what his motivations and his will are like, and what are his resources and plan of acting. By the same token, such men must themselves always hide their own enthusiasms and desires by adroit techniques of pretense. Watchful, skillful, armed and ready, they should wait for an opportunity to avenge themselves and not miss it when it presents itself. They should be forever mindful of their own interests; they should never spare their enemies unless they want to harm them still more grievously, like rams who build up striking power by rearing back, so as to butt all the more savagely.

"In punishing their enemy they will use things, not words; 13 deeds, not empty show. They will conceal the anger in their minds with a kind and winning manner; they will account everyone's words as equally untrustworthy. They will trust no one, but they will pretend to trust everyone. They should fear no man, but should train themselves to applaud and flatter everyone while in their presence. Anyone who shows himself trained and ready in this way will be regarded by the vulgar as honest; he will maintain his position among the learned; and everyone will fear and respect him, particularly when they see you adhering to their whole way of life down to the last detail, as though following a textbook. Otherwise, if you neglect your own interests, if you give in to the impudent, if you tolerate those who annoy you, the licentious will daily become more insolent towards you because of your patience, and this will further induce aggressive drunks to target you with their unwelcome attentions."

14 'Sed quid plura? Omnino illud unum iterum atque iterum iuva-
bit meminisse, bene et gnaviter fuscare omnia adumbratis quibusdam signis probitatis et innocentiae. Quam quidem rem pulchre
assequemur si verba vultusque nostros et omnem corporis faciem
assuefaciemus ita fingere atque conformare,[14] ut illis esse persimi-
les videamur qui boni ac mites putentur, tametsi ab illis penitus
discrepemus. O rem optimam nosse erudito artificio fucatae falla-
cisque simulationis suos operire atque obnubere sensus!'

15 Haec Momus. At Pallas et Minerva interea constituerant Iovis
arbitrio relinquere ut provideret turbulentone et concitato ad
omne facinus Momo deorum sacrum insigne commodent.[15] Verum interea exulem perquam benigne conveniunt, multa spe confirmatum hortantur ut malit summi deorum regis quam legatorum
manu divinitatis insigne suscipere.

16 Nullam recusat Momus conditionem, modo ab terrarum incolis
diffugiat, et quam quidem ipse sibi personam gerere imperarat,
impraesentiarum apud legatas belle ac sedulo initam agit. Quadam
enim simulata simplicitate et bonitate coepit collacrimari, et acclinato vultu inquit se quidem non ignorare quam intersit maximi
optimique deum regis manu ornari se atque restitui, fateri quidem
tantorum se putare munerum esse immeritum, daturum tamen
operam ut Iovi ceterisque diis, quoad in se sit, perspectum et cognitum reddat se neque immemorem esse neque ingratum accepti
beneficii; idque sperare se assecuturum, quandoquidem agendo
recte omnem exspectationem bonorum de se longe superare instituerit, et fracturum invidorum inimicorumque erga se conatus et
impetum patientia atque rebus his omnibus quibus ad gratiam et

"In short, it will be advantageous above all to call this one thing 14
to mind over and over again: hide all your plans carefully and well,
covering them with signs of trustworthiness and innocence. I shall
carry this off brilliantly once I get used to molding and shaping my
words, expressions, and my whole appearance so that I seem iden-
tical to those who are deemed good and meek, even though I am
completely different from them. Oh, what an excellent thing it is
to know how to cover and cloak one's true feelings with a painted
façade of artificiality and studied pretense!"

Thus Momus. Meanwhile, Pallas and Minerva determined to 15
leave it up to Jupiter to decide whether he wanted to bestow the
holy flame of the gods on a turbulent troublemaker like Momus.
In the meantime they met graciously with the exile and fortified
him with hope. They impressed upon him that he might prefer to
accept the gift of divinity from the king of the gods himself rather
than from the hands of the king's ambassadors.

Momus refused none of their conditions, so long as he could 16
escape from the earth-dwellers. He began on the spot to play brilliantly and with great zest before the ambassadors the role that he
had commanded himself to play. Feigning simplicity and goodness,
he started to weep, and bowing his head, he said he was not unaware how important it was to be honored and restored at the
hands of the greatest and best king of the gods. He confessed that
he thought himself unworthy of such great gifts, but that he
would do his utmost to show Jupiter and the rest of the gods, insofar as he could, that he remembered and was grateful for what
they had done for him. He hoped he would succeed in this, since he
had resolved, by behaving well, to far surpass all their expectations
of good for him. Through long-suffering he would shatter the
plots and attacks of those who envied and hated him and by every
other means he would incline them to graciousness and goodwill.
He said that, overwhelmed by prolonged calamity and worn down
with hardship, he had learned to endure adversity and to bear it

benivolentiam flectantur;[16] se quidem longa perdomitum calamitate atque aerumnis confectum didicisse perpeti adversa et facile
moderateque ferre si quid forte suam praeter sententiam et volun-
tatem exciderit; quibus rebus fiat ut possit non invitus illatas iniurias ad se non recipere et susceptas funditus oblivisci. Demum cupere et ad felicitatem putare id, sibi ut detur locus quo melioribus
et bene consulentibus pareat atque obtemperet.

17   Itaque haec Momus cum ornate copioseque disseruisset, qui
coeperat esse veterator, ficto vultu suspirans, 'Et quid agimus?' inquit. 'Abite vos dignae caelo, deae, ac redite ad vestras delicias, sinite miserum et infelicissimum exulem versari in sordibus et squalore! Sinite me in luctu, in solitudine degere et calamitatem qua
oppressus obrutusque sum ferre, quandoquidem ea tanta est ut ad
miseriam addi amplius nihil possit.' Hic deae quadam permotae
misericordia, multa ad consolandum prosecutae, medium inter se
Momum excepere atque ad superos adduxere.

18   Ad Iovem igitur cum appulisset Momus, pro suscepta assentatoris persona regis genua amplexatus veniamque pacemque compositis verbis deprecatus, non, uti concupisset, exceptus exstitit
benigne ab Iove. Nam adversus Phoebum factus iratior Iuppiter
intumuerat et ad redarguendi Phoebi quam ad salutandi Momi
causam erat occupatior. At miser Momus, rerum istarum ignarus,
suas rationes malo iniri apud superos exordio interpretatus, penitus concidit. Et quo se verteret non inveniens, quasi indicta ad iudices die reum se accitum atque adductum putare et pro capite
causam meditari quo dicendi genere culpam ab se suorum scelerum amoveret, quibusve deprecationis et commiserationis locis Iovem mitigaret secum ipse commentari occeperat.

19   Interea qui ab Iove scrutatum missus fuerat, Mercurius, rediens
refert Phoebum ipsum illico adfuturum, neque, quod inimici ca-

temperately and with ease if he were deprived of something contrary to his expectation and desire. As a result, he was able to keep himself from taking offense at injuries done to him and could forgive entirely injuries he had received. Finally, he said that he desired and believed it would conduce to his happiness to be allowed the opportunity to submit to and obey his betters and those of sound judgment.

And so when Momus—who had begun to be a sly old fox— 17 had explained this elegantly and at great length, he sighed with a false expression and said, "What should I do? Leave me, goddesses, worthy of heaven, and return to your pleasures, let a wretched and unhappy exile be cast into poverty and filth! Let me live in grief and loneliness, let me bear the catastrophe which struck me down and crushed me! This catastrophe is so great that nothing further can be heaped upon my misery." At this point the goddesses, deeply moved with pity, consoled Momus at length, and placing him between them escorted him up to the gods.

When Momus was brought before Jupiter, he embraced the 18 knees of the king in his assumed role of flatterer, and begged for pardon and clemency with well-chosen words. But he was not as graciously received by Jupiter as he would have liked. Jupiter in fact had gotten into a towering rage at Apollo, and he was more preoccupied with rebuking that god than with greeting Momus. However, the unfortunate Momus, unaware of this circumstance, thought that he had made a bad start with his plans among the gods, and completely collapsed. He did not know which way to turn. Just as a defendant who is summonsed and hauled before judges on the appointed day rehearses his case and thinks desperately what language he can use to absolve himself of guilt, so Momus began to formulate mentally which appeals to clemency and mercy might soften Jupiter's wrath.

Meanwhile Mercury, whom Jupiter had sent to investigate, re- 19 turned to report that Apollo himself would arrive momentarily. It

lumniis insimularant, aut Aurorae illecebris et amoribus detineri
aut suam per superbiam exsequi officium dedignari, verum immani quadam votorum phalange obiecta impediri[17] quominus ad
regiam Iovis arcem pro vetere more et consuetudine, ut assolent
dii, singulis diebus regem consalutatum[18] et veneratum ascenderet.
Hic Iuppiter, remissa frontis severitate, in Momum versus 'Nos'
inquit 'vota istaec tua, Mome, ni modus adhibeatur, obruent,' dictisque paululum conticuit. At Momo id Iovis dictum illico in animum induxit ut faceret coniecturam se aliquid turbarum suis votis
concivisse, idque cupidissimo rerum novarum tam fuit voluptati ut
non potuerit non oblivisci maeroris sui, conceptamque animo lae-
titiam nequivit non propalare. Secundo enim optatissimoque flagitiorum suorum successu gestiebat atque intra se 'Peream' aiebat 'ut
libet, modo, quod videre videor, hic aliquid laeserim.'

20   Interea Iuppiter ad Minervam Pallademque versus inquit
'Quin[19] et Virtutem vobiscum una reduxistis? Quid ea? Quid rerum agit?' Hic deae se quidem, pro vetere legatorum more, curasse
in sua profectione aliud nihil respondere praeter unum id, cuius
gratia proficiscerentur, ac satis quidem se superque habuisse negotii in uno Momo pervestigando, quando, ut miseri calamitosique
faciunt, in solitudine et squalore abditus latitaret. Coepit ergo Iuppiter de Momo sciscitari Virtutemne apud mortales viderit. Hic
Momus, dura suspicione perculsus ne quid ea interrogatio ad factum ab se vitium spectet, expalluerat et obmutuerat. Sed brevi
sese colligens, obducta ad speciem comiter fidentis fronte, subridens 'Num tu, o dignissime deorum princeps, quae apud mortales
in dies gerantur' inquit 'ignoras?'

was not the case, as his enemies had slanderously insinuated, that he had been delayed by the snares of Aurora's love, or that he had disdained to perform his duty out of pride. Instead, he had been hindered by a vast phalanx of prayers, so that he couldn't get up to Jupiter's royal citadel, in accordance with his long-standing custom and habit, to wait upon the king and pay his respects, as the gods usually did on a daily basis. Thereupon Jupiter, relaxing his severe expression, turned to Momus, and said, "These prayers of yours, Momus, are going to ruin us unless some limit is imposed." So saying, he fell silent for a little while. But this statement of Jove's immediately caused Momus to surmise that he had caused some disturbance with those prayers of his, and this brought so much pleasure to his subversive spirit that he could not but forget his suffering and reveal the pleasure the thought had given him. He was exultant at the longed-for success of his crimes, and said to himself, "Damn me if you please, but it looks like I've caused some damage here!"

In the meantime, Jupiter turned towards Minerva and Pallas, 20 and said, "Why haven't you brought Virtue back with you? How is she? What's she doing?" At this point the goddesses—in the time-honored way of ambassadors—said that they had done nothing more during their mission than their instructions had called for. They had had their work cut out for them with the job of tracking down Momus, since he was in hiding, lurking in solitude and squalor as the wretched and unfortunate usually do. Then Jupiter began to ask Momus whether he had seen Virtue among the mortals. Momus, struck by the hard suspicion that the question had been asked with a view to exposing the crime he had committed, grew pale and silent. Nevertheless, he quickly collected himself, and arranged his features in the guise of a trustworthy friend. Smiling, he said, "Surely you, O most worthy prince of the gods, are not unaware of what is happening on a daily basis among mortals?"

21 'Mitte' inquit Iuppiter 'quae norimus, dic quod rogere.' Tum
Momus iterato titubare et quo ea spectent verba dubius expave-
scere, sed iterato ab Iove admonitus ut responderet, sui memor ad
belle initas artes dissimulandi rediit atque hic inquit 'Mercurius,
qui omnium sollertissimus est, si quid eum novi, ubi ea consideat
tenet, qui quidem non iniuria dearum pulcherrimam Virtutem
unice amet. Et dulces amores tuos, o Mercuri, quamdiu sines abs
te abesse?'

22 Hic Mercurius cum arrisisset,[20] asseveravit seque Iovemque
deosque reliquos omnes adeo fuisse hac una votorum cura perpe-
ditos ut nullis rebus praeterquam votis vacare occupatissimis diis
licuerit, et putare se quidem optime consultam deam a tantis rerum agendarum molestiis secessisse. Momus hac de re iterato recreari, iterato efferri incredibili gaudio, et cum Virtutem deam videret apud Iovem deosque desiderari, ut erat mirus[21] admodum
redditus veterator, eleganti vocis, vultus gestusque artificio totum
sese ad fingendum comparat.

23 Et superiorem illam quam recensuimus historiam refert de suis
perpessis rebus, sed ita ut dum mortalium expromeret scelera, tum
quidem maxime hominum causam tueri et erratis velle veniam im-
petrare diceres. Etenim aliis ex fabulis insinuatione adducta eo
devenit ut quasi non ex proposito, sed ipsa ex re admonitus in id
incideret, ut enarraret irrupisse proceres in templum, tumultu ex-
territos adulescentulos deos a matre[22] restitisse variasque in formas versos sibi a consceleratorum temeritate et audacia cavisse.
Subinde annectebat se quoque gravissimis iniuriis affectum, et me-

"Never mind what I know," snapped Jupiter, "answer the ques- 21 tion!" Again, Momus began to falter. Not knowing where the question was leading, he became frightened, but after being once again admonished by Jove to answer, he regained his self-posses- sion and turned again to the arts of dissimulation, in which he had made so promising a beginning. He said, "Mercury is the most quick-witted one here, if I know him at all; he will know where she is, as he has a special love for Virtue—not without reason, for she is the fairest of all goddesses. So, Mercury, how long are you going to let your sweet love be absent from your side?"[3]

Here Mercury started to laugh, and stated that he, along with 22 Jupiter and all the other gods, had been so preoccupied with this one problem of prayers that there had been no opportunity for the gods, extremely busy as they were, to think about anything else. For his part he thought that the goddess was well advised to stay away from so much troublesome business. Once again, Momus was gladdened; once again he was carried away with incredible joy. When he saw that the goddess Virtue was missing from the court of Jupiter and the other gods, like the wonderful old fox he had now become, he set about reinventing himself entirely, contriving a well-chosen range of voices, expressions and gestures.

He told the story of his sufferings which we have already re- 23 counted, but he told it in such a way that, though he highlighted the crimes of humanity, you would have thought that he wished above all to defend the humans' cause and seek forgiveness for their mistakes. Working his way casually and indirectly from other tales he arrived, as though led thence by the subject-matter itself and not of set purpose, at a place where he might relate how the mortal chiefs had burst into the temple, and how the youthful gods, terrified by the disturbance, had been left behind by their mother and had turned into various shapes, thus escaping the dar- ing and wicked mortals. He appended a story about his own griev- ous injuries, and how he had escaped, losing half his beard. He

dia deperdita barba diffugisse. Itaque his admodum rationibus nihil praetermisit quod valeret[23] ad odium adversus homines excitandum, in eoque omnem vim orationis exposuit, ut indignissime factum id dii statuerent.

24   Confabellantem Momum Iuppiter audiens et hi qui aderant dii nimirum commovebantur cum ceteras ob res, tum ob iniquam indignamque Virtutis deae calamitatem. Alia ex parte non poterant non facere quin in cachinnum irrumperent ridiculos Momi casus intellegentes. Quos cum ita vidisset affectos, Momus 'Quantum ista in re' inquit 'quam dicturus sum valeam prudentia, vestrum erit iudicium: ego vero sic de me ipso testor, summa fide adduci ut haec referam. Tibi quidem o rerum conditor, Iuppiter, omnia probe et praeclare fore constituta sentio quae quidem ad imperii decus et ornamentum faciant, ni forte illud, quantum videre licet, desit, quod quae apud mortales agantur habes neminem qui ad te referat, et eam gentem, mihi crede, minime neglexisse oportet.'

25   Cum haec dixisset, Iuppiter, secum ipse suspensus, innuens affirmavit uni se huic rei cupere providisse, sed in tanto suorum numero aegre ferre quod haberet neminem, ex animi sui sententia, quem volentem et ad rem exsequendam non ineptum possit mittere. 'At habes quidem' inquit Momus 'cui recte ac tuto eam demandes provinciam, ut promptiorem accommodatioremque dari si optes, numquam alibi invenias. Habes enim ex me natam Famam, omnium pervigilem et, quod ad rem conferat, celerem pedibus et pernicibus alis ut nihil supra. Tum est illa quidem mei cupidissima atque observantissima, ut hoc tibi spondeam pro accepto abs te beneficio: eam quaeque imperaris, mea praesertim causa, mature

made sure not to omit from his account anything that would have the effect of exciting hatred against humankind, and the whole force of his words was such as to make the gods decide that the affair had been highly disreputable.

Jupiter listened carefully as Momus told his tale, and the other gods present were deeply unsettled by all of his stories, but in particular by the unfair and undeserved misfortune of the goddess Virtue. But at the same time, they could not stop themselves bursting into laughter when they learned about the ludicrous trials of Momus. When he saw how they had been affected, Momus said, "You be the judge how much prudence I am showing in what I'm about to discuss. I swear by my life that I've been led to mention the subject in good faith. I know that you, O Jupiter, creator of the world, have arranged all things with admirable excellence which might bring embellishment and ordered beauty to your empire. But perhaps there is one thing, I might observe, that's missing: you have no one to report to you what's going on among the mortals—and believe me, that's a race you really shouldn't neglect."

Privately, Jupiter was uncertain what to make of Momus' remarks, but he nodded and said yes, he had wanted to make provision for this, and it was annoying but he really didn't really have anyone among the vast number of his associates whom, in his opinion, he could send, someone who was willing and able to carry out the job. "But you do," replied Momus, "you *have* someone to whom you can properly and safely entrust this task. You couldn't wish for anyone better prepared and better suited to the job than my daughter Rumor, the most vigilant of all beings and, more to the point, incomparably swift on her feet and her agile wings. Besides, she is truly loving and respectful towards me, so that, in return for the benefits I've received from you, I can guarantee you this. Whatever you command she will execute, for my sake especially, quickly, reliably, and with great energy." Jupiter

24

25

summa fide et summa diligentia exsecuturam.' Habuit Momo gratias eam ob commonefactionem et pollicitationem Iuppiter. Ergo Momus 'Hoc pro beneficio' inquit 'si beneficium potius quam officium id supplici et calamitoso Momo putandum est, peto abs te, benignissime Iuppiter, ut si qua in illa procreanda forte videar amorum culpa obnoxius, eam ereptae barbae doloribus compenses.' Risere atque re cognita indulsere.

26   Hunc risum intercepit iratae Iunonis adventus. Nam dum apud Iovem sic confabularentur, evenit ut Pallas Minervaque sese e corona subriperent Iunonique ut gratificarentur abscederent; et Iunonem, quod in Momum esse infestam vetere contumelia meminissent, qua de causa sacrum deorum ignem inclusum gemma[24] reddere Momo destitissent edocuere. Illis ea de re collaudatis, Iuno ad Iovem irrupit ardua, irarum impotens, torvo aspectu, atque illic habere quidem se inquit quippiam quod de rebus maximis cupiat conferre, amotisque arbitris sic orsa est: 'Et quidnam esse causae dicam, mi coniunx, ut fieri te in dies etiam maioribus in rebus neglegentem intuear?[25] Pigetne te Iovem esse? Pudetne te haberi regem et omnia licere ex arbitrio, qui tibi paratum imperii aemulum induxisti? Vel quidnam fuit causae ut quam tu rem fastidias, eius tu rei auctorem improbum et factiosum probes? Inimicos eosdemque abiectissimos ornabis, tuos vero, quoad in te sit, omnium esse indecentissime acceptos voles!

27   'Extorres, proscriptos pessimeque de deorum genere meritos, etiam invitos, in caelum accersiri iubes, me vero quae te, quae Iuno, measque preces respuis! Tu aedes auro, tu fores, tecta, gradusque auro, aureas columnas, aurea epistylia, parietes auro gemmisque pictos ac redimitos quibus visum est condonasti, uxore

thanked Momus for the advice and for his promise. So Momus replied, "In return for this favor — if it must be reckoned a favor rather than a duty from Momus, the unfortunate suppliant — I ask you, most gracious Jupiter, that if I am to be held blameworthy for begetting her, thanks to a guilty love, you should balance this against the sufferings I endured when my beard was torn out!" The gods laughed, and after hearing the story, forgave him.

Juno's arrival in a rage put an end to the laughter. For while this 26 conversation was taking place at Jupiter's house, Pallas and Minerva slipped away from the audience and went off to pay their respects to Juno. Because they remembered that Juno hated Momus owing to an old insult, they explained to her why they had held back from handing over to Momus the sacred fire of the gods enclosed in a jewel. Praising them for this decision, Juno rushed off to find Jove, her face twisted by a towering and uncontrollable rage. She said that she wished to speak with him about something extremely important. The onlookers were dismissed, and she began in this vein: "May I ask why on earth, my dear husband, I see you day by day becoming more careless about even very serious matters? Are you sick of being Jupiter? Are you so ashamed of possessing a kingdom and arbitrary power over everything that you have introduced someone who is prepared to rival your sway? Why on earth did you give your approval to this factious doer of evils that you yourself abhor? You'll honor your enemies, even the lowest of them, but you'll do everything in your power to have your own family treated in the most disgraceful way!

"Exiles, outlaws, those who have deserved the worst and are 27 hated by the divine race — you'd have people like these summoned to heaven, even against their wills, while you reject me, the Juno who . . . , who you . . . and my prayers! You've handed out golden palaces, doors, roofs, golden stairs, gilded columns, gilded architraves, walls painted with gold and studded with jewels to whom you liked, while you overlook and neglect your wife. *They* occupy

praeterita et neglecta. Lautissimas illi aedes incolunt, at et[26] quinam? Mercurius deorum scurra et temulentus Mars et pellex Venus — infelix Iuno, despecta Iuno! O nos miseras, a nostri coniugis beneficentia excludimur!

28   'Adde quod et[27] nostras sedes, quas hinc reiectae incolebamus, cum essent nulla re alia praeter puritatem et sordium vacuitatem honestae, tu amantissime, tu coniunx, replesti foedissimorum votorum obscenitate: me dignam profecto hac mea in te perenni fide et constantia, in quam istarum purgamenta reicias! Sed liceat deorum regi ornare quos velit, ac velit quidem publicum odium, istum nefarium et consceleratissimum Momum, ad se recipere, regni consortem facere, sui et suorum oblitus; aulas uxoris ita foedari votorum illuvie patiatur ut vel iumenta Phoebi subisse[28] respuant ac pro foetore horrescant.

29   'Sed non hic committam amplius ut frustra apud obstinatum aspernatorem[29] graves meas iniurias deplorem. Satis obtudi aures tuas, Iuppiter, satis frustrata sum. Et quid iuvat aeternum poscere quod semper negetur, ni forte studeas ut continuo aliquid curarum ad veterem dolorem accumules?[30] Non rogabo, non profecto prosequar, ut qua in re tibi sum voluptati dum nostram importunitatem flocci pendis et omnia negas deprecanti,[31] in ea mihi sim gravis nimium rogando. Tu sequere negando et aspernando iam quae ultro erat officii tradere.

30   'Sed si per te licet, agedum: num illud oportuit, cum aliorum commodis etiam infimorum tam multa contulisses, hoc etiam[32] animadvertere, ne indecentius uxor quam caelicolarum infima plebes[33] habitaret? Et quanti erat elargiri uxori a Iove optimo et maximo, non sine lacrimis precanti, quod indignissimis ultro ero-

the most luxurious houses, and who are they? Mercury, the jester of the gods, drunken Mars, that tart Venus . . . O unhappy Juno, neglected Juno! Oh, how wretched I am, shut out from the generosity of my own husband!

"And another thing: the house I live in (after being ejected from 28 this one), whose only distinction was that it was clean and empty of trash, you, lover boy, dearest husband, have filled with filthy junk, your votive offerings! Oh yes, I certainly deserved *that* for my unbroken loyalty and constancy towards you: that you should dump your refuse on me! But the king of the gods can honor whom he will, and he wants to welcome that public nuisance, that impious scoundrel Momus, and make him his royal consort, forgetting his nearest and dearest. He lets his wife's house become so filthy with that votive trash that even Apollo's horses, revolted by the stench, would refuse to enter.

"But I'm not going to stand here any longer, vainly bewailing 29 my injuries at the hands of someone so stubborn and indifferent. I've belabored your ears long enough. I'm frustrated enough. What good is it to keep requesting eternally what will always be denied, unless you're eager to add more immediate worries to more durable sufferings? I won't ask—no, I won't go on troubling myself with endless asking, giving you the pleasure of despising my importunity and denying all my requests. No, you just go on denying and spurning what it's your duty to give willingly.

"But come on then, if you have the guts: since you've devoted 30 so much energy to the well-being of others, even the lowest of creatures, shouldn't you take some notice that your wife is living less decently than the lowest class of god? How much would it have cost High and Mighty Jupiter to give his wife something she'd begged for in tears, something you've lavished freely upon the lowest of the low? What if I'd demanded bigger things? All I've asked for is for you to put at my disposal, so as to embellish my house, such of the mortals' votive objects as are made of gold. I've

gasti? Quid si maiora expostulavissem? Nihilo enim plus rogaba-
mus dari quam ut ad aedium nostrarum ornatum vota mortalium
quae essent aurea commodares; idque tamdiu supplex orans, obtestans, coniunx, tandem[34] abs te haud usquam[35] potero exorare?
Mi vir, semperne eris in Iunonem durus? Quod si te mea in causa
nequeo flectere, at, mi vir, illud liceat admonuisse tua praesertim
causa, ut videas quos ad te recipias, quibus credas, cui committas
teque remque maiestatemque imperii tui. Hunc tu Momum si satis noris, etiam atque etiam quae commonefeci pensitabis.'

31   Haec Iuno. Cumque unas et item alteras lacrimulas tenui velo
abstersisset, quaeque de Momi animo erga Iovem vereretur sub-
texuit et omni dicendi qua poterat arte gravissimos infigere aculeos
suspicionum elaboravit; subinde iterato ad vota expostulanda orationem deflexit. Cui Iuppiter 'Esse et ego quid hoc dicam causae,'
inquit 'o coniunx, quod numquam te non iratam offendo? Dolet
me tui et curarum tuarum, quas nimirum esse alioquin leves, sed
ad te sollicitandam plus satis graves intueor. Et quid agis, Iuno?
Semperne sic novas res aucupaberis et captabis, quo me vexes?
Quid est quod me tibi purgem? Aurea dixti velle habere vota ut
coaedificares. An parum tibi apud nos suppeditat aedium ubi
splendide lauteque habites, ni et novas tibi arces construas?

32   'Sed vince, coniunx, habe tibi vota aurea, cape ab obstinato
frustratore quae imperas. Tu modo ne nobis istas leges imposuisse
prosequare, ut quae facta velim tu reddere infecta cures. Pone tuas
istas malo suspiciones dicere quam simultates, deque Iove posthac
sperato meliora. Neque enim adeo me Iovem esse oblitus sum ut
non prius quae facto opus sint mediter quam facta velim, tum et
quae me deceant ita prospicio ut nusquam mei me paeniteat consi-

been begging for this forever on bended knee, imploring you, husband, but do I ever get what I want from you? Dearest husband, are you always going to be so harsh towards Juno? If I can't make you relent for my sake, please let me advise you, dear, for your own sake, so that you'll see the kind of people you've taken up with, whom you are trusting, to whom you've committed your person, your state and the dignity of your rule. If you reckon you know enough about this Momus, then just keep thinking over what I've told you."

Thus Juno. When she had wiped away one, then another tear- 31 let with her finely-wrought veil, she wove together all her fears about Momus' intentions towards Jupiter. Using all her powers of speech she hammered away at the nails of her suspicions. Then she turned once more to the subject of the votive offerings she was demanding. Jupiter replied, "I, too, have a question, O wife. Why is it that I never encounter you except when you're angry? I do sympathize with you and your concerns. Trifling though they are, I see that they are still serious enough to worry you. But what are you up to, Juno? Why are you always hunting and fishing for new things to vex me? Why should I justify myself to you? You've said that you want to have the golden offerings to use for building.[4] Isn't our house, where you live in great splendor and luxury, enough for you, that you have to build a new fortress for yourself?

"Well, you win, wife, take your golden offerings, take what it is 32 you're demanding from this stubborn old cuss. Just don't try to lay down the law to me, so that you're always trying to undo what I want done. Get rid of those suspicions of yours — I prefer to call them that, rather than quarrels — and after this, try to show a little more confidence in Jove. For I've not so far forgotten that I'm Jupiter that I will things to be done before thinking about what needs to be done; and I also look out ahead of time the action that suits me so that I never regret my own advice. It's the negligent and thoughtless man who is thrown off course by trifling suspicions —

lii. Neglegentis potius esset atque inconsulti levium suspicionum occursu, quibus omnia referta sunt, ab instituto deici. Non tamen hinc est ut me admoneri abs te feram moleste, sed defatigari delationum ambagibus, utcumque id fiat, stomachor. Tu contra aeque, Iuno, admonentem Iovem ne despice; hoc est quod abs te impetrasse velim, quod item frustra aeternum petivi, ut cum parere dideris, Iuno, tum corum qui imperent consilia et gesta pensites atque corrigas. Interea quae tua fieri causa voles, et Iuno, et coniunx, Iove audiente volenteque assequere.'

33   Itaque haec Iuppiter, et in ea re consulto commotior videri multo voluit quam esset, id quidem cum ut coniugis vehementiam retunderet, tum ut Palladi pro non exsecuto in legatione imperio honestius succenseret. Ac fuit quidem ea de re in dicendo usus voce ita elata ut a corona deorum, qui tum semoti astabant, exaudiretur. Missa abs se Iunone, varia secum ipse de uxore repetens conticebat; ceteri dii veluti attoniti ob regis iniucunditatem obmutuerant.

34   Sed tulit casus ut Momi quodam facto insperato Iuppiter unaque dii omnes ad risum excitarentur. Namque Iunone apud Iovem quae recensuimus disputante, Momus de Mercurio interrogarat quidnam id ita esset, cur Phoebum ad Iovem salutandum proficiscentem vota interpellarint. Cui Mercurius in hunc modum responderat: 'Mortalium quidem vota cum multis de causis, tum quod plena venirent ineptiarum, ut erant aspernanda ita aspernabantur. Ea de re Iuppiter diique omnes iusserant ab his[36] caelicolarum sedibus expurgari atque excludi. Ut maiora omittam, in votorum numero erant quae nasum aduncum oculosque perturgidos strumamve informem emendari expostularent, eoque devenerat res ut, quod longe fastidias, acu aut fuso amisso votis deos poscere auderent.[37] Sed haec erant levia: illud erat gravius, quod quo erant

and there are always suspicions. I don't mean that I'll take it badly if you advise me on something, but I *am* angry and tired of these indirect, evasive charges, wherever they come from. But as for you, Juno, don't disregard Jove when he gives you good advice. The one thing I want from you — the one thing I've eternally sought for in vain — is that you to learn to *obey*, Juno. Then you can weigh and correct the plans and actions of the people in charge! But in the meantime, Juno, my dear wife, take what you want for yourself; Jupiter hears your plea and wills that it be so."

Thus Jupiter. He deliberately wanted to seem much more upset about the matter than he actually was, not only to dull the force of his wife's harangues, but also to help inflame righteous anger against Pallas for not having carried out his command during the legation. He spoke so loudly about the matter that he was overheard by the circle of gods, who were standing some distance away. He sent Juno away, and then, after muttering to himself various remarks about his wife, he fell silent. The rest of the gods grew quiet, as though dazed by the foul mood of their king.

Then Momus by chance did something unexpected that made Jupiter and all the other gods laugh. While Juno and Jupiter were having the dispute I recounted, Momus asked Mercury why the mortals' offerings had prevented Apollo from going to wait upon Jupiter. Mercury answered him like this: "The offerings of the mortals had to be discarded for many reasons, but in particular because they were arriving full of foolish nonsense; so we did discard them. That's why Jupiter and all the other gods ordered them to be cleaned out and kept out of the homes of the sky-dwellers. I won't go into the whole business, but among the prayers were requests for the repair of a hooked nose or bulging eyes or an unsightly tumor. Things deteriorated to the point where people were daring to pray to the gods for a lost needle or a spindle, which was really annoying. But this was nothing; it was a far more serious matter that the hatred, fear, anger, pain and other rotten and cor-

33

34

vota ipsa pleraque omnia referta odiis, metu, ira, dolore et huiusmodi putidis corruptisque pestibus quae hominum pectoribus im-
mersae haerent,[38] eo aulas omnes caeli obscena taetraque odoris
foeditate et nausea complerant. Illudque inprimis superi abhorre-
bant atque exsecrabantur, quod et inter vota comperiebantur quae
parentum, quae fratrum, quae liberorum virique inprimis necem
atque interitum exposcebant. Quid et quod magis oderis? Vota
audebant facere quibus urbium provinciarumque ultimum exitium
atque excidium flagitarent.

35   'Sed anceps ac diutina fuit deliberatio cunctane vota caelo ex-
terminarent atque reicerent. Vicit tamen eorum sententia, qui aurea retinenda consulerent. Nunc hoc successit incommodi, exclusis
votis, ut multa votis poscere mortales assueti, votis vota dum non
audiantur addere non cessent,[39] quo fit ut incredibili votorum vi
aethera occupentur, votis Phoebo via intercludatur,[40] votis Iunonis
area consternatur,[41] ipsi denique inter se dii votorum gratia grave
inire certamen parati sint. Ergo tu, Mome, his tuis inventis omne
caelum, omnes caelicolas exerces.'

36   Hanc Mercurii orationem Momus audiens non potuit ipsum se
continere quin prae animi laetitia in maximum cachinnum irrumperet ita ut omnium ora in se converteret. Ac rogatus quid ita
inepte ridendo insaniret, illico versipellis, se recipiens, inquit 'Sane
rideo, Mercuri, quod aiebas mortales votis poscere ut indecentes et
male dolatos vultus suos reconcinnaretis. Enim fabri sitis omnes
dii oportet puellarum gratia, siquidem una sola in puella pro eius
animi sententia construenda quidquid ubique est artis artificiique
consumitur. Pro et quae ora et quos vultus domo afferunt!'

rupt plagues which lie deep in the human heart and which filled all of their prayers, were sticking to these votive objects, so that foul and revolting smells and nausea filled every dwelling in heaven. That was the main reason the gods were cursing and shrinking back in horror: because they kept discovering among these prayers ones that begged for the slaughter and death of parents, brothers, children and especially husbands. What could be more despicable? They even dared pray for the ruin and destruction of whole cities and provinces.[5]

"But the gods were undecided and there was long deliberation 35 about whether all votive offerings should be banished from heaven and rejected. In the end, the opinion prevailed of those who advised keeping just the golden offerings. But now this problem arose: although their offerings were being kept out, humans had grown so used to asking for numerous things with them that they wouldn't stop piling request upon request, even when they weren't being answered. Hence, because the air was filled with an incredible numbers of prayers, Apollo's route was blocked by prayers, Juno's forecourt was strewn with prayers, and the gods were ready to come to blows—all because of prayers. So you, Momus, are really keeping all of heaven, and all the heaven-dwellers, busy with this invention of yours."

Momus, listening to Mercury's speech, could not stop himself 36 from bursting into a great guffaw out of sheer joy, and every face turned towards him. The gods asked him why he was going out of his mind with idiotic laughter. The shape-changer immediately pulled himself together and said, "I'm laughing, Mercury, because you said that mortals were asking you in their prayers to fix their ugly and badly chiselled features. Of course all you gods need to become craftsmen to please girls, since it would take every art and artifice there is to fix up just one girl in accordance with her liking. Good heavens, what faces and looks these girls bring outdoors!"

37   Hinc exhilaratus Iuppiter non tam Momi salibus quam gestus insipiditate, qui dedita opera et studio se ridiculum exposuerat, arrisit; perinde eos, qui tum illic aderant deos, inprimisque Momum, ridendi cupidus vocavit ut secum esset in cena. Ridebis atque admiraberis Iovemque Momumque, nam in cena non facile dici potest quam inter epulas praeter omnium opinionem iocosum se Momus exhibuerit, multa referens quae suum per exilium pertulerat cum ridicula, tum et digna memoratu.

38   Inter quae illud fuit, ut referret omnes quidem se voluisse hominum vivendi rationes et artes experiri, quo reperta commodiore acquiesceret. In singulis quidem elaborasse ut studio et diligentia coniuncta exercitatione et usu evaderet in egregium artificem; nullam tamen ita didicisse ut sibi satis instructus videretur, tam comperisse omnes artes eiusmodi ut quo plura quae ad peritiam faciant usu et doctrina sis assecutus, eo plura discernas tibi deesse ad cognitionem. Sed eas omnes quae apud homines inter egregias habeantur vivendi artes reperisse eiusmodi esse, ut sint longe minus utiles minusque commodae ad bene et beate[42] vivendum quam sapientis hominis cogitata ratio postulet.

39   Atqui, ut a primariis et honoratissimis incipiat, militiam sibi inprimis visam percommodam. Id quidem, cum alias ob res, tum quod per eam virorum principes reddantur, potentatus nanciscantur, posteritatisque fructum assequantur. Accedebat eo ut arma sibi potissimum eligenda duceret quod se ab armorum periculo immortalitate immunem meminisset, ac fuisse quidem militem se beneque rem gessisse manu et animi viribus, postremo ductitasse exercitum, instruxisse acies, exercuisse classem, suos vidisse titulos victoriarum quam plurimos excepisse frequentissimos civium plausus et congratulationes.

40   Sed brevi odisse castra, vexilla, arma, classica, omnemque virorum strepitum fremitumque. Non id quidem satietate aut fastidio

Jupiter smiled, amused not so much by Momus' wit as by his   37
silly gestures, for Momus was purposely putting on a ridiculous
show. He did it so well that Jupiter, wanting to laugh some more,
asked the gods who were present, especially Momus, to dine with
him. You will laugh and wonder at both Jupiter and Momus, for it
is not easy to describe how unexpectedly funny Momus showed
himself to be at that dinner, telling many hilarious and memorable
stories about his experiences during his exile.

Among his anecdotes, he told how how he had wanted to try   38
out every human calling and way of life, so as to ascertain which
was the best. In every one of them he had worked hard so that by
study and diligence, joined with practice and repetition, he would
turn out to be an outstanding craftsman. He added, though, that
he had not learned any skill well enough to regard himself as ade-
quately instructed in it. He had found that many arts were such
that, the more you got the hang of them through reading and
practice, the more you realized you lacked true understanding.[6]
He had found that all those callings men considered most presti-
gious were far less useful and less conducive to a good and happy
life than the considered reflection of a wise man would expect.

Nevertheless, so as to begin with the principal and most honor-   39
able métiers, it seemed to him, first of all, that the military life
would be highly advantageous. Apart from anything else, the military produced leaders of men, gave rise to potentates, and brought
lasting fame. Moreover, he believed arms were a particularly good
choice for him, as he remembered that he would be immune to the
dangers of arms thanks to his immortal nature. As a soldier he
had acquitted himself well physically and mentally; in due course
he had led an army, set up battle-formations, conducted naval ma-
neuvers, and had witnessed his numerous claims to victory greeted
by the citizenry with frenzied applause and congratulations.

In a short time, however, he had grown to hate military camps,   40
standards, weapons, trumpets, and all the clashing and raging of

quodam iteratae gloriae, sed iusta rectaque minime insolentis viri
ratione, quandoquidem in his omnibus rebus quae ad arma spectent nihil inveniri intellegeret quod saperet aequitatem, quod non
esset alienum a iustitia, quando item in omni illa armatorum multitudine intueretur nihil quod quidem ad humanitatem aut pietatem spectaret, omnia cerneret ad utilitatem, ad animi libidinem,
ad rerum temporumque suorum rationem et conditionem per vim
nefasque referri, nulla fortibus certa aut merita referri praemia,
omnia imperiti vulgi iudicio et opinione pensari, res consiliaque
eventu putari, praemia non virtuti sed audaciae et temeritati referri.

41   Sinere se pericula et labores quos in sole et pulvere nocteque[43]
sub umbra et[44] divo obire oporteat. Sed illud non praeterire, quod
inter sanguinis vitaeque suae prodigos, alieni cupidos, impuros,
impios, diritate immanitateque taeterrimos, in faece et sentina perditissimorum et a suis patriis sedibus perpetratis flagitiis profliga-
torum, inter ruentium templorum stragem, fragorem, fumum ci-
neremque versandum esset,[45] ut tota illa in re bellica nihil se
invenisse Momus deieraret quod satis delectaret praeter id, quod
interdum, stulto et vesano furore conciti, turmae atque manipuli
armatorum mutuum in ferrum praecipites ruerent. Operae quidem pretium esse coram intueri[46] portenta illa impurissima et pestes hominum properantium in mortem suique similium scelere et
manibus contrucidari.

42   Voluisse et regem fieri se, quod proxime ad deorum maiestatem
regium imperium arbitraretur ac magni quidem duxisse olim vereri observarique se a multitudine, eamque praesto adesse, pendere
ad obsequium, parere dictis. Item magnifice habitare, honorificen-

men. This was not because he'd had enough or because he was bored with his repeated glories, but came rather from the just and right reasoning of a modest man. He realized that in all that pertained to war he had found nothing that smacked of fairness, nothing not utterly alien to justice. He saw that in all that crowd of soldiers, there was nothing that showed respect for humanity or piety. He saw that everything turned on utility, on animal lust, on the disposition and condition of time and circumstance, as executed by violence and wickedness. The brave received no certain or deserved rewards; everything was weighed by the judgement and opinion of an ignorant rabble; plans and circumstances were judged by their outcome; and rewards were given not to virtue, but to reckless audacity.

He could let pass the dangers and hardships he had had to undergo in the sun and dust, at night, or sheltering under the open sky. But he could not escape the fact that he had to live among men who were prodigal of their own blood and life while lusting for those of others, impure men without religion, men marked by frightful cruelty, the dregs and scum of the most accursed races, men in flight from their native lands because of the crimes they had committed, surrounded by slaughter, infernal din, and the smoke and ashes of ruined temples. Momus swore solemnly that in the whole business of war he had found nothing that made him happy except, now and then, watching troops and companies of armed men, stirred up into a mad rage, running headlong into each other's swords. That ungodly and monstrous plague of men rushing to their death, slaughtered by the wickedness and violence of others like them, had been worth seeing personally.

Momus said that he had then wanted to become a king, for he thought royal power was nearest the majesty of the gods. He reckoned it would be a great thing to be feared and respected by the multitude and to them nearby at his service, hanging around obsequiously, obeying his commands. At the same time, he could

41

42

127

tissime progredi, laute ac splendide convivari et concelebrari. Principio quidem veritum ne id sibi foret arduum assequi atque difficile, quoniam multos videbat ea una in re nanciscenda frustra maximis laboribus et ultimo discrimine contendisse, perpaucos attigisse.

43   Sed animadvertisse duas ad principatum patere vias breves et haudquaquam difficiles. Unam quidem, quae factionibus et conspirationibus muniatur, hanc teneri expilando, vexando, collabefactando, sternendoque quicquid tuis curriculis obiectum ad interpellandum offenderis. Alteram vero ad imperium viam bonarum esse artium peritia bonorumque morum cultu ac virtutum ornamentis deductam atque aptam, qua quidem te ita compares, ita exhibeas hominum generi oportet, ut te[47] gratia et benivolentia dignum deputent, unum te in suis adversis rebus adire, tuis potissimum assuescere consiliis et stare sententiis condiscant.

44   Neque enim ullum in terris vigere animans quod ipsum sit homine contra servitutem magis contumax; contra item homine ipso fingi posse nihil ad mansuetudinem tractabilitatemque propensius. Sed scire imperium agere artis esse minime vulgaris. Quod si pecudes brutaque et quae ad feritatem agrestem nata sunt usu domita reguntur et certa quadam disciplina continentur, quid hominem ad facilitatem frugalitatemque vitaeque natum societatem non[48] moderabimur arte et ratione, quandoquidem iusta et recta imperantibus, ut videre licet, sponte ultroque obtemperet?

45   Sed imperium postquam[49] adeptum partumve est rem esse procul dubio difficillimam imperantibus asserebat. Nam eo cum sis adductus loco ut tua neglegere, aliena curasse oporteat, cum item tua unius cura et sollicitudine multorum otium et tranquillitatem tueri ac servare opus sit, quid potest in vita difficilius dari atque laboriosius? His addebat publica esse negotia omnia penitus ardua

dress magnificently, be laden with honors on his royal progresses, feast and carouse in luxury and splendor. At first, he was afraid that it would be arduous and hard to accomplish, since he saw that many men were competing vainly, with the greatest effort and risk, to achieve this one thing, but that very few had achieved it.

But he'd noticed two short and not at all difficult routes lead- 43 ing to kingship. One relied on factions and plots, and could be followed by plundering, ravaging, destroying, and razing to the ground anything that got in your way. The other route to power lay through knowledge of the liberal arts, through the cultivation of a fine character and through the acquisition of attractive virtues. That's how you position yourself in such a way—that's how you appear to the human race in such a way—that they learn to regard you as worthy of favor and goodwill, that they turn only to you in times of trouble, that they learn to seek out your views and abide by your counsel.

There is on earth no creature more contemptuous of servitude 44 than man, but at the same time there is no creature so readily tamed and handled. But knowing how to exercise power is no common art. If cattle, brute beasts and animals born to the wild are tamed and ruled through practice, if they can be controlled by a certain strict discipline, then why shall we not use art and reason to control man, who is born with easy, temperate habits and a propensity to social intercourse? Doesn't he freely and spontaneously obey (as one may see) persons who give him just and proper commands?

But Momus went on to claim that power, once it has been ac- 45 quired or created, is undoubtedly a most burdensome thing for rulers. What could be more difficult and laborious than to reach a state in life when you have to neglect your own affairs and look after those of others, when you need to use your own effort and energy to watch over and safeguard the ease and tranquillity of the many? He added that all public business was an uphill battle and

atque impeditissima, in quibus[50] si tua unius utaris opera non
sufficias, et aliorum si utaris opera casibus id atque periculis refertissimum sit; neglegere vero quod sit officii cum ad dedecus et
ignominiam, tum ad calamitatem exitiumque redundet. Denique,
si rem satis spectaris quod isti imperium nuncupant, id profecto
publicam et intolerabilem esse quandam fugiendarum rerum servitutem intelleges.

46   Ceterum nummularias ceteras quaestuosasque artes et facultates ultro abdicatas ab se esse voluisse, quod vel satietatem ex copia,
vel fastidium ex usu, vel taedium[51] ex quaestu praebeant, vel si tandem cupiditate adducaris ut tibi plura esse velis quam oporteat,
fore ut[52] sordidam illiberalissimamque sollicitudinem afferant.[53]

47   Postremo nullum genus vitae se aiebat comperisse quod quidem
omni ex parte eligibilius appetibiliusque sit quam eorum qui quidem vulgo mendicant, quos errones[54] nuncupant. Hanc esse quidem omnium unam facilem artem, in promptu utilem, vacuam incommodis, plenam libertatis ac voluptatis. Quam rem ita esse
multa cum festivitate Momus cum plerisque aliis argumentis, tum
his rationibus demonstrabat.

48   'Etenim sic' inquit 'dicunt quidem geometrae, quaeque versen-
tur in arte sua aeque teneri a quovis rudi discipulo atque ab erudi-
tissimo, modo semel ea percepta sint. Idem ferme ipsum in hac erronum arte evenit, ut uno temporis momento perspecta planeque
cognita atque imbuta sit. Sed in hoc differunt, quod geometra in-
structore qui futurus est geometra[55] indiget, erronum vero ars
nullo adhibito magistro perdiscitur. Aliae artes et facultates habent edocendi tempora, ediscendi laborem, exercendi industriam,
agendive quendam definitum descriptumque modum; item admi-
nicula, instrumenta et pleraque istiusmodi exigunt atque deside-

filled with obstacles. If you tried to go it alone you wouldn't be able to do it, but if you relied on other people you'd have endless misfortunes and dangers. Yet neglect of your duty would lead to shame and ignominy as well as to calamity and destruction. In the end, if you looked closely enough at the thing men call power, you'd realize that it was really a kind of intolerable public servitude that one would do well to avoid.

Momus said that he'd wanted to keep his distance from the ruck of money making and acquisitive arts, since the abundance of riches made you feel glutted, the use of riches led to disgust, and the pursuit of riches led to boredom. If you were motivated by cupidity to seek more for yourself than was appropriate, then riches brought you sordid and ignoble anxiety.

In the end, he said, he'd found no way of life more eligible and desirable in every way than the life of common beggars, whom people call vagabonds.[7] Momus said that this was the only easy profession out of them all: convenient, useful, harmless, full of freedom and pleasure. With great wit, he went on to prove why this was the case, using many other arguments in addition to the following reasons.

"Geometricians say that everything studied in their discipline can be understood equally well by an inexperienced pupil or by an expert, once it has been initially grasped. More or less the same thing happens in the beggar's profession: at the same moment you realize what the job is, it all becomes crystal clear to you and you can slip into the role. Yet there's one difference. A would-be geometrician needs a geometrician as his instructor, while the beggar's art can be learned without a teacher. Other arts and skills require time for instruction, hard work while learning, application while practicing, and a strict, systematic method of procedure. They also need and want tools, equipment and other things of that kind. Only the beggar's profession does not require these. The one skill it needs is carelessness, negligence, and a complete lack of every-

46

47

48

rant: quae hac una in arte minime requiruntur. Una haec artium est incuria, neglegentia inopiaque rerum omnium, quas aliis in rebus ducunt esse necessarias, satis fulta atque tuta. Hic non vehiculis, non navi tabernave opus est; hic non decoctoris perfidia, non raptoris iniuria, non temporum iniquitas metuenda est. Hic nullum congeras capital praeter egestatem rogandique impudentiam[56] oportet, ac tua ut perdas, aliena ut roges nihil plus negotii est quam ut velis id ita mereri de te. Adde quod aliorum sudore et vigiliis erro pascitur, suo quantum libeat otio abutitur, rogat libere, negat impune; capit a quibusque, nam et miseri ultro offerunt et beati non denegant.

49   'Eorum vero quid referam libertatem atque solutam vivendi licentiam? Rides impune, arguis impune, obiurgas, garris tuo quodam iure impune. Quod illi ad dedecus ignominiamque deputant verbis cum errone contendere, quod illi statuunt flagitio manum impotenti inferre, id ad regni quasdam conditiones et leges facit. Posse quae velis et nullos habere dictorum factorumque censores, ea demum regnandi suffragia et praesidia sunt. Neque illud concedam regibus ut divitiarum usu magis quam errones fruantur: erronum theatra, erronum porticus, erronum quicquid ubique publici est. Alii in foro ne considere neve altercari quidem voce paulo elatiori audebunt, et censoria veriti patrum supercilia publico ita versantur ut nihil sine lege et more, nihil pro voluntate et arbitrio audeant. Tu, erro, transverso foro prostratus iacebis, libere conclamitabis, faciesque ex animi libidine quaecumque collibuerint.

50   'Duris temporibus ceteri maesti mutique tabescent, tu saltabis, cantabis. Malo regnante principe alii diffugient errabuntque exilio, tu arcem tyranni concelebrabis. Hostis victor insolescet, tu solus tuorum intrepidus coram astabis. Et quod quisque summo labore capitisque periculo sibi accumularit, tu illius quasi debitas tibi dari

thing thought necessary in other situations—for it is sufficiently bolstered and secure as it is. Beggary does not require vehicles, neither a ship nor a shop. It need fear neither the treachery of the bankrupt, nor the injury of the thief, nor the injustice of the times. Here you need amass no capital apart from neediness and impudence in asking for things. Losing your own property and asking for someone else's is no more trouble than wanting to do yourself a favor. Moreover, a beggar grazes on the sweat and hard work of others, he misuses his leisure as he pleases, he asks freely, says no with impunity, and takes from everyone, because the wretched give voluntarily and the fortunate won't refuse.

"What shall I say of the liberty and the carefree *joie de vivre* of   49
beggars? You laugh with impunity, you criticize with impunity, you scold, you chatter with impunity: that's your right. That people think it a shameful ignominy to bandy words with a beggar and a crime to lay a finger on someone so powerless—such attitudes create the laws and usages of your realm. That you can do what you like and that you have no one to censure your words and deeds—that's what in the end supports and protects your rule! I won't allow that kings enjoy the use of riches more than beggars: the theaters belong to beggars, the porticoes to beggars—in fact, every public place belongs to beggars! Others wouldn't dare sit in the forum and bicker with a slightly raised voice. Afraid of the raised eyebrows of their elders, others don't dare do anything lawless or immoral in public, they'll do nothing of their own free will and choice. While you, beggar, will lie lounging around the forum, shouting freely, doing whatever takes your fancy.

"When times are hard, other people languish, sad and silent,   50
while you dance and sing. When a bad prince reigns, others will escape and wander in exile; you will frequent the tyrant's citadel. The enemy conqueror will wax arrogant; you alone of all your countrymen will face him fearlessly. From what every man accumulates for himself with great labor and risk of life you demand

primitias expostulabis. Est et illud quod ad rem egregie faciat, ut
cum nemo sic viventi invideat, tum et ipse nullis invideas, quandoquidem in aliis cernas nihil quod non facile possis assequi, dum
velis.

51   'Adde his quod erronis conditio ita est ad quamvis artium alia-
rum accommodata, ut quoquo te contuleris recte ac digne fecisse
videare, quod quidem ceteris mortalium haud aeque evenit: nam
et levitatis putatur suam cui[57] assueverit artem linquere et non
sine dispendio ad alias transmigratur. Neque illos audiendos puto
qui quidem hanc unam erronum sectam dicant plenam esse incommodorum. De me illud profiteor, ceteris omnibus in artibus
unas et item alias plerasque res offendisse quae et durae et acerbae
fuerint quaeve, cum eas noluerim, tum hisdem illis aegre carere
non potuerim. Nam omni quidem in artificio[58] multa sunt, insita
natura et quasi innata, quae etsi gravia et molesta sint, ferenda tamen sunt his qui in ea velint versari. At hac in sola una erraria (ut
ita loquar) disciplina et arte nihil umquam offendi quod quidem
ulla ex parte minus placuerit. Nudos vides errones sub divo atque
duro in solo accubare: eos contemnis, despicis una cum vulgo
atque fastidis.[59] Vide ne teque vulgusque errones ipsi contemnant
atque despiciant! Tu aliorum causa facies multa, erro nec tua nec
aliorum causa facit quippiam: sibi facit quicquid facit.

52   'Quid hic referam quam sint illa quidem inepti et stulti hominis
quae vulgo admirantur, toga, purpura, aurum, mitra et huiusmodi? Aut quis non irrideat cum videat te vestium gravi involucro
et implicamento obligatum atque compeditum prodire, ut aliorum
oculis placeas? Hoc non facit erro, ergo ridet. Tune sanus non ca-
vebis tibi esse vestium pondere infensus? Tune, ut lautior et cul-

the first fruits, to be given you as though they were your due. Another distinct advantage of the trade is that no one envies your living this way, and you yourself envy no one, since you don't see anything others own that you couldn't easily get if you wanted to.

"Moreover, so easily is the beggar's life adapted to any other 51 profession you please, that you will be admired whatever activity you take up. The same can't be said for the rest of mankind: for somebody who repeatedly abandons some trade he has been following and changes to another at great expense is thought to be a lightweight. Nor do I think we should pay attention to men who say that the beggar's calling alone is full of troubles. For my part, I confess that in all other professions I encountered one or another hard and bitter thing that I did not want but could not do without. In every profession there are many burdensome and irritating things, essentially and (as it were) congenitally linked to it, which people who want to engage in that profession must tolerate. Only in the discipline (as I may call it) and art of beggary did I not encounter anything which displeased me in the least. You see naked beggars lying down in the open air and on the hard earth: you scorn them; you despise them with the mob; you are revolted. But watch out that the beggars don't scorn and despise both you and the mob! You might do many things for other people, but the beggar does nothing either for you or for others. Whatever he does, he does for himself.

"What can I say about those things that only foolish and dull 52 men tend to admire, such as the toga, purple, gold, miters and so forth? Who wouldn't laugh to see you walking about bound and fettered in a heavy carapace of draperies, just to please other people's eyes? The beggar does not do this, and so he smiles at you. If you were sane, wouldn't you avoid the self-hatred of heavy clothing? Wouldn't you refuse to have your limbs held down and constricted in accordance with other people's ideas, just so that you could appear well turned out and respectable? We should use

tior videare, non recusabis habere membra ad aliorum arbitrium occupata et obstricta? Veste utemur[60] ut tegamur, non ut admiremur. Imbrem et frigora qui veste proteget, erit is quidem satis et ad usus commoditatem et ad naturae decus ornatus.

53 'At solo cubabit erro—et quid tum? Ne vero si somnus aderit apertioribus obdormies oculis nudo in pavimento quam inter peristromata? Ac cygnis[61] quidem dedit natura plumas ut integerentur, non ut ad lectorum delicias conferrent: tibi si tantum dedisset somni quantum subiecit strati ubi dormiens accumbas, procul dubio perquam maximum dormitares. Fitque is quem natura dedit ad requiescendum locus et sedes usu in dies mollior atque salubrior, quod, si quid ad delicias desit, pro pulvinari praesto erit fessis somnus.

54 'Ceterum, conscendat in contionem erro, dicat eadem quae quivis stragula veste indutus orator dicit: cuinam maior confertiorque accurret audientium corona? Quem attentius audient? Quo perorante magis commovebuntur? Cui tota in causa vehementius assentientur? Magna est in rebus gravissimis horum disciplinae hominum auctoritas, ut nihil supra. An[62] tu non interraro videbis ebrii et deliri erronis dicta accipi pro vatum monitis, eademque seriis in rebus referri ac si oraculi essent ore decantata?

55 'Sed de his alias, ad me redeo. Quid illud, et quanti erat arduis me et periculosissimis in rebus hominum aeque atque in levissimis versari animo aequabili, nullam in partem commoto? Quam quidem rem tu, o Iuppiter, deorum princeps, si sapis, optas atque maiorem in modum posse concupiscis. Et quidnam est quod ad fructum otii et specimen amplitudinis maiestatisque decus faciat

clothes to cover ourselves, not to attract admiration. The man who uses clothing to fend off rain and cold is the one who has embellished himself in accordance with practical utility and natural propriety.

"So the beggar sleeps on the ground — so what? When you're 53 sleepy, do you sleep with your eyes shut less tightly because you sleep naked on the pavement rather than in bedclothes? Nature gave swans feathers to cover themselves, not to make luxurious beds. If your sleep was as deep as your mattress was thick, no doubt you'd sleep a tremendous amount when you lay down to sleep. The place nature gave you to sleep with practice becomes softer and healthier each day, and although it might lack comfort, sleep will be there to serve as a couch for the tired.

"Now suppose a beggar gets up to make a speech. Let him say 54 the same things that some toga'd orator says. Which one is going to attract the larger and denser throng of listeners? Which one are they going to listen to more carefully? Whose peroration is going to move them more? Whose whole case are they going to agree with more strongly? At moments of crisis, the authority of those who follow the discipline of begging becomes incomparably great. Won't you sometimes see the sayings of a drunk and delirious vagabond taken for the warnings of prophets and cited in crisis situations as though they'd been chanted from the mouth of an oracle?

"More of this elsewhere. To get back to me: why was it, how 55 important was it, that I lived among humans, in challenging and highly dangerous times as well as in the most frivolous of times, without ever losing my equanimity? If you were wise, O Jupiter, prince of the gods, you too would wish for and desire greatly this ability. What is more conducive to the enjoyment of leisure, gives a greater proof of power and confers more honor on royal majesty than to be capable and composed, as though there were no form of

magis quam ita sese habere paratum et compositum, ut nullis uspiam rerum motibus de statu decidas?

56   'Nuntiabantur gravia, quae ceteri omnes exterriti pavefactique
horrescebant: novos invisosque liquores ex duro silice manasse,
mediisque ex fontibus arsisse flammas, tum et montes inter se
arietasse. Stabat attonitum vulgus, trepidabant patres, omnia erant
in metu et in sollicitudine rerum futurarum. Alii publicam ad ea
lutem advigilabant, alii suis commodis servandis insanibant, aut
spe agitati aut metu. At Momus, curis vacuus, in quodcumque velis latus dulce obdormiscens nihil sperabat, nihil metuebat, in-
terque stertendum illud usurpabat dicere: "Quid tum, Mome, et
quid haec ad te, ad quem neque pauperiem afferent neque quippiam auferent?" Narrabantur et rerum monstra: alios strata mari
via obequitasse, alios per silvas perque saltus traduxisse classem,
alios subfossis montibus media per saxa intimaque per viscera
terrae suos traxisse currus, alios immani strue caelum aggressos
petere, alios flumina et lacus eripuisse mari atque exstinxisse, mediumque intra[63] aridum terrae solum acclusisse maria.

57   'Haec admirantibus ceteris atque stupentibus, Momus illud as-
suescebat dicere: "Enimvero,[64] Mome, et hoc nihil ad te." Ferebant
locupletissimos amplissimosque orbis reges innumerabili hominum manu impetum inter se facere, contegi caelum sagittis, flumina sisti cadaveribus, mare hominum cruore excrescere. His rebus cognitis ceteri, prout rerum suarum ratio et studia ferebant,
aestuabant variis animorum motibus; solus Momus illud observabat dicere: "Et istuc, Mome, nihil ad te." Spectabantur agrorum
incendia, vastitates, populationes; audiebantur cadentium virorum
gemitus, ruentium tectorum fragor, calamitosorum eiulatus; haesi-

political agitation anywhere that might cast you down from your estate?

"Grave tidings were made known which struck everyone else 56 with fear and horror. New and strange liquids were flowing from hard flint, flames were burning in the middle of fountains, mountains were colliding with each other.[8] The common people were dazed, the city fathers trembled, all things were in a state of fear and anxiety about the future. Some watched over the safety of the public, others went mad trying to preserve their own goods, stimulated by hope and fear. But Momus, free of care, whatever turn things took, went on sleeping sweetly, hoping for nothing and fearing nothing. Between snores, Momus would habitually say, 'What then, Momus? What's it to you? They can't make you poor and they can't take anything from you.' Monstrous portents were recounted. Some people had ridden through a road that stretched across the sea, others had sailed a fleet through woodland passes, still others had dug through mountains, driving their carts right through the middle of the rocks and through the very bowels of the earth. Some built enormous structures to reach the sky; others had diverted and drained rivers and lakes, and had enclosed seas in the middle of dry land.[9]

"While everyone else was amazed and dumbfounded, Momus 57 said, 'Is that so? But Momus, that's nothing to you.' People said that the richest and greatest kings of the earth were attacking each other with innumerable hosts; that the sky was covered with arrows, the rivers were blocked with corpses, and the sea was rising with the blood of men. When others learned these things, they would seethe with various emotions, as their reason and passions led them. Only Momus watched and said, 'This, too, Momus, is nothing to you.' People would see fires in the fields, devastation, plundering; they would hear the groans of fallen men, the crash of falling roofs, the wailing of the distressed. There would be hesitation, quakings, running. There would be din, clashing, and uproar

tabatur, trepidabatur, discursitabatur; strepitus, crepitus, fremitus
totis triviis, totis angiportibus. At Momus resupinus nudis femini-
bus oscitans alucinabatur,[65] et quid sibi tanti tumultus vellent ne
rogabat quidem nisi neglegenter sane atque morose. Tum si quis
coram tantos turbines et rerum tempestates deplorare aggrediebatur, Momus, perfricato crure, aiebat: "Nequedum, Mome, quicquam est hic, quod quidem tibi recte curet dormi."

58   'Quid postremo? Quo hos atque illos animis affectos atque perturbatos mihi ludos facerem, cum eos coactis circulis collatisve ca-
pitibus serio aliquid ordiri atque conferre spectabam, repente eo
advolabam, istic assistebam, ab his petebam, assiduus efflagitabam
ut aliquid ad pietatem elargirentur inopi atque egeno; illi indigna-
bantur, ego mea gaudebam importunitate; illi nostram odiosam in-
tempestivamque scurrilitatem exsecrabantur atque excandescebant,
Momus ridebat.'

59   Itaque Momus huiusmodi toto ridente caelo referebat. Sed Iuppiter, cum satis risissent, Momum facetias istas recensentem interpellavit. 'Atqui' inquit 'heus Mome, num et, quod aiunt, figulus
figulo faberque fabro, ipsum idem aeque erronibus evenit, ut inter
se invideant?' Tum Momus: 'Enimvero[66] et quis huic invideat qui
prae se ferat miserum esse se?' Tum Iuppiter: 'Ni fallimur, invide-
bit quisquis prae illo qui admodum miserabilis sit, volet sese dignum videri misericordia. Quod ni istuc siet,[67] fateor una haec tua
erronum vita est non modo, uti aiebas, vacua incommodis, sed
egregie directa ad quietem atque summam ad felicitatem apta, ut
eam huic nostrae deorum beatitudini esse longe anteponendam
statuam.[68] O malum maximum invidia, maximum invidia, maximum malum!'

60   Tum Momus 'Admones,' inquit 'o Iuppiter optime et maxime,
ut ipsum me accusem: audies rem festivam. Versabatur inter phi-

at every crossroads and in every alleyway. But Momus would lie back, yawning and dreaming about naked thighs. He wouldn't even inquire how such a tremendous tumult might affect him, except rather offhandedly and peevishly. Then, if anyone in his presence started to lament the great storms and tempests of the times, Momus, rubbing his shin, would say, 'This isn't anything you need to worry about, Momus; go back to sleep.'

"So what happened in the end? In order to make a game out of this and that emotional and distraught person, when I saw them gathering in circles, putting their heads together earnestly, planning and setting things in order, I would fly there immediately and beg insistently for something to be given, for religion's sake, to the poor and needy. Some would get angry, and I'd be gleeful at my importunity. Others would curse and burst into a rage at my odious and untimely wit, and Momus would laugh." 58

Thus Momus was telling stories like this, to the laughter of all heaven. But when they'd had a good laugh, Jupiter interrupted Momus in the midst of his droll tales. "But look here, Momus, doesn't what people say happens between potter and potter and smith and smith happen to beggars too, namely that they hate each other?" — "But who could hate someone manifestly wretched?" Momus replied. — "Unless I'm mistaken," Jupiter answered, "someone who wishes to seem worthy of compassion will himself experience hate when faced with someone who is *really* miserable. But if this isn't the case, then I'll admit that this beggar's life of yours is not only free from disadvantages — as you have been saying — but also remarkably conducive to peace and the highest happiness, so that I believe it should be preferred to our divine beatitude. O envy, greatest of evils — greatest, greatest of evils!" 59

Then Momus said, "You remind me, great and powerful Jupiter, that I should be censuring myself. Listen to this jolly story. Among the philosophers lives an egregiously worthless fellow, and 60

losophos egregius quidam nebulo, quem unum si spectes facile credas principem esse abiectissimorum hominum: ita corporis forma
et omni membrorum ornatu se agebat inter errones insignem
atque nobilem. Describam tibi hominis speciem et habitum. Aderat illi os impressum, mentum obductum, cutis hispida, crispissata
atque ab genis pro palearibus dependens, omnis vultus perfuscus,
oculi turgidi et aperte prominentes, horumque alter luciosus, alter
sublippus et ambo perverse strabi. Naso tam erat multo ut non
hominem sed nasum existimes ambulare. Pergebat procurva cervice et inversa in sinistrum humerum, collo protenso et acclinato,
ut terram non prospicere oculis sed auricula diceres; surgebat scapularum[69] una in strumam pergravem, incedebat gradu lato, tardo,
vasto, sed lassis artubus et quasi longo morbo sphondylibus disso-
lutis ad cuiusque pedis motum innutabat. Sino vestitum et reliquum apparatum, saccos[70] centipelles, lacernam atavam lacerna-
rum, in qua mille parturientes mures nidificarant; pendebant[71]
humero pera, calathus atque cantharus sordibus obsceni, foetore
exsecrabiles.

61   'Huic me fateor homini fortassis interdum invidisse, non quo
esset ille quidem ita informis, sed quod non obscure perspiciebam
pluribus hunc videri dignum pietate, cum esset non pietate sed potius odio dignissimus. Tum et illud pigebat, quod errones nimium
multos volitare foro conspiciebam. Unum profecto erat in tota illa
erronum arte quod animo ferebam minus aequo: id erat cum la-
trantes et infestis dentibus nudos talos appetentes caniculas pueri
adversum me concitabant. Et quam sint illi quidem molesti scio
vobis non facile posse persuaderi, sed ea irritamenta si maximis
diis accidissent, nihil in rerum orbe universo est quod illis inveniri
posset laboriosius. Sed de his alias.

62   'Nunc vero ut ad rem redeam, hoc est ut affirmem apud mortales nihil inveniri commodius erronum vita, siquidem et facilis et

if you saw him you would easily believe that among the lowest of the low he was the chief. Thanks to his height and well-knit limbs, among beggars he used to pass for noble and distinguished. Let me describe the man's appearance and clothing. He had a flattened face, a long chin, rough and wrinkled skin that hung from his cheeks in dewlaps. His whole face was swarthy, his eyes swollen and protruberant: one of them was fishy, the other bleary, and both of them squinted askew. His nose was so big that you'd think it was no man, but a nose that was walking around. This man used to go about with his head twisted back onto his left shoulder, his neck straining sideways, so that you'd think he was looking at the ground with his ears, not his eyes. A hunchback, he walked with a long step, slow, ungainly, with tired joints and muscles wasted as though by a lengthy disease, and his head bobbed up and down whenever he moved either foot. I pass over his robe and the rest of his outfit, his motley beggar's sacks, his cloak — the grandfather of all cloaks — in which a thousand pregnant mice had built their nests. From his shoulder hung a little satchel, a bowl and tankard that were disgusting with dirt, vile with filth.

"I admit that I sometimes hated this man, not because he was   61 so ugly, but because it was obvious to me that most people thought he deserved reverence, while in fact he deserved hatred more than anything else. At that time it also annoyed me that I used to see far too many beggars flitting about the forum. I admit that there was one aspect of the beggar's trade that I could never bear with equanimity, namely, when boys used to set barking dogs on me, which made for my bare ankles with their vicious teeth. I know it will be hard to persuade you just how annoying this was, but if these irritations had ever befallen the greatest gods, you'd find nothing more troublesome in the entire universe. More of this later.

"To return to the subject, I maintain that there's nothing more   62 advantageous on earth than the life of a beggar, since it's both easy

pacatissima est, siquidem huic neque calamitas officere neque improbitas adimere quicquam potest, siquidem in ea nihil inveniri potest quod doleas.' 'O te igitur stultum' inquit Iuppiter 'si tanta bona reliquisti, ad superos ut conscenderes! Vide, Mome, quid recites, non potuisse in te apud mortales ea quae apud nos divos plus satis possunt. Quid est quod nequeat improbitas?'

63   Hic Momus coepit deierare numquam se fuisse minus affectum curis quam cum esset erro, numquam praeter semel tota illa in vita doluisse, atque id quidem re alioquin levi obtigisse, sed non tamen indigna memoratu. Incidisse enim ut offenderet quendam ascripticium servulum ex ergastulo qui detrectantem et calcitrantem asinum fuste cuderet. Primo coepisse efferate excandescentem illum ridere, post id incidisse in mentem ut repeteret quam ab pauperum numero iumentis debeatur, quae si forte desint, fiat ut divites velint portari a pauperibus. Ea de re indignatum coepisse redarguere atque increpare his verbis: 'O bipes indomite et servum pecus, non cessabis furere? Ne tu non intellegis quam huic animantium generi debeatur, quod ni essent tu tuique similes pro iumento sarcinas atque impedimenta ferres?'

64   Haec dixisse Momum. At illum, ut erat immanis, relicto asino obiurgatorem petisse et dixisse 'Quin immo tu pro asino feres?' fusteque ipso quo asinum percusserat reddidisse Momum onustum plagis. Adfuisse tum illic nonnullos viros probos qui servum hunc dictis castigarent et factum maledicerent atque condolerent; Momum vero affirmasse id factum optime, quandoquidem, maximis hominum aerumnis neglectis, asini incommodis moveretur.

and tranquil, since calamity can't get in your way and wickedness can't take anything from you, and since it is completely free of pain and grief," — "How stupid you must be, then," said Jupiter, "if you left such great goods behind, to ascend into heaven! Look what it is you're saying, Momus: that while you were among the mortals [as a beggar] you were invulnerable to evils which have more than enough power over the gods. Is there really anything invulnerable to wickedness?"

At this point, Momus began to swear that he had never been 63 less stricken with cares than when he had been a beggar. He said he had never suffered pain more than once during that whole life, and that had occurred for a trivial reason, but one which was still worth recording. He happened to meet a little peasant[10] just out of the workhouse, who was beating a stubborn and recalcitrant donkey with a stick. At first he had laughed at the fellow who was so carried away with anger, but then he began to reflect how much the tribe of paupers owed to beasts of burden: for if by chance there weren't any, then the rich would want to be carried on the shoulders of the poor. Angered by this thought, Momus started to rebuke the slave, shouting, "You savage biped, you servile beast, why don't you give up this rage of yours? Don't you understand what we owe to this breed of animal? Don't you know that if they didn't exist, you and people like you would be carring bundles and burdens in the place of pack-horses?"

These were Momus' words. But the slave, who was enormous, 64 abandoned the donkey and lunged at his critic, saying, "Oh, indeed, you take yourself for an ass, then?" And with the same stick he had been using to beat the donkey he belabored Momus. Several decent fellows were there who rebuked the slave, condemned what he'd done, and offered their condolences. But Momus declared that he had deserved it, seeing how he had been affected by the discomfort of a donkey, after having ignored the worst sufferings of mankind.

65   Tanta Momi lepiditate nimirum captus, Iuppiter edixit ut suis aedibus posthac uteretur perfamiliariter. Quam quidem rem cum ex Iovis imperio factitaret — vide quid possit principis erga quemvis gratia et frons — Momum, publicum caelicolarum odium, abiectum, despectum diisque[72] omnibus pessime acceptum, ut primum videre factum[73] principi familiarem et gratum,[74] illico bene de illo sentire dignumque ducere cui sese ultro ad amicitiam offerrent, observarent, colerent. Idcirco Momum singuli deorum adire, consalutare, gratificari dictis et factis certabant.

66   Quo in numero atque errore cum plerique omnes, tum et Pallas dearum una (ut ita loquar) mascula, et Minerva, cunctarum decus et lumen artium, versabantur. Et erit operae pretium legisse qualem se Pallas Minervaque dea gesserint, quo etiam in diis naturam mulierum recognoscas. Nam illae quidem, quod intuerentur beatissimum principem Iovem, cui relictum esset nihil quod amplius cuperet praeterquam ut perpetuis voluptatibus frueretur, Momi scurrilitate delectari, idcirco[75] movebantur ut de publicis deque privatis rebus suis plurimum cogitarent. Et cum essent non ignarae quid in cuiusque animum et mentem possint conspersae verborum aptis temporibus maculae, illius praesertim qui quidem ex arbitrio ad te sive otiosum sive sollicitum habeat aditum, iam tum animis erant vehementer commotae. Et[76] cum meminissent ab se proxima ignium iniuria fore lacessitum Momum, non temere vereri coeperant ne diligens sollersque sector aliquid iocosa illa sua assiduitate adversi moliretur.

67   Sed, uti erant mulieres, consilio usae sunt muliebri, minime opportuno minimeque attemperato. Enimvero[77] Minerva qua callebat dicendi arte convenit Momum, ac de sacrorum ignium facto ex ignaro fecit ut esset certior, dumque suadere institit non id sua

Captivated by Momus' wit, Jupiter decreed that he should here- 65
after treat the royal dwelling as his own. After he began to take advantage of the privilege accorded him by Jove's command — you see
what the grace and favor of a prince can do for someone! —
Momus, who had been the sky-dwellers' public enemy, an object of
loathing and contempt, avoided by all the gods, now, once the gods
saw him made the prince's favorite, began to be highly regarded by
them. They considered him a worthy fellow, willingly admitted
him to their friendship, respected him and courted him. Thus,
each one of the gods competed to visit Momus, to hail him and to
gratify him by word and deed.

Among this group, deceived along with everyone else, were 66
Pallas, the masculine goddess (if I can call her that), and Minerva,
the ornament and light of all the arts. It is well worth noting how
Pallas and Minerva conducted themselves, so that you may come
to recognise the female character even among the gods. The goddesses saw that the most blessed prince Jupiter, who had no other
wish than to enjoy eternal pleasure, was delighted by Momus'
buffoonery, and this provoked them to think hard about their own
public and private affairs. They were well aware what effect derog-
atory words might have if sprinkled into someone's mind at an op-
portune moment, especially the words of someone who had access
to you at their own pleasure, whether you were occupied or at leisure. This realization now made them distraught, especially when
they remembered that Momus had recently suffered injury at their
hands over the fire [of the gods], and they began to have a well-
founded fear that this zealous and guileful courtier might be preparing some hostile plot in the midst of all his humorous attentions.

Being women, however, they used their women's judgment, 67
which was inopportune and maladroit. Minerva approached
Momus using the rhetorical arts she knew so well and informed
him about the affair of the sacred flame, which he hadn't known

quidem fore amissum opera, ut tanto deorum dono Momus frau-
daretur. Omnem legationis offensionem explicavit, affirmans id
sibi nusquam potuisse venire in mentem, ut aggrederetur quippiam quominus bene de se deque deorum genere meritus Momus
ex Iovis decreto et voluntate ad superos rediret honestior. Sed fateri suum errorem, se quidem Palladi et armatae et praepotenti
deae sic petenti non fuisse ausam non obtemperare, neque mirandum Palladem hoc tentasse, quae quidem Fraudi deae plurimum
debeat; quin et indulgendum si studiis coniunctissimae deae in adversarii gloria non augenda[78] mutuo opitulentur. Ceterum orare ne
quid sibi succenseat, sed posthac malit sui[79] cupidam experiri
quam odisse immeritam.

68   Momus, etsi acrem animo ex ea re indignationem concepisset,
tamen, quod simulare dissimulareque omni in causa decrevisset,
tenui[80] oratione et levibus dictis Minervam ab se missam fecit, ac
inter cetera illud adiuravit, non id ad se accipere ut iniuriarum velit reminisci cum alias ob res, tum ne eam animo ferat molestiam
quam vindicandi cura et sollicitudo soleat afferre; meliorem posthac optare inimicis atque obtrectatoribus suis mentem, qui si tandem esse infesti non desinent, ad officium tamen ducet[81] ut suas
esse partes deputet ferendis adversariis palam facere quali sit cala-
mitosus infelixque Momus animo redditus miti et mansueto.

69   His acceptis responsis Minerva abiit, sed vixdum ex ea aula ex-
cesserat cum e vestigio Pallas, hisdem animi suspicionibus excita
quibus et fuerat Minerva, ad Momum appulit suadereque institit
astu et artibus Minervae adductam se ut de Momo non benemere-

about before, all the while trying to persuade him it was not through any omission on her part that Momus had been defrauded of this great gift of the gods. She recounted the whole mishap of the legation, declaring that, for herself, it could never have entered her mind to attempt anything to prevent Momus, so well deserving of himself and of the race of the gods, from returning among the divine beings in accordance with Jove's command and will. She admitted her mistake: she had not dared to disobey the request of Pallas, that well-armed and mighty goddess. She was not surprised that Pallas had tried this, given how much she owed to the goddess Mischief. But one should forgive them if those two goddesses, who worked hand in glove, were helping each other in their efforts to check the increasing fame of their adversary. She begged him, however, not to be angry with her; but hereafter he should prefer to test her goodwill towards him, rather than hate her when she didn't deserve it.

Momus, although he took bitter offence at this, had decided to 68 simulate and dissimulate in every situation, and so he dispatched Minerva with gentle speech and mild words. Among other things he assured her that he did not want to take it on himself to remember injuries, mostly so that he would not have to endure the mental distress normally brought on by an anxious concern for revenge. He said that he was hoping for a better attitude from his enemies and critics in the future, and if they would not in due course cease their hostile behavior, he should have to regard it as his duty to tolerate his adversaries, so as to make known how the blighted and unhappy Momus had been rendered gentle and meek of spirit.

When she heard his answer, Minerva departed, but she had 69 scarcely left the palace when Pallas, provoked by the same suspicions as Minerva, instantly pushed her way up to Momus. She tried to persuade him by cunning and artifice that it was Minerva's fault that she had behaved badly towards Momus. She was very

retur, cuius quidem erroris maiorem in modum paeniteat veniamque poscat. Non fuit aliud frontis aut verborum ad dissimu-
lationem in Momo adversus Palladem quam fuisset ad Minervam;
ardebat tamen et dolore et iracundia ut vix compesceret lacrimas.

70   Sed hunc animi dolorem Themis deorum apparitoris adventus
sustulit, qui Iovis iussu ad sollemne convivium Herculis Momum
accersiturus[82] advenerat. Cupiebat enim Iuppiter, ut multas alias
superiores, sic et cenam apud Herculem ducere lepiditate Momi
voluptuosissimam. Verum id longe evenit secus quam voluisset.
Nam cum inter cenandum pleraque dicta ultro citroque a com-
messantibus iactarentur et praesertim ab Hercule nonnulli sales
reiterarentur, rogareturque Momus ut veterem illam historiam
enarraret, quo pacto apud philosophos avulsa barba diffugisset,
Momus hos intuens ita ridicule in se affectos non potuit facere
quin stomacharetur. Aegre enim ferebat non illud sat videri Iovi et
diis semel atque iterum succincte et breviter audisse, ni et rursus
in convivio, in quo maximorum deorum flos et nitor discumberet,
quasi epularum obsonium et mensae condimentum Momum ad
irridendum deposcerent.

71   Qui ergo in hanc usque diem fuerat ex studio ludus iocusque
omnium ordinum sua affabilitate, is nunc sibi contumeliae loco as-
cribebat se invitari non honoris gratia, sed ad risum. Accedebat
quod novissimam animo personam imbuerat, superiore illa
omissa. Namque posteaquam intellexerat plurimi se ab deorum
vulgo fieri ob principis gratiam, rerum suarum successu (uti fit)
elatus, coeperat spe et cupiditate maiora appetere de se atque, intermissa pristina conveniendi festivitate, per maturitatem et gravitatem sensim elaborabat ut dignus videretur apud Iovem gratia et
apud caelicolas auctoritate. Quae cum ita essent, factum est ut,

sorry indeed for her mistake, and asked for forgiveness. Momus used no less dissimulation in his words and expression with Pallas than he had with Minerva. But he was so inflamed with pain and anger that he could barely control his tears.

However, the arrival of Themis, the attendant of the gods, alle- 70 viated his woe.[11] At Jupiter's command, this messenger had come to summon Momus to Hercules' solemn banquet. Jupiter wanted Momus' wit to make the banquet at Hercules' house, like many other previous banquets, a highly entertaining one. But it turned out far otherwise than he had wished. While they were at table, the dining companions bandied about many words, and Hercules in particular repeated a number of jokes. Momus was asked to tell the old story of how he had fled from the philosophers and had had his beard torn off. Momus, seeing how ready they were to laugh at his expense, could not contain his irritation. It annoyed him that Jupiter and the other gods did not seem satisfied to hear the story told succinctly once or twice, but that yet again, at a ban- quet where the cream of the divine race were reclining, they were asking Momus to make a fool of himself, as if he were the victuals for a feast or the seasoning for a dish.

Thus the man who until that day had purposedly laid himself 71 out to be the prankster of all the orders, now took it as an insult that he had been invited for his humor rather than as an honor. In addition, he now laid aside his previous mask and put on a novel one. When he realized that the mob of gods valued him because of the prince's favor, carried away (as usual) by success, his greed and sense of entitlement made him start to seek greater things for himself. He abandoned his humorous approach to social inter- course, and through mature behavior and seriousness he worked gradually to make himself seem worthy of Jupiter's favor and de- serving of authority among the gods. Thus it came about that, having taken offense at the rudeness of the diners and especially of

convivarum et maxime Herculis petulantia offensus, pulcherrimo quodam commento insolentes bellissime castigatos reddiderit.[83]

72   Se quidem, inquit, numquam non fecisse libenter ea omnia quae maximis diis grata intellegeret, nequedum id sibi inpraesentiarum videri molestum si suo etiam cum dolore tam[84] praeclare de se meritorum voluptatibus satisfaceret. Malle quidem tristem turbulentissimorum suorum temporum memoriam delesse ex animo quam totiens refricasse, sed suis recensendis aerumnis venire quandam annexam complicatamque rationem gratiarum pro accepto ab deorum rege beneficio, cuius quidem meminisse procul dubio gaudeat, ac futurum quidem sempiterne inscriptum animo beneficium quod acceperit, et numquam non retributurum officio quod potuerit. Exilii quidem sui poenam fuisse numquam sibi adeo acerbam et molestam quin de genere deorum superum bene fore merendum statuerit; doloris sui poenam erroris culpa[85] mitigasse. Inde illud fuisse, ut quae sibi in dies forent mala subeunda, ea quidem cum moderate, tum et fortiter atque constanter perferret.

73   Sed quantis rerum adversarum cumulis obrueretur non facile dici posse. Inter quae illud inprimis angebat, quod nullae salvis deorum rebus darentur occasiones quibus qualis demum esset Momus praeclare agendo ostenderet. Accidisse ut qua in re se pulcherrime officio fungi intellegeret quamve unice atque maxime curaret, in ea nimium multos, nimium acres, nimium infestos oppugnatores atque hostes offenderet, quorum de vita et moribus dicendum sibi sit prius; mox de illorum gravissimis sceleribus pauca ex incredibili numero facinorum, quae ad rem faciant, referentur.

74   Esse apud mortales genus quoddam hominum, quos si spectes progredi oculis in terram defixis, fronte corporisque habitu ad omnem veterem morem et honestatem quadam scaenica superstitione

Hercules, he punished those arrogant folk beautifully, making use of a delicious scheme.

Momus said that he had always gladly done everything that he 72 thought would please the greatest gods. Even in the present circumstances, it seemed to him no trouble to use his own pain to delight people who had deserved so well of him. He would prefer that the sad memory of his tumultuous experiences be blotted out of his mind rather than massaging them over and over. But to recount his hardships was an implicit way of thanking the king of the gods for the favor he had received, a favor that beyond doubt it delighted him to recall. The benefit he had received would forever be inscribed upon his heart, and he would always wish to repay it with whatever service he could perform. The punishment of his exile had never been so bitter and distressing that it lessened his resolve to deserve well of the race of gods. The remorse he felt for his mistake had softened the pain of punishment. Thus he had been able to bear with moderation, and also with bravery and constancy, whatever evils he had had to undergo from day to day.

But Momus could not easily describe the great heap of misfor- 73 tunes that had overwhelmed him. Among these, the most distressing had been the absence of opportunities — as the gods' affairs had been going so well — to show through distinguished deeds the sort of person he was. It happened that whenever he thought he could discharge some task with distinction and carry it out uniquely well, he would encounter too many bitter enemies and hostile opponents. He would first have to describe their behavior and way of life, then he would mention a few of the most serious and relevant crimes among their innumerable acts of wickedness.

Among humans there was a certain kind of person, whom you 74 would be likely to revere if you saw them processing with their eyes fixed on the ground, their expression and comportment betokening an old-fashioned kind of morality and honesty, laid on

composito, facile venerere; sin vitae consuetudinem et studia ad
omnem flagitii turpitudinem pronam et praecipitem respectes, merito oderis. Hos quidem sese spectatores dici rerum voluisse, ac
esse quidem eos pro nominis dignitate ingenio praeditos alioquin
non tardo neque hebeti, sed tam praeclarae atque excellentis virtutis lumina, si qua in illis sunt, foedissimarum sordium cumulis
perdidisse. Quaesivisse illos titulo cultusque parsimonia non vitae
modum, sed inanis cuiusdam gloriae levem auram et famae[86] im-
meritae rumorem apud eos quibus parum essent cogniti; eosdemque tam inepte, tam intemperanter esse ambitiosos ut rerum
quae sint omnium pulchre et praeclare nosse causas profiteantur.

75 Horum duas primum de diis exstitisse sententias, subinde multas et varias manasse opiniones, non tam multitudine quam disceptantium deliramentis repudiandas. Sed inter omnes quaenam
sit maiore digna odio nondum satis constare. Nam alii ullos esse
deos penitus negare: orbem rerum concursu quodam fortuito mi-
nutissimorum, quo sunt omnia referta, corporum esse factum
casu, non deorum opere aut manu constructum. Alii deos esse
cum ipsi non credant (nam si crederent aliter viverent), credi tamen vulgo velint sua praesertim causa, id quidem ut venerentur, ut
arma, castra imperiaque sua deorum metu muniant atque ad stabi-
litatem firmitatemque corroborent.[87] Cui sententiae illud addunt,
ut se quidem esse deorum interpretes, cum nymphis, cum locorum
numinibus magnisque cum diis grandia habere rerum agendarum
commercia excogitatis vanitatum figmentis assimulent.

76 Cum his adeo sibi fuisse certamen varium atque laboriosum,
hic ut deos esse ostenderet, illic ut non esse deos tales probaret
quos scelerosi mortales suorum facinorum auctores sociosque ha-

with an almost theatrical scrupulosity. But when you observed that their habits of life and interests made them incline towards everything vile and disgraceful, you would have good reason to hate them. These men wanted to be called observers of affairs and indeed they deserved the name, being gifted with intellects that were anything but slow and weak, but whatever lights of excellence and virtue there were in them had been lost under a heap of stinking filth. In name only and with economy of effort they sought, not the virtuous mean in life, but a mere aura of empty glory and the rumor of unmerited fame among those who did not know them well. They were so crassly, so immoderately ambitious that they claimed to have a beautiful and distinctive explanation for everything.

At first, there existed among them two opinions about the gods, but afterwards many different ideas poured out of them. These ideas were to be rejected not so much for their number but because of the ravings of the disputants. It wasn't yet evident which of all these ideas deserved the most scorn. Some utterly denied that any gods existed, and said that the universe was not created by the hand or work of the gods, but by chance—that is, by the fortuitous collision of tiny particles of which everything was constituted.[12] Others did not themselves believe the gods existed—for if they *did* believe, they would be living differently—but for their own sakes they still wanted that belief to be common, so that they would be held in awe and so that they could use the fear of the gods to fortify and render impregnable their arms, their camps and their empires. To this view they added the practice of pretending to be the interpreters of the gods, inventing vain fictions to suggest that they were holding lofty exchanges with nymphs, tutelary spirits and even with important gods.

Momus had had a long and varied struggle with them, now to show that the gods existed, now to prove that the gods were not the sort of beings who would co-opt wicked mortals to be the as-

75

76

beant. Sed ita congressum in certamen ut cum eloquentem ipsa causa faceret, tum se dicente veritas ipsa atque ratio facile tutaretur atque defenderet. Ac pro deorum quidem re satis commodam sibi atque accommodatam fuisse contra philosophos orationem, pro salute autem sua et pro capitis sui periculo parum se sibi utilem patronum exstitisse. Quo enim deorum rationibus inservierit studio et contentione qua debuit, eo sibi pessime consuluisse: gravem subisse invidiam, acerba odia adversum se excitasse ambitiosorum immodestissimorumque hominum, qui quidem eiusmodi sunt ut omnia possint facilius perpeti quam videri cuiusquam[88] prudentiae et consilio acquievisse.

77   Accessisse et tertium quoddam genus hominum, sane doctrina et praeclaris artibus excultissimum, sed nimis cupidum laudis et gloriae, qui quidem non fortiter factis aut recto rerum agendarum consilio fructum posteritatis mereri, sed umbratili quadam confabellandi arte suum commendare nomen immortalitati affectent.[89] Hos per contiones vagari solitos, nihil sibi assumentes certi atque constantis quod affirment, praesertim apud eos qui usu et exercitatione rerum sapere quicquam videantur, sed novis in dies assentationum artibus auditorum aures aucupari et popularium de se admirationem captare, non tam multitudinis sensum atque cogitationes flectendo et diducendo,[90] quam ad multitudinis nutum sua omnia instituta vertendo in dies et immutando, et in ea re verumne an falsum, rectumne an pravum[91] id sit quod dicendo tueantur minimi eos pendere: illud omnibus nervis eniti, ut prae ceteris recte sensisse in suscepta altercatione videantur.

78   Horum se amplitudine et impetu orationis interdum rapi et obrui solitum, ut quid respondendum esset non succurreret. Posse illos copia verborum, posse eruditione, posse usu ut nihil sit,

sociates and agents of criminal acts. He had descended into the
lists with the idea that the cause itself would make him eloquent,
and also telling himself that truth itself and reason would safeguard and defend him with ease. His speech in defense of the gods
against the philosophers had been effective and appropriate, but
he had not proven a powerful advocate in his own defense, or able
to counter the threats to his own life and safety. The zeal and exertions he had employed in his proofs of the gods' existence had not
served him well in his own case; he had suffered profound envy
and had provoked the bitter hatred of ambitious and shameless
men, who were the sort of persons who could bear anything more
readily than yielding to someone else's wisdom and counsel.

He had met a third kind of men, highly educated in distin- 77
guished branches of knowledge, but too eager for praise and glory.
They did not try to earn fame from brave deeds or wise counsel,
but aimed to commend their names to immortality through aca-
demic theorizing. They liked to wander into debates, taking up no
fixed or consistent position, especially when faced by persons who
seemed to know something from actual experience. Instead, day
after day, they tried to ensnare the ears of their audience with
novel arts of flattery and to win popular acclaim for themselves,
not so much by leading and influencing the thoughts and passions
of the multitude as by adjusting their own principles on a daily basis to fit the crowd's approval. They did not consider in the slightest whether the position they were defending was true or false,
right or wrong. All their efforts were directed at seeming to be
more perceptive than all the rest in whatever debate they had
taken up.

As a rule, Momus was carried away and overwhelmed by the 78
breadth and power of their speech, so that he could not quickly
come up with an answer. Those men were so powerful in the
abundance of their words, in their training and long practice that
there was nothing they wanted that they couldn't accomplish

modo velint, quod vel dicendi facultate vel adepta iam tum auctoritate nequeant.

79   Hoc ex genere hominum quendam, cum de diis disputaretur,
his verbis orsum fuisse dicere: 'Non is sum, o viri optimi, qui nullos esse deos et inane volvi caelum ausim affirmare, inveterata praesertim in animis hominum opinione de diis, quos tamen vestrum
nemo, ni fallor, est qui ullos esse certa praestantique[92] ratione au-
deat affirmare. Sed illud interdum occurrit, ut possim[93] dubitasse
quid illud sit, cur patres et piissimos deos superos nuncupemus.
Quaeso, adeste animis et pro vestra humanitate quae dicturi sumus[94] attendite: novas inauditasque de rebus optimis disputationes ex me audisse, ni fallor, minime pigebit.

80   'Fingite adesse hic primos illos parentes nostros quos diis proximos arbitramur et eos, hac nostra hominum qua constituti sumus
miseria perspecta,[95] ab Iove hominum patre et deorum rege pro
nondum obsoleta parentis gratia ita rogare. "Utrumne illud, o pater Iuppiter, statuemus officium fuisse piissimum, ut, quoad in te
fuerit, omnia esse nobis per te erepta volueris, quae quidem optanda homini ducerentur?"[96] Quis illud a quovis irato patre etiam
in perditos liberos animo umquam ferat aequo et moderato, ut
quos haberi suos velit eosdem inferiore sorte quam bruta pleraque
animantia agere vitam patiatur? Sino vires, velocitatem, sensus
acuitatem, quibus longe homines a bestiis superamur. Cervisne
atque cornicibus[97] tam multos vitae annos dedistis ut degerent,
homines vero, quorum id intererat, vel maxime superum causa, per
quos templa, sacrificia et ludorum magnificentia, a quibus omne
sacrorum specimen religionisque honos colitur, tum primum inter
nascendum consenescere atque deficere, et antequam se in vita

thanks to their speaking ability and the authority they had acquired.

One of this sort, disputing about the gods, began to speak as 79
follows: "I am not the kind of person, gentlemen, who would dare
claim that there are no gods and that the heavens turn in a void,[13]
especially as there is in the human mind a deeply rooted belief in
the gods. Yet, unless I'm mistaken, none of you would dare claim
that there was an eminently convincing rational proof for the existence
of any of them. But from time to time it happens that I'm
able to doubt why it is that we call the heavenly gods 'fathers' and
'most holy.' Please listen and kindly pay attention to what I'm
about to say: unless I'm mistaken you won't be displeased to
hear my new and original discussions of these highly important
matters.

"Imagine that those first parents of ours were present, those 80
whom we believe to have been close to the gods. Imagine that they
saw the wretched condition this human race of ours is in, and in
the name of some vestigial parental feeling called upon Jupiter, father
of men and king of the gods, in this way. 'O Father Jupiter,
should we conclude it to be an act of the strictest piety that you
will to tear away from us, as much as you can, everything men believe
they want?' Who could ever bear without emotion — even in
the case of depraved children — that any father, however angry,
would permit those whom he wishes to be considered his own
children to suffer a worse lot in life than that of the greater part of
the brute animals?[14] I grant that animals far surpass humans in
strength, speed, and sharpness of senses. But why give deer and
crows many years to live out their lives, but will that humans shall
grow old and die from the first moment of their birth? Why rush
them off to death before they have established themselves in life,
while they are just beginning their strivings? It makes a difference,
most of all as regards the interests of the gods, since it is man who
builds temples, offers sacrifice, and holds magnificent games; it is

constitutos sentiant in ipsoque aliquid incohandi conatu ruere in mortem voluistis?

81 'At sit mors, deorum sententia, quidam exitus ab aerumnis sitque perinde mors bonorum optimum quod a malis adimat. Mortem ego facilius crederem esse non malam si eam sibi deos arripuisse perspicerem,[98] donumque non delaudarem si ab his esset deditum qui malorum tantorum causa non fuissent.[99] Verum quid hoc? Ceteras prope res omnes quae quidem ulla ex parte possent placere superi occuparunt, mortem longe ab se exclusere.

82 'Quid est bonarum rerum omnium quod sibi non vindicarint superi atque ascripserint? Nostros dii Ganymedes, nostras dii naviculas, nostras dii coronas, lyras, lampadas,[100] turibulos, crateras, nobis quicquid belli, venusti lautique invenere sustulerunt atque asportaverunt[101] in caelum: in caelum lepusculos, in caelum caniculas, in caelum equos, aquilas, vultures, ursas, delphinas,[102] cete.[103] Quod autem nostris delectentur, quod monstra hinc rapta in deliciis habeant non doleo, sed ne probo quidem. Illud doleo, beatos illos superos nostris non moveri incommodis, et cum patres sint, tam de nobis mereri pessime[104] quis animo ferat non aegro et perturbato? Nos, deorum filios, deteriore esse in sorte constitutos quam pecudum filios quis possit ferre? Ne vero nos, si filii sumus, si patres ipsi sunt, tam maximi eorum regni participes facere non[105] oportuit? At illi filios a patriis sedibus pepulere, beluis caelum replevere; homines exclusos voluere, monstris caelum refertum reddidere. Et quantine putabimus nos hydras atque hippocentauros potius factos non esse quam homines?

83 'At hominum gratia tam multa in medium effudisse deos praedicant, quae quidem cum ad usum, tum ad voluptatem atque ornamentum faciant: fruges, fructus, aurum, gemmas et huiusmodi.

man who worships you with every kind of rite and religious honor.

"Suppose, as the gods think, death is a kind of exit from trou- 81 ble; suppose it is even the best of goods, in that it frees us from evils. I should more readily believe that death was not an evil if I saw the gods appropriating this 'good' for themselves; I should not dispraise it were it not given by those who are themselves the cause of great evils. And why don't the gods appropriate death? They have taken over almost every other good that could possibly please them; but they've kept far away from death.

"Which of all good things have they not arrogated and assigned 82 to themselves? The gods have stolen and taken away our Gany-medes, our boats, our crowns, lyres, lamps, censers, drinking bowls — whatever beautiful, attractive, and luxurious possessions of ours they could find. They took to heaven bunny rabbits, pup-pies, horses, eagles, vultures, bears, dolphins and whales. It doesn't pain me that they enjoy our possessions, that they prize the mon-sters they've seized from here, although I can't approve of it, ei-ther. It pains me that those blessed gods are not affected by our hardships, and since they are 'fathers', how can someone not be upset at the terrible treatment we get from them? Who can stand the fact that we, the sons of the gods, have a lot inferior to the sons of cattle? Shouldn't we — if we are their sons, if they are our fathers — shouldn't we also share in their enormous kingdom? But they have forced their children from their parental estates and have filled heaven with wild beasts; they've willed to shut men out of heaven and fill it with monsters.[15] So why should we set any value on the fact that we have been created men rather than hy-dras and centaurs?

"They say that the gods have poured out many blessings for 83 mankind's sake, useful, delightful and ornamental things, such as crops, fruits, gold, jewels and the like.[16] So it will be helpful to consider among ourselves whether what people say is really true. If

Haec igitur iuvet inter nos considerasse, itane sint uti ferunt: quod
si quis deos ea fecisse asserat ut his nobis illudant, nostras spes et
exspectationes frustrentur, fortassis non mentiatur. Quotus enim
quisque est qui istiusmodi non appetat volente deo, quotus est qui
adipiscatur deo non repugnante, quotus est qui adeptis fruatur aut
gaudeat?

84   'Sed ea demum cedo fecerint hominum causa, quaero bono-
rumne an malorum? Si bonis providisse dicent, quaeram quid igitur ea bonis non erogent,[106] improbis non auferant? Cur eadem
optimis adimant et scelestissimis condonent? Eccam pietatem probis dedere, ut quae ad necessitatem faciant omnia per industriam,
vigilias laboremve quaeritent; impiis vero, audacibus deorumque
contemptoribus, etiam adiecere quae nimia penitus sint.

85   'Sed quid ego ullos ab deorum iniuria excipiam, cum videam
eos in universum mortalium genus tam multa intulisse, quae interdum si quid furere desinant sibi non licuisse optent? O diis invisum genus mortalium, quandoquidem, praeter eas gravissimas res
quas recensuimus, dolorem quoque febremque atque morbos et
acres pectoris curas et turbidos praecordiorum impetus et saevissi-
mos animi cruciatus importarunt! O nos extrema in miseria gravissimis durissimisque aerumnis obrutos mortales, quos ita vexant,
ita in dies afficiunt malis superi ut cum numquam vacare calamitatibus liceat, tum et assiduis acerbissimisque in casibus semper
nova dolendi ratio insurgat atque immineat, quoad perpetuo in
luctu homini vivendum sit, et ita vivendum ut omni in vita hora
nulla succedat horae similis.

someone were to maintain that the gods have done these things to mock us, to frustrate our hopes and expectations, perhaps he wouldn't be lying. How many individuals are there who, compelled by the divine will, don't actually go in for these things? How many are there who do obtain them, but in the face of opposition from divine forces? How many are there who really enjoy and take pleasure in what they've obtained?

"But let's grant that the gods have done these things for the 84 sake of human beings. I ask: good human beings or bad ones? If they say that the gods look out for the good, I'd ask: why then don't they bestow them on the good and take them away from the bad? Why do they take them away from the best men and give them to the most wicked? Look how they impose on righteous folk a sense of justice, forcing them to meet all their basic wants through industry, sleeplessness and hardship, while they open-handedly reward the impious, the licentious, and the blasphemers of the gods.

"But why should I except anyone from the injuries of the gods, 85 when I see these gods inflict so many evils on the whole human race, evils they would wish they hadn't been allowed to inflict, if they would ever come to their senses. O, how the human race is loathed by the gods! As well as those dreadful evils I've listed, they also give us grief, fever, diseases, bitter woes in our hearts, stormy emotional outbursts, and brutal psychological torment! Alas for us mortals, plunged into extreme wretchedness under the heaviest and hardest of burdens! Alas for us, whom the gods so torture, so afflict with daily evils, that we are never free of calamity. Even in the midst of continual, bitter misfortunes some new form of suffering is always rising up to threaten us. To that extent mankind always has to live in sorrow and lamentation; we must always live in such a way that not one hour of our existence resembles the next.

86 'Vel quis vestrum[107] est, viri optimi, qui sibi commodarum rerum omnium quippiam relictum sentiat praeter eas tantum res,
quibus ademptis, omnino futuri simus nulli? Lucem, undas, fruges
et eiusmodi non est ut nostra potius quam ceterorum animantium
causa fore producta assentiamur. Loquendi usum et vitae modum,
quo esset alter alteri adiunctior, coacti necessitatibus ipsi adinveni-
mus; cetera omnia nobis erepta brutis fuisse condonata vestrum
quis ignorat? O nos igitur iterum male acceptos! Quid admisimus[108] miseri mortales ut, rebus omnibus quae gratae commo-
daeve sint ereptis,[109] aerumnis et difficultatibus obruti vitam miseram degamus?

87 'Sed sint illi quidem dii caelo digni, optima omnia mereantur:
nos mortales, ad miseriam nati, obrui cumulis malorum non recu-
semus. Tametsi de omni deorum genere quid possit quispiam in-
terpretari, quis est vestrum quem id fugiat? Quid tamen sentiam
ipse non est ut referam; vos id adeo statuetis quid tota in re assentiri oporteat, quandoquidem ex nostro mortalium numero dicun-
tur aliqui ad deorum numerum[110] augendum conscendisse. At voletne ille quidem ex medio[111] hominum grege abreptus et inter
beatissimos rerum dominos ascitus, voletne, inquam, ille venerari
et coli et metui, tantarum sese rerum gradu et sede et maiestate dignum deputans? Cui forte iterato si via sit hac sibi plane cognita et
explorata qua conscenderit ad superos redeundum, quidvis facilius
possit quam caelicolam fieri. Multa praestitit occasio, multa tulit
necessitas, sed plura adiecit hominum improbitas atque stultitia,
quibus rebus summorum forte deorum aliqui vel inviti in id amplitudinis rapti sunt ita adeo ut se mirentur unde tantum siet.

88 'Et quam commodius cum illis ageretur, si se nossent pro dignitate deos gerere! Quod si nostrum quispiam homunculorum talem

"Is there any one of you gentlemen who believes that any of   86
life's advantages has been left to him, beyond those things without
which we would die? We would all agree that light, water, corn
and things of that kind were produced as much for the sake of the
other animals as for our sake.[17] We ourselves, compelled by necessity, have devised the use of speech and social organization. Who
among you doesn't know that everything else has been ripped
from us and given to the brute animals? Again, how badly we have
been treated! What crime did we miserable mortals commit, that
everything pleasing and helpful was taken away, that we now live
out a wretched life ruined by troubles and difficulties?

"But let's suppose that these gods are indeed worthy of heaven   87
and deserve only the best, while we mortals, born to sorrow, will
not resist being overwhelmed by a heap of troubles. Has it escaped
any of you what anyone could figure out about the race of the
gods? It's not necessary to tell you what I think of them myself;
you can draw your own conclusions in this whole matter from the
fact that some of our mortal number are said to have risen to augment the number of the gods. But will a man who has been
snatched from the middle of the human flock and co-opted to join
the blessed lords of nature — will he, I say, really want to be regarded with awe, worshipped and feared, and believe himself worthy of a position and a seat among great affairs? If by chance he
had to return to the gods a second time by the same way he'd as-
cended, a way tested and well-known to him, he could become
anything more easily than a heaven-dweller.[18] Chance and necessity have offered many opportunities, but the wickedness and folly
of mankind have added still more occasions for some to be lifted
up to the height of the highest gods, even without their willing it,
so that they wonder themselves how they got there.

"How much more easily we could deal with them if they knew   88
how to conduct themselves like gods! If one of us little men discharged his administrative functions as the majority of the great

se exhibeat in rebus administrandis qualem plerique magnorum deorum se habent, merito plecteretur. Sed tu deosne esse hos putes, qui res mortalium tam supine desidioseque neglegant, aut hos qui monstra, ut videre licet, inprimis colant, ulla rerum piissimarum procuratione dignos putabis?

89   'Scio quid hic respondeas; dices: quid mirum si nimia in licentia constituti insaniunt; si dum omnia posse quae velint sentiunt, hi quidem velint omnia quae possint, et quae demum velint, licere omnia arbitrantur? Atqui id ita liceat diis: spreta hominum causa, cum Ganymede[112] inter epulas volutari, nectare et ambrosia immergi.

90   'Nobisne non licebit tantis miseriis moveri? Non licebit opinari superos deos aut nullam[113] gerere mortalium curam, aut si gerant odisse? Et quid iuvat tantis supplicationibus obsecrationibusque pacem deum alias res agentium, aut mala reddentium, exposcere? Desinamus inepti eos sollicitare irritis cerimoniis qui, voluptatibus occupati, sollertes agentesque oderint. Caveamus inutili nostra superstitione de his velle benemereri, qui quidem aut nulli sunt aut, si sunt, infesti[114] semper ad miseros mortales malis conficiendos vigilant.'

91   Huiusmodi fuisse ambitiosi illius orationem Momus rettulit, et hac sese oratione adiuravit ita commotum dictorum petulantia et flagitii indignatione ut prae ira vix manum continuerit, nec dubitare quin si Iuppiter ipse optimus maximus, omnium mitissimus, diique piissimi et modestissimi adfuissent impudentissimumque illud oratoris os et intolerabilem gestus verborumque iactantiam atque magnificentiam fuissent intuiti, illico in illam omnem scele-

gods do, he would be punished, and rightly so. Do you think that
these beings are gods, who treat mortal affairs so apathetically? Do
you think these beings, whose primary role is to take care of monsters (as one may see), deserve to have oversight of the holiest
things?

"I know what you'll say here; you'll say: why be surprised that 89
they act like madmen when they're set up to have such an excess
of freedom? So long as they think they can do anything they want,
is it any wonder that they in fact want to do everything they can,
and that they end up believing everything they want is allowed?
Indeed, what would seem to be allowed the gods is this: to spurn
the concerns of humans and to roll under the dinner table[19] with
Ganymede, soaked in nectar and ambrosia.

"Will it not be allowable for *us* to get angry at so much wretch- 90
edness? For *us* to believe the gods above either have no concern for
mortals, or hate us? What good are all these supplications and entreaties, asking for peace from gods who are either occupied elsewhere or actively doing us harm? Let's stop being so foolish and
bothering them with pointless rites. The gods are taken up with
their own pleasures; they hate ingenious and active people. We
should beware this useless superstition of ours which makes us
want to deserve well of the gods. Either the gods do not exist at
all, or if they do exist, they are always hostile to wretched mortals,
actively seeking to do them harm."

Momus reported that the speech of this presumptuous individ- 91
ual had been like that, and he had been so distressed by the pro-
vocative and scandalous tone of this oration that he could scarcely
restrain himself from hitting the man out of sheer anger. He had
no doubt that Best and Greatest Jupiter, the gentlest of all gods,
and the other holy and well-behaved gods who were present, had
they seen the orator's utterly impudent face, his insufferable way of
gesticulating, his boastful and ostentatious words, they would
immediately have passed judgement and hurled their biggest thun-

stissimam familiam litteratorum omnem vim fulminis effunden‧
dam iudicassent, quo philosophos omnes totis cum gymnasiis et
libris et bibliothecis absumerent.[115] Verum se pro suorum temporum conditione et necessitate temperasse iracundiae; pro suscepti
tamen negotii ratione non potuisse non facere quin in id erumpe-
ret verborum, ut inter admonendum eos, qui de diis ita obloque-
rentur, hortaretur iterum atque iterum prospicerent ne quid de
his, a quibus tantis tamque divinis prosecuti essent beneficiis, aut
perperam perverseque opinarentur aut male mereri aggrederentur,
caverentque nedum deos negent; demum sentiant praesentes esse
eos atque piissimorum et impiissimorum, proborum et improborum habere discrimen. Postremo illis optavi[116] ut ea mens erga superos sit quae suo sit sine detrimento et[117] malo.

92   Hic igitur ambitiosos illos, qui omnia possent moderatius perpeti quam videri cuiusquam prudentiae et consilio acquiescere,
consensione facta insurrexisse. Et quod Momi praesertim admonitiones dedignarentur, a quo iam pridem multis victi disputationi-
bus capitali odio dissiderent, idcirco[118] furore concitos irruisse
atque vim illam ab[119] se persaepius alibi enarratam intulisse; sed
petere se ab Iove optimo et maximis diis ne huic mortalium insi-
pientiae succenseant, potius quae se digna sunt suam per indul-
gentiam atque beneficentiam cogitarent[120] et prodesse mortalibus
perseverent, Momi incommodis atque iniuriis posthabitis.

93   Haec Momus submissa et inflexa voce tristique fronte referens,
animo erat alacri, cum ceteras ob res, tum quod deos atque inprimis Iovem dictorum aculeis commoveri non obscure perpendebat.
Perspiciebat enim obmutuisse Iovem et digito hospitalem mensam
subincussisse; ergo intra se gaudio exsultabat. Quam rem intuens

derbolt at that whole criminal clan of literati, so that all philosophers, with their gymnasia, books and libraries, would be consumed by flame. But Momus, because of his own circumstances
and exigencies, had tempered his fury. Still, for the sake of the
business he'd undertaken, he couldn't help one outburst, in which
he had warned them against speaking ill of the gods and urged
them again and again to make sure they didn't start to alienate or
think anything wrong or perverse about those beings who had bestowed so many divine benefits upon them. They should be careful not to deny the gods; for in the end they would realize that the
gods did exist and were quite able to make distinctions between
pious and impious, good and bad men. Finally, he expressed the
wish that they should adopt an attitude towards the gods which
would not be to their detriment and harm.

Hereupon these presumptuous men, who could tolerate any- 92
thing more calmly than seeming to comply with someone else's
wisdom and advice, came to an agreement among themselves, then
rose in rebellion. In particular they spurned the warnings of
Momus, for whom they had a deadly hatred, having been bested
by him for a long time in numerous debates. That was why they
came down upon him furiously and inflicted that violence which
he had told them about so often on other occasions. But he besought Jove the Best and the greatest gods not to become angry
with this instance of mankind's folly, but rather plan deeds worthy
of themselves with indulgence and good will, and continue to help
mortals, ignoring Momus' injuries and misfortunes.

Momus told this story in a meek and quavering voice and with 93
a sad face, but his mind was keen, mostly because, as he shrewdly
assessed the situation, the gods and particularly Jove had been
deeply shaken by his barbed words. Noticing how Jupiter had
fallen silent and was tapping his fingers on the table, he was inwardly gleeful. Hercules, perceiving this, smiled and said, "For my
part, I appeal in turn to *you*, Momus, not to get angry if I show

Hercules subridens 'Te' inquit 'ego item, o noster Mome, testor, ne quid ipse succenseas si qua ex parte mortalium causam non esse apud Iovem omnino desertam cupio.' Et ad Iovem versus, 'Indulgendum sane, o Iuppiter, est' inquit 'mortalibus errore praesertim consilii adversus ignotum apud se Momum desipientibus, quandoquidem apud superos Momus ita se gerit ut non facile nosci et alius videri possit plane quam sit. Sed cavendum item est ne quis in aliorum incommodum atque detrimentum plus sapiat plusve teneat artium fallendi quam ingenia bona et simplicia deceat. Quid illi mortales possint eloquentia ex Momo perspicue licet intellegere, qui tam exquisita excogitataque suadendi ratione instructus de mortalium gymnasiis ad superos rediit. Sed de Momi dictis deque tota causa quid a Iove optimo et maximo sentiri deceat in promptu est; quid vero statuisse debeat, alii viderint.

94   'At tu, Mome, illud velim tecum deputes, an hic aut locus aut tempus idoneus accommodatusve sit, ut in convivio de his rebus iniucundissimis disputes, ut capitis causam agites? Quid tibi voluisti, Mome? Utrum philosophos atque eruditos ad invidiam trahere, an deos lacessere dictis et ironia? Sed nos, o superi, tam grandi accuratque Momi oratione commoti, quid faciemus? Illudne praeteribimus, quod meminisse oportet, quamdiu fuerint mortales, tamdiu fuisse et opinionum errores et studiorum varietates et disputationum ineptias?

95   Sed tu, deorum gravissime, agedum Mome: negabisne cum his studiosorum familiis, in quas tu tam atrocissime invehebare, aeternum fuisse quandam perennem inquisitionem veri atque boni? Negabisne philosophorum opera effectum ut genus mortalium seque suamque sortem non ignoret? Non erit ab re neque ab offi-

some concern that the cause of the mortals not be entirely abandoned in Jove's court."[20] He turned to Jupiter. "O Jupiter, you should forgive the humans' foolish error of judgment, especially as it regards their actions against Momus, a person unknown to them. For even among the gods Momus behaves in such a way that he is hard to know and may seem otherwise than he really is. One should be careful, likewise, to prevent someone from learning and mastering more of the arts of deceit, to the misfortune and detriment of others, than is fitting for good and sincere people to learn. What eloquence these mortals are capable of may be learned clearly from Momus, who has returned to heaven from the gymnasia of the mortals outfitted with that meticulous and studied technique of persuasion. But it's obvious what Best and Greatest Jupiter ought to think about Momus' words and about this whole case; others will see to what he ought to decide.

"As for you, Momus, I want to know whether you consider 94 this banquet an appropriate time or place to debate such unpleasant matters and to conduct cases of capital importance? What were you after, Momus? Did you want to make philosophers and learned men odious, did you want to harass the gods with your words and your irony? But what shall we do, fellow gods, shocked as we are by Momus' solemn and studied speech? Shall we let pass something we ought to remember: that for as long as there have been mortals, there have been erroneous beliefs, conflicting passions and absurd debates?

"But come now, Momus, gravest of the gods, will you deny 95 that, in the case of these scholarly clans against whom you rant so dreadfully, there have always been ongoing investigations into the true and the good? Will you deny that it is through the efforts of the philosophers that the human race has come to know themselves and their lot? It will not fall outside the subject or my obligations, Momus, if I respond to your provocation. What mortal man was ever so insolent that he deemed himself worthy of the

cio, Mome, si abs te provocatus congredior. Etenim quis umquam apud mortales tam protervus inventus est qui se maximorum deorum amplitudine et maiestate dignum deputet? Quis est qui non se quidem tam multis quae a diis susceperit bonis prope indignum deputet? An erit ullus amens adeo furoreque adeo perditus quin mentem, rationem, intellegentiam rerumque memoriam et eiusmodi, quae longum esset prosequi, cum praeclara praestantissimaque et summo deorum beneficio esse concessa hominibus, tum et ipsis a diis, inprimisque a mente divina[121] atque ratione ducta asserat atque confirmet? Haec ut homines dinoscerent et profiterentur, viri docti et in gymnasiis bibliothecisque, non inter errones et crapulas educati, effecere dicendo, monendo, suadendo, monstrando quod aequum sit, quod deceat, quod[122] oporteat, non popularium auribus applaudendo, non afflictos irridendo, non maestos irritando.

96 'Fecere, inquam, docti ipsi, suis evigilatis et bene diductis rationibus, ut honos diis redderetur, ut cerimoniarum religio observaretur, ut pietas, sanctimonia virtusque coleretur. Atqui[123] haec quidem eo fecere quo ceteros meliores redderent, non quo sibi inanem ullam gloriam aucuparentur. Qui tametsi gloriae cupiditate commoti tantas vigilias, tantos labores, tam multa diligentia et cura res arduas et difficiles suscepissent atque obivissent? Quis erit deorum omnium qui illis, praeter te unum, Mome, succenseat? Quis erit deorum omnium praeter te unum, Mome, qui illos non de se benemeritos fateatur? Quis erit quin[124] illis, praeter te unum, Mome, habendas gratias, diligendos, iuvandos servandosque non affirmet?

97 'Deorum autem cultores atque observatores, quales illi cumque sint, nostro pro officio, o superi, ne vero non fovebimus, eorum saluti non prospiciemus, eorum causae, commodis rationibusque

greatness and majesty of the mightiest gods? Where is the man who does not think himself unworthy, or nearly so, of the many good things he has received from the gods? Will there be anyone so mad, so consumed by anger, that he will not maintain and affirm that thought, reason, intelligence, memory, and other such faculties too numerous to list are splendid, excellent things, granted to mankind with the highest divine generosity, and also things that derive from the gods themselves, primarily from the divine mind and reason? Learned men and persons educated in gymnasia and libraries—not among vagabonds and drunkards—have worked so that mankind shall understand and confess these truths. They have done so by talking, advising, and persuading men of the fair, the fitting and the obligatory—not by seeking popular applause, not by mocking the afflicted or disturbing those in grief.

"Learned men, I say, through their deeply-meditated and well-constructed arguments have been responsible for the honor paid to the gods, for the performance of religious ceremonies and for the cultivation of piety, holiness and virtue. At the same time, they have acted in this way so that others would become better people, and not to chase any empty glory for themselves. Who, however motivated by the desire for glory, would take on such long vigils, such great hardships, such arduous and difficult obstacles with so much diligence and care? Who of all the gods would get angry with them—except you alone, Momus? Who of all the gods would not confess that they had earned good treatment—except you alone, Momus? Who would not say that they deserved thanks, affection, help and support—except you alone, Momus? 96

"Isn't it our duty, O gods, to foster those who worship and respect divine beings—as these men surely do? Shouldn't we look out for their security? Shouldn't we be of service to them in their problems, their interests and their reasonings? Momus, with his deep devotion to the cause of the gods, hates these men, who have 97

non opitulabimur? Eos demum[125] per quos haec tam digna, tam grata, tam accepta constent, per quos dii putemur et veneremur, Momus, deorum causae affectissimus, caelo annuente atque impune oderit! Sicine studio et contentione rationibus deorum inservire didicisti, Mome, ut qui illic apud mortales quo colamur,[126] veneremur, supplicemur providerit, effecerit, instituerit, eum hic[127] tuo dicendi artificio et verborum ambagibus inducas in odium eu periis? Quod si nescias, philosophi, Mome, philosophi, inquam, hi sunt omnes inter mortales a quibus superi multa et praestantissima ad maiestatis decus imperiique columen cum acceperint, tum se accepisse non infitientur, quibusve et superi omnia pietatis officia cum debeant, tum et deberi fateantur. Et diligunt quidem eam studiosorum familiam, Mome, superi magis quam ut dictis tuis commoti eos velint perdere; potius cupiunt eos[128] esse non infelicissimos, ac merito id quidem, nam hi ratione et via assecuti sunt ut sit nemo quin[129] deorum vim et numen esse non sentiat atque profiteatur et se ad bonos mores rectamque vitae normam accommodet.

98 'Neque tamen velim Momum nostrum, deorum festivissimum, tam esse erga mortalium[130] genus iratum deputes ut eos oderit, qui fortasse quempiam ex mortalibus asciverit inter superos. De me adventicio novoque deo hoc testor, a me plurimum deberi Momo quod filiae iusserit ut ad vos me sublatum afferret. Et te laudo, Mome, si tuam erga mortales mentem et animum bene interpretor, qui Iovem admones ut malit quae suae sint beneficentiae meminisse quam quae[131] aliorum sint iniuriae, si ad iniuriam pensandum est quod inconsulti homines admiserint.

99 'Ideo, ni fallor, pertinet, o Iuppiter, ut sic dixisse velit Momus: tu quidem[132] cum insipientibus non succensueris, officii erit sa-

established so much that is worthy, esteemed and deserving of thanks, who have upheld the existence and worship of the gods. And he does it with impunity, with divine approval! Is it thus, with this battling zeal, Momus, that you've learned to serve the interests of heaven, so that with rhetorical artifice and verbal subtleties you bring odium upon the very men by whose foresight, activity and teaching we are worshipped, venerated and supplicated? If you don't know it, Momus, it's the philosophers — I repeat, the philosophers — from whom, of all mortals, the gods have undeniably received the most excellent support for the splendor of their majesty and the exaltation of their power. The higher beings should owe them a debt of reverent service and should confess this debt. The gods *love* this clan of scholars, Momus, and, far from wanting them damned in agitated response to your words, they do not want them to be wretched. And rightly so, since they have succeeded in bringing it about that no one may not perceive and confess the power and divinity of the gods, and conform himself to good morals and a right standard of living.

"I do not want you to think that our dear Momus, the most entertaining of the gods, has been so angered by the human race that he has grown to hate them. After all, it's possible that he has himself been responsible for co-opting one of the mortals into the divine race. I give you the example of my own arrival as a newly-made god: I owe Momus a great deal because he ordered his daughter to carry me up among the divine race. And I praise you, Momus, if I understand rightly your attitude and intention towards mortals, for advising Jove to remember his own beneficence rather than the injuries of others — if actions committed by thoughtless men should be thought of as injuries. 98

"Unless I am mistaken, O Jupiter, this is the true relevance of Momus' words: since you do not show anger towards fools, it will be your duty to show all favor and benevolence towards wise men who have deserved excellently of the gods. When Jupiter shall will 99

pientibus et optime de diis meritis omnia ad gratiam et beneficentiam referre. Quod cum fecisse volet Iuppiter, o superi optimi,
et quosnam deliget,[133] quos ornabit, quos caelo dignos putabit?
Eosne qui omnia turbent, nihil pacati, nihil quieti possint aut meditari aut exsequi, an eos potius quos ratio quaedam non ab scur-
rarum improbitate ducta, sed a virtute parata et constituta aditum
sibi ad Iovis deorumque gratiam et benivolentiam patefecerit? Qui
suo studio, diligentia, opera, labore, periculo plurima perquisierit,
multa invenerit, nihil praetermiserit, omnia tentarit in mediumque
contulerit quae quidem ad hominum usum, ad vitae necessitatem,
ad bene beateque vivendum conferrent, quae ad otium et tranquillitatem facerent, quae ad salutem, ad ornamentum, ad decus publi-
carum privatarumque rerum conducerent, quae ad cognitionem
superum, ad metum deorum, ad observationem religionis accom-
modarentur!'

100   Hanc Herculis ad Momum orationem et animos utrimque iam
ad altercationem paratos occupavit atque avertit repens exauditus
ad caeli vestibulum strepitus; ad quem dinoscendum cum relictis
poculis advolassent, evenit ut in grandem inciderint admirationem, conspecto e regione maximo atque omni colorum varietate
ornatissimo arcu triumphali, quem quidem Iuno coaedificarat au-
roque votorum conflato operuerat, tanto et operis et ornamenti artificio insignem atque illustrem ut caelicolarum optimi architecti
fieri id negarint[134] potuisse, et pictores fictoresque omnes sua esse
in eo expingendo atque expoliendo ingenia superata faterentur.
Alia ex parte successit ut maiorem in modum demirarentur quid
sibi cumulus illic maximorum deorum intra se tumultuantium et
ad caeli regiam infesto gradu properantium vellet.

101   Ergo et illuc versus[135] oculis et hic auribus arrecti et animis in
partes utrasque solliciti pendebant. Illud interea effecit ut acrius

to have done this, O best of the divine race, whom, pray, shall he choose, whom shall he honor, whom shall he reckon worthy of heaven? Those who disturb everything, who can neither plan nor perform any peaceful and quiet action? Or those for whom a pathway has been opened to the favor and good will of Jupiter and the gods by Reason — a Reason not influenced by worthless and wicked persons, but formed and fixed by virtue? Such men have inquired widely with zeal, diligence, effort, toil and danger; they have discovered many things and neglected nothing. They have tested everything and made publicly available whatever contributes to human use and need and to living well and blessedly; whatever makes for ease and tranquillity; whatever conduces to the security, embellishment and honor of public and private affairs; and whatever befits the knowledge and fear of the gods, and the observance of religion!"

A sudden noise coming from the entranceway to heaven interrupted Hercules' speech to Momus and averted a quarrel between the two gods, who were now spoiling for a fight. Everyone put down their goblets and rushed out to find out what had caused it. They experienced a great feeling of wonder on seeing across from them a huge, richly decorated and polychrome triumphal arch. It had been built by Juno and covered with gold melted down from votive objects.[21] So remarkable and splendid was the workmanship of the monument and its decoration that the greatest architects among the heaven-dwellers would have said it was impossible to build. All the painters and sculptors admitted that their own talents had been surpassed by the painting and finishing of that arch. Looking in another direction, they wondered still more, asking themselves what was the significance of that roiling crowd of great gods who were hurrying at a menacing pace towards the heavenly palace.

The gods were in a state of uncertainty, anxiously turning their eyes in one direction, their ears in another, and their minds in

100

101

commoverentur, quod vixdum eo appulerant, cum illico Iunonis illud vastum et immane tantarum impensarum opus labans corruit,
cuius fragore et sonitu subincussa caeli (uti sunt aenea) convexa
maximum dedere sonitum, quem ab resonantis testudinis tinnitu
exceptum musici notantes ad memoriae posteritatem Iunonis illud
caducum fragileque opus Tinnim[136] nuncuparunt. At postea id
corrupto vocabulo Irim vulgo appellarunt.

102   Iuppiter vero ceterique caelicolae cum aliunde, tum hinc quam
in omni re agenda sit ratio, mens institutumque muliebre inconsultum et penitus ineptum annotarunt; subinde re ipsa admoniti
manifesto perspexere coepta mulierum eo semper[137] tendere, ut
aliquid discordiarum discidiorumque exsuscitent.

103   Nam etsi inter eos qui tum adventarant deos aliquid fortassis
aderat quominus unanimes atque concordes essent, ad veteres tamen simultates Iunonis novissimum factum magnas contentionum
acrimonias excitarat. Quas ubi ad Iovem detulissent, conversus ad
Herculem Iuppiter, animo vehementer commotus, 'En' inquit 'et
quanti est nos esse principes? Quid homines querantur nullam sibi
advenire horam horae persimilem, nihil ad animi sententiam secundare?[138] Nos et dii et rerum principes integram unam sumere
cenam vacuam molestia non poterimus! Quosnam accusem? Isto-
rumne studia importuna et insanas cupiditates an meam potius
desidiosam facilitatem, qua fiat ut cum licere sibi per me omnia ar-
bitrentur, tum et interdum plus satis iuvet delirare?

104   'Quidvis malim fore me quam principem,[139] dum quibus prae-
sis, quorum commodis advigiles, quorum quietem et tranquillitatem curis et laboribus tuis praeferas, neque beneficii neque officii
memores in te sint, dum assiduis futilibusque expostulationibus
obtundere atque variis agitare sollicitudinibus non desinant. Sem-

both directions. They were shocked even more by the fact that they had hardly arrived on the spot when that vast and ruinously expensive work of Juno's tipped over and collapsed. The crashing sound bounced off the dome of heaven (which was made of brass) and gave out a great ringing sound, leading the writers of music among them to give posterity a name for Juno's ephemeral construction: "the Ringer." But afterwards the word became corrupted, and people commonly called it "the Rainbow."[22]

Jupiter and the rest of the heaven-dwellers took note that on 102 this as on other occasions the methods, ideas and decisions of women in every undertaking were ill-advised and inept. Soon thereafter, they learned from experience in the clearest possible way that women's undertakings always led to division and discord.[23]

Although the gods who had turned up by that point had reason 103 to be something less than unanimous and harmonious, Juno's latest act had provoked great acrimony and contention, reviving old feuds. When the quarrels were brought before Jupiter, he turned to Hercules and said, with deep emotion, "You see how much trouble it is being a prince? Why should men complain that no hour comes along which resembles the last, and that everything goes wrong for them? Even we gods and rulers of nature can't get through an entire dinner without trouble! Whom should I blame? Their importunate passions and mad desires, or my own lazy and compliant character, which makes them think that I'll let them get away with anything, and also sometimes does more than its share to provoke their ravings?

"I would have preferred anything to being a prince.[24] The peo- 104 ple you lead, whose welfare you watch over, for whose tranquillity and quiet you offer up your own cares and toils — these people forget your benefits and their obligations to you, they never stop harassing you with their ceaseless, pointless demands and their ever-changing worries. Won't you ever stop, you noisy lot, renewing

perne, o meum convicium, semperne causis expostulationum inno-
vatis me coram contendere ad simultatem perseverabitis? Quotiens vestra sedavi iurgia, quotiens a contumelia coercui, a rixa
distraxi, ab insania revocavi? Quotiens hos nostros tumultus op-
pressi? Thetim accusabat olim Vulcanus – tritaeque iam tum
vestrae hae fuere fabulae – quod splendorem lucemque omnis suae
dignitatis pollueret atque exstingueret. Vulcanum Diana silva-
nique dii accusabant quod umbratiles suas amoenasque sedes ho-
stili impetu immanique iniuria populare atque vastare aggrederetur. Hos accusabat Aeolus[140] quod Zephyro et Noto et Austris et
Aquilonibus ceterisque suis commilitonibus alas expilarent pen-
nasque decerperent, quas monstris navigiorum adigerent.[141] Aeo-
lum[142] accusabat Neptunus quod misceret[143] omnia otiumque
atque aequabilitatem suarum regionum funditus perturbaret.
Neptunum rursus et Thetis accusabat quod se impio hospitio ex-
ciperet nitoremque atque illibatum virginitatis florem auderet vio-
lare.

105   'Nunc et nova discidiorum discordiarumque materia oborta est:
Iunonem accusat Neptunus quod votorum purgamenta aedifica-
tionisque rudera in aram Neptuniam per contemptum et contumeliam eiecerit. Ceres ne suum in solum reiciantur repugnat; ea
item Vulcanus negat posse commode suis in officinis apud se re-
cipi. Et harum querelarum ad me irrequieta immodestissimorum
iurgia referuntur! Ego delirantibus meas patientissimas aures prae-
beo; isti nostra abuti patientia non cessant, nihil verentur. Quid
hoc petulantiae est? Numquamne erit ut hac vestra garrulitate
mutuo vos lacessere nosque obstinate obtundere desinatis? Liceat
per hanc nostram patientiam insanire, at pudeat olim de nobis demum abiecte atque impudenter sentire. Annon illud est impu-
dentiae, quae quisque fastidiat esse apud se, ea in principis gremium velle reicere?

your causes of complaint and conducting your quarrels in front of me? How often have I settled your quarrels, how often have I restrained you from insulting each other, broken up your fights, brought you to your senses? How often have I quelled these tumults of ours? Once Vulcan accused Thetis[25]—these stories of yours are always so familiar!—of having stained and wiped out all the light and splendor of his dignity. Diana and the woodland deities accused Vulcan of trying to ravage and despoil their shady and idyllic habitat with his vicious and outrageous attacks. Aeolus[26] accused *them* of stealing the wings from Zephyr, Notus, Auster and Aquilo[27] and the rest of their comrades-in-arms and of plucking their feathers, which they then attached to carven monsters on the prows of ships. Neptune accused Aeolus of churning everything up, claiming that he utterly disturbed the peace and even tenor of his kingdom. Thetis in turn accused Neptune because he had carried her off with no regard for the ties of hospitality and had dared to pluck the shining and untouched flower of her virginity.

"And now new causes of upheaval and discord have arisen! Neptune accuses Juno of throwing discarded offerings and surplus construction materials onto his watery altar out of scorn and a wish to be insulting. Ceres resists having them cast onto her ground; Vulcan says that he cannot accommodate them in his workshops. And the unceasing litigation arising from these unruly quarrels is brought before me! I lend my long-suffering ears to lunatics, and they, fearing nothing, won't stop abusing my patience! What impudence is this? Will you never stop assailing one another with this chattering of yours, will you never stop belaboring me with your obstinacy? As far as I'm concerned you can go on ranting, but at some point you should be ashamed to treat me with such disrespect. What is this impudence, that everybody wants to throw into the lap of their prince all their own petty annoyances? 105

106   'Vota mortalium deponi recusant apud se; quo alibi ponantur
non patet locus. Ad me itur, expostulatur ut inde atque inde adimam. Quid hoc? An aliud est quam efflagitare ut quae illis ingrata
sint, quae obscena illis videantur, quae desertis et incultissimis suis
in vastitatibus excepisse nolint, ea in regium triclinium reiciantur?
O nos miseros, si impudentissimis obtemperandum sit, et infelicissimos, si his imperandum sit apud quos nulla est principis reverentia, nulla aequi, nulla pudoris observatio! Putabam me ali-
quando magna diligentia compositis rebus, et distributis pro
dignitate imperii,[144] ab his praesertim molestiis vacaturum. Nunc
ne id Iovi maximo rerum principi deorumque regi liceat, non caelicolae modo sed, quod vix ferendum est, homunculi obstant.

107   'Sed quid ego in hanc unam pestem animantium (ne dicam homines) irascar? Hoc nimirum nostra effecit nimia facilitas: dum
omnibus obsequi ultro cupimus, omnium in nos temeritatem il-
leximus. Dederam mortalibus, ut duras et indomitas eorum mentes nostrorum munerum commoditate[145] mitigarem atque beneficiis ad bene de nobis sentiendum flecterem, plura longe quam
optare homines sit fas. Namque principio dederam amoenissimum
odoratissimumque perpetua florum copia ver. Cupere se illi quidem dixere ut quam fructuum spem flores prae se ferrent mature
traderem. Ea de re aestatem adieci, eique rei Vulcani fabros omnemque ignium officinam exercui, quorum manu et opera intimis
ab radicibus sucus in baccas educeretur atque in ramos fru-
ctumque concresceret. Quid tum? Demum saturi, fructuum copia
delectari se admodum atque cupere dixerunt ut pristinum ver restituerem.[146] Cessi quidem eorum libidini: collegi idcirco ab omni
natura gignendarum rerum igniculos atque baccis quasi thesauris

"They refuse to place the mortals' votive offerings in their houses, although there's nowhere else to put them. They come to me, they ask me to take the offerings away from this place or that. What is the meaning of this behavior? How is it different from asking that whatever they dislike, whatever offends them, whatever they don't want to take into those vast, unfurnished, empty halls of theirs, be offloaded into the royal dining room? Oh, how wretched We are, if We must comply with the demands of the impudent! How miserable, if We must govern those who have no reverence for their prince, no sense of justice and shame! I used to think that once I had sorted everything out carefully, once I had delegated power according to merit, I would be free from troubles like these. Yet now it's not just the sky-dwellers who are preventing Jove, greatest prince of the universe and king of the gods, from taking his ease, but also — something hardly to be borne — those little humans!

"But why should I get angry at this unique plague among animals (not to call them men)? Of course, my excessive good nature has brought this about. Eager to gratify everyone, I have caused everyone to treat me thoughtlessly. To soften their thick and wild heads with useful gifts, using kindness to make them think well of me, I gave mortals more things than it is right for humans to expect. First I gave them Spring, so sweet and fragrant, with its perpetual abundance of flowers.[28] They said they wanted me to bring to maturity that hope of fruits which the flowers had shown. So I gave them Summer, too, and set to work Vulcan's craftsmen and all his fiery shop, making sap flow from the deepest roots into the berries and making branches and fruit grow. What then? They said that they were satiated and had really enjoyed the abundance of fruit and now wanted me to bring back Spring. Yes, I gave in to their desires, and so collected from the whole of nature little fires to make things grow, enclosing them in nuts, fruits and berries as though in treasure chambers, feeding them with vital spirit so that

106

107

183

inclusos fovi spiritu, quo ad veris opus atque ornamentum serva-
rentur.

108   'At improbi illi, tantorum a me acceptorum commodorum im-
memores, ingrati, indigni mortales, novarum semper cupidi rerum
temporumque, suique admodum impatientes, dum quae a me aut
petant aut optent non habent amplius, dum ultro eis commodo
quae ne optare quidem audeant si modestiores sint, pro accepto
beneficio nihil plus est quod referant quam merum odium. Nunc
aestum, nunc algores, nunc ventos exsecrantur, et nos ea facere accusant quae suam in rem non sint, neque verentur dicere nos ea facere quae vesani amentesque non facerent. Sed merito accusant,
nam eos prosequimur beneficiis, quos furialibus Erinybus[147] perse-
qui opus est. Sed satis superque furoribus exagitantur, quandoquidem se deorum superum haeredes deputant regnique partem de-
poscunt. Aut quis maior inveniri potest furor quam versari in
errore, trahi libidine, impelli audacia, velle indigna, appetere immoderata, suis bonis nusquam nosse perfrui, aliorum praemiis dolere, quae quidem sua socordia atque ignavia recusent refugiantque
consequi?

109   'Et breve sibi datum vitae spatium condolent qui supini tam
multis perdendis horis otio abutantur, et inter senescendum nihil
agendo marcescunt! Morbos et aerumnas a diis importatas praedicant. De his quid est quod dicam, cum sit homo homini aerumnarum ultima? Pestis est homo homini! Tu tibi, homo, tua voraci-
tate, tua ingluvie tuaque intemperantissimae libidinis incontinentia
effecisti ut doloribus excruciere, ut morbo langueas, ut ipsum te
male ferendo perdas. Dolet mortalium dementiae et mallem mo-

they might be conserved for the activity and embellishment of Spring.

"But these wicked people forgot that they had received so many 108 favors from me—those ungrateful, undeserving mortals, always craving change and novelty, always so discontented! While they had nothing more to ask or hope for from me, while I had freely granted them things which (if they were humbler) they wouldn't dare even to wish for, all I get from them in return for the benefits they've received is pure hatred. Now they curse the heat, now the cold, now the wind. They accuse Us of doing things which are not in their interest, and aren't afraid to tell Us that We are doing things which madmen and lunatics wouldn't do. This is a just accusation, for We have honored them with favors when We should have honored them with a visit from the raging Furies! But they've been driven by furies enough and more than enough already, for they regard themselves as the heirs of the gods and demand a portion of our kingdom. Indeed, what behavior is more fury-like than roiling in error, than being pulled by lust and driven by presumption, than wanting what you don't deserve and desiring what you shouldn't have, than never knowing how to enjoy your own blessings, than always grieving at the successes of others—successes that apathy and laziness have led you yourself to pass over and avoid?

"And they complain that they are allotted a brief span of years, 109 when they abuse their leisure by spending so much of it on their backs, and grow feeble with age doing nothing! They go around preaching that the gods have sent diseases and hardships. What can I say about this, since man is the worst hardship man must endure? *Man* is the plague of man! You, man, thanks to your greed, your gluttony and your inability to control your intemperate desires, have made sure that you're tortured by pain and enfeebled by disease; you've damned yourself by your own evil conduct. The madness of mortals grieves me, and I'd prefer that they had been

destiori esse praeditos ingenio. Sed quid agam, quo me vertam? Quis ab importunissimorum catervis obsessus opportunum sibi uspiam consilium reperiat? Quis tam ferreus, tam ad omnes lacessentium impetus expositus atque obfirmatus erit, qui haec diutius perferat? Hinc altercantium inter se expostulationibus obtundimur, hinc votis aut potius exsecrationibus obruimur. Nec tantarum molestiarum vexationumque ullus adinvenietur modus? At invenietur quidem. Quid tum? Quo fruantur mundus non placet. Hic status, haec rerum conditio gravis intolerabilisque est. Novam vivendi rationem adinveniemus: alius erit nobis adeo coaedificandus mundus. Aedificabitur, parebitur!'

110   Obmutuerant irato Iove ceteri omnes dii. At Momus, sentiens quid suis esset consecutus artibus in perturbandis tantopere et deorum et hominum rebus, exsultabat animo sibique congratulans gloriabatur quod ex tam raro laedendi genere suas deprompsisset[148] vindicandi facultates, quas quidem ridendo prosequeretur. Verum, ut ad suas dissimulandi artes rediret, composito ad mansuetudinem vultu, subridens 'Adsis, quaeso' inquit 'o Iuppiter, et quae dixero, si per tuam facilitatem licet, consideres sintne ex tua re an non. Hominum improbitate inprimis quantum videre licet offenderis, ac merito id quidem. Quis enim praeter te illorum ineptias diutius perferat? Et soleo saepe ipse mecum quaerere[149] unde sit quod nulla re sis magis quam facilitate et mansuetudine ingratis atque immeritis homunculis parum acceptus.

111   'Sed vide par ne sit hos labores suscipere alium coaedificandi orbem ut ingratissimorum querelas fugias, vide ne id deceat tantis coeptis hominum insaniam velle habere castigatam. Tu tamen de tota re pro tua prudentia cogitabis. Quod si tandem istos voles ho-

endowed with less ambitious intellects. But what should I do, where should I turn? Who can ever get useful advice when he's beseiged by troops of importunate people? Who is so steely, so resolute in the face of every attack, that he could tolerate this any longer? On one side I'm being buffeted by the demands of people wrangling amongst themselves, on the other I'm being overwhelmed by prayers, or rather curses. Will there never be an end to such annoyances and irritations? But suppose one is found. What then? They don't care for the world they enjoy. This situation, this state of affairs is grave and unbearable. We shall invent a new way of life; We shall have to construct another whole world from the ground up. It shall be built, it shall be created!"

Jupiter's anger struck the other gods dumb. But Momus, realizing that his own machinations had succeeded in disturbing so greatly the affairs of both gods and men, rejoiced in his heart. He congratulated himself, proud that he had found in so rare a form of causing distress a means of exacting revenge, and that he could continue to employ that means for his own amusement. But to resume his arts of dissimulation, he arranged his face in a mild expression, smiled and said, "Please listen, O Jupiter, and consider, if your good nature will permit it, whether what I say is to your purpose or not. As far as one may see, it is man's wickedness that primarily offends you, and rightly so. Who besides you could have endured their folly for so long? I often ask myself why it is precisely for your good nature and gentleness that you are so little regarded by these ungrateful and undeserving little men. 110

"But consider whether it is reasonable to take on the task of constructing another world from the ground up just to escape the complaints of ungrateful men. Consider whether it is fitting that you should want to punish the madness of men with such an enormous enterprise. You will think the whole matter over with your usual prudence. If in the end you want to penalize men for their boldness and impudence, then I know what you need to do, 111

munculos pro sua temeritate atque procacitate multatos reddere, novi quid facto opus sit, potius quam ut tantam aedificandi rem aggrediare. Illi quidem, quod praeter cetera animantia erecto ad sidera spectanda vultu perstent, idcirco ex deorum se ortos genere praedicant et sua interesse deputant nosse quid quisque superum agat aut meditetur. Adde quod dictis factisque caelicolarum redarguendis delectantur et deorum vitam et mores censoria quadam lege praefinire atque praescribere non pudet. Qui si mihi credideris, Iuppiter, iubebis[150] eos pedibus sursum versus et ima cervice obambulare manibus, quo et a ceteris quadrupedibus differant, et manum a furtis, rapinis, incendiis, veneficiis, caedibus peculatuque abque[151] taeterrimis reliquis, quibus assuevere, flagitiis conferant ad perambulandi usum.

112   'Sed muto sententiam. Novi eorum mentes atque ingenia: pedibus ipsis furari, pedibus involare et cuncta perpetrare scelera triduo condiscent, ut nihil fieri posse commodius censeam quam ut muliercularum illis numerum ingemines. O quantum dabunt poenarum, quantos qualesque et quam assiduos cruciatus experientur! Animorum est carnifex mulier curarumque flamma furorisque incendium atque omnis tranquillitatis et otii pestis, calamitas[152] atque pernicies. Sed hic iterum verto sententiam: deorum me superum movet ratio. Nam unam admodum si addideris hominum generi feminam, tantum illa quidem ciebit malorum, tantas vexationes, tantos rerum turbines et tempestates excitabit ut non dubitem futurum quin ea, profligatis atque prostratis rebus hominum, caeli quoque fundamenta collabefactata ac penitus convulsa reddantur.'

113   Tum Iuppiter ad Momum annuens 'Sicine' inquit 'Mome, etiam dum seria agantur te exhibes ridiculum?' Tum Momus 'Enimvero'[153] inquit 'recte admones: desino te ad risum et iocum verbis illicere et quod instat agam. Tu, o rerum princeps, agedum, ac si

rather than undertaking such an extensive building project. Men lay claim to being born of the divine race on the grounds that they, unlike other animals, stand erect with their faces looking towards the stars, and so think it their business to know what each of the heavenly race does and thinks. They take great pleasure in refuting the words and deeds of the sky-dwellers, and they have no scruples about prescribing and delimiting with their moral censures the life and behavior of the gods. If you'll rely on me, Jupiter, order them to walk on their hands, with their heads down low and their feet in the air. This will distinguish them from all the other quadrupeds, and it will oblige them to use their hands to move around, thus disabling them for theft, pillage, arson, poisoning, murder, embezzlement and the rest of the foul acts they normally get up to.

"But no, I've changed my mind. I know their dispositions and abilities: within three days, they'll learn how to steal with their feet, to attack with their feet, and commit every other crime. No, I can think of nothing more suitable than to double the number of silly little women among them. My, how they'll be punished, how numerous, various and constant shall be the torments they'll experience! A woman is an executioner of souls, a bonfire of cares, a blaze of fury, the plague, destruction and ruin of all peace and relaxation. But, no, I've changed my mind again; I must take account of the effect on the gods. For if you add just one woman to the race of men, she will stir up so much evil, so much vexation, so many whirlwinds and tempests that I don't doubt that, once she has overthrown and destroyed human affairs, she will shake and subvert the foundations of heaven itself!" 112

Jupiter, nodding towards Momus, said, "So, even when serious matters are afoot, you're still playing the buffoon?" Momus replied, "Oh, right, thanks for reminding me. I'll stop making you laugh and will get on with pressing concerns. Come on, prince of the universe, I'd really like to know, if your good nature thinks it 113

fas per tuam facilitatem[154] est sic sciscitari, pervelim quidem intellegere tuane an deorum an hominum gratia et causa instituas novum exaedificare mundum. Ego de me hoc fateor, non is sum qui existimem habere te quippiam quod in tam pulchro absolutoque opere atque perfecto amplius desideres, neque video cur in quo perficiendo omnem diligentiam tuam, omnes ingenii vires exposueris, in eo innovando aliquid immutari posse, nisi forte in deterius arbitreris. Sin aliorum te ratio in tantis coeptis commovet et ita decresti velle illis morem gerere quorum causa haec aggrederis, scrutandas tibi primum eorum sententias censeo quorum te causa et commoditas moveat, ne forte[155] his quibus gratificari studeas fias ingratus, tuis frustra susceptis laboribus atque impensa.

114   'Et ea in re ediscendum principio iudico cupiantne illi quidem orbem novari an corrigi, proxime intellegendum quamnam statuant futuri operis optimam esse descriptionem. Interea ad deliberandum erit aliquid dandum spatii, quo aliud sit cogitandi, aliud agendi tempus. Ceterum redarguendi ineptias, seu sint illi quidem dii seu sint illi quidem homines, semper erit tibi, ni fallor, integrum semperque patebit idem ipsum, ut possis ex sententia quicquid ad istorum poenam statuas oportere. Verum id egisse intempestive, quod mature possis facere, haudquaquam sapientis est, et omnis quidem maxima ex parte opera quae immatura est cum perditur, tum etiam laedit. Vota demum, si videbitur, poteris interea eo loci ad litoris margines exponere, quo mare ab tellure et ab his aer distinguitur. Id si feceris, erit istorum nullus qui sibi fieri iniuriam possit merito affirmare, et e medio quod amplius litigent tolletur. Adde quod eo erunt loci vota exclusa, ut ea nullibi esse possis dicere.'

115   In hanc Momi sententiam Iuppiter facile adduci passus est, eamque dii omnes comprobavere. Itaque extremis inde litoribus ad mare vota distenta exstant, esseque vota minutas illas ampullulas

right to ask, whether you've decided to build a new world for your own sake or for that of the gods and men. For my part, I admit that I shouldn't have thought that you'd need anything more in such a beautiful, finished and perfect work. And I don't see why, after expending all your care and intellectual power on perfecting it, you'd imagine you could change anything by updating it, except possibly for the worse. But if the interests of others have stimulated you to so great an enterprise, and you've made your decision wishing to oblige those for whose sake you began it, then I reckon that you should first canvass the views of those for whose sake and whose happiness you are acting. Otherwise, in trying to please them you may make yourself unpopular, and waste your effort.

"I think the first thing to find out is whether they want the world to be entirely changed or just fixed up before working out the best plan for this project. In the meantime, let's devote some time to thinking this through: thought and action should be separate phases. Unless I'm mistaken, you will always have full powers to correct folly, whether that of the gods or that of men, and you will always have the opportunity to inflict whatever punishment on them you think right. It is hardly the mark of a wise man to do hastily what he could do after mature reflection, and any work which is for the most part premature is likely to be unsuccessful, even harmful. If you like, you can set out the votive offerings at that point by the edge of the seashore where the sea, the land and the air separate. If you do that, not one of them will be able claim with justice that he or she was slighted, and you'll remove from sight what they're quarrelling about. Moreover, as the offerings will be cut off from place, you'll be able to say that they aren't anywhere."[29] 114

Jupiter readily let himself be led by Momus' opinion, and all the other gods approved. And so the offerings were laid out along the furthest shores of the sea, and people said that the offerings were 115

praedicant quae quidem illic luculentae et quasi vitreae splende-
scunt.[156] Quae cum ita essent, laeti dii ab Iove discessere.

116   At Fraus dea, Momi dicta pensitans, quam ea quidem in se ha-
berent vim ad animos in quamvis partem concitandos facile per-
spexit: miro illum callere doli artificio atque ad fingendi fallen-
dique usum nimium posse Momum intellexit. Ea de re omnem
simultatem sibi adversus Momum longe evitandam posthac indixit
atque, ut sibi adversarii gratiam conciliaret, quanta licuit arte frontem, vultum, gestum[157] ad venustatem, affabilitatem comitatemque
confingit atque conformat.

117   Momus, veteris acceptae ab dea Fraude contumeliae memor,
pro novissimo ab se suscepto vitae instituto gnaviter[158] docteque
scaenam agere perseverat. Longum esset referre quam se quidem
quisque eorum compararit atque gesserit optimum simulandi artificem, dum arte ars utrimque illuderetur. Tandem eo ventum est
ut inter congratulandum dea Fraus de Momo quaereret quisnam
sibi Hercules sua lautitiae et mensarum apparatu videretur, qui
quidem unus deorum omnium maximum optimumque caelicolarum principem hospitio atque convivio suscipere ausus sit. Cui
Momus 'En' inquit 'et quid putes? Annon dignus erit Hercules
quem tu Momo praeferas, quem tibi ad gratiam et benivolentiam
spreto me adiungas?' Tum dea: 'Sicine agis mecum, Mome? Egone
tibi, quicum vetus et dulcissima est consuetudo et familiaritas,
alium quempiam praeferam? Sed de his alias. Illud, quaeso, dicito:
tune[159] Herculem ipsum apud mortales noras?'

118   Tum Momus 'Tu' inquit 'demum uti coepisti sequere, novos in
dies amores sectare,[160] at Fraudi id liceat deae.[161] Quid tum adeo?
Semperne oportebit his curis et suspicionibus excruciari eos qui te

little flasks that shone there luminously, like glass. When this was done, the happy gods left Jupiter alone.

But the goddess Mischief, thinking about Momus' words, saw 116 with ease the innate power they had to impel people's minds in any given direction. She realized that Momus had excessive power from his skill in the marvelous artifice of deceit and in the practice of trickery and illusion. So she declared that henceforth she would absolutely avoid all quarrels with Momus, and to win back her enemy's favor, she used all her arts to mould her face, mien and bearing to express charm, affability and friendship.

Momus, mindful of the insults he had received from Mischief 117 in the past, persevered in acting his part with great industry and shrewdness in accordance with the plan of life he had most recently taken up. It would be a long business to recount how each of them readied and deployed their best skills of deception; how, on both sides, art fooled art. Finally it came to the point that Mischief, while congratulating him, asked Momus who this Hercules thought he was, with his luxury and his ostentatious banquets, and how he, alone among all the gods, had dared to invite the best and greatest prince of the gods to his banquet as a guest. Momus replied, "Look, what do you think? Isn't Hercules a worthy fellow? Hercules, whom you prefer to Momus? Hercules, whom you admitted to your grace and favor after rejecting me?" The goddess said, "Why do you treat me like this, Momus? Do you think that I'd prefer anyone else to you, with whom I have so old and sweet a relationship? We'll talk about this some other time. But tell me this, please: did you know Hercules when you were living among mortals?"

Momus replied, "So you're going to continue just as you've be- 118 gun, chasing new lovers daily . . . well, of course the goddess Mischief is allowed to do that. So what then? Must you always torture with these worries and suspicions men who love you more than their own selves? So you're crazy about Hercules, you're obsessed

plus se ament?' Verum Ierculem ames, Ierculem cogites, Herculem loquaris, Momum despexeris. Num etiam ludum facies?'

119   Tum dea meretricias inire blanditias, et cum cetera tum illud 'Me miseram' inquit 'atque infelicissimam, si quid de me venire tibi in mentem potest, ut putes me istiusmodi amantium genus cupere! Hos ego Hercules non penitus abhorrendos ducam atque fugiendos, qui quidem ingenio elati, animis tumidi, successibus gloriosi, imperiosi, importuni, omnia sibi quae eorum postulet libido deberi deputent? Vel qualem ego illum erga me futurum interpreter, qui deorum principem alienis convitare in aedibus integra cum divorum contione ausus sit? Et huic tam insolenti quid erit quod negasse tuto possim, si forte illi me dedicem?[162] Servire[163] id quidem esset, non amare. Sed hac in re Martis prudentiam requiro, qui[164] adventicium caelicolam levissimumque hospitem apud se tantisper insanire possit perpeti.'

120   Tum Momus, despecta scintillula unde in Herculem posset aliquam ignominiae notam inurere, illico eam arripuit inquiens 'Non est is quidem Hercules qui non didicerit et imperare et parere, ut[165] temporum suorum exigat ratio. Sed ne adeo quidem imperiosus est ut te eum odisse censeam.' Tum dea 'Ain vero' inquit 'parere didicisse Herculem? Audieram quidem istuc, sed invidia dictum rebar.' Tum Momus subridens 'Et quidnam' inquit 'illud est quod audieras?' Tum Fraus: 'Vis me dicacem reddere, tam belle interrogando! Sed non invita amanti parebo amans. Audieram Herculem hunc ipsum servisse apud mortales. An[166] vero, mi Mome, id est uti ferunt? Quid taces?'

121   Tum Momus gestu concitato et aspectu indignanti 'En' inquit 'credin me posse tuum esse ludum diutius? Convivarit Hercules, quid ad te? Lautus sit Hercules, quid ad te?[167] Amas Herculem,

with Hercules, you talk to Hercules — and you scorn Momus. Do you want to make a laughing stock of me?"

The goddess then embarked on meretricious flattery, and 119 among other things said, "Oh, how wretched I am, how miserable, if you can imagine that I'd want lovers of that kind! Personally, I think these Hercules types should be shunned and avoided, these men who are so full of themselves, so stuck-up, so boastful about their successes, so bossy and demanding, these men who think their libidos should get whatever they ask for. What should I make of the intentions of someone who dares dine in other peoples' houses with the whole of the divine assembly? What could I safely deny to such a bold person, if I were to give myself to him? I would be his slave, not his lover. But in this matter I require the prudence of Mars, who can endure an upstart god and an unreliable guest raving madly in his house all the time."

Then Momus, seeing the spark of an opportunity to brand 120 Hercules with shame, leaped upon it and said, "Hercules is certainly not the kind of person who hasn't learned how to command and obey as circumstances require. But I shouldn't think he's so imperious that you should hate him." The goddess replied, "Has Hercules really learned to obey? I had heard that, but I thought it was said out of spite." Momus smiled and said, "And what, please, did you hear?" Mischief replied, "You ask me so nicely because you want to make me gossip! But since I'm in love, I don't mind obeying my lover. I heard Hercules was a slave when he was among mortals.[30] But is it true, Momus, what they say? Why are you silent?"

Momus, with an impatient gesture and indignant expression, 121 said, "Look, do you think that I can be your plaything any longer? Hercules throws a dinner-party, what do you care? Hercules has a luxurious lifestyle, what do you care? You love Hercules, that's what you care about! You won't make me angry with you: I shall love a woman who doesn't deserve me and who doesn't return my

ergo id ad te! Non tamen efficies ut tibi succenseam: amabo immeritam at amabo invitam!' Hisque dictis fronte ad simulationem
iracundiae vehementius obducta sese inde surripuit. Ab se dis-
cedentem dea intuens, secum ipsa immurmurans inquit 'Vale,
Mome! Tu quidem constirpata atque abstersa barba tectior ado-
pertiorque a mortalibus redisti quam abieras. Vale, vale!'

love!" With these words, he furrowed his brow more violently, in a semblance of anger, and stole away. The goddess, seeing him depart, murmured to herself, "Goodbye, Momus! Though your beard was ripped off and removed there, you've come back from earth more secretive and mysterious than when you left. Goodbye, goodbye!"

LIBER TERTIUS

1 Superiores, credo, libri rerum varietate et iocis delectarunt: fuit etiam quippiam in illis, ut videre licuit, quod quidem ad vivendi rationem et modum conferat. Qui sequentur libri nulla erunt ex parte aut iocorum copia aut insperatarum rerum eventu et novitate[1] superioribus postponendi et, ni fallor, eo erunt fortasse hi anteponendi superioribus, quo maiora atque digniora recensebuntur. Videbis enim quo pacto salus hominum deorumque maiestas et orbis imperium fuerint ultimum paene in discrimen adducta, et hac in re tam seria tamque gravi admiraberis tantum adesse ioci atque risus.

2 Sed ad rem proficiscamur. Itaque indicarat Iuppiter venisse in animum sibi ut deorum hominumve causa alium vellet orbem condere. Quod quidem institutum cum maiores, tum et minores dii mirum in modum comprobabant. Namque, uti fit, ad suos usus et commoditates eam rem interpretantes, quisque sibi prospiciebat; et[2] qui fortassis erant inter caelicolas ignobiles atque alioquin privati, facile in eam spem adducebantur, ut sibi persuaderent a rerum novarum casibus aliquid adminiculi atque occasionis ad se honestandum appariturum. Et contra qui auctoritate dignitateve praestabant non posse Iovem arbitrabantur tantis in rerum motibus primorum procerum carere consilio, quo fiebat ut sibi praescriberent hanc ipsam rem ad sui status robur et firmitatem fore accessuram. Hinc minores quidem dii quibus poterant artibus suadendi apud Iovem instabant ut pro suscepto instituto rem exsequeretur. Tum et primates optimatesque deorum causae huiusce-

BOOK III

The previous books, I think, gave pleasure through humorous in- 1
cidents and through the variety of their subject matter. But as one
may see, they also possessed material which helps bring reason
and due measure to one's life. The books that follow are by no
means inferior to the previous ones in the abundance of their humorous incidents and in the original outcomes of their surprising
events. Unless I'm mistaken, they should perhaps even rank ahead
of the earlier ones, as they recount greater and loftier events. You
will see how the salvation of mankind, the majesty of the gods and
the government of the world were brought almost to a final crisis,
and you will marvel at how many jokes and laughter can accompany such serious and weighty matters.

But let's get on with the story. Jupiter had proclaimed his intention 2
of building another world for the sake of gods and men. Both the
greater and lesser gods heartily approved of the plan. As usual, everyone was looking to see how the idea would affect themselves,
sizing it up in light of their own interests and advantage. Those
sky-dwellers who were not nobles and had no public position were
led to persuade themselves with facile hope that this new state of
affairs would give them the means and opportunity to move up in
the world. Those who were foremost in authority and dignity, on
the other hand, reckoned that Jupiter could not cope with such a
great universal change without a leadership council, so that they
would be well placed to increase the strength and security of their
own position. Hence the lesser gods urged Jupiter to carry out the
project he had undertaken, using as much persuasive skill as they
could muster, whilst the noblest and highest-ranking gods thought

modi satis admodum suffragabantur tacendo et interdum annuendo.

3   Sed qua esse opus arte apud principem intellegebant, ea tum docte utebantur. Suas quidem in agendis rebus cupiditates atque affectus dissimulando obtegebant, et quae inprimis affectabant, ea levibus quibusdam verborum indiciis sibi haudquaquam satis placere ostentabant, quo eorum consilium, cum rogarentur, utilitati principis ac reipublicae magis quam privatis emolumentis et studiis accommodatum videretur. Neque praeterea deerant ex deorum optimatibus qui quidem, seu quod animi quadam integritate atque maturitate in rebus Iovis versarentur, seu quod prudentis et bene consulti ducerent plus semper in omni re putare incommodi[3] subesse quam appareat, Iovem idcirco admonerent ut tanto in opere incohando iterum atque iterum cogitaret, ne quid in perficiundo offenderet quo tanti coeptus interpellarentur: et praecavendum quidem cum alias ob res, tum ne facti pigeat, ne quid in experiundo invisum atque impraemeditatum irrumpat, quominus res ex sententia succedat.

4   Accedebant et ii qui propriis commoditatibus consulentes nullam rem aliam curabant praeter id, ut Iovem a suscepto innovandarum rerum instituto amoverent. Namque Iuno, votorum affluentia facta aedificatrix, quidvis poterat perpeti magis[4] quam hominum populos perire, huicque causae praeter[5] Herculem, qui quidem in servandis hominibus officio fungebatur, Bacchus et Venus et Stultitia dea et huiusmodi plerique alii, quod ab mortalium numero egregie colerentur, maximopere favebant. Tum et Mars, quod Aerugine architecto struendo porticu aeneo uteretur, cui centum columnas ferreas levissime rasas et perpolitas adamantinasque tecto tegulas destinarat, Iunoni ad res hominum servandas ultro sua et studia et operas accommodabat.[6] Namque ab hominibus quidem non modo materia et huiusmodi in dies suppeditaba-

that to advance their own cause it was enough to keep silent and nod every so often.

They knew what strategy they needed to use on the prince, and they deployed it craftily. They used dissimulation to conceal their desires and aims. Their words were casual, and they made a great show of hardly caring for the things they actually wanted most. Thus their advice, when solicited, seemed suited to the interests of the prince and the commonwealth rather than their to own private desires and emoluments. Nor were there lacking among the noblest gods some who, whether because they were conducting Jove's affairs with integrity and mature judgement, or because they thought it the role of the prudent and well-informed always to be finding more difficulties in every matter than there appeared to be, were advising Jove to think repeatedly about how to set on foot such an immense project in such a way that he would not meet obstacles while building which would interrupt the whole enterprise. He should be careful for other reasons, but also so that he wouldn't regret what he'd done. They said that while he was trying different things out, he shouldn't hurry and do something eccentric and ill-considered, so that things wouldn't go as planned. 3

There were also gods who thought only of their own interests, and whose sole concern was to deflect Jupiter from the renovation project he'd taken up. Juno, for example, who had set up as a builder thanks to the influx of votive offerings, could not bear the destruction of mankind. She greatly favored humans, as did Hercules, who was discharging his office of looking after mankind, as well as Bacchus, Venus, the goddess Folly and the other gods like them whom mortals worshipped with particular fervor. Mars too decided to put his resources at Juno's disposal to save the humans, because he was employing Rusty the architect to build a bronze portico, on which would be placed one hundred iron columns, very finely planed and polished, with adamantine tiles for the roof. Every day the humans were supplying him not only with building 4

tur, verum et quo tersissimas redderet columnas callos atque sudo-
rem excipiebat. Ergo ii quidem dii summopere elaborabant
dissuadendo, hortando, poscendo ne quid temere aggrederetur.

5   At[7] Momus ipse secum, rerum tantarum perturbatione motus,
'Profecto' aiebat 'est quod fertur, nullam inveniri tam amplam voluptatem quae non pusilla sit, ubi tu aliis nequeas impertiri.
Quanta mea haec esset voluptas, si haberem quicum possem explicare sine periculo! O me beatum, qui potui verbis adducere principem ut tantas res aggrederetur! Verum commovi hactenus, nunc
impellendus est. Sed quid ago? Multorum invidiam in me compa-
rabo. Et quid tum? Oderint illi quidem ut libet, modo sim uni
huic cordi. Is me Iuppiter dum non respuet, dum excipiet (ut facit)
benigne, plus satis habebo fautorum. Vel quis est qui deliro cum
principe non insaniat? At vincat, uti aiunt, malum. Ergo tu,
Mome, una cum grege id suadebis fieri, quod si forte iam factum
sit vituperes? Et quidni? Id agam, ut quaeque placere principi sentiam, eadem quoque probare me ultro[8] ostentem. Et quid ago? O
me iterum felicissimum, qui meis artibus ita mihi rem hanc para-
verim, ut regem me admodum esse caelicolarum sentiam! Quid
erit posthac quod nequeat Momus, quando inieci inter proceres
quo maximis inter se studiis contendant atque ita contendant ut
sic[9] me inde[10] habituri forte sint arbitrum? Hic igitur opus est in-
sistam. Atqui dissentiant quidem inter se conferet, quorum erga te
impetum metuas. Nam si qui horum in te insultarint, tu ad hos alteros confugias, ubi tot conspiratores adiunges tibi quot erunt hi
ad quos concesseris. Sed de his videro quae tempus feret; interea
iuvat de Iovis in me gratia et benignitate melius mereri. Commiti-
ganda quidem et commoderanda eius mihi est animi concitata ratio. Quid si[11] ei tradam optimas illas commonefactiones de regno
quas olim apud philosophos collectas redegi brevissimos in com-

materials, but also with the tough skin and the sweat he needed to polish his columns. So these gods worked hard in opposition, exhorting and demanding that Jupiter not act rashly.

But Momus, excited by the great upheaval, said to himself, "It's just as people say: even the greatest pleasure becomes trivial if you can't share it with someone. How great my pleasure would have been, if I had someone I could safely tell about it! Oh, what bliss, that I was able to talk the king into attempting this enormous enterprise! Yet so far I've only gotten him started; now I must push him forward. But what am I doing? I'll bring down everyone's hatred upon my head. So what, then? Let them hate as they like, so long as I am dear to this one person. As long as Jupiter doesn't reject me, as long as he applauds me—as he does now—I will have more than enough supporters. Who wouldn't play the madman, when the prince himself is insane? As they say, let evil triumph! So you'll go along with the herd, Momus, suggesting something that you'll only criticize if it ever gets done? Certainly, why not? I shall happily show my approval of whatever I know pleases the prince. What am I doing? How doubly blessed I am! Through my arts I've arranged things so that I feel that I am the real king of the gods! After this, what won't Momus be able to do, now that I have meddled among the leading gods so that they fight each other with the greatest ardor, and fight in such a way that they shall even perhaps have to adopt me as their mediator? So I must press on with the matter. It's highly convenient for those whose attacks you fear to be quarreling among themselves. Thus, if some of them insult you, you can change sides, and you'll be able to surround yourself with as many co-conspirators as you left behind. I shall see what time will bring, but in the meantime, it's best to increase Jupiter's favor and benevolence towards me. I must soften and moderate the excited state of his mind. Why don't I pass on to him those brilliant observations on kingship that I once col-

mentariolos? Profecto, si legerit, sibi rebusque suis commodius consulet.'[12]

6   At Iuppiter, uti est vetus quidem et usitatus mos atque natura nonnullorum, ferme omnium principum, dum sese graves atque constantes haberi magis quam esse velint, illic illi quidem non quae ad virtutis cultum pertineant, sed quae ad vitii labem faciant usurpant; quo fit ut cum quid forte prodesse cuipiam[13] polliciti sunt, in ea re apud eos minimi pensi est fallere, et fallendo perfidiam et perfidia levitatem atque inconstantiam suam explicare cognitamque reddere. Cum vero molestos nocuosque se cuivis[14] futuros indixerint, omni studio et perseverantia libidini obtemperasse, id demum ad sceptri dignitatem regnique maiestatem deputant; itaque in suscepta iracundia plus dandum pertinaciae quam in debita gratia retribuendum fidei statuunt.

7   Sic hac in re Iuppiter neque odia dediscere suo cum animo neque non meminisse iniuriarum apud alios videri cupiebat. Sed cum nullam inveniret novi condendi mundi faciem atque formam quam huic veteri non postponeret atque despiceret, cumque intellegeret se initam provinciam satis nequire commode per suas ingenii vires obire, instituit aliorum sibi fore opus consilio. Sed ita peritorum[15] sensus et mentes captare affectabat, ut si quid forte dignum laude a quoquam in medium exponeretur, nullos inventori honores aut gratias deberet, sibi vero invidiam hanc novandarum rerum inventi gloria pensaret. Idcirco unum olim atque alterum deorum quos esse acutiores opinabatur atque inprimis Momum, quem unum multo praestare ceteris omni laude ingenii existimabat, detinebat verborum ambagibus atque cum iis flectebat sermones longa insinuatione, quoad illecti quid de tota re sentirent

lected from the philosophers and wrote down in notebooks? If he reads them, it will certainly profit him and his affairs."

Such were Momus' thoughts. But Jupiter? It is an ancient and 6 ingrained characteristic of some (indeed, nearly all) princes to want to be considered grave and steadfast rather than actually being so. In this way princes seize upon courses of action that cause them to descend into vice rather than cultivate virtue. When they promise something that may perhaps benefit someone, in that matter they regard lying as a thing of minimal importance, and their lying exposes their treachery, and their treachery in turn advertises their total lack of gravity and steadfastness. On the other hand, when they proclaim that they will vex and harm someone, then yield to their desire with zeal and persistence, they believe that this will add to the dignity of their scepter and the majesty of their reign. That's why they decide to be more pertinacious in discharging their anger than in properly rewarding loyalty.

Thus in this matter Jupiter did not want it to seem as though 7 he had forgotten how to hate and did not remember slights others had dealt him. But he could find no appearance or form of the new world he was to found that he didn't think contemptibly inferior to this one. When he realized that his own abilities would not be enough to carry out his intended task, he decided he would have to seek the advice of others. He hoped to appropriate the judgment and ideas of experts, and if one of them should propose something praiseworthy, he would not owe any honor or thanks to the inventor, but the glory of the invention would compensate him for the unpopularity of the innovation. To this end he engaged one after another of the gods in subtle discourses — the gods he considered to be the smartest, and Momus in particular, whom he thought excelled all the rest in intellectual distinction. With them he steered discussions through long and winding paths, so that they would be lured into volunteering their opinions about the whole business. Jupiter found no one whose industry he could

expromebant. Nullos inveniebat quorum industriam probaret, ingenio perquam paucissimi excellebant, rari qui cogitandi labores et investigandarum rerum studia non refugerent: omnes tamen ita se gerebant ut eos facile intellegeres videri velle apud Iovem plus sapere longe quam saperent.

8   Sed cunctorum una ferme erat sententia, ut quos apud mortales omnia nosse praedicant, philosophos consulendos assererent: illos quidem complura de iis rebus maximis et gravissimis[16] solitos cum[17] mandare litteris, tum in dies accuratissime pervestigare, et nihil esse rerum omnium de quo non audeant propalam disceptare; valere quidem ingenio et suarum artium cultu ut, si curam et diligentiam adhibeant, facile omnem difficultatem absolvant.

9   Cum audiret Iuppiter philosophos tantopere universo a caelo comprobari, non facile dici potest quam eos desideraret coram congredi et colloqui. Quod ni superiorem invidiam nova invidia coacervare esset veritus, fortassis[18] adducebatur ut omnes illas philosophantium catervas cuperet inter deos caelicolas asciscere, quo deorum senatum tam illustrium patriciorum splendore ornatissimum redderet sibique prudentissimorum consilio imperii sui rationes communiret. Vicit tamen quod in mentem venit non esse ex usu ut eos haberet apud se quibus non imperandum, sed ob insignem gravitatem atque dignitatem esset obtemperandum, habendos quidem apud se eos praesertim a quibus observari[19] se[20] metuique sentiat, non quos vereri oporteat. Accedere et illud, quod eos recusaret qui se recte facere edocerent, et eos sibi dari cuperet qui quaeque ipse ediceret[21] facere non recusarent.

10   Quae cum ita essent, diu multumque deliberabat quemnam ex suis ad philosophos consulendos mitteret: qua in disquisitione facile sensit quam non bene secum ageretur, dum nulli tam multos

commend; only a very few stood out for their intelligence; and rare were those who did not shirk the bother of thinking and the effort of investigating. But all of them acted in such a way that you'd naturally think they wanted Jove to believe they were wiser than they actually were.

But almost all of them agreed about one thing: they maintained 8 that the philosophers should be consulted — the mortals who, they claimed, knew everything. The philosophers were in the habit of committing their thoughts on such important and serious matters to writing, and also of investigating them carefully every day; there was no subject they dared not debate openly. In fact, they were so brainy and their skills were so honed that they could solve any problem easily, if they were careful and diligent.

When Jupiter heard that all of heaven had such a high opinion 9 of philosophers, it is hard to describe how much he longed to meet and talk with them personally. If he had not feared to pile new unpopularity upon the unpopularity he already enjoyed, he might have been induced to co-opt all the bands of philosophers into the ranks of the heavenly gods. In that way he might embellish the divine senate with the luster of these illustrious gentlemen and fortify his system of empire with the advice of the wisest men. What decided him against this, however, was the thought that he was little used to being surrounded by men whom, instead of commanding, he would have to obey, in deference to their extraordinary gravity and dignity. He still felt that he should surround himself with men who would obey and fear him, not intimidate him. Another consideration was his rejection of men who would teach him to act rightly, and his preference for men who would not reject his edicts.

This being the case, he deliberated for a long time over which 10 of his ministers he should send to consult the philosophers. While mulling this over, he soon realized that he was not in a good position. He could not find one person in all of his numerous house-

inter suos familiares adinvenirentur quorum posset opera praeclaris in rebus uti. Ac doluit quidem suos omnes tam esse omnino rudes atque imperitos ut nihil bonarum artium tenerent, nihil homine dignum nossent praeter id quod longo servitutis usu didicissent: id erat[22] ad regiam lauto apparatu esse, ad principem assistere, appellentes arte quadam plaudendo[23] excipere, confabellari, assentari, detinere, ut[24] eos omnes cuperet ab se mittere atque amovere. Sed novos deligere quorum sibi essent mores ignoti minime conducere suis inceptis arbitrabatur.

11   Idcirco, ne hac praesertim in re quam esse penitus occultissimam cuperet sese aliorum fidei atque taciturnitati committeret, instituit posito regio fastu solus atque ignobilis mortales adire philosophos tum consulendi, tum multo et visendi[25] gratia. Sed prius, quo praestantissimorum philosophorum nomina, notas, effigies sedesque condisceret,[26] habuit apud se Momum et quantum potuit quae ad rem facerent longis sermonibus expiscatus est. At hos inter sermones incidit ut de sinu Momus paratas[27] tabellas Iovi porrigeret his dictis: 'Fides amorque quo in te affectus sum, Iuppiter, efficit ut meas ipse partes duxerim aliquid studii et operae in tuis servandis atque augendis rebus exponere, quoad id possem. Idcirco ea sum aggressus cogitatione et meditatione quae ad imperii tui decus et dignitatem spectare arbitrabar. Tu ea, cum tibi erit otium, ex istis tabellis quibus mandata sunt cognosces, hac lege, ut quaeque tibi in his prudentiae partes minus satisfecerint, eas tu fidei acceptas referas.'

12   Susceptis Iuppiter tabellis et ab se misso Momo tabellas ne aperuit quidem sed neglectas reiecit in penetrali, seque ad iter accinxit animo admodum alacri et prompto. Sed istiusmodi obivisse pere-

hold he could employ on such an important task. He lamented the fact that all of his household were so completely inexperienced and ignorant that they knew nothing of the liberal arts. They knew nothing worthy of man apart from what they had learned from the long practice of servitude, that is, to be well dressed around the palace, to attend the prince, to receive visitors with artful bowing and scraping, to tell stories, to flatter, and to buttonhole. Jupiter wished he could banish them all from his presence. On the other hand, he thought that choosing a new retinue with unknown habits would not fit his plans at all.

Consequently, since he did not want to entrust this top-secret 11 affair to the loyalty and discretion of others — but also, still more, so that he could see the philosophers with his own eyes — he decided that he would set aside his kingly pride and visit the mortals alone and in humble guise. But first, so as to learn the names, distinguishing features, appearances and abodes of the most distinguished philosophers, he invited Momus to his palace and tried to fish for as much pertinent information as he could in long-winded discussions. In the midst of this talk, Momus brought out from inside his robe the notebooks he'd prepared for Jupiter, saying. "The loyalty and love I feel for you, Jupiter, made me conclude it was my duty to offer a portion of my own studies and labors, insofar as I could, to preserve and enlarge your power. So with thought and reflection I undertook something that I thought would have in view the honor and dignity of your empire. When you get the chance, look at what I've written in those books, with the understanding that whatever fails to satisfy your wisdom will at least be received as tokens of loyalty."[1]

Jupiter picked up the books, and dismissed Momus. He didn't 12 even open them, but threw them down unread in his private quarters, then eagerly prepared for his journey. But in the end he regretted having made this sort of pilgrimage. For as soon as he came down to earth, he happened to go into the Academy, where

grinationem postremo tulit ingrate. Namque ut primum ad mortales appulit, in Academiam forte ingressus, complures illic variosque mortalium repperit huc et illuc et omnes per angulos vagando quaeritantes ac si abditum aliquem noctu comperisse furem elaborarent. Quos adeo sollicitos intuens[28] Iuppiter obstupuit ipsoque in gymnasii vestibulo haesitavit. Mox ubi eos vidit lucilucas musculas blateas inter digitos gestantes atque his quasi in umbra positis pro igniculis utentes risit, quoad ex quaeritantibus quidam 'O' inquit 'insolens! Ne tu et nostrum Iovem philosophorum percontatum[29] accessisti?' Tum Iuppiter 'Et quemnam' inquit 'perconter?' Tum illi 'Platonem' inquiunt 'naturae monstrum, quem quidem hoc esse in gymnasio certo scimus, sed quo eum comperisse loco detur non habemus. At eius interdum audire visi vocem sumus[30] interdumque eius ob oculos facies obversari credita est: verum ille nusquam minus. Sed quid agimus? Heus, et tua ubinam luciluca est?' His verbis Iuppiter in suspicionem incidit atque pertimuit ne ii, quos omnia etiam occultissima nosse sibi persuaserat, ludicra istac veluti scaena exprobrarent sacrum ab se deorum insigne fore ita contectum ut cum adesse coram deus intellegeretur, tamen nusquam satis dinosceretur. Idcirco illinc secedens iam tum accusare initam profectionem suam incipiebat.

13   Interea sensit seducto quodam in viculi spatio intra putidum reiectumque dolium multo hiatu oscitantem quempiam seque versantem. Quo cum appulisset propius et in dolio coactum hominem in globum demiraretur, accidit ut solis radios qui adinfluebant interciperet. Ergo inclusus ille torvis oculis taetraque voce increpans 'Apage te' inquit 'hinc, o insolens spectator! Si dare potis non es, ne adimito solem.' Tum Iuppiter, tanta abiectissimi hominis acrimonia concitus et rerum quae ageret prae indignatione oblitus, 'Tibi' inquit 'aeternum si velim solem dabo atque rursus adimam.' Haec ille cum audisset, caput e dolio quasi testudo proferens multa coepit conclamitare voce: 'Accurrite, adeste populares!' quoad multitudo artificum advolavit. 'Hunc' inquit 'Iovem

he came across a large assortment of mortals wandering here and there and in every corner, searching as though they were trying to find a thief who had hidden there during the night. Jupiter was astonished to see what they were doing, and he hesitated on the very threshhold of the school. Then when he saw that they were holding fireflies between their fingers, using them like little torches in the shadows, he laughed,[2] whereupon one of the searchers said, "You rude fellow! So you too have come to interrogate our Jove of the philosophers?" Jupiter replied. "Whom should I be interrogating?" — "Plato," they said, "the prodigy of nature! We know for sure that he's in the school, but we haven't been able to figure out where. Once or twice, we seemed to hear his voice, or we thought that we had caught a glimpse of his face: but he wasn't really there.[3] So what can we do? And where's your firefly?" These words made Jupiter suspicious, and he feared that these men, who (as he had convinced himself) knew everything, even the greatest secrets, would embarrass him about his silly bit of play-acting, and would reproach him for having hidden the sacred token of the gods in such a way that up close you could see he was a god, but you couldn't tell who he was. So he departed, and began to regret having made the trip in the first place.

Next, in a secluded piazza of a small town, he noticed a man 13 rolling around in a stinking and abandoned tub, yawning with his mouth wide open. As he drew nearer, wondering how a man could be balled-up and forced into a tub, he happened to block out the sunlight that was streaming down.[4] At this, the man shut inside glared at him and chid him in a croaking voice, saying, "Get back, you peeping-tom! If you can't give me the sun, then at least don't take it from me!" Provoked by this low fellow's acrimony, Jupiter in his anger forgot his mission and retorted, "If I wanted to, I could give you the sun forever, and take it away, too." When the man heard this, he lifted his head out of the tub like a tortoise and began shouting in a loud voice, "Hey, everybody, get over here

comprehendite, ac cogite ut puteos atque cuniculos vestros sole oppletos reddat.'

14   Hic Iuppiter, superiores Momi deaeque Virtutis casus repetens, nihil erat malorum quod non ab insolenti quae circum irruerat multitudine exspectaret, beneque secum actum deputabat si nihil plus quam dimidia multatus barba tam inepti sui consilii poenas lueret. Hunc ita perterritum et titubantem intuens ex iis qui congruerant[31] unus paterfamilias, homo sane frugi, 'O' inquit 'hospes, sine hunc cynicum philosophum dignam se vitam degere, quandoquidem nihil sibi esse rerum omnium relictum velit, praeterquam ut possit omnibus maledicere et mordere.' At Iuppiter, ubi hunc esse philosophum intellexit, nimirum ad conceptum metum addit novam suspicionem, istic se quoque agnitum existimans. Ergo nihil sibi antiquius ducit quam ut confertissima ex plebe se illico proripiat atque abducat.

15   Itaque secedens, procul respectat quempiam mediam in convallem sub pomeriis urbis obscena inter animantium cadavera considere atque cultro hos atque hos, seu canes seu mures, concidere atque praesecare.[32] Id sibi cum visum esset opus partim mirabile,[33] partim ridiculum, procedebat ut rem cognosceret. Eo cum propius accessisset constitit; at homo Iovis adventu nihil commovebatur. Sed a finitimis laribus interim subaudito mulieris cuiusdam eiulatu, quae filii mortem deploraret, ab secandorum[34] animantium opere paululum destitit, atque Iovem despectans et subridens 'Num tanti est' inquit 'velle quod nequeas?' Id dictum Iuppiter non, ut erat, in eam dictum, quae filium forte immortalem fore optasset, sed in se dictum pensitavit. Et discedens 'Quid hoc mali est' inquit 'apud mortales? Ne vero et stulti etiam philosophantur?' Iamque decreverat ad superos redire, ne quid gravioris incommodi subiret.

quick!" so that a crowd of laborers rushed over. "Get this — it's Jupiter! Make him fill your tunnels and pits with sunshine!"

Jupiter, remembering the earlier misfortunes of Momus and the   14
goddess Virtue, expected all kinds of evil from the insolent crowd
that had gathered around him. He reckoned that he would get off
lightly if he only lost half of his beard as payment for his foolish
decision! One fatherly type, a decent fellow, who had gathered
with the others, saw that Jupiter was terrified and quaking, and
said, "Stranger, let this cynic philosopher live the life that suits
him, for he wants nothing apart from the opportunity to curse and
carp at everything." But once Jupiter found out that the man was a
philosopher, unsurprisingly he added new suspicion to the fear he
already felt, believing that he had once again been recognised. The
most important thing, he reckoned, was to break away from that
pack of plebeians and escape.

So Jupiter withdrew. Far away in the distance, at the bottom of   15
a ditch running along the boundaries of a city, he saw a man[5] sitting down among disgusting animal corpses. The man was cutting
and slitting some of them, both dogs and mice, with a knife. The
activity seemed both amazing and ludicrous, and Jupiter set off
to investigate. He came up close to the man and stopped, but
the man paid no attention to him. At that moment, however, a
woman's cry rang out of a nearby house: she was lamenting the
death of her son. The man stopped his project of animal dissection, looked at Jupiter and smiled. "Is it of such importance," he
said, "to want what you can't have?" Jupiter thought that the man
was not talking about the woman who had prayed for her son
to be immortal, although in fact the man was referring to this.
Instead, he assumed that the saying was directed against him.
Walking away, he said, "What is this evil? Do even the stupid play
the philosopher among mortals?" He decided to return to the
gods, so that he would not have to face any more serious unpleasantness.

16   Ex urbe igitur excedenti evenit ut cum propter[35] vallum atque
saepem horti cuiusdam pervaderet, sensisse visus sit nonnullos intus disceptantes de diis et maiorem in modum altercantes. Astitit.
Hic altercantium unus elata voce forte sic dicere aggressus est: 'Ut
intellegatis quid sentiam, hoc affirmo: rerum orbem non factum
manu, neque tanti operis ullos inveniri posse architectos. Immortalem quidem ipsum esse mundum atque aeternum; et cum tam
multa in eo divina et quasi mundi membra conspiciantur, statuo
totam hanc machinam deum esse. Si ullus in rerum natura deus
aut mortalis aut immortalis est, qui vero contra periturum mundum opinetur? Num is insanire quidem posse deum putabit, an
ipse potius insaniet, ubi non conservatorem tantorum tamque ab-
solutorum operum deum, sed peremptorem futurum possit arbi-
trari?' Alius contra 'At ego' inquit 'sic censeo, infinitos in horas
concrescere et consenescere capacissimum per inane mundos mi-
nutissimis corpusculis concurrentibus atque congruentibus.' 'Num
tu' inquit igitur alius 'deos tollis? Cave te esse ita impium sentiant:
sunt enim omnia plena deorum.'

17   Haec audiens Iuppiter obstupuit atque non satis, prout sua ferebat suspicio, demirari poterat unde in hoc genus hominum tantum cognitionis incessisset ut se post saepem et vallum abditum et
delitescentem agnoscerent. 'Non igitur est' inquit 'ut hic tuto esse
diutius possim apud mortales' caelumque idcirco petiit, tanta de
philosophis imbutus opinione ut incredibili arderet cupiditate
ediscendi quid demum docti illi pro suis institutis rebus decerne-
rent. Neque dubitabat illos quidvis rerum obscurissimarum atque
difficillimarum nosse et posse, quorum tam praeclara in se dino-
scendo exempla spectasset. Et hanc opinionem augebat quod in
Academia vidisset ex quaeritantibus illis aliquos nitenti barba et
lauto apparatu, fluenti ab humeris purpura, leni incessu, commo-
deratis oculis obambulare ut eos caelo dignos et deorum habendos
magistros existimaret.

Leaving the city, he came up near a trench and hedge enclosing 16
someone's garden.[6] Inside, he glimpsed several people who were
discussing the gods and arguing vehemently. Jupiter froze. One of
the debaters began to speak, saying in a loud voice: "Let me tell
you this, so you'll know what I think: no person's hand made the
universe, and you could never find an architect for such a big job.
The world itself is immortal and eternal, and since so many things
in it look like parts of the divine, I argue that the whole edifice is a
god. If there is in nature any god, either mortal or immortal, who
would claim that the world will perish? Won't you have to think
either that the god could be mad, or that you yourself are mad to
be able to reckon that a god would not preserve such a great and
perfect work, but destroy it instead?" Another man replied, "But I
think that infinite worlds develop every hour in the void and die
out, as the result of the collision and attraction between the small-
est atoms." — "So," said another, "would you take the gods out of
it? Be careful or they'll think you're a blasphemer, for the gods are
present in everything."[7]

Jupiter listened in stunned silence. Prompted by his paranoia, 17
he couldn't marvel enough at how the human race were so intelli-
gent that they realized he was hiding out of sight behind the
trench and hedge. "I can't be safe here any longer among mortals,"
he said, and made for heaven, filled with such a high opinion of
the philosophers that he had a burning desire to know what those
learned men would think of his own enterprise. Jupiter did not
doubt that they both would know about and have power over the
most obscure and difficult matters, for he had seen impressive examples of how they were able to recognize him. What he had seen
in the Academy had reinforced his opinion. Among the seekers,
there had been some men with snow-white beards walking about
looking well-groomed, with purple robes flowing from their shoulders, easy of step and placid of gaze, whom Jupiter thought worthy of heaven and of being the gods' teachers.

18   Sed pro instituto, cum operis gloriam sibi concupisceret et id
suo se ingenio assequi non posse animadverteret, commento ad
eam rem usus est eleganti. Namque accito Mercurio edicit uti ad
se Virtutem deam ab inferis reducat: dedecere quidem tam insignem et praestantissimam dearum in tantis rebus agendis non ac-
civisse. Neganti Mercurio deam male a superis diis atque inferis
acceptam et ea fortassis de causa latitantem facile posse comperiri,
'Apud philosophos illos tuos' inquit Iuppiter, 'ni fallimur, invenies,
qui se totos illi dedicarunt.'

19   Tum Mercurius 'Cave,' inquit 'o Iuppiter, ullos inveniri posse
putes tam vanos atque mendaces. Ut rem teneas, de illis ipse nonnumquam, quod Virtuti afficior, quaesivi eamne deam viderint: illi
eam quidem apud se perquam familiarissime diversari deierant, at
demum dea nusquam minus.' Tum Iuppiter 'Tu tamen'[36] inquit
'abi et percontare,[37] sic facto opus est.' Id ita agebat Iuppiter quod
norat quam esset quidem Mercurius curiosus quamque novis in
dies iungendis hospitiis paciscendisque commerciis delectaretur,
quo futurum prospiciebat ut lingulax deus aliquid a peritissimis
philosophis acciperet, cum de rebus deorum quae sciret et quae
nesciret omnia suo pro more conferret, et id quidem peropportune
ad suas institutas res fore ut referret.

20   Interea apud superos studia partium tantas in simultates et fa-
ctiones excreverant ut omne caelum non minus quam tres esset in
partes divisum. Namque hinc[38] Iuno, quae aedificandi libidine in-
sanibat, quam poterat maximam suarum partium vim et manum
et bonis et malis artibus cogebat ad hominumque salutem tuen-

But since in accordance with his plan he wanted all the glory of the project for himself, and realized that his own abilities were unequal to carrying it out, he used a well-crafted fiction to compass his end. He summoned Mercury, and told him to bring him back the goddess Virtue from the lower world. He said that it was unseemly not to recall such a remarkable and outstanding goddess when important enterprises were underway. Mercury said she would not be easy to find, as the goddess was unwelcome both among the heavenly gods and among those of the underworld, and for that reason she would perhaps keep out of sight. "Unless I am mistaken," Jupiter said, "you'll find her among those philosophers of yours, who are entirely devoted to her."

Mercury replied, "Don't ever think you're going to find any men as unreliable and deceitful as that lot. Just so you understand the situation: because I'm involved with Virtue I sometimes used to ask the philosophers whether they'd seen her. They swore that she dwelt among them in the closest friendship, but it turned out that the goddess had never so much as visited them." — "You get going and ask," said Jupiter, "that's what you need to do." Jupiter behaved thus because he knew how curious Mercury was, and how he delighted in forging new friendships and new business relationships every day. He foresaw that the little chatterbox of a god, while conferring as was his wont about all the affairs of the gods — the ones he knew about and the ones he didn't — would acquire from the best-informed philosophers, and report back to him, information that might be of considerable value for Jupiter's projects.

Meanwhile, among the gods, partisanship had grown into feuds and factionalism so that all of heaven was divided into no less than three parties. On one side was Juno who, crazed with passion for building, had put together by good arts and bad the very largest force of partisans she could, and arrayed them with a view to protecting the safety of the mortals. On the other side, a troop of middle-class gods and other persons out of sympathy with the sta-

18

19

20

dam instruebat. Hinc³⁹ contra turma illa popularium et eorum⁴⁰ quidem quibus non ex sententia cum statu rerum suarum agebatur sponte congruebant, sed immoderatam rerum novandarum cupiditatem qua flagrabant studio gratificandi deorum principi honestabant. Medium quoddam tertium erat genus eorum qui cum ignobilis levissimique esse vulgi caput grave et periculosum putarent, tum et cuiquam privatorum subesse recusarent, contentionum eventum sibi etiam⁴¹ quiescentibus exspectandum indixerant, ea mente, ut in quamcumque visum foret partem tuto attemperateque prosilirent suisque motibus⁴² rem quoquo versus vellent ex arbitrio traherent. Hi demum omnes apud Iovem unam eandemque rem sed variis diversisque causis et rationibus poscentes instabant. Alii enim ut pro exspectatione succedentibus rebus congratularentur; alii ut rebus non ex sententia succedentibus mature providerent; alii ut occasionibus praestitis attemperate uterentur. Id autem erat ut olim quid de orbe innovando Iuppiter statueret enuntiaret.

21 Quae cum ita essent, Iuppiter, ut molestam odiosamque ab se assiduitatem sollicitantium excluderet, fretus inprimis legatione Mercurii, quo sibi persuaserat futurum ut apud rude vulgus deorum multum gratiae et gloriae pulcherrimo aliquo philosophorum invento assequeretur, edicit proximis caelicolarum Kalendis se contionem habiturum et quae decreverit explicaturum et omnibus deorum ordinibus satisfacturum. Sed haec Iovem spes de Mercurio multo fefellit.

22 Nam cum adivisset Mercurius terras et positis talaribus Academiam, philosophorum officinam, peteret, evenit ut Socratem philosophum ipso in angiportu solitarium offenderet. Quem cum nudis vidisset pedibus et trita veste astantem, ratus plebeium quempiam, eo ad hominem se fronte qua erat liberali et indole ni-

tus quo gathered spontaneously.⁸ This group dignified its burning desire for revolution by presenting it as a desire to gratify the king of the gods. In the middle was the third faction of gods who thought it a serious and dangerous undertaking to head an ignoble and fickle crowd, and also refused to obey someone who was not in public life.⁹ They said that they would serenely await the outcome of the fight, and intended to jump safely and at the appropriate moment onto whichever side seemed likely to win. They would then use their influence to inflect the situation in the direction they wanted. All these gods in due course pressed in on Jupiter, demanding one and the same thing, though they were impelled by different causes and reasons. Some congratulated him that things were proceeding as expected; others were offering sage advice on the grounds that things were not proceeding according to plan; while still others were simply opportunists. But what they all wanted was for Jupiter to tell them what he had decided with regard to renewing the world.

In this situation Jupiter was relying chiefly on Mercury's embassy to shut off this annoying and odious stream of overwrought gods. He persuaded himself that as a result of the embassy, he would win great glory and gratitude from the ignorant mob of gods thanks to some wonderful idea of the philosophers. He decreed that he would hold a council of the gods on the next Kalends,¹⁰ when he would explain what he had resolved and would satisfy all the ranks of the gods. But Jupiter was greatly deceived by the hope he had placed in Mercury.

For when Mercury reached earth, he took off his winged sandals and made his way to the Academy, the philosophers' workshop. There at a side-gate he happened to encounter Socrates the philosopher, who was all by himself. When Mercury saw him standing there with his bare feet and threadbare robe, he thought Socrates was just some commoner, and so went over to him with a gentlemanly demeanor and a, well, godlike superiority and said,

mirum divina confeit. 'Atqui heus' inquit 'homo! Ubinam hi sunt,
apud quos viri et docti et boni fiunt?' Socrates, ut erat mirifica
praeditus affabilitate et comitate, peregrinum conspicatus adule-
scentem forma egregium facieque insignem, pro innata sua consuetudine coepit callida illa qua assueverat disserendi ratione alios
ex aliis allicere sermones, quoad et qui esset Mercurius et qua de
re appulisset et quid superi pararent omnia exhausit.

23   Interea ex Socratis auditoribus unus et item alter accesserat,
quos cum non paucissimos pro re agenda Socrates adesse intellexisset, manum in Mercurium primus iniecit. 'Atqui adeste' inquit
'familiares! Apprehendite hunc, alioquin indole nobili et liberali
praeditum sed inaudita incredibilique insania laborantem. O de-
terrimam hominum conditionem! Quam multos habet ad nos per-
turbandos aditus atque[43]aditus insania! Quid ego nunc querar furere alios amoribus, odiis, cupiditatibus, libidinibus — quid hoc?
Hic se Mercurium praedicat[44] et ab Iove demissum[45] Olympo
ut Virtutem quae ab caelo exulet deam pervestiget ubinam sit, ac
parasse quidem caelicolas orbem rerum evertere et eum cupere in-
novare. Quis hic furor est?' His auditis, qui Mercurium prehende-
rant in maximos risus exciti, cum neglegentius Mercurium observarent, Mercurius, ut erat pedibus celer, ipsum se eripuit fuga.

24   Et casu devenit in viculum ubi intra dolium Diogenes inhabita-
bat, quo in loco seducto et arbitris vacuo ab cursu fessus constitit.
Interea improbus quidam lenonis puer, adiecto fuste quem manu
ebrius gestabat, Diogenis dolium putre et vetustate penitus confectum multa vi illisit atque confregit, ac mox inde e conspectu evolavit. Ea contumelia percitus Diogenes, quasso ex dolio prosiliens,
cum alium neminem praeter Mercurium videret, rapto eodem quo

"Hallo there, my good fellow! Where are the men by whom mankind is made both learned and good?" Socrates, a man of wonderful affability and graciousness, seeing a young traveller with an outstanding physique and a handsome face, started, in accordance with that congenital habit of his, to use clever dialectical methods to deduce one thing from another and squeeze out every detail concerning who Mercury was, why he had come to earth, and what the gods were planning.

Meanwhile, one after another of Socrates' students approached, 23 and when Socrates realized that not a few people were watching what he was doing, he first laid his hand on Mercury, and said, "Come here, friends! Seize this man! He's blessed with a noble and gentlemanly character, but is laboring under a strange and incredible madness. O, how horrible is the human condition! How many ways upon ways does madness have to disturb us! How lamentable it is that this one rages with love, that one with hatred, desire, or lust . . . but what is this one's problem? He claims that he's Mercury, that Jupiter has sent him down from Olympus to search for the goddess Virtue, who was exiled from heaven — and he says that the gods are planning to destroy the world and want to rebuild it. What is this madness?" When they heard Socrates, the men who had grabbed Mercury guffawed loudly. In so doing they kept a less than watchful eye on him and Mercury, who was swift of foot, tore himself away and fled.

By chance he came upon the village where Diogenes was living 24 inside his tub. In this remote place, where there was no one to see him, he came to a halt, exhausted from running. Meanwhile, a wicked boy who worked for a brothel-keeper had drunkenly picked up a club, which he beat with great force against Diogenes' tub, almost entirely dilapidated with decay and old age, and broke it. Then he ran out of sight. Diogenes, infuriated by this insult, leapt out of the shattered jar, and when he saw no one apart from Mercury, he snatched up the same club with which he had been

esset lacessitus fuste, sedentem petit.[46] Mercurius atroci et insperato insultu absterritus voce maxima coepit popularium opem
atque auxilium acclamitare, et in Diogenem versus, qui se inter
acclamandum percussisset, 'Sicine' inquit 'in liberum hominem
atque immeritum facis iniuriam?' At Diogenes contra 'Sicine tu'
inquit 'a servo tibi iusta atque emerita rependi doles? Tu impure,
tu sceleste, tu iniustus exstitisti, qui quidem quietum lacessere, qui
domum diruere, qui ex laribus sedibusque detrudere insontem
non sis veritus. Tua est, adeo tua haec intolerabilis iniuria! Nam
meo quidem in facto non iniuria sed error est: nam cervicem quidem, non quam incussi genam petebam fuste!'

25   Ad Mercurii voces pauci accursitarant; ii, re intellecta, hortati
sunt ne in philosophum istiusmodi esset iratior. Dehinc, ad Diogenem versi, redarguendo his verbis usi sunt: dedecere quidem qui
se philosophum profiteatur non temperasse iracundiam, et quam
rem in hominum vita tantopere improbent, eam ab se non habere
alienam flagitium esse. Postremo addebant nihil esse turpius quam
egenum et destitutum hominem per impatientiam delirare. At
contra Diogenes 'En' inquit 'admonitores audiendos, qui mea in
causa eum velint esse me, qui ipsi in aliena non sint: meum tu me
iubes dolorem ferre patienter, cum alienum tu ne feras quidem
moderate.'

26   Ergo Mercurius decedens sic secum stomachabatur: 'Hisne credam qui asserant illud hominum genus fore sapientissimum quod
litteras tractent, qui re ipsa sint stultissimi? Mirabar quidem si una
cum sapientia tantum posset odium sui persistere. Nudi ambu-
lant, sordide vivunt, doliis habitant, algent, esuriunt. Quis eos ferat, qui sese non ferant? Sibi omnia denegant quae ceteri concu-

assailed and set upon the sitting Mercury. Mercury, terrified by
this vicious and unexpected attack, began to shout for help in a
loud voice. He turned to Diogenes, who was beating him as he
shouted, and said, "Why are you harming an honorable and innocent man?" Diogenes retorted, "Why are you sorry that a slave is
paying you back your just deserts? You filthy, lawless scoundrel!
You had no scruples about attacking a peaceful man, destroying
his house, and casting an innocent man out of his home and
dwelling. You—yes, you!—have committed this intolerable outrage! What I'm doing isn't an outrage, but a mistake: instead of
hitting your face with this club, I should have broken your neck!"

A few people ran up when they heard Mercury's plaintive cries,   25
and once they understood what had happened, they urged him
not to get too angry against a philosopher of this type. Then they
turned to Diogenes and reproached him, saying that it was unseemly that a man who called himself a philosopher could not
control his anger. They said it was a disgrace not to be free oneself
of a vice philosophers had so vehemently condemned in human
life. Finally, they added that nothing was more shameful than for a
poor and needy man to go out of his mind with impatience. But
Diogenes in reply said, "Oh, so I must heed admonitions from
those who want me, for my own sake, to act like him—while they
themselves can't act that way for the sake of somebody else. You
bid me bear my own sufferings patiently, when you wouldn't even
bear another's sufferings calmly."[11]

Thus Mercury left, muttering furiously to himself: "Should I   26
trust those who claimed that philosophers are most wise just because they are literate, when in reality they are utterly stupid? I
wonder that such wisdom can co-exist with such self-loathing.
They walk around naked, they live in squalor, they inhabit tubs,
they're cold and hungry. Who could stand them, when they can't
stand themselves? They deny themselves everything that other
people desire. Isn't it madness to refuse to enjoy things that con-

piscunt. Ne vero is non furor est nolle rebus perfrui quae ad
cultum, ad victum faciant, quibus ceteri omnes mortales utantur?
Quod si plus ceteris in ea re sapere se arbitrantur, superbia est,
stultitia est, ut eos aeque errare aliis in rebus, quas nosse
profiteantur, deputem. Quod si se reliquis esse hominibus[47] in ur-
banitatis officio similes recusant, exsecrabilis quaedam eos incessit
feritas atque immanitas. Sed istos sordidissimos sinamus esse miseros, quoad invisa istiusmodi philosophandi ratione vitam degant
illepidissimam.'

27   Hisque dictis rediit ad superos, Iovemque salutans subridens
inquit 'Qui aliorum sensus et mentem indagaturus accesseram, in-
veni qui mea secreta omnia exhausit.' Mercurium Iuppiter et[48] tam
cito et liventi cum gena redisse advertens[49] remque percontatus,[50]
non facile dici potest ex istius peregrinatione plusne voluptatis an
tristitiae exceperit. Voluptati quidem fuit ridiculam totius peregrinationis historiam intellegere,[51] dolori vero fuit quod penitus nihil
pro exspectatione factum sentiebat. Sed cum satis Mercurium esset allocutus et non cessaret Mercurius omni dictorum contumelia[52] philosophos prosequi, 'Vide' inquit Iuppiter 'ne tua[53] verborum intemperantia tibi vitio sit atque effecerit ut quos vituperas, hi
meritas abs te poenas desumpserint. Novi quid dicam: plus sapiunt illi quidem rerum occultarum quam opinere. Quid si praesenserint suis investigandi artibus te, Mercuri, esse eum qui se
apud me insimulare levitatis assueveris?' His dictis Mercurius
animo factus perturbatior e Iovis conspectu sese abdicavit.

28   At Iuppiter, suarum rerum statum repetens, in tanta consiliorum inopia qualecumque in mentem incidit consilium arripuit.
Apollinem, quem unum omnium deorum sapientissimum et sui
cupidissimum habebat, amotis arbitris apud se habet et admonet
quaenam sibi rerum difficultates instent. Non multo abesse Kalen-

tribute to a decent appearance and good nutrition, things that all
other mortals use? If they think they know more than the rest on
this subject, it is just pride and folly, which makes me wonder
whether they don't make just as many mistakes in the other subjects they profess to know about. And if they refuse to adopt civil
forms of behavior like other men, then a deplorable wildness and
barbarism has come upon them. But we permit those filthy men to
be wretched, as long as they live their gross way of life according to
some odious philosophical system."

With these words Mercury returned to the gods. He greeted 27
Jupiter, smiled, and said, "I went to investigate the feelings and intentions of others, and I met a man who found out all my secrets."
Jupiter, noting Mercury's swift return and his red cheeks, ques-
tioned him about what had happened. It would not be easy to say
whether he derived more pleasure or sadness from Mercury's travels. He was entertained to hear the ridiculous story of the journey,
but was unhappy to realize that nothing had gone as planned.
When he had spoken enough with Mercury and the latter would
not stop attacking the philosophers with every variety of insult, Jupiter said, "Look, don't let this verbal incontinence of yours become a vice and cause those whom you've attacked to pay you your
just deserts. I know whereof I speak: these men know more secrets
than you might think. What if they have foreseen, Mercury, with
their investigative skills, that you would charge them with fickle-
ness in my presence?" These words made Mercury even more
upset, and he withdrew from Jupiter's presence.

Jupiter, reconsidering the state of his affairs, was perfectly clue- 28
less about what to do, and so seized upon the first idea that came
to mind. He cleared the room, keeping Apollo by his side, for he
considered Apollo to be the wisest of all the gods, and also the one
who was fondest of him. He advised him of the difficulties of the
situation at hand. The prescribed Kalends were not far away, and
he had no edict to deliver to the Senate and People of the Gods.

das praestitutas; quid senatui populoque deorum ex edicto referat deesse; demum cetera omnia, praeter suam Mercuriique peregrina- tionem ad philosophos factam, explicat. Postremo rogat uti quam possit opem atque auxilium suis iam prope afflictis rationibus affe- rat. Omnem Apollo in tuenda servandaque principis bene de se meriti maiestate pollicetur curam, operam atque industriam adhi- biturum, modo tantis rebus agendis valeat ingenio, fidem vero et diligentiam profecto non defuturam neque ullos pro commodis et emolumentis Iovis recusaturum se labores,[54] pericula, difficultates. Illud videat, ne quod se velit facere, id cum iis conveniat quae sibi in mentem venerint.

29   Nam versari quidem apud mortales genus quoddam hominum, qui philosophi nuncupentur, quorum sint plerique ausi novas atque inauditas commentari formas orbis: hos se aditurum et consulturum, neque futurum ut vereatur in dubiis rebus eos consulere, qui bonis artibus et disciplinis innitantur. Amplexatus Apollinem Iuppiter atque exosculatus 'Nunc' inquit 'resipiscere a maximis animi curis per te incipiam, o Apollo. Novi sollertiam, novi et vigilantiam tuam: omnia de te spero quae huic causae op- portunissima accommodatissimaque sint. I, sequere, faciam qui- dem ut sentias te adversus memorem accepti beneficii functum fuisse officio.'

30   Tum Apollo, se accingens ad iter capessendum, 'Agesis' inquit 'aliudne me velis?' Tum Iuppiter 'Recte' inquit 'nam est apud mor- tales Democritus quidam minutis animantibus caedendis nobilis. Sanusne an insanus sit, varia est opinio. Sunt qui philosophum, sunt qui delirantem praedicent. Pervelim fieri certior quanti homo sit.' Tum Apollo: 'Tantumne hoc est, quod cum maxima novandi orbis cura apud te conveniat? Sed rem expediam: hicque tibi iam

He explained everything, omitting only his and Mercury's journeys to the philosophers. Finally he asked Apollo what he could
do to help, what aid he could provide in this near-crisis situation.
Apollo promised to apply all his efforts and toil to guarding and
keeping safe a prince to whose majesty he owed so much, to the
extent that his abilities were equal to such important affairs. But at
least Jove could count on his loyalty and hard work, and he would
not shirk any efforts, dangers, and difficulties on behalf of Jove's
well-being and interests. Apollo asked Jupiter to consider whether
an idea that had just occurred to him accorded with what Jupiter
wanted to do.

Among the human race, he said, there lived a certain kind of   29
men called philosophers, and many of them had dared to specu-
late about new and strange worlds. Apollo said that he would go
to them and consult them. He would not be afraid to consult
them in this doubtful situation, for they relied on the liberal arts
and disciplines. Jupiter embraced Apollo, kissed him, and said,
"Now, thanks to you, I can begin to shake off the enormous mental strain I've been under. I know your ingenuity, and I know your
vigilance. I expect that the whole business will go as favorably and
as fittingly as possible with you in charge. Go, do get on with
things, and I shall make you feel that you have discharged an office
on behalf of someone who remembers favors."

Apollo, preparing himself to embark on the journey, said,   30
"Come now, is there something else you want from me?" — "Yes,"
said Jupiter. "Among mortals there is a man called Democritus
who is famous for killing little animals. Opinions differ as to
whether he's mad or sane. Some people call him a philosopher,
others say he's a lunatic. I would dearly like more information as
to what kind of a man he is." Apollo replied, "What's so important about that, when you've got the great burden of building a
new world? But I'll tackle the problem. Here, let me find that out

id inventum dabo.' Ergo sua ex crumena, qua sortes inerant, hos eduxit versiculos:

> Quae tamen inde seges? terrae quis fructus apertae?
> Gloria quantalibet quid erit, si gloria tantum?

Lectis versiculis, 'Omnium hic' inquit 'stultissimus est mortalium!' Subrisit Iuppiter. 'Atqui adsis,' inquit 'sortem iterato educito et spectato sitne itidem quem dixero sapiens an insipiens.' Eduxit Apollo hos alteros versiculos:

> Scire erat in voto damnosa canicula quantum
> raderet augusto.

'Ergo' inquit 'omnium is quidem sapientissimus est!' Hic vehementer arridens Iuppiter 'O te' inquit 'ridiculum! Et quasnam sortes esse has tuas dicam, quae ex stultissimo tam repente queant sapientissimum reddere Democritum? Neque enim alium appellare succurrebat?' Tum Apollo 'At' inquit 'in promptu est quo haereat res. Sic interpretor: sciscitanti[55] Apollini, cuius est diem illustrare, sortes diurnum qualem se habeat Democritus hominem decantarunt. At subinde Iovi, cuius praeter id quod aliis impertitus sit, sua sunt reliqua omnia, qualem aeque se Democritus reliquo habeat tempore sortes liquido explicaverunt, ut sentire nos hic oporteat hominem hunc noctu sapere perpulchre, eundemque interdiu insanire.' Risere atque abiit Apollo.

31   Iuppiter vero plenus spei per alacritatem Kalendas exspectabat. At cum ipsae[56] advenissent Kalendae et in arcis atrium dii cum sollemnium causa, tum et contionis ineundae gratia laeti frequentes venissent, Apollo vero nusquam[57] appareret, incredibili maestitia Iuppiter affectus prope contabescebat. Iam Fata, quorum erat

for you right now." From his purse, which contained fortunes, he drew out these little verses:

What crops, what fruits come from the plowèd earth?
When glory's all there is, what is that glory worth?[12]

Having read the verses, he exclaimed, "The man is the biggest fool of all mortals!" Jupiter smiled. "Please, try another fortune, and let's see whether the man I mentioned is wise or foolish." Apollo pulled out this second set of verses:

He was to learn how much an unlucky deuce
shaved off an honorable prayer.[13]

"There you go," he said, "that man is the wisest of all mortals!" Jupiter, laughing heartily, said, "What a ridiculous fellow you are! What should I say about these fortunes of yours, which can so suddenly turn Democritus from the stupidest into the wisest of men? It doesn't occur to you to appeal to another fortune?" Apollo said, "But it's obvious what it means! I interpret it like this: when Apollo, who illuminates the day, asks, the oracle chants what kind of man Democritus is to be considered by day. But it clearly explained to you, Jupiter, the one in charge of everything else, what kind of man Democritus is to be considered the rest of the time. So we ought to see that this man is most wonderfully wise at night, and a raving lunatic during the day."[14] They laughed, and Apollo departed.

Jupiter, full of hope, keenly awaited the Kalends. But when the 31 Kalends arrived, and the gods crowded happily into the atrium of the citadel, both for the solemn rites and also to attend the assembly, Apollo was nowhere to be seen. Jupiter, profoundly depressed, nearly fainted away. The Fates, whose job it was to look after the sacred fires, were trying to carry on as usual. Elsewhere, a dense crowd of gods asked whether Jupiter was going to call the assembly, since this was the reason why they had been summoned in the

muneris sacros curare ignes, facere pro more aggrediebantur. Alia ex parte confertissimi dii poscebant ut ab Iove contio indiceretur, cuius ergo inprimis acciti convenissent. Ille vero, quod esset nihil commentatus, ad tantam de se exspectationem progredi refugiebat. Sed praescriptam de contione habenda legem suo facto rescindere neque ex gravi principis officio neque ex sua re ducebat,[58] quod intellegebat quanti[59] intersit minime volubilem minimeque variabilem haberi Iovem quantumque conferat eos qui rem publicam moderentur ita sua omnia quadrare (ut sic dixerim) instituta, ut in recto aequabilique consilio facile acquiescant. Ergo ut aliquid rerum agendarum festinantibus interiaceret atque intermisceret, quo interea deorum desideria ab causa hac sibi difficili et gravi diverteret et distineret, imperat Fatis sollemne incohent: mox se adfuturum atque cetera expediturum.

32   Itaque stant Fata lautissimo habitu manu postes attinentes ac deorum dearumque ingredientium ordines recensent[60] igniculosque flamines, quos deitatis exstare ad verticem insigne dixeram, caelicolis instaurant.[61] At Iuppiter interea inter cunctandum secreta obclusus aula sollicitudinibus curisque obruitur. Tandem egressus potius ut aliquid ageret quam ut quid ageret intellegeret, in templum se infert. Illic sollemne rite ac pro vetere more sanctissime peracto, dum senatus deorum Iovem salutatum aggrederetur, unus ferme omnium maximorum principum, Apollo, desiderabatur. Erant idcirco qui Apollinis contumaciae succenserent. Iuppiter neque purgare absentem neque moderate pati obtrectatores, et dici non potest quam perplexe sese agitaret animo atque in omnes partes haesitaret. Tandem incidit in mentem ut Momum regem institueret senatus comitiorumque principem faceret, non quo illum tantis honoribus dignum censeret, verum ut ostenderet audacibus

first place and why they had turned up. Jupiter, having made no preparations whatever, shrank from going forward in the face of such high expectations. But he thought it was neither in accordance with the solemn duty of a prince nor with his own interests to rescind by his own act the law concerning the conduct of assemblies. Jupiter understood how important it was that he not be thought in the least changeable and fickle, and how advantageous it would be for those who ruled the state that all of his ordinances should (so to speak) square with each other, so that people would readily acquiesce to rulings that were fair and just. Therefore, to give the throng something to do, and to confuse the situation so that he might divert and distract the gods' desires from this problem which was so tricky and serious for him, he ordered the Fates to begin the solemn rites, saying that he would soon be there and would get on with the rest of the assembly.[15]

And so the Fates stand in their sumptuous costumes, holding the gates fast with their hands. They review the ranks of gods and goddesses as they file in, and they renew the priestly flamelets of the sky-dwellers, which flicker forth as a sign atop the gods' heads, as I explained. Jupiter hung back, skulking in a secret part of his palace, paralyzed with worry and care. Finally, he went outside, just for the sake of doing something rather than because he knew what to do, and entered the temple. There, the solemn and holy rites having been conducted in accordance with ancient custom, the divine senate of the gods went up to Jupiter to greet him. Only one of the greatest princes, Apollo, was missing, and some people there were angered by Apollo's insolence. Jupiter could neither justify Apollo's absence nor calmly tolerate that god's critics, and I can't express how baffled he was and how he hesitated about everything. Then it occurred to him to appoint Momus king of the senate and leader of assemblies. This was not because Jupiter thought him worthy of such great honors, but because he wanted to show several overbold and ambitious gods that he would do ev-

32

ambitiosisque nonnullis deorum se ad illos augendos atque ornandos ultro omnia sponteque velle conferre qui quidem non imperare, sed obsequi et gratificari didicissent.

33   Itaque iubet in comitium classes deorum immittat ordinibusque universos considentes habeat, apudque populum verbis Iovis ita agat: cupere quidem Iovem quae ageret quaeve meditaretur omnia omnibus vehementer placere et decresse quidem singulis, quoad in se sit, morem velle gerere; quae res cum ita sit, adductum se ut priusquam suam proferat sententiam optet fieri certior ex tota mundi congerie sitne quippiam quod velint servari ad novum opus integrumque transferri potius an[62] funditus velint everti universa atque perfringi. Tum et de tota re edicit ut quid quisque tum suis,[63] tum communibus rationibus conducere arbitretur licenter aperteque disputent: non adfuturum se in contione utili consilio, quod cavisse velit ne qui forte humiles dii et in publicis insueti praesentiam regis vereantur ac perinde dicere quae sentiant retardentur.[64]

34   Haec mandata maximarum insperatarumque fuere perturbationum causa. Quam rem futuram Momus, ut erat acutus atque ingenio excitus, fortassis animo praesagibat, sed Iovi, cui iam pridem suum dedisset consilium inscriptum tabellis, sollicitare novissimis admonitionibus non audebat; tamen conferre arbitrabatur quoquo pacto Iovem ab inconsiderata innovandarum rerum libidine interpellaret. Idcirco 'Si tuam per facilitatem' inquit 'licet, Iuppiter, quaeso, tabellasne, quas a me pridie accepisti, legistin?' 'De his alias' inquit Iuppiter 'colloquemur: nunc quod instat agito.' Tabellas Iuppiter ne sibi quidem traditas meminerat.

35   Ardentem alacritate[65] contionem offendit Momus et studio rerum novarum obsequentissimam adeo ut vix crederet[66] tam volen-

erything in his power to advance their careers and honor them, if they learned not to rule, but rather to defer to him and humor him.

So Jupiter bade Momus send into the assembly the different 33 classes of gods, have everyone sit down in their ranks, then act as his spokesman. Jove (Momus should say) wanted everyone to be delighted with everything he was doing and planning. He had decided to gratify each of them individually, as far as he could. This being the case, before handing down his own decision, he wished to learn what they wanted to do with the materials that constituted the world, whether they wanted some of them kept for the new project and transferred in their entirety, or whether they wanted the universe to be completely destroyed and broken into pieces. He said that they should all freely and openly debate what each of them believed should be done about the whole matter, both in their own and in the communal interest. He said that he would not himself be present at the assembly advisedly, because he wanted to make sure that the king's presence would not intimidate the lesser gods and those unused to public debate, and prevent them from saying what they felt.

These instructions caused a vast and unexpected uproar. Being 34 acute and mentally alert, Momus perhaps had an inkling of what would happen, but he did not dare bother Jupiter with new advice, since he had long since given him his counsel, written down in the notebooks. Nevertheless, he decided that he would confer with Jupiter in order to block somehow the latter's ill-considered urge to change the universe. So he said, "Jupiter, will your good nature permit me to ask a question? Did you read the notebooks I gave you yesterday?" — "Let's talk about those another time," said Jupiter. "Let's deal with the present crisis." Jupiter did not even remember that he had been given the notebooks.

Momus encountered an assembly burning with eagerness and 35 extremely amenable to revolutionary zeal, and he could hardly be-

tes ac libentes obtemperare. Sed illico ut coepit mandata Iovis explicare et se regem senatus contionisque principem gerere, sensit tantam in singulis animorum fieri commutationem ut ad vultus frontisque tristitiam addi amplius nihil posset. Non est ut referam quantum invidiae ob id adversus Momum, quantum querimoniarum adversus Iovem insurrexerit et apud proceres et apud infimos plebeios. Nullorum erat oculis aspectus Momi non gravis atque invisus, Momi verba omnibus molesta, Momi facta singulis infensa. Quin et tantum flagrabat odii in Momum ut se in faciem sentiret exsecrari, et quoquo versus vertebat oculos, illic spectabat explodentes et contumeliosum quippiam ad sui fastidium gestientes. Qui tamen omnes etsi ita essent animati ut vix a Momo refractis subselliis impetendo manus continerent, tamen sese ab iracundia Iovis maximi metu revocabant atque coercebant.[67]

36   Tandem rogatus primam dixit sententiam Saturnus voce ita suppressa, verbis ita raris gestuque ita defesso ut potius conatum loqui quam locutum diceres. Pauci reliquum sonitum vocis immurmurantis excepere; aliqui tamen ferebant Saturnum dixisse se quidem petere ut suae senectuti veniam darent si quid minus orando posset, quando et latera et pectus quassum et imbecille haberet attritis consumptisque viribus senio.[68] Proximo loco Cybele, deorum mater, rogata, diu nutans oreque admodum pro vetularum more irruminans, cum satis diuque suos respectasset ungues, 'Enimvero'[69] inquit 'de his[70] rebus gravissimis atque rarissimis cogitasse oportuit.' Tertia fuit Neptuni[71] sententia. Is quidem, acri voce atque aspero tono tragicoque quodam dicendi more sententiis tritis et locis communibus late diffuseque vagatus, quidvis aliud potuit videri velle dicere quam quod ad rem qua de agebatur ulla ex parte pertineret. Successit Vulcanus,[72] et is quidem suam omnem orationem hac una in re consumpsit, ut affirmaret vehemen-

lieve how willing they were and how pleased to defer to him. But when he began to explain the commands of Jupiter and to conduct himself as king of the senate and leader of the assembly, he noticed a great change of attitude, so that their faces set in the severest possible expressions. There is no need to describe how much hatred was directed at Momus on this account, how many complaints were levelled against Jupiter by both the leading gods and the lowest class of gods. Everyone looked at Momus with somber and hate-filled expressions, they all loathed Momus' words, and every single person was bitterly hostile to Momus' deeds. So much hatred for Momus flared up that he realized they were cursing him to his face, and wherever he turned his eyes, he saw gods jeering at him and gods making insulting gestures to provoke him. Though the whole lot of them were roiling to the point that they could scarcely restrain themselves from shattering the benches and attacking Momus with them, they checked and controlled themselves out of fear of great Jupiter's anger.

At length, when the first view had been solicited,[16] Saturn   36
spoke, but in a voice so low, with such few words and with such tired gestures that you'd think he was trying to speak rather than actually speaking. Few gods caught the sound left by his mumbling voice. Others, however, reported that Saturn had asked them to excuse his old age if he could not speak any better—his ribcage and chest were battered and frail, and his strength was worn down and devoured by old age. Next Cybele, mother of the gods, was asked to speak: she nodded for a long time and chewed her gums as old women do. When she had looked long enough at her nails, she said, "Certainly we should think carefully about these serious and unusual circumstances." Neptune's opinion came third. This god, in a harsh, cutting voice like that of a tragic actor, wandered widely and vaguely through trite notions and oratorical commonplaces, giving the impression that he preferred to speak on any subject other than the matter at hand. Vulcan came next, who

ter admirari se quidni sint in deorum numero plurimi[73] tanto prae
diti ingenio ut de rebus his quorum gratia convenerint docte atque
erudite norint disseruisse.

37   Mars vero, cum ad se ventum esset, nihil plus habere se quod
pro re diceret affirmavit quam ut polliceretur accinctum paratissi-
mumque arbitrio imperioque Iovis Martem adfuturum et praesta-
turum quidem operas demoliendo convellendoque mundo. Plutonis oratio avaritiam sapere visa est, quod se habere attestatus sit
modulos novissimi operis perquam pulcherrimos quos proferret,
modo quid prius paciscerentur: suos enim labores atque industriam nullis propositis praemiis decresse non condonare. Hercules, praestita occasione ut diu multumque praemeditatam orationem de suis laudibus tam celebri tamque in confertissima contione
recitaret, sibi haudquaquam defuit. Sua gesta magnifice extulit et
grandia de se in posterum pollicitus est; demum de tota re se ad
Iovis sententiam referre dixit.

38   Venerem risere dii quae excogitasse nova quaedam miri artificii
deierabat, ni paululum quippiam totam rem plurimum impediret,
sed optimum[74] rerum magistrum, speculum, consulendum. Diana[75] inventuram se optimum quendam architectum pollicita est,
sed negare id genus artificum velle imperitis censoribus subesse, ne
quod arte ab se elaboratum sit alii, ut aliquid fecisse videantur,
mutando vitient atque depravent. Iunonem callidiorem putarunt,
quae plures fieri mundos variis formis suadebat et hos atque alios
habendos ad satietatem.

39   Cum autem ad Palladem ventum est, ea, uti ex ante composita
constitutaque scaena cum Iunone ceterisque illarum partium con-
spiratoribus convenerant, se habere enuntiavit quae cum Iove ipso
de iis rebus conferat. At, quibus mandatum negotium erat, unus et

spent all his time detailing his astonishment at how many there were among the gods who knew how to discourse brilliantly and learnedly upon the subjects they'd come to discuss.

Mars, when it was his turn, asserted that he had nothing to say 37 on the subject except to promise that he, Mars, would be armed and equipped to execute the judgment and command of Jupiter, and that he stood ready to offer his aid in breaking up and destroying the world. Pluto's speech smacked of greed. He announced that he had some lovely little world-renewal kits he could offer, but only after a price had been agreed upon, as he had decided not to sacrifice his labor and effort without some prospect of profit. Hercules, presented with the opportunity to recite a long and carefully rehearsed speech in praise of himself at such a famous and crowded assembly, did not fail to do himself full justice. He richly extolled his own actions and he promised that he would do great deeds in the future, and in the end, regarding the matter at hand, said he would follow Jove's decision.

Venus made the gods laugh when she swore that she had 38 thought up some wonderfully clever and original ideas, except that one teensy thing was hindering her plan, but she would consult that best of teachers, the mirror. Diana promised that she would find the finest architect, but said that an artist of his class would not defer to amateurs. He wouldn't want other people to spoil and pervert the unique creations of his art just so they could appear to have had their imput. The gods thought Juno cleverer; she urged them to create many worlds of different kinds, making one after another until they had had enough.

Then it was Pallas' turn. Having planned and orchestrated the 39 scene ahead of time with Juno and the rest of the conspirators in their faction, she declared that she would have to consult personally with Jupiter himself about these matters. But then a couple of the gods, acting on instructions, engaged loudly and with artful deceit in a prearranged altercation among themselves. They up-

item alter deorum prae constituta inter se arte et fraude magnis
vocibus redarguere eiusque superbiam increpare, quae tantos deos
totamque contionem indignam putet cui pro communi utilitate
meditata communicet. Illa altercari; hinc ex ordinibus plures studiis partium excitari: in convicia conveniunt, inglomerantur, con-
strepunt. Quem tumultum atque ordinum perturbationem spectans Momus, supra quam ceteri omnes voce illa sua boanti hos
atque hos increpans, ita conclamitabat ut solus ipse tanto ex convi-
cio audiretur.

40   At cum sedare tumultuantem contionem iterum atque iterum
frustra tentasset, commotus facti obscenitate excanduit, quoad
plurima per iracundiam dixit immoderata, inter quae excidit ut diceret non iniuria apud mortales veteri sanctissimoque more et lege
observari ut publicis abigerentur excluderenturque mulieres. Addi-
dit his etiam Momus ut diceret: 'Etenim quaenam temulentissi-
morum lustra iis comitiis comparabimus?' Quae[76] dicta ab tota
contione audita cum animos cunctorum iam tumidos atque indi-
gnatos offendissent, ut erant iam tum primum concepto odio irritati, 'Sicine' inquiunt 'Momus hic sua cum demorsa barbula ab
exilio erit restitutus ut nostram ad ignominiam novus exsistat censor?' Hunc[77] contionis animum intuens Fraus dea, tempori inser-
viendum rata, ad Iunonem advolat, monet, hortatur beluam hanc
nimia licentia insanientem atque temere[78] insultantem coerceat.

41   Itaque Iuno, sponte sua iam pridem satis in Momum commota,
nunc deae Fraudis impulsu concita, sese praecipitem[79] ad facinus
inauditum dedit. Reiecto enim pallio, 'Adeste' inquit 'matronae!
Tuque, Hercules, huc ocius trahe Momum! Sic soror et coniunx
Iovis imperat.' Paruit haud invitus Hercules, Momumque in hunc
atque in alterum manuque voceque sese agitantem[80] per capronosum[81] illud[82] quod fronti sublime imminet sinciput prehensum, ut

braided her for her arrogance, because she thought the great gods and the entire assembly unworthy of hearing her thoughts on matters of common interest. She disputed their remarks, and then a number of them, roused from their places by partisan zeal, came together in an uproar, turning themselves into a howling mob. Momus, seeing the tumult and disorder in their ranks, in a thunderous voice that carried over all the rest reproved first one then another group of gods, roaring so loudly that he alone could be heard above the clamor.

But after trying in vain again and again to calm the tumultuous 40 assembly, he grew extremely angry. Provoked by its disgraceful behavior, his wrath led him to make a number of intemperate observations. Among other imprudent remarks, he said that the mortals were right to observe the ancient and holy custom and law whereby women were sent away and excluded from public business. He added, "Can the most drunken debauches compare with this gathering?" These words, heard by the entire assembly, offended the already enraged and indignant minds of everyone present, and rubbed raw the hatred they had earlier conceived for him. They said, "Has this Momus, with his chewed-off little beard, been restored from exile to be made a new censor for our humiliation?" The goddess Mischief realized the assembly's mood and decided to take advantage of the opportunity. Flying to Juno, she advised and exhorted her to bridle this beast, who was raging with absolute license and recklessly insulting the gods.

Juno of her own accord had been angry with Momus for a long 41 time, but now, provoked by the goddess Mischief, she flung herself headlong into a shocking and outrageous deed. Flinging off her cloak, she said, "To me, matrons! You, Hercules, drag Momus here quickly! Jupiter's sister and wife commands it." Hercules was by no means reluctant to obey. He seized Momus, screaming and punching, by the goatlike hair hanging down over his forehead, and being overwhelmingly strong, he slung Momus over his shoul-

erat praepotens, ita suum in dorsum reiecit ut resupinum contorto
collo ad Iunonem quasi truncum apportaret. E vestigio innumerae
iniectae manus misero. Nihil plus dico: Momus quidem mulierum
manu ex masculo factus est non mas, omnique funditus avulsa vi-
rilitate praecipitem in oceanum deturbarunt. Inde Iunone duce ad
Iovem properant iniuriisque deploratis efflagitant ut aut publicum
ipsum odium Momum releget aut universum dearum populum in
exilium abigat: non posse quidem deas matronas tuto[83] his in locis
degere ubi funestum exitiosumque id monstrum versetur. Qua de
re etiam additis lacrimis obtestantur ut malit unius conscelratis-
simi poena tot suarum necessitudinum et optime de se meritarum
precibus salutique consulere quam perditissimi unius gratia omni
de caelo duriter mereri.

42   Id Iuppiter, etsi facti exemplum magis quam factum ipsum non
probaret, tamen ne non concedendum quidem multitudini statuit
quod tantopere affectaret atque exposceret. Semper enim multitudinis motum atque impetum fuisse reipublicae periculo ni compri-
matur, et alium non adesse comprimendi modum nisi ut obtemperet.[84] Tum aliqua item ex parte eam rem ita cecidisse ferebat
minime moleste, maxime quod gravi illa esset hoc pacto[85] sollicitudine factus liber qua non mediocriter angebatur, cum non haberet
quid contioni exspectanti se dignum referret. Ergo cum annuisset
garrientiumque muliercularum strepitus quievisset, pauca de rixae
istiusmodi indignatione[86] succinctis verbis perstrinxit, ac se eam
quidem perdendi Momi libidinem in tales tamque multas sibi con-
iunctissimas et carissimas incidisse ait dolere[87] magis quam ut au-
deat improbare: illud maluisse factum non impetu, non praecipiti
consilio cum[88] multas alias ob res, tum ut liceret pacata et quieta
contione frui, quoad quid instituisset commonefaceret. Sed
quando per Momi calamitatem (ne dicat per suorum immode-

der, face down like a log, his neck twisted back, and brought him to Juno. Immediately countless hands grabbed at the wretched god. I shall not elaborate, but in the hands of the women, Momus went from manly to unmanly. They tore off his entire manhood and flung it into the ocean. With Juno in the lead, they hurried to Jupiter. They bemoaned their injuries and demanded that he should either banish Momus as an object of public hatred or send the whole divine populace into exile. The matron goddesses could not dwell safely in places infested by that deadly and destructive monster. In tears they besought Jupiter to consider the prayers and the safety of so many of those bound to him by ties of obligation and merit. He should prefer to punish one thoroughly wicked individual rather than to lose the sympathy of all heaven.

Jupiter disapproved of the precedent set by the deed rather than   42
of the deed itself, but he decided he could not but yield to the multitude in what it so ardently demanded. Riots and assaults by the multitude, he believed, were always dangerous to the state if not suppressed, and there was no other way of suppressing them apart from complying with the mob's demands. Then again, on the other hand, Jupiter reckoned, the episode had not turned out all that badly. The event had freed him of a serious problem that had given him no little trouble: that he did not have an appropriate decision to put before the expectant assembly. Consequently, after nodding his approval and quieting the clamor of the chattering ladies, he restricted himself to a few brief remarks about the unseemliness of a quarrel of this kind. Not daring to reprove them, he said he was grieved that the desire to destroy Momus had taken hold of so many important goddesses so near and dear to himself; for a variety of reasons he would have preferred that the deed had not been done from impulse, in summary judgement, but mostly because they might have profited from a peaceful and serene debate before hearing what it was he had decided. But since this would not now be appropriate owing to Momus' misfor-

stiam) id non liceat, ducere ait se commodius non agere id nunc
quod decreverat, et non invitum velle supersedere quando videat
commotos et perturbatos procerum animos; sed propediem ad senatum de tota republica relaturum quae excogitasset utilia et admodum necessaria.

43   Et cum tandem ex aula egrederetur[89] indomitus ille feminarum
vulgus, casu fit illis obviam Apollo a mortalibus rediens. Quem
cum vidissent, quod et vatem et praeclarum futurorum coniecto-
rem putarent, non sine causa consulto abfuisse a tumultu interpre-
tati sunt. Ideo innutantes 'Hui' aiebant 'improbe, quam[90] solus sapis,[91] quam belle scisti uti foro et vitare illepida!' Fiebat idcirco ad
Apollinem concursus iamque ad vestibulum astabant pressi, quod
multis exeuntibus atque redeuntibus constiparentur. Quam[92] inter
frequentiam forte aderat et dea Nox, quae una furtis faciundis mirifice delectatur et in ea re ita scite perdocta est ut vel oculos Argo,
si velit, furari possit. Ea ut pendentem ab Apollinis latere crumenam sortibus turgidam animadvertit,[93] ita abstulit ut id facinus
omnes penitus latuerit. At Apollo, salutatis his atque his, intelle-
ctaque contionis historia, laetabatur cum ceteras ob res, tum quod
in rem Iovis cecidisset. Eoque admodum exhilaratus ad Iovem ingressus, quod minime rebatur, tristiori quam erat par exceptus est
fronte ab Iove.

44   Etenim Iuppiter ceteris amotis: 'Et quidnam tam sero tar-
dusque redisti?' Tum Apollo 'Nihil habui rerum' inquit 'aliud
quod agerem quam ut tua sedulo matureque imperia exsequerer.
Sed me illi ad quos accessi philosophos, dum ita instructi sunt ut
nihil expromant rerum reconditarum nisi id sit maximis verborum
involucris implicitum, longis ambagibus detinuere invitum quidem, tamen eos audiendos putabam quando exspectationi tuae

tune (he would not say owing to the intemperance of his relatives), he had decided he could not usefully go forward with what he had decreed. He would not be unwilling to prorogue the assembly in view of the excited state of mind of its leaders, but he would shortly divulge to the senate his thoughts as to what was useful and vitally necessary in all affairs of state.

When the wild mob of women finally left the palace, they hap-   43 pened to meet Apollo on his way back from earth. When they saw him, they inferred that, being a prophet able to foresee future events, he had deliberately and with reason absented himself from the riot. So winking at him, they said, "Ho there, you rascal! You're the only smart one, how clever you were to stay outside and avoid that mess!" A crowd then gathered around Apollo, packing into the vestibule, wedged together by the gods leaving and enter- ing. The goddess Night happened to be among the throng. She took an amazing pleasure in stealing, and was so clever at it that she could have even stolen the eyes of Argos, had she wanted.[17] When Night noticed the purse bulging with fortunes hanging from Apollo's side, she stole it, her crime passing completely unno- ticed. Apollo, greeting people left and right, heard the story of the assembly. Among other reasons he was delighted because the situ- ation had fallen out to Jupiter's advantage. In a state of exhilara- tion he went in to see Jupiter, but to his surprise Jupiter received him looking more severe than usual.

Jupiter dismissed everyone else, and said, "So why have you re-   44 turned so late and in such a dilatory fashion?" — "I fully intended to carry out your commands diligently and on time," replied Apollo. "But when I reached those philosophers, they were so well informed that they could not explain any obscure matters without wrapping them in the thickest blankets of words. Though unwill- ing, I was enmeshed in their long-winded quibblings. But I still thought I should hear them out, for I was determined to satisfy your expectations with the utmost care. To speak frankly, they are

omni studebam diligentia[94] satisfacere. Ac sunt profecto ad unum omnes verbosi. Unum excipio Socratem, nisi forte quibusdam minutis interrogatiunculis interdum quasi aliud incohans vagetur: qui tamen, utcumque est, mihi semper visus est frugi, illique volens favi fudique in eum tantum mearum rerum quantum sat sit ad sinistros gravesque casus evitandos. Semper eius abstinentia, continentia, humanitas, gratia, gravitas, integritas unaque et veri investigandi cura et virtutis cultus placebit. Is omnium unus opinione longe praestitit, dum ex eo elegantem et dignissimam memoratu disceptationem accepi; quam quidem, cum audies, credo non gravate feres me in ea perdiscenda paululum supersedisse, et fortassis non infitiaberis tuas ad rationes bene componendas adhiberi posse nihil accommodatius. Quod si vacas animo ad has res audiendas, eam tibi succincte et breviter enarrabo.' Tum Iuppiter: 'Cupio, narra: sapientum quidem sermonibus[95] et dictis delectari, etiam ubi nihil afferant praesentibus causis emolumenti, conferet.'

45   Tum Apollo 'Duo' inquit 'fuere homines inter philosophos apud quos aliquid grave et cum ratione constans audierim: Democritus et Socrates. Dicam de Socrate si prius de ipso Democrito dixero quae te ab tua ista insolita tristitia frontis ad risum hilaritatemque restituant. Audies rem cum[96] festivam, tum et plenam maturitatis.

46   'Democritum offendi inspectantem[97] proximo ex torrente raptum cancrum vultu ita attonito, oculis ita stupentibus ut prae illius admiratione una obstupuerim. Cumque plusculum astitissem, coepi hominem compellare; at ille ab suo, si recte interpretor, somno quo apertis oculis habebatur nequiquam excitabatur. Commodius ea de re duxi Democriteam illam (ut ita loquar) statuam relinquere quoad sponte sua expergisceretur, quam illic frustra tempus perdere. Itaque alias alibi catervas conveni philosophorum,

chatterboxes to a man. I make exception for Socrates, although even he sometimes wanders through trifling little questions as if he were aiming at something else. Still, however that might be, he always seemed an honest fellow to me, and wishing to show him favor, I infused as much of my prophetic skills into him as would suffice him for avoiding serious misfortunes. His abstinence, self-control, humanity, graciousness, seriousness, integrity, and his unique concern for investigating the truth and cultivating virtue always pleased me. He had the best reputation of all the philosophers. I heard him give an elegant and memorable disputation, and when you hear it, I think you won't be angry with me that I lingered a little to learn it carefully, and perhaps you won't deny that it is highly relevant and useful for solving your own problems. Concentrate on listening to it; I'll summarize it for you." Jupiter said, "Do tell me, I'd like that. It's profitable to enjoy the speeches and sayings of wise men, even when they aren't relevant to the case at hand."

"There were two men," said Apollo, "among the philosophers 45 from whom I heard things that were weighty and logical: Democritus and Socrates. I'll get to Socrates, but first I'll tell you something about Democritus that will change this unwonted severity of yours into laughter and merriment. You'll hear a story that is both jolly and full of ripe wisdom.

"I met Democritus when he was inspecting a crab he'd caught 46 in a nearby stream. His expression was so startled and his eyes were so full of amazement that I too was dumbfounded just from wondering at him. When I got a little nearer, I started to accost the fellow, but he would not be shaken out of the snooze he was having with his eyes wide open, if I understand rightly. I thought it would be better to leave that Democritean statue (so to speak) alone until he snapped out of it, rather than wasting time there in vain. So I met with other troops of philosophers in another place. And who would not disapprove of their behavior? Who would

quorum mores quis non improbet? Et vitam quis non oderit?
Dicta vero et opiniones quis aut interpretetur aut probet? Adeo
sunt obscura, adeo ambigua, ut nihil supra.'

47   Tum Iuppiter arridens 'An'[98] inquit 'o Apollo, tu quidem, qui
interpretandi mirus es artifex, istorum dicta non interpretaberis?'
'At' inquit Apollo 'de me profiteor omnia posse facilius: ita sunt illa
quidem partim varia et incerta, partim inter se pugnantia atque
contraria. Sed de his alias. Illud sit ad rem, quod cum inter se hoc
genus hominum nulla in ratione conveniant, omnibus opinionibus
et sententiis discrepent, una tantum in stultitia congruunt quod
eorum quivis ceteros omnes mortales delirare atque insanire deputat praeter eos quibus fortassis eadem aeque atque sibi sunt vita,
mores, studia, voluntas, affectus viaque et huiusmodi. Adde quod
quisque probat alios non probare, quae oderit alios non odisse,
quibus moventur alios non moveri: id demum ad iniuriam deputant. Hinc difficile dictu est quantae et quam multae manarint inter eos lites et controversiae, dum et contumeliis et vi etiam, si
possint, alios omnes sui esse imitatores velint, ut vix feras[99] tantam
in sapientiae professoribus versari insaniam.'

48   Tum Iuppiter: 'Quid ego philosophos mirer[100] velle ceteros suo
arbitratu degere, cum et plebeios video in horam, prout sua fert libido, a superis poscere imbrem, soles, ventos atque etiam fulgura
et huiusmodi?' Tum Apollo: 'Quid ceteri faciant non refero. De iis
hoc statuo eiusmodi esse, ut dum quisque sua stultitia orbem universum agi[101] optet dumque nihil constantis certique habent, statuo, inquam, futurum ut, si eorum velis audire ineptias, oporteat
infinitos et momentis temporum varios mundos profundere aut assiduis deprecantium querelis insanire.

49   'Haec de universo philosophorum genere dicta sint. Ad Democritum revertor. Ad hunc igitur iterato rediens offendo hominem

not hate their manner of living? Who could either understand or sanction their words? Their words are more obscure and more ambiguous than anything!"

Jupiter smiled, and said, "So even you, Apollo, the amazing 47 master of interpretation, could not interpret their words?" — "I could do anything more easily than that, I admit," said Apollo. "Some of their words are ill-assorted and vague, others are self-contradictory and inconsistent. But more of this later. The point is that mortals of this kind do not agree with each other; they disagree in all their thoughts and opinions. Only in their stupidity do they agree. They think that all humans are mad and insane apart from those who happen to have the same way of life, customs, enthusiasms, desires and emotions as they do. Moreover, what one approves the others do not approve, what one hates the others do not hate, what moves one leaves the rest indifferent — and that they consider an insult! It's difficult to describe how great and numerous are the quarrels and disputes that spring up among them, and they use insulting language and violence, too, if they can, to force everyone else to imitate them, so you'd scarcely believe that professors of wisdom could be subject to such madness!"

Then Jupiter said, "Why should I wonder that the philoso- 48 phers want others to live by their rules, when every hour I see even the common folk demanding things like rain, sun, winds, and even lightning from the gods as their desires dictate?" — "I'm not talking about what the others do," Apollo replied. "As far as the philosophers are concerned, I'm convinced that as long as each of them wants to run the world in accordance with his own foolishness, as long as they have no consistency or conviction . . . I'm sure, I tell you, that if you want to heed their follies, you should create an infinite number of worlds that change every minute or you'll go crazy from the incessant complaints of your petitioners.

"What I've said applies to philosophers as a class. Now I'll 49 come back to Democritus. When I went back to him again, I

perscindentem cancrum quem spectare attonitum dixeram, can-
crumque ipsum obtenso vultu pronisque luminibus introrsum per
viscera scrutantem et dinumerantem quicquid nerviculorum ossi-
culorumque inesset. Saluto hominem, at ille nusquam minus. Non
possum facere quin ipsum me rideam: audies, o Iuppiter, ridiculam rem. Incidit enim in mentem ut caepe quoddam ex proximo
agro desumerem atque medium perciderem meque homini adige-
rem; quo facto coepi eius gestus et motus imitari. Pressabat ille os,
ego itidem pressabam; cervice ille in hanc ruebat aurem, ego itidem in hanc; praegrandes ille exporgebat oculos, ego itidem. Quid
multa? Omnia enitebar ut me illi praeberem similem, et habebam
quidem me homini prope imitando parem ni illud interturbasset,
quod Democrito exstabant oculi siccitate insignes, nobis vero ob
molestam caepae acrimoniam oculi erant praegnantes lacrimis.

50   'Quid multa? Hoc ludicro[102] invento assecutus sum quod serio
nequivissem, ut colloquendi daretur locus. Me enim despectato
subridens "Heus" inquit "tu, quid facis lacrimans?" Tum ego contra despectans: "At enimvero tu quid facis? Quid rides?" "Te" inquit ille "prius rogaveram." "Tibi" inquam "ipse prius respondi."
Paratum inde adeo litigium videns grandius arrisit. "Atqui quando
ita evincis" inquit "referam de me quale nostrum foret opus. Ego
enim multam dederam operam ut brutis eviscerandis (hominem
quidem ferro lacerare nefas ducebam) intellegerem quasnam primum in animantibus malum, iracundia, sedes occuparet: unde
tanti motus effervescerent, quibus facibus mentem hominis exagi-
taret omnemque vitae rationem perverteret. Ea enim[103] re inventa,
multa in hominum vitam me reperturum putabam commoda et
utilissima.[104] Videbam in plerisque animantibus quaedam quae
mihi plane satisfacerent, sed ne in homine quidem intellegebam
unde tam multa insurgerent quae ad stultitiam facerent.

found the man dissecting the crab he had been looking at in amazement, as I mentioned. He was scrutinizing that same crab with his head bent over it, looking down into its innards, counting how many little nerves and bones were inside. I greeted the fellow, but he didn't give me the time of day. I can't help laughing at myself: listen to this ridiculous incident, Jupiter. It occurred to me to pick an onion out of a nearby field, slice it through the middle and force myself on the man's attention. When I had done this, I began to imitate his gestures and movements. He grimaced, I grimaced in the same way; he jerked his head to one side, I did the same; he popped out his enormous eyes and I did too. In short, I did everything I could to look like him, and I almost had the man down, except for the fact that Democritus' eyes were remarkably dry, while mine were streaming with tears from the onion.

"In short, thanks to this ridiculous device I achieved what I 50 could not when I'd been serious: I got the chance to talk to him. He looked me over and, smiling, said, 'Hey, you, what are you crying about?' Then I looked him over too and said, 'Well, what are you doing? Why are you laughing?'[18] — 'I asked you first,' he said. — 'I answered you first,' I replied. Seeing that he was about to get into a lawsuit, he smiled broadly. 'Okay, you win,' he said, 'I'll tell you what sort of work I'm doing. I've spent a lot of effort disembowelling animals (I thought it was wrong to cut a human being with my knife), so that I can learn where anger, the primary evil of living beings, originates from: where these powerful emotions boil up from, the fiery sources which agitate the human mind and pervert the rational order of life.[19] If I could discover that, I think I could discover a great deal that would be very convenient and useful for human existence. I've found certain things in a number of animals that give me distinct satisfaction, but in the case of the human body I haven't yet understood the multiple sources and causes of stupidity.

51 "'Quae compereram haec sunt: nam sucum quidem inveniebam ad inter praecordia inhaustum ab spirantibus animi igniculis coqui[105] in sanguinem ita ut variarum quibus constet partium variae fiant segestiones, quarum una quidem, quae ex levissima sanguinis exspumatione adnatet, colligitur et vasculo a natura coacto et coaptato commendatur.[106] At solere liquorem hunc figura ignibilem, sive commotis praecordiis sive admisso visceribus intimis incendio, fervere[107] atque candescere eiusque acutissimas scintillulas segestione levigatas, aestu impulsas, volitare canalibus et ad rationis usque sedes sese attollere atque pervadere suoque appulsu acri atque temulento inflammari et conflagrare intima naturae omnia, quoad mentem lacessendo tumultuantem reddat.

52 "'Haec ita esse in aliis quidem animantibus clare perspexi. At nunc animal unum hoc quod inter manus est, cum natura mihi ad omnem duelli audaciam et ferocitatem pulchre adornatum videretur, diligentius recognoscendum arbitrabar. Huic thorax, huic manicae, huic nihil non opertum squamis adesse natura voluit, cumque arma scirem amoto irarum impetu esse penitus mollia et inutilia, non iniuria opinabar huic etiam dedisse naturam multa ad incessendam[108] iracundiam fomenta atque irritamenta. Ea vero ubinam haereant nusquam invenio,[109] et quod magis solliciter[110] accedit, quod ne cerebrum quidem hoc in animante comperio. Et opinari non adesse uno hoc in animante cerebrum vetat[111] ratio: quod enim animal movetur loco, cerebrum habeat atque inde vigeat necesse est, quandoquidem omnes nervorum fibrae a cerebro ipso fluant. At hoc, cui tam multorum membrorum et robusti et varii motus suppeditent, qui carere possit cerebro non intellego." Haec Democritus.

53 'At ego, ut viderer quoque philosophari, contra sic orsus sum dicere spectare quidem me in eo quod manibus haberem caepe de-

"'What I have discovered is this: I found a juice that circulates 51
near the stomach and is heated in the blood by little fires breathed
into it by the soul.[20] Thus it forms various decoctions of the
different parts of which it consists. One of these decoctions swims
along, forming the lightest foam on the blood, is collected and
sent to a little vessel formed by nature for the purpose. This humor is usually flammable in form, either because of the turbulence
of the stomach or because of fire hidden in the innermost organs.
So it seethes and blazes, and its brightest sparks are broken down
into the decoction; buffeted by heat, they move quickly through
the vessels and lift themselves up to the seat of reason, which they
pervade. By their sharp and intoxicating pressure they inflame and
set fire to all the innermost parts of the temperament, and to that
extent set upon the mind, throwing it into a disturbed and pas-
sionate state.

"'I have observed this phenomenon clearly in other animals. 52
But I think I need to explore this singular animal in my hands
more carefully, an animal which nature beautifully equipped to
fight with boldness and ferocity. Nature gave it a breastplate and
greaves and completely covered it with armor plating, and since I
knew that arms are utterly feeble and useless if you take away the
force of anger, I correctly held that nature must have given it numerous fuels and irritations to provoke anger. But I have never
found out where they are located, and what is more worrying, I
have never even found the creature's brain. Reason forbids that
this creature is alone in lacking a brain. Because the animal moves
in space, it must have a brain and a source of activity, seeing that
all nerve fibers flow out from the brain. I don't understand how it
can lack a brain when it has available to its many limbs so many
vigorous and varied motions.' Thus Democritus.

"So that I, too, could look like a philosopher, I started to say 53
that I, on the contrary, was scrutinizing the onion in my hands to
determine whether the gods would destroy the world or preserve it

moliturine sint superi dii mundum an perpetuo servatui. Tum ille
"O te" inquit "haruspicem lepidissimum! Unde tibi novum hario-
landi hoc genus arcessivisti?"[112] Tum ego "Atqui" inquam "istuc
recta et a vobis philosophantibus diducta fit ratione, qui quidem
maximum esse caepe mundum asseveratis." Tum ille "Facis tu" inquit "adeo venuste, qui parvo in orbe maximi mundi casum quaeris! Verum et quidnam? Quid hisce in extis caepariis, quid ingrati
invenisti quod plores?" Tum ego "Viden" inquam "istic diviso in
caepe litteras c atque o? Num[113] eas clare aperteque admodum sentis quid proloquantur?" Tum ille: "Quid, tune loqui caepe, cum et
caelos cantare aliqui dixerint, existimabis?" Tum ego: "Minime,
sed prae se ferunt. Iunge o atque c: aut occidet, inquiunt, aut cor-
ruet. Disiunge: nonne itidem enuntiant, corruiturum[114] orbem?"
Tum ille vehementer ridens "Tu" inquit "igitur, o piissime, orbis[115]
excidium atque interitum ploras! Sed heus tu! Ubinam huius qui
nunc constat mundi rudera superi reicient, si demoliri aggrediantur?" Hoc dictum, quod sapiens et ad nostram rem accommoda-
tissimum videretur, effecit ut obmutescerem atque mecum ipse di-
cerem: "Habes tu quidem cerebrum quod te non habere fueram
dicturus, quando illud in cancro quaereres."

54   'Haec de Democrito hactenus. Nunc ad Socratem illum redeo,
virum omni virtutis laude insignem. Hunc repperi quadam in taberna coriaria suo pro more de quodam multa interrogantem. Sed
ea prorsus nihil ad nos.' Hic Iuppiter: 'Nempe et perquam insignem praedicas virum, qui apud coriarios diversetur! Verum agedum, quaeso, o Apollo: quidnam id erat quod interrogabat Socrates? Est enim ut cupiam de eo audire quae vere sua quidem sint,
non quae aliena fictione Socratis dicantur.'[116] 'Nempe tum, si recte
memini, his verbis utebatur: "Agesis, o artifex, si quid tibi in mentem veniat ut velis optimum calceum conficere, num tibi corio esse

forever. Democritus said, 'Oh, what an amusing diviner you are! Where did you get this new kind of prophecy?' — 'Right reason and you philosophers, who claim that the great world is an onion, led me to it,' I replied. 'You're doing something beautiful,' he said, 'seeking the fate of the great world in such a little sphere![21] But what's the matter? What have you found among the onion's innards so unpleasant that it makes you cry?' — 'Do you see in this halved onion the letters C and O? Isn't it clear and obvious what they are telling us?' — 'What, do you think onions talk, just as some people say that the sky can sing?'[22] — 'They don't talk, but they do reveal,' I retorted. 'Join the O and the C: it means either "it is knocked over" or "it collapses." Separate the letters: do they not spell out the same thing, "the orb will collapse?"'[23] Laughing heartily, he said, 'So, O holiest of men, you are weeping for the ruin and destruction of the world! But look here, where are the gods going to put the raw material the world is made of, if they decide to destroy it?' I was speechless at this remark, which seemed to me a profound one and highly relevant to our problem. I said to myself, 'You really do have a brain, though I wouldn't have said you had one when you were looking for a brain in that crab.'

"So much for Democritus. Now I come back to Socrates, a distinguished man universally praised for his virtue. I found him in a cobbler's shop, asking lots of questions, as is his wont. But nothing he said there concerns us." At this point Jupiter said, "Oh, the man you're talking about must be very distinguished indeed, since he associates with cobblers! But come on, Apollo, please; I want to know: what was it that Socrates was asking about?[24] I long to hear the genuine sayings of Socrates, not things other people make up and attribute to him." — "But of course! Well then, if I remember correctly, he used these words: 'Tell me, craftsman, if you intend to make an excellent shoe, don't you decide to use the best leather?' — 'I do decide that,' said he. Then Socrates said, 'Do you

54

opus statues optimo?" "Statuam" inquit ille. Tum Socrates: "Qualecumque ne dabitur corium ad id opus: accipiesne an putabis interesse ut ex multis commodius eligas?" "Putabo" inquit. Tum vero
Socrates: "Quo id pacto" inquit "dinosces corium? An tibi aliud
quod experiundo videris corium peropportunum et accommoda-
tissimum propones tibi, cuius comparatione hoc tuum pensites et
quid cuique desit ampliusve sit apertius discernas?"[117] "Proponam"
inquit ille. Tum Socrates: "Qui vero optimum illud condidit
corium, casune an ratione assecutus est ut illi nullae adessent
mendae?" "Ratione potius" inquit artifex. "Et quaenam" inquit Socrates "illa fuit ratio ad id munus obeundum? Eane fortassis quam
condiendi corii usu et experientia perceperat?" "Ea" inquit artifex.
"Fortassis" inquit Socrates "aeque ac tu in seligendo ita ille in pa-
rando corio similitudinibus utebatur, partes partibus integrumque
integro comparans, quoad futurum corium omnibus numeris responderet suo huic quod menti memoriaeque ascriptum tenebat
corium." "Est" inquit ille "ut dicis." "Tum" inquit Socrates "quid si
ille numquam fieri vidisset corium? Eam optimi corii conficiendi
descriptionem et similitudinem unde hausisset?"'

55   Hic Iuppiter, qui attentissime omnia haec Socratis quaesita adnotarat, rupit incredibilem quandam in admirationem Socratis
atque 'O' inquit 'virum admirabilem! Nequeo me diutius continere
quin clamem "O" iterum "virum admirabilem!" Sino illud, te, o
Apollo, quamquam esses personatus, ab Socrate fuisse cognitum.
De illo enim sic est quod audeam affirmare, novisse[118] et qui sis et
quid negotii ageres et quid tibi velles: denique omnia cognovisse.
Nam est ea quidem mentis perspicacia in occultis quibusque rebus
pervestigandis apud philosophos, quantum re periclitatus sum,
cum communis et quasi peculiaris, tum genere ipso tanta ut supra
sit quam possis credere. Et novi quid dicam, et expertus novi. Verum vide quam bellissime te cognito et causa intellecta satisfecerit.

take whatever leather is on offer, or do you think it makes a difference to choose the best leather from among those offered?' — 'That's what I think,' he said. — 'And how do you know the best leather? Do you do anything else but see which leather will be most fitting and suitable, and use the comparison to evaluate it and decide clearly whether it is too small or too big?' — 'That's my position,' he said. — 'Does someone who works with the best leather rely on chance or method to verify that there are no faults in it?' asked Socrates. — 'Method,' said the craftsman. — 'And what method did you use to perform the job? Does one perhaps learn it from the experience and practice of preparing leather?' — 'Yup,' said the craftsman. — 'Perhaps' said Socrates, 'you used analogous procedures both to select and to prepare the leather, comparing parts with parts and the whole with the whole, so that the future leather corresponded with mathematical precision to the leather recorded in your mind and memory.' — 'Whatever you say,' replied the craftsman. — 'So what happens,' said Socrates, 'if a man has never seen leather made? Where does the description and likeness of the best kind of leather to prepare come from?'"

At this point Jupiter, who had been noting most attentively all of Socrates' questions, gave vent to his incredible admiration for Socrates, saying, "What a wonderful man! I can't keep myself any longer from shouting it out again: what a wonderful man! It goes without saying, Apollo, that although you were disguised, Socrates still knew who you were. In fact, I daresay that he knew who you were and what business you were conducting and what you wanted: in short, he knew everything. Philosophers just have that mental acuteness when it comes to secrets or subjects for investigation, as I know from experience. They take in so much of the general, the specific and the generic — more than you would believe possible. I know what I'm talking about, and I know from experience. You see how beautifully he satisfied himself once he recognized you and grasped your motives. I know where your ambigu-

Sentio quo tuae tendant verborum amphibologiae, Socrates! Aut enim ad huius similitudinem in quo fabricando omnes pulchritudinum formas expressi restituendus erit mundus, aut plures tentandi quoad fortassis casus absolutiorem aliquem afferat. Sed quid tum, quid postea?'

56   Tum Apollo: 'Enimvero[119] negavit artifex se id scire quod rogasset atque obmutuit. Illico ipse me ingressi, consalutavi, ille me per hospitalissime benignissimeque accepit. Multa in medium contulimus quae longum esset referre, sed eorum quae nostram ad rem conducerent illud placuit inprimis quod pluribus interrogatiunculis conclusum dedit, et fuit huiusmodi: namque hunc[120] quo omnia contineantur mundum talem nimirum exstare ut alibi reliquerit nihil quod addi adiungive sibi a quoquam possit. Cui si nihil addi, nec diminui; si non diminui, nec corrumpi. Nam cui addes, quod alibi esse non possit? Aut qui corrumpas, quod diduci nequeat?'

57   Hic Iuppiter: 'Tritum istud et vulgatum quidem est dictum, utcumque sit, quod minime cum illo superiori de corio compares.' Tum Apollo: "Cave iis rebus diiudicandis, o Iuppiter, opinioni quam veritati assentiaris. Vide ne te nimia quae apud te viget istius viri auctoritas in errorem trahat atque detineat: nihil enim tantas habet vires ad suadendum quam gratia, nihil quod veritatem obnubilet aeque atque auctoritas. Pythagoras auctoritate assecutus est ut quae diceret[121] vera an falsa essent sui nihil curarent, omnia assentirentur, nihil auderent negare, nihil non crederent: denique vel ineptissima etiam vellent haberi pro certis et testatis apud ceteros, ut etiam cum se ab inferis esse reducem praedicaret iurarent vera praedicare.'

ous words are going, Socrates! Either I must restore the world in the likeness of the one I made when fashioning all the forms of beauty, or I should experiment with numerous worlds until chance happens to produce a more perfect one.[25] But what then, what happened next?"

"Well," said Apollo, "the craftsman said that he had no idea 56 what Socrates was asking about, so he remained silent. At that point I entered and greeted Socrates, who received me like a kind and gracious host. We talked over many things which it would take a long time to recount, but of the matters relevant to our problem, I liked particularly what he said at the conclusion of his line of micro-questions, namely, that this world, as it contains all things, is evidently such that nothing exists outside it that could be added or taken away from it by anyone. If one can't add to it, neither can one take from it, and if one can't take from it, then it can't degenerate. For how can one add something to a world out-side of which nothing can exist? And how can you destroy some-thing that can't be disaggregated?"[26]

Jupiter said, "That's a commonplace, trite thing to say, however 57 it may be, and you can't put it in the same class as the previous discourse about leather." — "In judging such matters, O Jupiter, be careful to agree with the truth, not opinion. Make sure that your exaggerated enthusiasm for Socrates' authority doesn't lead you into error and trap you; nothing has more power to convince than charm, and nothing clouds over the truth like authority. Pythag-oras[27] acquired so much authority that his followers didn't care whether what he said was true or false, but they assented to every-thing, did not dare deny anything and wouldn't disbelieve any-thing he said. In the end, they wanted to take even the the silliest doctrines as certain and proven, so that even when he claimed that he had come back from the underworld they swore that his claims were true."

58   Tum Iuppiter: 'Attemperate quidem in haec incidimus. Eram enim percontaturus[122] quidnam istiusmodi celebres, Aristotelemne, Platonem Pythagoramque ipsum et eiusmodi philosophos adivisses. Et quid igitur? Num ab his quippiam rari et reconditi attulisti?' Tum Apollo: 'Aristotelem' inquit 'repperi, contuso pugnis Parmenide et Melisso, nescio quo minuto philosopho, gestientem et cum quibusque obviis rixantem ac intolerabili quadam superbia et incredibili arrogantia vetantem quosque prae se quicquam proloqui. Theophrastum vidi maximam suorum scriptorum pyram instruere ut eam incenderet. Platonem erant qui dicerent abesse longe apud suam illam invisam quam coaedificasset politiam. Pythagoram audiebam paucis superioribus diebus in gallo quodam fuisse cognitum eundemque fortassis nunc inveniri posse in pica aut loquaci aliquo in psittaco: solere quidem illum per varia diversari corpora.'

59   Hoc loco Iuppiter 'O' inquit 'Apollo, quam cuperem quempiam istiusmodi in cavea domi habere philosophum! Quam meas regni res inde praeclare constitutas ducerem! Quid censes? Possetne ulla prehendi industria?' Tum Apollo:[123] 'Et quidni id posset qui nosset venandi artes, modo illum norit?' Tum Iuppiter: 'Istuc difficile, vili in corpore philosophi mentem intellegere.' Tum Apollo: 'Immo vero facile, ubi advertas.' Tum Iuppiter: 'Obsecro, tuisne id fortasse artibus et sortibus?' Tum Apollo: 'Maxime, vel etiam inprimis propositis praemiis assequemur ut sese illi ultro offerant.' Tum Iuppiter: 'Malo tuas in illis dinoscendis artes experiri. Age, quaeso, specta ubi sint locorum.'

60   Tum Apollo cum istac pro re suas vellet sortes consulere et ruptam ligulam abrepta crumena intueretur, maxima coepit voce indignissimum facinus in se admissum deplorare. Et quod familia-

"We've happened on this subject at a good moment," said Jupiter. "I was about to inquire what other famous philosophers you've met. Did you meet Aristotle, Plato or Pythagoras himself? Surely you brought back from them some unusual and recondite piece of knowledge?" — "I found Aristotle gesticulating," replied Apollo, "having just beaten up Parmenides[28] and Melissus[29] (some trifling philosopher or other). He fought with every man he met, and with unbearable insolence and incredible arrogance he forbade everyone else to express themselves. I saw Theophrastus[30] assembling a huge pyre of his writings to burn them. Some said that Plato was far away, at that invisible polity he'd constructed.[31] I heard that a few days beforehand, Pythagoras had been recognized in the form of a cock, and, that perhaps now he could be found in the form of a magpie or a chattering parrot.[32] He was always one for changing bodies." 58

At this point, Jupiter said, "Oh, Apollo, how I'd love to keep a philosopher like this in a cage at home! How excellent it would make me at settling the affairs of my kingdom! What do you think? Is there some way of getting one?" — "Why couldn't an expert hunter do it, provided he could recognize one?" said Apollo. — "That's the tricky part: to perceive the philosopher's mind inside his vile body." — "No, on the contrary," said Apollo, "that's easy, when you pay attention." — "How's that, please? Do you perhaps use your oracular arts and fortunes?" — "Yes, indeed," said Apollo, "or we could even offer a reward first, so that they'd give themselves up voluntarily." — "I'd rather employ your skills for tracking them," replied Jupiter. "Go on, I implore you, look and see where they are." 59

Apollo wanted to consult his own bag of fortunes about this, but found that the strap had been broken and that his purse had been snatched. In a loud voice he started deploring the base crime that had been committed against him. Since Socrates had associated with him on a rather familiar basis, he persuaded himself and 60

rius apud Socratem foret versatus, sibi id fecisse furtum blanditorem Socratem persuadebat et adiurabat. Longum esset referre quibus verborum conviciis philosophum[124] prosequeretur: scurram appellabat et fabrorum ludum. Tum et illud addebat, non iniuria Momum praedixisse tales fore mortales ut etiam, sin aliter nequeant, pedibus ipsis furari aggrediantur.

61 Cumque satis deferbuisset ac verborum iactantia acquievisset, eum intuens Iuppiter 'Num' inquit 'o Apollo, cancrum te Democriti esse quam qui sis tantis conceptis irarum motibus praestaret? Cancro quidem, cum sit furoribus vacuus, omnis armorum nervorumque vis ad lacessendum suppeditat; tibi cum ira flagres, cum tui vix compos sis, nihil ad prosequendam vindictam relictum est. Quid facies? Quos petes? Qua ratione aut ab sontibus poenas desumes aut insontes afficies? Illis quidem quid auferes boni cum nihil habeant? Quid afferes mali cum paupertatem et dolorem et istiusmodi penitus nihil timeant?'

62 Tum Apollo: 'En monitorem percommodum, qui minima offensus molestia orbem velit ruisse, et me, qui tantas amiserim divitias, ut temperem iubeat! Et possum quidem aestu sitique mortales perdere, Iuppiter, mortales, inquam, perdere.'

63 Tum Iuppiter: 'Vel possis quidem quidvis malorum; tu tamen nihil feceris, quandoquidem nihil deinceps apud superos constituetur quod ipsum non pateat mortalibus. Namque philosophi quidem aut suis, quibus callent, occulta pervestigandi artibus, aut tuis sortibus adiuti omnia praevidebunt quae acturi simus et pro summa sua sapientia vitabunt. Quare malo tuos istos animi aestus sedes. Desine casum hunc longius deplorare. Collige ipsum te! De istis quidem improbissimis multandis alias erit ut mature cogitemus, tametsi opinor alibi accidisse ut tantas divitias amiseris.'

swore up and down that that smooth talker, Socrates, was the thief.[33] It would take a long time to repeat the abusive language Apollo hurled at the philosopher: he called him a clown and the laughing-stock of craftsmen. He added that Momus had been right to predict that mortals would start to steal with their feet if they had no other means.

When Apollo had cooled off a bit and moderated his language, 61 Jupiter looked at him and said, "Surely, Apollo, you'd be better off as the crab of Democritus than as yourself when you're in such a rage? For since the crab is free of anger, it possesses the full force of its weapons and sinews to attack, but when you flare up in a rage, when you're out of control, you've no resources left for exacting revenge. What are you doing? Whom do you seek? By what reasoning do you take punishment from the guilty and inflict it on the innocent? How are you going to strip goods from those who have none? How are you going to inflict ills on those who have no fear of poverty or pain?"

"Well, you're a fine one to advise me," Apollo replied, "the fel- 62 low who wants to destroy the world when he encounters the slightest annoyance! But when I have lost such extraordinary riches, you tell me to calm down! I too can kill mortals with heat and thirst, Jupiter — I repeat, I too can kill mortals."

"Of course you can do evil," said Jupiter. "But you will do noth- 63 ing of the sort, because from now on the mortals will know everything that happens among the gods. Using either their own art of finding out secrets, at which they're so clever, or with the help of your fortunes, the philosophers will be able to foresee what we're about to do, and thanks to their great wisdom they'll be able to avoid it. So I would prefer that you calm your overheated mind. Don't lament this misfortune any longer. Pull yourself together! In good time, we shall consider how those wicked men should be punished, although my view is that you lost your riches somewhere else."

64   Tum Apollo 'Recte' inquit 'admones. Iam monenti pareo, et
unum est quod me recreet: habeant illi quidem sortes, interpretandi[125] modum et rationem nusquam habituri sunt. Sortes levi labore reintegrabimus; illis curarum plus et sollicitudinis quam com-
moditatis et opportunitatis redundabit a sortibus.'

65   Dum haec apud superos agebantur, Aestus, Fames, Febris et
eiusmodi, quod audissent finem atque interitum rebus parari, quo
repentinum futurum laborem in tot mortalium milibus mactandis
minuerent, iam tum primum coeperant vexare humanas res mul-
taque viventium capita absumpserant. Quibus calamitatibus acti,
hominum genus, quod deos votis aureis maiorem in modum moveri animadvertissent, ludos voverunt diis maximos, et eos dictu
incredibile quam grandi apparatu et theatri et scaenae quantave
impensa ornarint. Sino musicos, ludiones, poetas, quorum innu-
merabilis populus omnibus ab provinciis exterisque usque ab orbis
oris confluxerat. Quicquid erat rerum dignarum ubivis gentium, id
ad templi,[126] ad sacrificiorum ad ludorumque ornatum convexe-
rant.

66   Sino cetera: illud operis vastitate non postponendum, quod
theatrum[127] circusque[128] maximus aureis velis pictis acu, opus vastum[129] et incredibile, superne et quaque circumversus integebatur.
Honoratissimis in gradibus maximorum deorum simulacra exstabant, omnia circum auro gemmisque nitebant. Et quod aurum
gemmasque vinceret specie quantum ab iis dignitate vincebantur,
omnia floribus conspersa ad venustatem conveniebant, omnia
sertis fumorumque deliciis odorata et redimita. Tabulae insuper
pictae alabastricaeque mensae et varia speculorum miracula ad
complendos non admiratione, sed stupore homines accedebant;
quin et, quo nihil esset non refertissimum rebus admirandis, ipsa

"You're right to admonish me," said Apollo, "and I'll obey your   64
advice. One thing consoles me: let them have the fortunes, as
they'll never have either the method or the rules for interpreting
them. It will be an easy job to reassemble the fortunes. They'll get
more care and worry from those fortunes than benefits and opportunity!"

While these events were taking place among the gods, Heat,   65
Hunger, Fever and others like them heard that the end and destruction of the universe was being planned. They immediately
began to torment the human race, and in order to reduce to man-
ageable levels the work of slaughtering many thousands of mortals
in a future catastrophe, they began to kill many among the living.
These disasters prompted the human race to pledge lavish games
to the gods, for they had noticed that the gods were powerfully influenced by golden offerings. It is incredible to relate their plans to
embellish the games with a grand theatrical spectacle, sparing no
expense. I shall pass over the innumerable crowd of musicians,
stage performers and poets who flowed in from all the provinces
and from all over the world. Whatever worthy things there were
among the nations were brought together to beautify the temples,
the sacrifices and the games.

I won't mention the rest, but I cannot pass over the vast project   66
of swathing the top and the sides of the theatre and the Circus
Maximus[34] in enormous gold-embroidered veils, an unbelievably
massive job. In places of honor stood statues of the great gods, all
shining with gold and jewels. But what surpassed the gold and
gems in beauty, as much as they themselves were surpassed in
value, were the flowers: the flowers strewn over the statues, adding
to their charm; the flowers woven into garlands, girdling the statues and perfuming them with delicious incense. Paintings, too,
alabaster tables and various miraculous mirrors were added, fill-
ing men not only with admiration, but also with dumbfounded
amazement. And so that no space would be left without some

item[130] singula intercolumnia singulis heroum statuis occupaban-
tur.

67   Tantis apparatibus superi ab coetu hominum dignari venera-
rique se advertentes[131] non poterant non facere quin commoverentur. Quo effectum est ut etiam hi qui fortassis aut studiis partium
aut suorum commodorum spe causae hominum adversarentur
sententiam verterent et partim misericordia, partim muneris ma-
gnitudine commoti superiorem suam de novandis rebus postula-
tionem reicerent. Qui vero hominum res salvas cuperent, quorum
erat princeps Hercules, apud Iovem instabant ut mallet de se bene
in dies promerentes mortales beneficio obstringere quam poenis
perdere: illud enim valere cum ad gratiam, tum etiam ad laudem,
hoc vero postremum nihil afferre emolumenti et plurimum posse
ad calumniae suspiciones augendas.

68   Et monebat ut diligentius pensitaret votane haec facta religione
haud minore quam impensa cum Momi calumniis conveniant.
Sintne illorum qui deos nullos putent an eorum qui se diis acce-
ptissimos et commendatissimos esse optent? Admonebat item
ut[132] Momi naturam et mores animo repeteret: demum statueret
an qui apud mortales, quibus esset odio,[133] deos invisos et infensos
reddere aggressus sit, idem apud superos, quibus se acceptum opinabatur, inimicos homines male afficere neglexerit; et quibus sit
Momus odiis praeditus erga mortales satis patere quidem cum
aliunde, tum illinc, quod antea paene quam eos vidisset foeda ob-
scenaque illa animantia, quae vix nominare sine flagitio possumus,
ad homines incessendos[134] produxerit. Quare illud cogitent superi,
an qui sui reprehensores superos fuerit tantis conatibus prosecutus, idem barbae demorsae contumeliam non curarit.[135] Postremo

wonderful object to fill it, every space between the columns was occupied by individual statues of heroes.

The gods noticed that they were being honored and venerated   67 by mankind with these extraordinary preparations, and they could not but be moved. As a result, even the gods who had opposed the human cause, either from partisanship or in their private interest, changed their stance. Motivated partly by mercy and partly by the magnitude of the offering, they revoked their earlier request to renew the world. On the other hand the gods who wanted to save the humans, led by Hercules, urged Jupiter to place the mortals under the obligation of his goodwill, rather than destroying them with punishment, for the humans were deserving well of him on a daily basis. They said that by helping them he would earn their favor as well as their praise, while punishing them would not bring any advantage, and could very well increase the mistrust of his detractors.

Hercules advised Jupiter to think carefully about whether these   68 offerings, which had been made with a sense of piety that equalled their expense, corroborated Momus' malicious words. Were they the offerings of men who thought nothing of the gods, or of men who wanted to be dear to the gods and warmly commended by them? Hercules advised Jupiter to think again of Momus' character and habits. Jupiter needed to decide whether Momus, who had tried to convince the mortals, who hated him, that the gods were odious and hostile, would miss the opportunity to harm his human enemies when he was among the gods, who liked him (as he thought). A variety of evidence pointed to Momus' hatred of mortals, but especially the fact that, almost before he'd ever seen them, he had invented awful and vile creatures to attack them, which we can hardly name without infamy. The gods should think about whether a person who had so exerted himself to pursue his critics among the gods would be indifferent to the insult of a bitten-off beard. In the end Hercules called to witness Shadow, the daughter

Umbram, Noctis filiam, obtestans Hercules affirmabat—id enim maximum est deorum iuramentum—quaeque insimulaverit in cena Momus adversus homines, eadem ipsa omnia sceleris et perfidiae esse refertissima, et Momi esse illa in deos nefanda, non[136] mortalium dicta, quibus frequens apud philosophos abuteretur.

69   His addebat non intellegere prudentissimos deorum quid sibi vellet Iuppiter. Si quid forte hoc pacto quaerat novandis rebus placere multitudini, aut si tantarum impensarum praemium[137] nihil praeter solum plebis plausum quaeritet, semper quidem adfuturos quibus non quaeque agas omni ex parte probentur, neque defuturos inprimis honestissimos deorum qui consuetas res desiderent magis quam ut novis delectentur. Tum et veteres illos optimos architectos qui tanta arte hunc qui exstet mundum peregerint[138] obsolevisse vetustate, et negare omnino omne id fabrorum genus fieri quicquam posse elegantius, ornatius atque ad perpetuitatem constantiamque aptius quam hoc quod factum tam omni ex parte perplaceat. Quod si tandem novos iuvet architectos experiri, satis patere quidem quid valeant cum aliunde, tum in Iunonis arcu exaedificando, quandoquidem non iniuria vulgo dictitent non aliam ob rem structum fuisse ita nisi ut inter struendum rueret.

70   Haec Hercules non modo Iunone Bacchoque et Venere et reliquis Iunoniae factionis complicibus suffragantibus aperteque iuvantibus edisserebat, verum et omni prope caelo probante et admodum consentiente. At Iuppiter[139] horum admonitionibus motus, cum[140] operis ineundi difficultate diffisus, tum etiam votorum[141] magnificentia illectus, facile de sua pristina sententia abduci se passus est. Ergo praestitam occasionem reiciendae ab se invidiae in Momum libenter usurpavit, tametsi cupiebat videri beneficii

of Night—for that was the gods' greatest oath—and swore that the anti-human stories Momus had fabricated at the banquet were full of wickedness and treachery. He said that it was Momus, not the mortals, who had spoken those blasphemies against the gods, often making ill use of them while disputing with the philosophers.

He added that even the wisest of the gods could not understand what Jupiter wanted. If perhaps he hoped to please the multitude with his project of renovation, or if the only reward he sought for so enormous an expenditure was the applause of the vulgar, there would still always be people who did not fully approve of all he had done. First of all, there was no shortage of honorable gods who preferred things as they were rather than delighting in novelty. Moreover, those excellent old architects, who had built this present world with such skill, were fading into old age. Hercules roundly affirmed that the whole genus of craftsmen could make nothing more elegant, more lovely and better adapted to permanence and stability than what had already been created, which gave universal delight. If Jupiter at this point preferred to try out new architects, they had clearly proved their worth both in other ways and in the construction of Juno's arch. It was widely and deservedly repeated that the arch had been built for no other reason than to collapse under construction.

Hercules' speech was supported and openly favored not only by Juno, Bacchus, Venus and the other members of the Junonian faction. In fact almost all of heaven approved of and fully agreed with it. So Jupiter, swayed by their advice, made diffident by the difficulty of the project, and attracted, too, by the magnificence of the offerings, easily let himself be diverted from his earlier decision. He gladly seized the opportunity presented to him of displacing hostility from himself onto Momus. Yet, although he was going to do this anyway of his own accord, he wished to seem to be doing it as an act of beneficence. So he said, "Sky-dwellers, it would be

69

70

gratia id facere quod esset ultro facturus. Idcirco 'Homines quidem' inquit 'vestras, o caelicolae, delicias, quanti semper fecerim
non est ut referam, ni forte hac spe qua vota ineunt homines ipsi
parum attestantur sibi esse perspectum et cognitum animum erga
se nostrum. Quis enim opem atque auxilium suis adversis in rebus
tanta spe atque exspectatione postulet nisi ab eo cui se carum et
commendatum meminerit? Neque velim existimeris me futili de
causa aut simulasse his non succensere qui praesentia fastidirent,
aut dissimulasse eorum nescire mentes atque sensus qui novas res
cuperent. Quod si quae in causa sint[142] diligentius pensitabitis,
non dubito factum meum ita probabitis ut fieri commodius nihil
potuisse affirmetis.

71   'Sino reliqua. Quid illud, quod patefactum quidem reddidi
multorum disquisitione apud multos qui numquam huc[143] mentem intenderant, orbem hunc rerum ita demum omni ex parte ab-
solutum pleneque perfectum esse ut addi amplius nihil possit?
Quo fit ut congratuler hinc omnes in posterum abstrusas, ut ita
dicam, futuras improborum expostulationes hac in re. Sed quo
ipse mihi vehementer placeam illud est, quod aperte atque perspicue cognovi quali essent plerique ingenio praediti vario et longe
alio quam ostentarent. Atque inprimis noster Momus praeclare ipsum sese indicavit quid fingendo atque dissimulando cuperet. Me
fateor Momi versutiae et commentitiae fallendi artes poterant adducere incautum ut vel Iunonem ipsam, amantissimam scilicet,
minus diligerem, id quidem maxime ubi eum fortassis putabam
malorum suorum taedio fractum atque effectum plane quem se
fingebat. Accedebat quod plura sapere variarum rerum usu et philosophorum commercio videbatur. Et bonis artibus excultum ingenium minime improbum et plurimum diligendum arbitrabar.

72   'Quid mirum igitur si huic quem diligerem, praesertim versuto
et callido, inconsulte quippiam credebam? Non refero quantopere

impossible to explain to you how highly I have always valued those humans, your darlings, if the humans themselves, by the very hope they place in their offerings, had not given such ample proof that they know and understand our attitude towards them. For who would ask for help and aid in adverse circumstances with such hope and expectation, unless it was from someone whom they remembered as fostering and supportive? I wouldn't have you think that it was for a futile purpose that I either pretended not to be angry at those who were averse to the present state of affairs, or disguised my knowledge of the intentions of the revolutionaries. If you weigh the issue at hand very carefully, I don't doubt that you will approve of my deed, and you'll agree that I couldn't have done anything more appropriate.

"Enough. By provoking a broad debate, haven't I made it obvi- 71 ous to many of you, even those who never troubled to think about it, that this world is absolutely complete and utterly perfect, so that nothing more could be added to it? So, I shall be pleased if from now on all expostulations of wicked persons on this subject shall be set aside. But where I've really pleased myself is in this: I now see clearly and in detail that many people have an intellectual makeup far different from the one they present to the world. Our dear Momus, first and foremost, gave a distinguished example of what he hoped to accomplish through dissimulation and pretense. I admit Momus' craftiness, his fanciful arts of deceit, were able to catch me unawares, so that I went off my Juno, that most loving of women, most of all when I thought that Momus was perhaps crushed by his hardships and had been changed into what he pretended to be. Moreover, he seemed to be wiser thanks to his varied experiences and his intercourse with the philosophers. So I concluded that his character, polished by the liberal arts, was not wicked at all; it was even lovable.

"Why then is it surprising that I unthinkingly trusted this man 72 I loved, especially as he was wily and clever? I shall not dwell on

elaborarit suadere, quanta sedulitate eniteretur impellere ut prae-
ceps novis rebus incohandis irrumperem. Ac mihi sapiens quidem
illud dictum saepius in mentem redibat: istos plus satis eruditos
minus esse probos quam par est. Et profecto sunt, ut videre licet,
minime puri et minime simplices. Nam alios facto et re se habent
quam fronte et gestu videantur, et insigni, quo plurimum valent,
acumine ingenii perverse ad malitiam abutuntur, et illic ubi ac pro·
bos et simplicissimos videri student, illic maxime fallunt dolo et
improbitate.

73   'Quam rem cum mature ita esse in Momo animadverterem, ferebam quidem iocosum illum quem se videri affectabat quemve
quasi personatus gestu verbisque agebat, ut intimum vafrum et
subdolum profundius scrutarer atque comprehenderem. Interea
cavebam omnia, credebam nihil. Nunc vero, utcumque res cecidit,
commode actum vobiscum interpretor, quando curarum et seditionum seminarium illud deturbastis. Mallem, ut dixi, sine multitudinis motu, sine tumultu, sed licuerit hoc Iunoni improbum
atque detestandum e numero deorum quoquo pacto extrudere
atque exterminare. Nostrae prudentiae erit, qui Momi acerbitatem
atque furorem novimus, providere ne quid superiores pristinas ad
perturbationes addat, quo iterato et deorum quietem et res humanas vexet.

74   'Ea de re sic institui: consceleratissimum rerum perturbatorem
Momum, deorum hominumque odium, quod nihil sinceri, nihil
sani, nihil pacati, nihil tranquilli aut cogitet aut studeat aut cupiat;
quod felicium et beatorum beneque constitutorum res atque rationes collabefactare, profligare atque funditus pervertere elaboret as-
siduoque enitatur; quod miseros et immeritos aerumna calami-
tateque obruere ac penitus obterere, quoad in se sit, nusquam
desinat, nusquam acquiescat; quod factiosis, audacibus, nefariis

the great effort he made to persuade me, the pains he took to rush me into starting a new creation. But that wise saying has come back to me often: men who are abnormally clever will be abnormally dishonest. And in fact, as one may see, these men are not at all pure-minded and not at all sincere. They are different in fact and reality from how they seem in their faces and gestures. They abuse their distinguished and powerful intellects, perverting them so as to perform malicious acts. And when they study to seem honest and natural, that is when they are at their wickedest and most deceitful.

"Although in due course I came to realize that this was true of 73 Momus, I tolerated him as the amusing fellow he wished to be taken for, as someone who simulated his movements and words as though wearing a mask. I did this so that I could watch my cunning and deceitful confidant more closely and catch him out. In the meantime, I was wary of everything, I trusted nothing. But now, as it turns out, I think I have done you a favor, for you have taken that sower of woes and rebellion out of your midst. As I said, I'd rather not have riots and disturbances, but I did let Juno drive out and banish this wicked and loathsome individual from the heavenly ranks, however she chose to do so. It will be left to my own prudence, as one who knows Momus' bitterness and fury, to make sure that he does not add further upheavals to those he has already caused, and thus once again disturb the peace of the gods and human affairs.

"So I decree as follows: whereas Momus, the wickedest dis- 74 turber of the universe, an object of hatred to gods and men, neither plans nor desires nor wishes for any pure, sane, peaceful or tranquil state; whereas he works for and tries assiduously to achieve the corruption, overturning and utter destruction of the affairs and right order of happy, blessed and well-established individuals; whereas he never rests, if he can, in his efforts to oppress and completely crush the wretched and undeserving with hardship

omnique scelere perditis utatur et faveat; quod deterrimos instruat
in facinus, incitet atque impellat; quod dictis factisque pestem
atque perniciem orbi rerum in horas commachinetur atque impor-
tet, quodque in dies nefandae et detestabili improbitati suae multa
adaugere accumulareque minime intermittat;[144] ne superos deos lacessere deorumque delicias, homines, opprimere atque conficere
pro sua libidine et desiderio amplius possit, intra oceanum mari
mum fore relegandum et catenis ad cautem commendandum ita ut
praeter summum os reliquo haereat corpore undis immerso aeternum.'

75   Hic Iuno prope exhilarata gaudio, Iovem exosculata 'Fecisti' inquit 'ut decet, mi vir. Sed unum est quod addi velim, ut qui tam
petulanter, tam impudenter[145] et praeter id quod seque nosque deceat in feminarum genus invectus est, Momum, ex semiviro reddas
ut sit prorsus femina.' Annuit Iuppiter. Relegatum ea de re com-
mutilatumque Momum posthac caelicolae commutilato etiam nomine 'humum' nuncuparunt.

and calamity; whereas he employs and shows favor to the quarrelsome, the presumptuous, the criminal and those lost to every form of wickedness; whereas he sets up the worst sort of persons in crime, inciting and urging them on; whereas hour by hour he plans and inflicts pestilence and destruction upon the world by word and deed; and whereas day by day, he never stops increasing and heaping up wickedness and hateful treachery — because of all this, and to prevent his being able to do anything more, out of lust or desire, to attack the gods above or oppress men, the darlings of the gods, let him be banished to the nearer shore of Greatest Ocean, and let him be bound to a rock in chains in such a way that, except for the top of his head, the rest of his body may be submerged beneath the waves forever."[35]

Juno was filled with delight at this, and kissed Jupiter lovingly, 75 saying, "You've done what's right, my dear husband. But there is one thing that I'd like to add. Momus has criticized women so petulantly and so rudely, going far beyond the bounds of decency both for him and for us, that I'd like you to turn him from a half-man into a complete woman." Jupiter agreed. And for that reason, the gods always called the banished and mutilated Momus "humus," mutilating even his name.[36]

LIBER QUARTUS

1   Vide quod possit improbitas et nequitia, ut cum eius esse exstinctam vim ad laedendum credas, reviviscat. Plus enim relegatus atque ad cautem obstrictus Momus dabit perturbationum quam hactenus dederit solutus et concitatus. Nunc dignosces uti Momo facinorum auctore deorum maiestas extremum in periculum sit adducta; tum et tantum aderit iocorum et risus ut prae his superiora fuisse iocis vacua deputes.

2   Iam vero omnis hominum, ut ita loquar, torrentes in urbem confluxerant ludorum spectaculorumque gratia. Canebant tubae, subaudiebantur tibiae ad modosque cadebant[1] crotala[2] et sistra et litui et omnis musica. Ipsae deorum superum testudines maximo istarum rerum concentu resonabant. Addebantur iis hominum murmur latum atque ingens multorumque multiplices variaeque voces et huiusmodi; quo insolito atque immani sonitu cuncti caelicolae ad rei admirationem exciti stetere.

3   Interea Stupor deus, omnium ineptissimus, quod[3] sese Momum imitans in gratiam Iovis aliquo dicto ridiculo cuperet insinuare, ut erat suapte natura subattonitus atque vastus, ad Iovem properans agresti voce 'Pro,' inquit 'o rex, tantum hominum confremuit istic subtus, ut si omnes excories procul dubio totum caelum contegas.' Cui Iuppiter: 'Censen tu hunc tantisper sapere? Et quid tum, o Stupor? Et quid tibi venit in mentem? Sed tu perbelle quidem commentatus es. Namque ipse quod semper frigeas, caelum cavisti ne nudum algeat.'

4   Risere dii. Hinc locis omnibus quibus terras contui possent late passimque, ut cuiusque oculi atque aures ferebant, spectabundi haesitabant. Eccam patriciorum pompam et civium ordines matro-

274

BOOK IV

But see the power of wickedness, and how villainy revives itself, 1
just when you think its capacity for harm has been exhausted. For
Momus, banished and fastened to a rock, wreaked more havoc
than he had ever done when he enjoyed freedom of action. Now
you will learn how the majesty of the gods was brought into extreme danger through Momus' criminal agency. There will be so
many jokes and so much laughter that you will think the earlier
books were quite humorless by comparison.

An entire river of humanity, so to speak, flowed into the city 2
to enjoy the games and spectacles. Trumpets blared, flutes were
dimly heard, castanets, rattles, cornets and all other instruments
sounded rhythmically. Even the lyres of the holy gods echoed to
this mighty harmony. A vast hubbub of people, the numerous and
varied voices of the throng, accompanied the music, so that the
sky-dwellers stood still, stirred with wonderment at the strange
and tremendous noise.

The god Stupor,[1] silliest of the gods, wanted to worm his way 3
into Jupiter's good graces with wit, in imitation of Momus, although by nature Stupor was thick-witted and oafish. He ran to
Jupiter and in his yokel's voice said, "Ho, King, there are so many
humans roaring together down there that if you tore their hides
off, you'd be able to cover the whole of heaven!" — "Since when do
you think you're a man of wisdom?" replied Jupiter. "What's next,
Stupor, what will you think of next? You've come up with a great
idea. As you're always cold yourself, you're taking precautions so
that the naked sky won't freeze over."

The gods laughed. They were lingering in every place from 4
which they could get a wide view of the earth, watching as eagerly

narumque deinceps nurumque greges cum sacris lustrare urbem:
aggreditur taeda et multa lampade noctem illustrem reddunt. Vir-
gines porticibus conspicuae urbem ornant atque carminibus can-
tuque ad saltum et thyrsum deos venerantur. Tantas res superi in-
tuentes obmutuerant atque uti quisque se receperat loco pendebat
maxime intentus, maxime stupidus.

5   Interea pro vetere more, quod quidem in Promethei calamitate
iam pridem factitarunt,[1] dii praesertim maritimi ad Momum consalutandum abque[5] animi miseria levandum plerique accesserant:
Naiades, Napaeae,[6] Dryades, Phorcaeque atque huiusmodi. At
Momus flammulas summo aethere deorum cervicibus colluce-
scentes, sublatis oculis quos fletu et lacrimis prope[7] consumpserat,
despicatus, quid sibi tanta repente oborta[8] caelo lumina peterent
rogavit. Cumque rem intellexisset,[9] tanti spectaculi invidia commotus, perquam longissimum imo ab pectore suspirium inter inge-
miscendum emisit, quo ex spiritus anhelitu fusca et atra nebula-
rum vis totum per aethera sublime astitit.

6   Qua visa, Momus[10] illico animum atque ingenium ut aliquid
pro sua consuetudine mali faceret contulit[11] atque adeo institit
precari eos deos qui aderant, quoad impetravit ab iis quae ad se
consalutandum accesserant nymphis ut,[12] quando aliud nequeant
suam ad salutem conferre, hoc unum ad levandas miserias gratissi-
mum beneficium condonent: nebulam ipsam quam valde possint
late distentam protrahant et producant montiumque cacuminibus
annectant, quo tam[13] inimicissimis[14] et pessime de se meritis superis voluptuosissimum suarum aerumnarum spectaculum interci-
piatur.

7   Calamitosi Momi precibus obtemperarunt nymphae pluri-
mumque in eo opere perficiundo laborantes desudarunt. Quo factum est ut cum delubra deum sacellaque atque aras adeuntes

as their eyes and ears would allow. Behold the procession of the patricians, the citizens in their orders, then flocks of matrons and young women, purifying the city with sacred rites! Torches of pinewood are brought forward, and the night is lit up with innumerable lamps. The most attractive maidens adorn the gates and honor the gods in bacchic dances, with song and music. The gods, watching these extraordinary events from their several coigns of vantage, had fallen silent, utterly absorbed, utterly dumbfounded.

Meanwhile, many deities, principally those of the sea, approached Momus to greet him and lighten the wretchedness of his spirit, in accordance with the custom they had long practiced in the case of Prometheus' calamity: there were Naiads, woodland nymphs, Dryads, sea goddesses, and other divinities of this kind.[2] Momus lifted his eyes, nearly consumed with weeping and tears, and saw the flamelets glimmering on the heads of the gods in lofty heaven. He asked them what so many lights, suddenly appearing in heaven, portended. When he heard the reason, he was stirred to envy by the great spectacle and amid his groanings let out a long, long sigh from deep within his breast, and the black and cloudy vapor from his exhalation covered the whole sky.

Seeing this, Momus immediately brought his mind to bear on causing some of his usual damage. He made an urgent plea to the sea gods that he might beg one most gracious favor to lighten his woes from the nymphs who had come to soothe him, since they could do nothing to save him. He would like them to spread out and expand that swollen cloud as widely as they could and fasten it to the peaks of the mountains, so that it would hide the highly enjoyable spectacle of his suffering from those gods who hated and had so mistreated him.

The nymphs obeyed the wretched Momus' entreaties and sweated mightily to accomplish the task. Thus it came to pass that, with the clouds blocking their view, the gods could not see the mortals going to the divine shrines, chapels and altars, but

mortales non perspici a superis nubium interventu sed solum audiri possent, superi sese in periculum dederint. Namque quod[15]
suas quidem laudes ad tibiam concinentes non audire modo, verum inprimis spectare quoque cuperent, quasi amentes e caelo
ad sua gaudia propius haurienda delabi instituerunt. Mortalium
ergo[16] tecta occupavere.

8 Solus Hercules, quod fortassis invidorum aemulorumque insidias reditusque difficultatem ad superas sedes vereretur, negavit
aut deorum maiestati convenire aut fieri id tuto posse, ut intra
mortalium coetus superi conscenderent et commiscerentur. Se
enim monstra terrarum immanissima et truculentissima prostravisse, subegisse, absumpsisse, hominum vero plurimorum impetum et temeritatem consentientem ne ferre quidem uspiam potuisse: facile[17] moveri et esse quidem opinionibus fluidam, animis
volubilem, libidinibus concitatam multitudinem;[18] facile impelli ad
quodvis facinus, neque apud multitudinem cogitari fasne sit an nefas id quod plurimorum consensus appetat; efferri indomitam et
ruere effrenatam; neque revocari, neque retineri, neque satis coerceri ullis prudentium monitis et rationibus aut bene consulentium
imperio posse; neque scire quidem vesanam multitudinem nolle
quod ad arbitrium possit, ac quae vero occeperit,[19] flagitiosa et
turpiane an non ea[20] sint non curare, modo perficiat; et atrocia
non intermittere ni prius aliud quippiam atrocius incoharit. Et
quod magis miretur, in hominum numero sapere quidem per se
ferme[21] singulos atque nosse quid rectum sit; cum tamen coiverint,
omnes simul facile insanire sponteque delirare.

9 Haec Hercules, sed dii spreto Hercule in theatrum ingressi,
atque inprimis Iuppiter pario ex marmore ingentes innumerasque
columnas, maximorum montium frustra,[22] gigantum opus, admiratur et tantas numero et tam vastas et in eam regionem locorum

could only hear them, and so the gods exposed themselves to danger. They craved not only hearing their own praises sung to the music of the flute, but especially watching the spectacle, so like lunatics they started to slip down from heaven so as to enjoy their pleasures at closer range. They took possession of the mortals' dwellings.

Hercules alone, perhaps because he was worried about the plots   8
of his enemies and rivals as well as the difficulty of returning to his celestial seat, said that gods descending and mingling in a crowd of humans suited neither the majesty nor the security of the divine race. He said that he had flattened, tamed and crushed the most gigantic and ferocious monsters on earth, but he had never been able to bear the violence and concerted recklessness of a human crowd. A mob is easily swayed, fluid in its opinions, changeable in its intentions, stirred up by its passions; it is easily driven to all kinds of crime, and cannot be made to consider whether the appetites of the majority are right or wrong; it is carried along untamed, rushes forward unbridled; it cannot be recalled nor restrained, and neither the rational suasion of the wise nor the commands of the right-thinking can control it. A demented mob doesn't want to know anything that doesn't suit its own pleasure, and doesn't care whether what it undertakes is pernicious and base, so long as it can have its way. It won't stop committing atrocities except to commit still worse atrocities. The amazing thing about mortals was that, as individuals, they were almost all wise and aware of what was right; but when they formed themselves into a group, they fell into a frenzied rage and spontaneously behaved like madmen.

So Hercules advised, but the gods ignored him and went into   9
the theater. Jupiter particularly admired the innumerable large columns of Parian marble—pieces carved from great mountains, a gigantic labor. The columns were so numerous and so vast that he was at a loss to imagine how they had been dragged there and

aut tractas esse aut erectas obstupescebat intuens, easque tametsi coram intueretur tamen fieri negabat posse tantum opus, et prae admiratione et vidisse et laudasse plus satis non intermittebat. Atque secum ipse suas ineptias accusabat consiliique tarditatem deplorabat, qui hos tales tam mirifici operis architectos non adivisset potius quam philosophos, quibus uteretur ad operis futuri descriptionem componendam. Evenisse quidem quod aiunt, ut quem semel sapere aliqua in re ubi ipse persuaseris, hunc semper sapere[23] et in omni re doctum esse facile credas. Haec Iuppiter.

10   Tandem lustrata urbe hominum turmae sua per deversoria corpori se cenisque dederant. Quae cum ita essent, incidit in mentem diis ut futuros postridie mane ludos scaenamque cuperent inspectare. 'Ergo, et quid agimus?' inquiunt inter se. 'Num ad nostras redibimus[24] sedes, an istic spectaculis visendis considebimus?' Spectaculorum erant omnes cupientissimi, sed alii alibi, aut caelo, aut templis pernoctandum statuebant. Postremo placuit sententia illius qui deorum quodam, ut opinor, fato admonuit uti se quisque in suum quod in theatro esset simulacrum converteret, quo abeundi redeundique viam et laborem vitarent quove cum dignitate et sine ullius iniuria dignissimis locis conquiescerent.[25]

11   Unum erat quod huic sententiae adversaretur: nam parum quidem occurrebat ubi locorum illinc abreptas statuas apte deponerent. Dum haec animis deorum volvuntur, Stupor deus, ut erat artubus torisque praepotens, rem se dignam aggreditur; nullis id quod paret indicans, atque se in pedes conicit ita vaste, ita dissolute, ut subito furore efferri bacchantem diceres, facinusque ipsum aggreditur alioquin ridiculum, sed pro re agenda eiusmodi ut fa-

erected. Although he saw them with his own eyes, he still said that such work was impossible. Full of wonder, he could not stop looking at them and praising them extravagantly. He cursed his own stupidity and deplored his lack of foresight in having consulted the philosophers rather than the architects of this stupendous work. He should have gotten the architects to draw up a plan of the intended project. It was just as people say: when you persuade yourself that someone knows something, you can easily convince yourself that they always know everything about everything. Such were Jupiter's thoughts.

At last, when the city had been ritually purified, the throngs of 10 humans devoted themselves to the refreshment of their bodies in their lodging-places. This being the case, the gods realized that they yearned to inspect the games and the spectacle which would take place early the next day. "What should we do, then?" they said to each other. "Should we return to our homes, or should we take our seats here to see the spectacle?" Everyone was longing to see the spectacles, but some proposed spending the night elsewhere, either in heaven, or in their temples. In the end one god's idea prevailed, to the ruin of the gods, in my view. He advised everyone to turn themselves into the likenesses of themselves which stood in the theater, so as to avoid the bother of coming and going, and so that they might rest comfortably in the best places, with dignity and without any injustice to others.[3]

There was one problem with this suggestion: they did not 11 know a convenient place to put the statues that they had taken from their niches. While the gods were mulling this over, the god Stupor, mighty in chest and limb, attempted something worthy of him. Not telling anyone of his plan, he suddenly took off so uncouthly, so wildly, that you would think he had been seized by sudden madness and was raving like a worshipper of Bacchus. He attempted something which would normally be thought ludicrous, but which under the circumstances the rest of the gods approved

ctum subinde omnes reliqui comprobantes imitati sint. Ad statuam enim in theatro positam sui similem applicans, hos atque
hos validiores deorum uti se adiuvent voce illa sua agresti advocat.
Mox subiectis scapulis illa se onerat. Erat autem statua ampla et
ponderis immanis,[26] tamen susceptam dorso solus asportavit[27] et
eam intra opacam silvam reposto in antro, obscuro loco, collocat.
Inde in theatrum sudore madidus rediens se vertit[28] in statuam
quam asportarat statuaeque[29] vacuum locum occupat. Id ipsum ceteri tametsi factum irriderent, sibi tamen faciundum[30] putarunt.
Itaque fecere, Stuporis exemplo, suam quisque quo visum est loco
statuam abdidere,[31] neque defuere Cupido, Mercurius et huiusmodi talarium alarumque adminiculis freti, qui extremo theatri
fastigio prostratas reliquerint.

12   Dum se sic[32] dii in theatrum dispositi ex animi libidine habe-
rent, res omnium ridicula, sed memoratu dignissima cum in silva
ad Stuporis statuam, tum et in theatro excidit. Nam in silva quidam[33] Oenops, philosophus idemque histrio, vetere illa Momi
contra deos disputandi flagitiosissima petulantia imbutus, dum
ad ludos concelebrandos properaret a praedonibus captus exstitit
multisque affectus plagis adducitur ad ipsam hanc specum in qua
statua Stuporis dei erat exposita.

13   Quo cum appulissent, praedones consilium ineunt praestetne
captum iugulare an vivum dimittere oculis effossis. At Oenops,
tanto in periculo constitutus, etsi in eam diem nullos deos, inane
caelum esse crediderat et praedicarat, nunc tamen ultimo in capitis
periculo constitutus seque salutemque suam coepit omnibus votis
commendare maximis diis.

14   Sed[34] consilio inter se habito praedonibus placuit habere quae-
stionem de homine et discere quanti se possit redimere. Erat nox

and copied. Stupor stood next to his own likeness in the theater, and shouted out in his yokel's voice for one or another of the strongest gods to help him. Bending his shoulders, he heaved the statue onto his back. The statue was large and enormously heavy, but on his own he carried it off and placed it in a hidden cave, a dark place in the midst of a shadowy wood. Dripping with sweat, he returned to the theater, turned himself into the statue he had carried off, and filled the empty place the statue had left. Although the others laughed at what he had done, they still reckoned they should do it too, so they followed Stupor's example. Each god hid his statue in a likely place. Cupid, Mercury, and other gods like them who could rely on their little helpers — their winged sandals and wings — did not hesitate to leave their statues lying flat on the topmost pediment of the theater.

While the gods arranged themselves in the theater as the whim   12
took them, a ridiculous thing, but one well worth mentioning, happened in the woods near the statue of Stupor and later in the theater. In the wood was a certain Oenops,[4] a philosopher and actor, who was imbued with Momus' inveterate and disgraceful impudence in disputing against the gods. When Oenops was hurrying off to celebrate the games, some robbers stopped him and took him prisoner.[5] They beat him severely, then took him to the very cave where the statue of Stupor had been placed.

When they had dragged him there, the robbers began to dis-   13
cuss whether it would be better to slit the prisoner's throat or send him away alive with his eyes gouged out. Oenops was placed in great danger, and although up until that day he had believed and proclaimed that there were no gods and that heaven was a void, being now in mortal peril he began to recommend himself and his safety to the greatest gods, using every conceivable prayer.

But the robbers, having finished their council, agreed that it   14
would be best to interrogate the man and learn how much they could get for his ransom. It was a dark and stormy night, so the

atra et intempesta: expediunt idcirco praedones quae ad cruciatum
faciant. Alii lorum comparant, alii virgas ulmo avellunt, alii ignem
cote excutiunt. Illis ita occupatis res evenit digna memoratu. Nam
primis igniculorum favillis collucescentibus videre visi sunt praedones in antrum quippiam, et quidvis id quam statuam eiusmodi
in loco adesse poterant opinari; dehinc maioribus admotis luminibus manifesto adesse deos animadvertentes obmutuerunt, et ea re
insperata perterrefacti e vestigio non sine clamore relicto captivo
abvolarunt.

15   Vidisses hos amissis armis quasi temulentos obiectam ornum
fugiendo impetere, alios inter cursitandum offensa roboris stirpe
ruere atque alios offensis prostratis sociis istuc versus et[35] illuc versus praecipites ruere, eosdemque illiso ore inter surgendum in-
terque spuendum cum cruore defractos dentes iterato sequentium
impetu quassatos ruere; alios vero,[36] viso deo, quasi alteram Stuporis statuam factos primum haerescere, mox formidine debilitatos
labascere.

16   Quae rerum et temporum suorum facies cum ita esset, non defuit sibi Oenops. Egressus enim antrum et turbam concussorum
profligatorumque contuens sese confirmavit. Inde, rapto de quodam telo, unum egregie stupentem excordemque factum metu per
capillum prehendit, prosternit revincitque loro quo se praedones
illi vincire[37] coeperant. Mox hominem prae se in urbem agit laetus
et animo secum adiurans nihil minus credendum posthac quam
nullos esse deos quos tam praesentes extremo suo in periculo com-
pererit.

17   Itaque haec in silvis Oenops. In theatrum vero ingressus, suos
colludiones qui se exspectabant offendit de se deque diis mereri
non bene, nam supersedentis tarditatem una et deos maximos

robbers prepared instruments to torture him. Some got leather thongs ready, others tore switches from an elm-tree, and others struck fire from flint. While they were thus occupied, something happened that is well worth recounting. When the first sparks of fire began to glow, the robbers thought they saw something in the cave. They could not imagine anything like a statue being in a place like that, so they brought up bigger torches. Seeing that gods were manifestly present, they were struck dumb; utterly terrified by this unexpected discovery, they abandoned their prisoner and flew away immediately, making a great racket.

You should have seen those men — flinging aside their weapons, behaving like drunkards, colliding with an ash-tree that stood in their way as they fled. Some tripped over tree roots as they ran away, others then stumbled over their fallen companions as they rushed headlong here and there, and when they got up, their heads injured, spitting out blood along with broken teeth, those rushing up behind them crashed into them. Others, however, having seen the god, first froze — looking like another statue of Stupor — and then fainted away from fright.

In such circumstances, Oenops rose to the occasion. He left the cave and, seeing the group of shaken and defeated men, recovered his strength. He snatched someone's weapon, seized by the hair one of the men, who was utterly bewildered and senseless with fear, threw him down and bound him with the very thong those robbers had begun to use on himself. Gleefully, Oenops soon drove the man back into the city in front of him. He swore to himself that from now on nothing was less credible than the non-existence of the gods, since he had found them to be so helpful in his moment of extreme danger.

These were Oenops' words in the woods. When he got to the theater, however, he met his fellow actors who were waiting for him, ready to abuse both him and the gods. They cursed both Oenops' unpunctuality and the fact that the great gods had kept

285

quorum causa vigilarent exsecrabantur. Id sibi primum visum est indignissimum, sed illud indignius, quod inter histriones servum quendam vino madidum ad Iovis statuam pleraque nefanda exsequentem offendit. (Pudet ea dicere: tamen institutum prosequemur.) Immingentem ebrium intuens, Oenops pro nova suscepta religione coepit gravissimis dictis increpando absterrere. At servus in eum versus 'Eia' inquit 'philosophe, adesne? Sicine mecum agis? Unde in te nova istaec repente religio incessit? Qui deos aeternum negasti, frigentem hic statuam fictaque simulacra veneraberis?'[38]

18   Haecque referens non imminxisse modo erat contentus, verum et alvi praeterea illic onus ponere parabatur. Hic Oenops 'O' inquit 'sceleste, non tu denique alium tibi locum ad tantam flagitii spurcitatem desumes?' Tum barbarus et ebrius ille servus 'Vos' inquit 'philosophi omnia esse deorum plena consuestis dicere.' 'At' inquit Oenops 'etiam praesentis deos irridens neglegis?' Tum barbarus 'En' inquit 'perdoctum philosophum! Deumne tu hoc frigens et vacuum simulacrum aut opinaris aut nuncupas, quod quidem vix igne et ferro adhibito fabri effecere ut vultus hominis potius quam monstri faciem imitaretur? Dic,[39] heus tu, o aeneum caput, quanto malleo, quantis follibus durum tuum istud os dolarunt fabri! Vel tu, Oenops, num simulacrum hoc vidisti ad publicum aquaeductum pridie patera istac calonibus aquam fundere? Demum[40] inutile istud aes, cui nihil invenias quod probes praeter artificis manum, Iovis instar venerabimur?[41] Est nimirum illud perpulchre dictum quod in cavea saepius decantari audio:

Qui fingit sacros auro[42] vel marmore vultus,
    non facit ille deos: qui rogat ille facit.'

them awake. This seemed most unworthy to Oenops, but it was even more unworthy to encounter among the actors a certain wine-soaked slave who was performing a number of vile acts near the statue of Jupiter. (It makes one blush to say it, but we have to follow the plot.) Oenops saw that the drunken man was urinating. Inspired by his new-found piety, he tried to scare him with threats. But the slave turned to him and said, "Hey there, philosopher, is that you? Why are you treating me this way? Where has this new religion of yours suddenly come from? You, a man who has always denied the existence of gods — are you now going to worship a lifeless statue and imaginary likenesses?"

The slave stopped speaking, and, dissatisfied with mere pissing, 18 he prepared to empty his bowels on the statue. — "Oh, you scoundrel!" cried Oenops, "choose another place for your filthy act!" — "You philosophers are always saying that everything is full of gods,"[6] replied the uncouth and drunken slave. — "What? Do you mock the gods and ignore them even when you are in their presence?" cried Oenops. — "What a brilliant philosopher you are!" said the uncouth fellow. "Would you call this lifeless and empty image a god, when craftsmen have barely been able, with fire and iron, to make it resemble a human being and not a monster? Hey, tell me, you bronze-headed fool, how many hammers and bellows the craftsmen used to fashion that brazen face of yours! Didn't you see his like the day before, Oenops, ladling out water for servants at the public aqueduct? Should we worship that useless bronze as the likeness of Jupiter, even though you'll find nothing to admire in it apart from the skill of the craftsman? That saying I've heard often recited in the theater is indeed wonderfully phrased:

> The man who shapes gods' faces out of marble or of gold
> Does not himself make gods; it's the one to whom it's sold."[7]

19 Tum Oenops et facti indignitate et dictorum petulantia commotus, 'Malam' inquit 'tuam in rem! Num desines de his tuis sceleribus cantando disputare? Apage te hinc!' At barbarus, dum se
Oenops iugulo apprehensum traheret, alvi afflatu perobscene con-
crepuit atque 'Apage tu' inquit 'te, profane, dum sacrum facio, o
interturbator! Num tu non perspicis quam hunc adolendi ritum
comprobent hi?' En iterum intonuit. Non potuit hoc amplius Oenops ferre, sed ebrium pugnis calceoque contusum suos intra foeto-
res[43] obvolvit atque gradibus praecipitavit. At multatus ebrius ore
illo suo liventi et male illibuto impudicissime plorans, 'Ego tibi,
quisquis es deorum,' inquit 'cuius causa haec pertuli, ut eveniant
aeque atque mihi evenere imprecor, quandoquidem hunc qui ullos
esse deos semper negavit, quod se imitarer tua causa tam impie in
me grassatus[44] exstitit.'

20 Iuppiter haec intuens intra se rem sic deputabat: 'Credin me
hoc noctis bene acceptum? Tametsi hic suo utitur officio: quid
aliud aut ebrius faciat, aut ab improbo audias? Adde quod probe
multatus luit: plus enim cruoris effudit quam ingurgitarit vini.
Quid quod ne tanti quidem haec sunt ut ludorum voluptatem re-
spuas? Sint histriones obsceni ut libet, modo nos in theatrum esse
nulli noscant. Sed quid agimus? Quid si praesenserint? Neque
enim illud factum frustra opinor, quod[45] praesentes esse deos philosophus ipse Oenops dixerit. Verum et quid demum, quid tum?
Utcumque ceciderit res, tamen praesente populo venerabimur.'

21 Haec cum effecisset Oenops, rogantibus[46] sociis quid ita religa-
tum adduxisset hominem et quid se praeter spem et exspectationem omnium ad religionis sanctimoniam dedisset, qui antea
nullos credidisset esse deos, ordine quaeque sibi apud praedones
accidissent recitavit. Sed ne satis quidem eum sibi notum esse[47]
deum auxiliatorem dixit, quo propitio rem tam fauste atque felici-

Oenops was angered by the slave's irreverent deed and insolent   19
words. "Go to hell!" he said. "Don't try to justify your crimes by
uttering such rubbish! Get out of here!" As Oenops grabbed him
by the throat and pulled him away, the uncouth fellow broke wind
with a thoroughly revolting noise and said, "*You* get out of here,
you blasphemer, you interloper! I'm performing a sacred rite!
Don't you know how much the gods like the smell of burnt
offerings?" And again he farted. Oenops, unable to bear this any
longer, beat the drunk with his fists and feet, rolled him in his
own excrement and threw him headlong down the steps. The
drunk, punished with a bruised and swollen face, wept shamelessly. "Whichever of you gods made me suffer this," he said, "I
pray that the same thing may happen to you as happened to me. A
man who always denied the existence of gods impiously beat me
up for your sake, because I was imitating him."

Jupiter, when he saw this, mulled the matter over. "Did I really   20
think that I would be welcome tonight? But still, the man was
only doing his job—what else would a drunk do, what do you expect to hear from a blasphemer? He's fully paid the penalty, and
he's spilt more blood than he's drunk wine. Are these incidents
important enough for you to forego the enjoyment the games will
afford? Let actors be disgusting if they like, so long as no one
knows we are in the theater. But what shall we do if they find out?
It was no accident, I think, that the philosopher Oenops said that
gods were present. But what will happen in the end, what will
happen next? However things turn out, we shall be honored by
the presence of the people."

After Oenops had punished the drunk, his companions asked   21
him why he had brought a man tied up like that, and why he, a
man who had previously not believed in any gods, had so unexpectedly devoted himself to pious acts. Oenops told them the
story of what had happened to him with the robbers. He said that
he hadn't taken a close enough look at the god who had helped

ter exsecutus sit, et idcirco magis atque magis cupere[48] sibi fieri cognitum cui habendae forent gratiae tanti beneficii. Non illum quidem sibi visum Iovem, non Phoebum, non Iunonem, non ex his celeberrimis et popularibus quibus templa constituta sunt, sed rarum illum quidem atque insolitum. Hic histriones 'At sunt quidem' inquiunt 'in theatro deorum omnium simulacra: ehodum,[49] revise omnes, ut facilem et beneficum cum salutarimus, tum eundem patronum nostris in malis auxilio advocemus.[50] Nam maiores illi dii iam tum fastidire humilium vota assueverunt.'

22   Itaque fit. Face igitur incensa circum statuas signaque omnia recensendo, dum horum atque horum vultus contemplantur, in Stuporem ipsum incidunt. Quo viso, Oenops venerabundus procidit eiusque pacem precatus locumque amplexatus adoravit. Viso Stuporis vultu et habitu, risere histriones taetram illius deformitatem. Nam stabat ille quidem ore late anhelanti, labio propendulo, oculis concretis, temporibus[51] lacunosis, auribus appensis, et omni denique facie ita affectus ut sui oblitus videretur. Cumque accuratius hunc ipsum deum respectarent proscaenici socii, eo maiores in cachinnos efferebantur atque 'En' dicebant 'strenuum, en fugatorem latronum!' Ergo Oenops 'Enimvero istuc quidem est' inquit 'quod in me susceptam deorum opinionem multo confirmet, ubi unus multos, inermis armatos, metuculosus audaces ad omnemque crudelitatem accinctos sola praesentia exturbarit atque profligarit.'

23   Haec de se coram Stupor deus audiens, etsi mente esset bardus et ingenio prorsus plumbeo, tamen neque laudibus non movebatur neque vituperatoribus non[52] irritabatur. Tamen sic secum rerum humanarum sortem atque conditionem versabat: 'Et quidnam hoc esse mali dicam apud mortales, ut praesentem deum irrideant, ab-

him, by whose favor things had turned out so luckily and happily for him. He yearned more and more to know whom he should thank for such kindness. It was apparently not Jupiter, Apollo, Juno, or any of those famous and popular gods for whom temples were built, but a rare and unusual deity. "But there are likenesses of all the gods in the theater," said the actors. "Here, have a look at them all, so we can salute this affable benevolent god, and invoke him as a patron to help us in our adversities. The more important gods usually turn up their noses at offerings from the lowly."

And that is what they did. Lighting a torch, they examined the statues and all their attributes, looking into the faces of each one. Finally they came to Stupor himself. When Oenops saw him, he fell on his knees to venerate him, prayed for his grace, kissed the ground, and started to worship him. When the actors saw Stupor's face and clothes, they began to laugh at his horrible ugliness. Stupor stood with his mouth gaping wide open, his lip jutting out, his eyes squinting, his temples sunken, his ears hanging down — in short, the whole set of his face seemed that of someone who was unconscious. The more closely the thespian companions inspected this god, the more they were convulsed with laughter. "Behold this doughty god!" they cried. "Behold the router of thieves!" So Oenops said, "Yes, here's the one that has strongly confirmed my new belief in the gods. Alone against many men, unarmed against the armed, calm in the face of the rash, by his mere presence he drove away and put to flight a gang which was ready for every kind of cruelty."

When he heard this, the god Stupor, although unimaginative and heavy-witted, was nevertheless moved by the praise and irritated by those who had abused him. He reflected thus on the lot and condition of mortals. "What can I say about this evil among mortals? They mock a god who's right in front of them, while they fear and dread the likeness of an absent deity! This one fellow, on the mere suspicion of a divine blessing, blotted out both his long-

22

23

sentis simulacrum vereantur atque pertimescant? Hic beneficii
suspicione ductus inveteratam contra deos opinionem opinio-
nisque pervicaciam obliteravit; hi sole, luna et istiusmodi manife-
stis deorum signis admoniti, quae se posse debereque credere
profitentur, infitiantur. Meum potuit aeneum simulacrum profano
in loco immanes et ferocissimos latrones a crudelitate absterrere,
metu deorum flectere, ad religionis cultum revocare; ipse deus et
praesens qui sum studiosos artium quae ad pietatem faciant et
gratificandis diis deditos nequeo modestiores reddere.[53] Aut quo
pacto istos ab impietate, si esse in nos impii prosequantur, revoca-
bimus?' Haec secum Stupor.

24   Oenops vero, cum satis esset veneratus fautorem deum, spectans non poterat pati tam neglectum esse hunc a quo beneficium
accepisset; idcirco rubiginem qua Stuporis facies admodum squa-
lebat ferro coepit abradere. Stupor vero deus abradentis molestiam
libenter abegisset ab se sed, ingenio tardus, quo id pacto posset
non habebat. Alia ex parte hominem quamvis inepte gratificantem
ferendum ducebat, rictu tamen oris interdum duriter abradentis
ferrum subterfugiebat. Hunc dii, illius memores dicti, qui ex hominum corio contegi posse caelum asseruerat,[54] risissent cum ab
homunculo prope excoriari intuerentur, sed eadem sibi durioraque
iam tum fieri ab hominibus posse intellegentes, magis ut proprium
periculum metuerent propensi erant quam ut alienam insulsitatem
riderent, et multa quidem ex parte se omnes aeque gravi fore nota-
tos rubigine non negabant.

25   Itaque haec in theatro. Quae scio videri posse iis qui nostris
opusculis legendis delectentur si non admodum, alioquin scurrilia,
at nostris ab moribus et scribendi legibus aliena, qui quidem semper et factis et dictis cavimus ne quid minus grave et sanctum ado-

standing disbelief in the gods and the obstinacy of his disbelief. These other men, though reminded by the sun, the moon, and similar manifest signs of divinity which they profess they can and ought to believe in, refuse to acknowledge them. My bronze likeness in a profane place scared off savage, vicious robbers from an act of cruelty, moved them with fear of the gods and converted someone to piety and worship; yet as a real and present god right here, I can't make men devoted to the arts (which are a source of religious feeling) behave more decently or act in ways pleasing to the gods. How shall I turn these men from impious acts if they continue to be impious towards me personally?" Thus meditated Stupor.

Oenops, when he had sufficiently worshipped his divine protec-   24
tor, could not bear to see how neglected his benefactor had become. He began to scrape away with a piece of iron the rust that completely marred Stupor's face. The god Stupor would gladly have done without the irritation of being scraped, but being slow-witted, he did not know how to. Besides, he thought he should endure the efforts, however inept, this human was making to please him. Every now and then, though, he flinched to avoid the hard iron scraper. The gods, remembering what Stupor had said about the sky being covered in human skin, laughed when they saw him being almost skinned by the little man. But when they realized that humans were capable of doing the same things — and even harsher things — to themselves, they were more inclined to fear for their own peril than to laugh at the stupidity of another. They mostly could not deny that they, too, were laden with thick rust.

All this took place in the theater. I know that, to those who en-   25
joy reading our little books, this circumstance may seem alien to my literary principles, if not positively vulgar, and I have always avoided in word and deed tackling subjects that were less grave and sacred than my literary conscience and piety would allow. But

riremur quam litterarum religio et religionis cultus pateretur. Sed si pensitaris quid conati simus cum totis libellis, tum hoc loco exprimere, intelleges profecto principes voluptati deditos incidere in opprobria longe iis graviora quam quae recensuimus. Eaque de re nos velim magis secutos initam institutionem iudices quam pristinam studiorum et vitae rationem. Sed plura fortassis diximus quam volebamus, pauciora profecto diximus quam postulaverit res. Verum de his hactenus: ad rem redeo.

26 Huiusmodi in theatrum[55] cum agerentur, novae item apud inferos rerum iucundissimarum et inprimis dignissimarum historiae initae sunt. Namque audierat Charon crebris defunctorum rumoribus proximum fore ut omnis mundus vastaretur, iamque coepisse Parcas et Hispides populare hominum familias, omnia consenescere tristitia et contabescere instantis ruinae periculo et metu. Eo Charon adeo priusquam opus tantum tamque ornatissimum deleretur instituerat hunc videre mundum, quem vidisset numquam visurusque postea esset numquam.

27 Sed tantae peregrinationis viam, ut puta ab inferis ad superos usque mortales, arduam esse audierat et paucissimis aut cognitam aut concessam non ignorabat. Idcirco inire temere non audebat, et ex omni defunctorum multitudine reperiebat neminem qui ullo abduci pacto posset ut non recusaret eo redire unde solutus taetro corporis carcere libens atque volens profugisset: eamque ad rem dehortandam mortalium aerumnas multa ex parte explicabant[56] et viventium mala[57] cum defunctorum libertate comparabant. Postremo affirmabant praestare quidvis malorum perpeti quam redire ad hominum vexationes obeundas.

28 Aderat fortassis inter defunctos Gelastus quidam philosophus alioquin non vulgaris, quem tamen Charon diutius neglexerat non aliam ob rem nisi quod, extrema egestate mortuus, non attulerat

if you think again of what I'm trying to express in all these books and in this passage specifically, you'll surely realize that princes who are devoted to pleasure commit far more disgraceful acts than any we've recounted. For that reason, I would have you judge me as someone who is following the logic of a given plot rather than some antique standard of life and learning. But perhaps we've said more than we wished, and we've surely said less than the circumstances demanded. Enough of this; I'll get back to the story.

While this was taking place in the theater, a new and delightful   26
adventure, and one particularly worth telling, was beginning in the underworld. Charon[8] had heard frequent rumors from the underworld that the whole world would soon be destroyed. The Fates and the Shaggy Ones[9] had already started to ravage the families of humans. Everything was grim and withered, and people were wasting away, beset by danger and the fear of imminent ruin. So Charon decided to see the world before such a great and exquisitely beautiful work was destroyed, for he had never seen it and would never be able to see it afterwards.

He had heard, however, that the route of this long journey,   27
namely, from the underworld to the mortals above, was tricky. He realized that only a few knew the route or were allowed to take it. He dared not set out rashly, and out of the entire crowd of dead souls he found no one he could convince on any account to travel with him. They all refused to go back to the place whence they had fled so happily and freely, released from the foul prison of their bodies. To discourage him, they listed at great length the hardships of the mortals and compared the woes of the living with the freedom of the dead. In the end, they declared that they would prefer to suffer any evil rather than return to face again the distresses of mankind.

Among the dead there chanced to be a certain Gelastus,[10] a   28
philosopher who was anything but ordinary. Charon had ignored him for a long time, simply because, having died in extreme pov-

quo portorium persolveret. Cum eo igitur paciscitur Charon, si se prius comitem apud mortales viaeque praemonstratorem praestet, gratis transvecturum.[58] Suscipit Gelastus id muneris tametsi invitus viaeque inscius. Sed quid ageret miser, cum solvendo non esset? An eo in loco aeternum consideret quo neque inter vivos neque inter mortuos censeretur? Nimirum ergo omnia et nota et ignota, dura acerbaque aggredi cogebatur, idque maxime cum neque ex amicis neque ex ditissimis quidem quispiam appellebat,[59] a quo daretur ut stipem mutuo rogaret: defunctorum enim nemini plus nummo uno ad portorii mercedem asportare a mortalibus umquam licuit.

29   Itaque Charon, dum ad iter accingitur, subducta navi multum ac diu cogitavit conferatne hanc alibi apud inferos relinquere. Tandem, quod ita praestare arbitrabatur, navim reversam sustulit suoque imposuit capiti ut staret quasi pusillo mapalio opertus, manuque remum collibrans graditur. Arduum et praeter aetatem firmissimum senem proficiscentem turbae demirabantur.

30   Verum illi inter pergendum in sermones incidere istiusmodi, ut quaereret Gelastus de Charonte quid ita navim portaret aut quidni praestitisset eam in litore subductam sinere. Cui Charon 'Et quid' inquit 'tibi defunctorum ineptias referam? Nemo est illorum quin me suis velit imperiis navigare. Quin et fuit pridie Polyphagus nescio quis, qui quidem rapto remo se pro argonauta gereret. Illum ego "Et quis tu?" inquam. "Classiumne fuisti fortassis praefectus in vita?" "At" inquit ille "nostra in familia olim fuere plures remiges." Ego illius insolentiam non tam admiratus quam ineptias risi, cum viderem tam impudenter et temere id[60] profiteri et aggredi cui esset rei[61] minime aptus. At ex comitibus defuncti unus "Mentitur" inquit "o Charon, ne pictum[62] quidem uspiam aut hic aut suo-

erty, he had not been able to pay his fare. So Charon made a bargain with him: if Gelastus acted as his companion among the mortals and as his guide on the journey, he would ferry him across to the underworld for free. Gelastus accepted his terms, although he was reluctant and unsure of the way. But what else was the wretched man to do, seeing that he couldn't pay? Should he have stopped forever in that place where he would be numbered neither among the living nor the dead? Naturally he had been forced to tackle everything known and unknown, harsh and bitter, mostly because no friends and no rich patrons arrived whom he might ask for a handout, and no one among the dead was permitted to bring from the mortal realm more than one coin for the price of his fare.

While preparing for the journey, Charon beached his boat and   29
thought long and hard about whether he should leave it somewhere in the underworld. In the end, reckoning it the best thing to do, he turned the boat over and carried it on top of his head, covering himself as though with a little hut. He then balanced his oar in his hand and set out. Crowds marvelled at the old man as he went along, hardy and powerful beyond his years.

As Charon and Gelastus went along, they fell into a conversa-   30
tion like this. Gelastus inquired of Charon why he was carrying the boat, and why he had not left it aground by the shore. "Should I tell you about the follies of the dead?" said Charon. "Every single one of them wants me to steer the boat at their command. Just yesterday there was somebody called Polyphagus who snatched the oar and began acting like an Argonaut.[11] I said to him, 'Who the hell are you? Were you an admiral maybe when you were alive?' 'No,' he replied, 'but there were once several rowers in my family.' I was surprised at his insolence, but I laughed still more at his stupidity when I saw how shamelessly and rashly he laid claim to and took on a task for which he was plainly not suited. Then one of the dead man's companions said, 'He's lying, Charon, neither he

rum aliquis vidit mare. Alpibus enim aeternum lapidicinis ascripti exercebantur."

31 'Is cum ita fuerit insolens, quales tu putas futuros ceteros aut tranandi studio aut insolescendi voluptate, si fortassis detur relicta illic navi occasio?' Hic Gelastus 'Quid' inquit 'illi quidem si neque insolentia neque arrogantia, sed discendi libidine id ita aggrederentur?' Tum Charon 'Novasne' inquit 'istic ut apud inferos artes condiscant? Minime: sed temerarii sunt. Vel quis hoc ferat ut Charontem remigare quisquam instruat?' Tum Gelastus 'Atqui hoc est,' inquit 'o Charon, quo fit ut abs te accepisse me iniuriam possim dicere. Tu quidem insolentes plerosque omnes istiusmodi transportasti, me vero, qui nulla ab re magis absum quam a petulantia et importunitate, longum repudiasti.' Tum Charon 'Negasne te' inquit 'petulantem atque importunum exstitisse an non?[63] Est non petulantia nostros sibi deposcere labores dari gratis? Nulla item importunitas est centies negatam rem dura et nusquam intermissa assiduitate expostulare?' Tum Gelastus: 'Deplorare meum incommodum erat istud, o Charon, non tuos labores poscere, quando tam difficilem te atque inexorabilem praestares erga me, qui nihil sibi relictum haberet rerum omnium quod conferret, praeter preces.' 'Atqui' inquit Charon 'suspendio opus fuit priusquam istud admitteres in te, ut tuae res omnes solis in precibus niterentur.'

32 'Id' inquit Gelastus 'fateor factum inconsulte, at factum tamen ratione fortassis non improba. Namque id quidem statuebam apprime fore philosophantis, ut quam curarum alumnam praedicant, pecuniam funditus a me abiciendam ducerem ac me totum rerum difficillimarum rarissimarumque cognitioni et studiis traderem animo soluto et libero.' Tum Charon 'O' inquit 'stultitiam irridendam si id credas, coercendam si id tentes, in rebus difficillimis et

nor any of his relatives have ever seen the ocean, even in pictures. They've always worked as forced laborers in Alpine quarries.'

"If this one man could be so presumptuous, how do you think 31 the rest are going to act — with their keenness to cross and their positive pleasure at lording it over me — if given the chance to get hold of my ship?" — "But what if they try, not out of high-handedness or arrogance, but out of a desire to learn?" — "Are they about to learn new skills in the underworld?" said Charon. "I hardly think so; but they are a reckless lot. It's outrageous that they try to teach *me* to row." — "I might observe, by the way, that in this regard you've done me an injustice, Charon," replied Gelastus. "You've carried across these high-handed fellows and many others like them, but for the longest time you have refused me, a man who has never succumbed to rudeness and importunity." — "Are you saying that you were not rude nor importunate?" answered Charon. "Isn't it rude to demand my labors for free? Isn't it importunate to ask a hundred times, tirelessly and without letup, for something you've been denied?" — "That was me deploring my misfortunes, Charon, not a demand for your services," said Gelastus; "you've always given me a hard time, you've never shown me any mercy, a poor fellow who departed the world bringing nothing to help him but prayers." — "You'd have done better to hang yourself," said Charon, "rather than allow yourself to depend only on prayers."

"I will admit that I acted misguidedly," replied Gelastus, "but I 32 did not act out of malice. I decided that as a philosopher — since people claim that money is the nurse of anxiety — it would be especially becoming for me to reject money utterly, and to apply myself completely, with a free and unencumbered mind, to the contemplation and study of difficult and unusual problems." — "What a laughable folly if you believed that, and how much this folly of yours needs to be held in check, if you tried to concern yourself with difficult and unusual problems with a free and unencum-

rarissimis, ac praesertim in paupertate, versari animo libero et soluto! Tu quidem, si forte dabitur ut possis id sine molestia, erunt
res ipsae non difficiles; sin erunt difficiles, plus olei et operae exi-
gent quam ut te animo esse curis vacuo possis affirmare. "Pecuniam demum curarum alumnam praedicant": quaeso, quinam id
praedicant? "Qui sapiunt" inquies. Tanti ergo est sapere apud philosophos, ut algendo et famescendo vitam precario et per mercedem trahere quam[64] in rerum opulentia affluentiaque malint? "At
tamen vivunt" inquies. Non est vivere, o Gelaste, sed luctari adversus mala! Dum ita te habes in vita ut esurias algeasque, hoc est ut
miser sis. Aut vos denique, et quid sapitis, in vobis inprimis sapitis
philosophi?'

33   'Num' inquit Gelastus 'quaeris "quid"[65] sapimus? Etenim omnia
novimus, siderum, imbrium, fulminum causas et motum; novimus[66] terras, caelum, maria. Nos artium optimarum inventores;
nos quae ad pietatem, ad vitae modum, ad hominum gratiam
conciliandam faciant nostris monitis quasi lege data praescribi-
mus.' Tum Charon: 'Egregios audio et venerandos homines, si se
aeque re operaque habeant atque dictis. Sed vos, dicito, iis vestris
legibus ut sint homines hominibus praesto, ut opera et obsequio
faveant et opitulentur etiamnum ascribitis?' Tum Gelastus 'Et istud' inquit 'ad officium inprimis ducimus.'

34   'Officii igitur erit' inquit Charon 'eos quibuscum degas levare
aerumnis, levare incommodis, fovere iuvareque opera?' 'Erit quidem' inquit Gelastus 'ut dicis.' 'Tu igitur officio legique hoc dato'
inquit Charon 'hanc praegravem cumbam adiutato ut feram.' Tum
Gelastus: 'Atqui est quidem tuum quoque hac in re pensandum
officium. Quare, Charon, videto ne praeter officium siet enecto
fame atque precario et per mercedem qui vitam traxit, tantum

bered mind, especially if you were poor! If you can do this without distraction, then the problems will not be that difficult, but if they truly are difficult, then they will demand from you more time and trouble, and then you can't claim that your mind is free from care. 'People claim that money is the nurse of anxiety' — *who* says that, if you please? 'The wise,' you will say. Among you philosophers, is so much value placed on wisdom that you prefer to live freezing and hungry, dragging out a beggar's existence by hourly labor rather than living affluently and opulently? 'But still, they're alive,' you'll say. That's not living, Gelastus, it's fighting off adversity! As long as you live your life hungry and cold, you're a wretched man. In the end, are you philosophers really wise in what concerns yourselves first of all, and in what does your wisdom consist?"

"Surely you're not asking in what our wisdom consists?" replied 33 Gelastus. "In fact, we know everything: the causes and movement of the stars, rain and lightning; we know about the earth, heaven and the sea. We are the inventors of the finest arts; our counsels are like legislation, prescribing that which conduces to piety, to a just mean in life and to goodwill among men." — "The people you're talking about must be excellent and venerable," said Charon, "if their deeds are up to their words. But tell me, do you still include it among those laws of yours that men should help their fellow men, that they should support, respect and work for each other's benefit?" — "We hold that as our principal duty," replied Gelastus.

"So it will be your duty," said Charon, "to lighten the cares of 34 those you live with, to relieve their troubles, to cherish and help them?" — "It is as you say," answered Gelastus. — "Well, if this is your duty and principle, help me carry this heavy boat!" — "But your own duty must also be carefully weighed in these circumstances. Consider, is it right to ask someone who lived his life dying of hunger, surviving on handouts and hourly wages, to carry such a great burden?" — "Carry the oar at least," said Charon. —

onus nobis velle imponere.' Tum Charon: 'At saltem remum.' 'Ne
tu negasti' inquit Gelastus 'licere apud inferos aggredi artes novas?
Calamum didici per aetatem tractare in vita, non remum.'

35   Itaque haec inter proficiscendum confabulabantur quoad perve-
nerunt ad extremum orbis limbum quem horizontam nuncupant,
geminae in quo e regione maximo interiecto secessu portae ab inferis patent, altera quae in oceanum, altera quae in continentem orbis dirigitur, estque harum una ebore apta atque intercrustata, altera vero cornu humilem ad cryptam adacta.

36   Placuit Charonti, quod satis aquarum per aetatem vidisset, tellure iter facere sed, quod rapido ascensu insuetoque peregrinandi
labore fessus desudaret, primo in pratulo recubuere. Est Charon
sensibus acutissimus, visu, auditu et huiusmodi supra quam possis
credere. Cum igitur ad eius nares florum, qui passim in prato
aderant, applicuisset odor, illico se ad flores ipsos colligendos et
contemplandos dedit tanta voluptate et admiratione ut ab iis aegre
ferret abstrahi.[67] Admonebat enim Gelastus plus itinerum super-
esse quam ut puerilibus florum deliciis legendis insisteret: maiora
enim esse quae aggrediantur, flores quidem suppeditari mortalibus
adeo ut etiam ab invitis conculcentur. Ille etsi nihil invitus magis
posset audire, ductori tamen parendum ducebat.

37   Dehinc inter proficiscendum Charon tantam in natura rerum
amoenitatem et varietatem spectans, colles, convalles, fontes, flu-
enta, lacus et huiusmodi, de Gelasto coepit quaerere unde tanta vis
pretiosissimarum rerum manarit mundo. Cui Gelastus, quo se di-
sertum philosophum ostentaret, huiusmodi ordiri orationem aggressus est: 'Principio nosse te oportet, o Charon, universa in[68] re-

"But didn't you say that one can't learn new skills in the underworld?" replied Gelastus. "In my mortal life, I learned how to use a pen, not an oar!"

Thus they talked as they went along, until they came to the farthest margin of the world, which people call the horizon. In this place there stand opposite each other, separated by a large isolated expanse, two gates opening onto ways out of the underworld. One gate leads to Ocean, the other leads towards the dry portions of the earth. One of them was inlaid and encrusted with ivory, but the other was decorated with horn and led to an underground passage.[12]

Charon had seen enough water in his life that he preferred to make his way by land. However, he was exhausted by the rapid ascent and by the unaccustomed effort of travelling, and was sweating freely, so the two men lay down to rest in the first meadow they came to. Charon's senses — his sight, hearing and other senses — were unbelievably acute. So when the fragrance of the flowers that filled the meadow reached his nostrils, he felt so much pleasure and wonder in gathering and contemplating those flowers that he could hardly be torn away from them.[13] But Gelastus warned that they had too long a journey ahead of them for Charon to indulge in the childish pleasure of picking flowers. They had far more important things to do, and the mortals had so many flowers that they trod them under foot even when they didn't want to. This was the last thing Charon wanted to hear, but he thought he should obey his guide.

So they forged on. Charon feasted his eyes on the pleasant variety of nature, on the hills, valleys, springs, rivers, lakes and other similar features, and began to ask Gelastus from what source this great abundance of precious things had come into the world. Gelastus, to prove that he was an articulate philosopher, undertook to set out a discourse as follows: "To start with, Charon, you need to know that throughout the natural universe, nothing is

35

36

37

rum natura nihil aut factum aut fieri posse vacuum causa. Causas quidem eas interpretamur quae ad motum conferant atque ad quietem. Quietem motus finem statuimus, motum vero intellegi volumus cum ex hoc fiat quidvis aliud. Et nosse oportet versari eum quidem motum aut in prima aeternaque rerum firmitate formis imbuenda aut in formarum mutabilitate varianda, quod naturae artificium alii opinati sunt in substantia accidentibus iungenda versari. Sed, ne longius frustra disputem, haec tu hactenus, o Charon, satis intellexistin?'

38 Negavit Charon grandioribus verbis pusilliora aut ordinatius confusiora audisse uspiam dici. Tum Gelastus aliunde repetito dicendi exordio rursus ordiebatur. Eum quidem qui principio quippiam facturus esset, mente et cogitatione sibi descripsisse quae facta cuperet hancque animo conceptam et consignatam speciem nuncupasse formam; proxime sibi comparasse, seu simplex illud fuerit seu mixtum coactumve partibus, quippiam cui aut formam adigeret et quasi obinvolveret aut quo formam ipsam compleret solidamque redderet: hoc vero postremum nuncupasse materiam. Sed ne potuisse opus nisi arte viaque adhibita perficere qua facile exque animi sententia materiae formam coniugaret et couniret:[69] idque artificium appellasse motum.

39 Hoc item Gelastus cum dixisset, interpellavit Charon. 'Atque' inquit 'ego quidem audieram mutua quadam concordique lite rerum omnia facta esse et in dies accessionibus decessionibusque minutarum partium immutari. Sed visne quid sentiam referam de te? Putaram vos philosophos omnia nosse sed, quantum ex te video, nihil nostis nisi ita loqui ut de rebus notissimis verba facientes non intellegamini.

made nor can be made without a cause. We interpret causes as things which contribute to motion or rest. We have decided that rest is the end of motion, but by motion we understand the process of one thing becoming something else.[14] You should know that motion has to do either with imparting forms to the original and unchanging structure of nature, or with changing the mutability of forms, because some people hold that the artfulness of nature consists of joining accidents to substance.[15] But I don't want to explain at length to no purpose — do you understand what I've said so far, Charon?"

Charon said that he had never heard anything more trivial explained more pompously, nor anything more muddled discussed more systematically. So Gelastus went back to the beginning, and started to explain again, from a different angle.[16] He said that the being who first wanted to create something used its intuition and reason to design for itself what it desired to make, and called this mental concept and impressed species a "form." Then the being prepared a substance — which was either simple or combined and molded from parts — a substance by which form could be impelled and enveloped or by which form might be rendered solid and complete. This substance he called "matter." But he could not perfect his work without recourse to an art or means by which he could join and unify form to matter easily and according to his liking, and this artifice he called "movement."

While Gelastus was explaining this again, Charon interrupted him. "So, what you're telling me is, everything is generated by means of reciprocal and harmonious struggle, and under normal circumstances things change because of the aggregation and disaggregation of minute particles. Do you want me to tell you what I think of you? I thought that you philosophers knew everything, but — from what I see of you — you know nothing except how to talk in such a way that you render incomprehensible the most well-known facts by the words you use.

40   'Vel quid ego tibi credam temere quando tu quidem, qui primus rerum conditor quid animo habuerit te non ignorare affirmas, profecto, quod pueris evenit, domum redeundi viam oblitus es? Quod si recte coniector, nos ad tartareas plagas te duce praelongo habito itinere redivimus. En atram Stygiae caliginem, en et istinc audisne fremitum et eiulatus excruciatorum sontium?' Dehinc lupum ostentans 'An[70] tu' inquit 'vides illic defuncti errantem animam?'

41   Hic Gelastus arridens 'Ne mirere,' inquit 'o Charon, namque non plus semel hac iter feci. Sed, quo rem intellegas, quae tibi eiulantis vox visa est litui est sonus a mortalium inde castris delatus aura et, ni fallor, secundas excubias canunt. Caliginem quoque ipse unde tanta sit miror;[71] miror[72] et ipsum te, qui defunctorum hic animas videre alias praeter me praedicas.' At Charon: 'Is profecto ipsus est rex: ehodum, o rex!' Tum Gelastus: 'Lupumne tu regem vocas? Id quadrupedum genus apud mortales etsi noxium est, mortale tamen[73] est animans[74] et longe ab hominum natura defunctorumque animis alienum.'

42   Interea lupus ipse multo morsu raptis quodam ex cadavere visceribus mandendo restitabat. 'Ergo tibi' inquit Charon 'iam fit ut assentiar: non enim apud inferos manducant. Sed illud animans putavi esse regem quendam quicum mea in navi Peniplusius[75] praeco elegantem habuit disceptationem, quam in reditu[76] narrabo, ut voles.' Tum Gelastus 'Volam' inquit 'sed tu reges esse lupos qui vidisti aut audisti umquam?' Tum Charon: 'O te philosophum quidem bonum, qui siderum cursus teneas et quae hominum sint ignoras! Ex Charonte adeo portitore disce ipsum te nosse. Referam quae non a philosopho — nam vestra omnis ratio nisi in argutiis et verborum captiunculis versatur — sed a pictore

"Why should I be rash enough to believe you, a man who   40
claims to know what the creator of everything had in mind but
has forgotten his way home, just like a little boy? For in fact, if I'm
not out of my reckoning, thanks to your guidance we've retraced
our steps the long way around to the shores of Tartarus! Look—
there's the black murk of the Styx, and can't you hear the groans
and wails of the guilty being tortured?"[17] Then pointing to a wolf,
Charon said, "Don't you see there the wandering soul of a dead
man?"

Gelastus laughed and said, "Don't be so surprised, Charon—   41
I've only made the journey here once, after all. But to clarify the
situation, what appeared to you to be a wailing voice is the sound
of a trumpet, borne on the breeze from the encampments of the
mortals. If I'm not mistaken, they're signalling the second watch. I
myself am wondering where all this fog is coming from, and I'm
also surprised at your claim to see other souls of the dead besides
me."—"Surely this one is the king himself?" said Charon. "Hey,
you there, king!—"Is it the wolf you are calling a king? That is a
species of quadruped, a mortal animal, and though harmful to humans it is far different in nature from humans and from the souls
of the dead."

Meanwhile the wolf himself had stopped to rip out the entrails   42
of some corpse, and was chewing on them vigorously. "Well, that
sight makes me agree with you now," said Charon; "nobody chews
in the underworld. But I thought that animal was the king with
whom the herald Peniplusius[18] held an elegant debate in my boat.
I will tell you about it when we return, if you like."—"I would like
that," said Gelastus, "but have you ever seen or heard of kings being wolves?"—"Oh, what a fine philosopher, who understands the
ways of the stars but not those of men! Learn from Charon the
ferryman to know thyself.[19] I will tell you what I remember hearing, not from a philosopher—for all your reasoning revolves only
around subtleties and verbal quibbles—but from a certain painter.

quodam memini audivisse. Is quidem lineamentis contemplandis plus vidit solus quam vos omnes philosophi caelo commensurando et disquirendo. Adsis animo: audies rem rarissimam.

43 'Sic enim aiebat pictor: tanti operis artificem selegisse et depurasse[77] id quo esset hominem conditurus; id vero fuisse aliqui limum melle infusum, alii ceram tractando contepefactam. Quicquid ipsum fuerit, aiunt imposuisse sigillis aeneis binis quibus altero pectus, vultus et quae cum his una visuntur, altero occiput, tergum, nates et postrema istiusmodi impressarentur. Multas formasse hominum species et ex his selegisse[78] mancas et vitio insignes, praesertim leves et vacuas, ut essent feminae, feminasque a maribus distinxisse dempto ab iis paulo quantillo quod alteris adigeretur. Fecisse item alio ex luto variisque sigillis multiplices alias animantium species. Quibus operibus confectis, cum vidisset homines aliquos sua non usquequaque forma delectari, edixisse ut qui id praestare arbitrarentur quas placuerit in alias reliquorum animantium facies se verterent.

44 'Dehinc suas quae obiecto in monte paterent aedes monstravit atque hortatus est ut[79] acclivi directaque via quae pateret conscenderent: habituros illic omnem bonarum rerum copiam, sed iterum atque iterum caverent ne alias praeter hanc inirent vias — videri arduam initio hanc, sed continuo aequabilem successuram.

45 'His dictis abivisse. Homunculos coepisse conscendere, sed illico alios per stultitiam boves, asinos, quadrupedes videri maluisse, alios cupiditatis errore[80] adductos in transversos viculos delirasse. Illic abruptis constreposisque praecipitiis sentibusque et vepribus irretitos pro loci difficultate se in varia vertisse monstra; et iterato

By himself this man saw more while looking at lines than all you philosophers do when you're measuring and investigating the heavens. Pay attention: you'll hear something that is very rare indeed.

"This painter used to say that the artificer of a great work had been selecting and purifying the material from which he was to create man. Some said the material was clay mixed with honey, others said warm wax. Whatever it was, people said that he should mold two bronze seals upon man, one on the chest, face, and the other parts seen from the front, and a second one on the back of the head, the back, the buttocks, and the parts seen from behind. The craftsman had fashioned many kinds of humans, and had selected from among them the defective ones and those marked by flaws, especially the light and vacuous ones, to make women of them, and he distinguished the females from the males by taking a little bit from the one and adding it to the other. Using other clay and a variety of seals, he made many other species of living things. When he had finished his work, and when he realized that some humans did not like their shape at all, he declared that whoever preferred to could change themselves into the shapes of other creatures they liked. 43

"He pointed out his house, conspicuous on a nearby mountain, and encouraged them to climb the steep and straight road that led to it. He said that they would enjoy there an abundance of good things, but he warned them repeatedly not to go there by any other road. This particular road might seem steep at first, but gradually it would become more level.[20] 44

"Having said this, he went away. The homunculi began to climb, but immediately some, in their folly, preferred to look like cattle, asses, and quadrupeds. Others, led astray by misguided desires, went on detours through the little hamlets they passed. There, in steep and echoing valleys, impeded by thorns and brambles, faced by impassable places, they turned themselves into assorted monsters, and when they returned to the main road, their 45

ad primariam viam redisse, illic[81] fuisse ab suis ob deformitatem explosos. Ea de re, comperto consimili quo compacti essent luto, fictas et aliorum vultibus compares sibi superinduisse personas, et crevisse hoc personandorum hominum artificium usu quoad paene a veris secernas fictos vultus[82] ni forte accuratius ipsa per foramina obductae personae introspexeris: illinc enim contemplantibus varias solere occurrere monstri facies. Et appellatas personas hasce fictiones easque ad Acherontis usque undas durare, nihilo plus, nam fluvium ingressis humido vapore evenire ut dissolvantur. Quo fit ut alteram nemo ad ripam non nudatus amissa persona pervenerit.' Tum Gelastus: 'O Charon, fingisne haec ludi gratia an[83] vera praedicas?' 'Quin' inquit Charon 'ex personarum barbis et superciliis rudentem hunc intorsi ipsoque ex luto cumbam obstipavi.'

46   Huiusmodi rettulerat Charon iamque non longe ab theatro aberant. Ergo de Gelasto sciscitatus didicit et quinam tantam molem coacervassent et quos ad usus haberetur. Et cum theatrum illud fabulis agendis factum intellexisset, vehementer risit hominum ineptias, qui tantos labores consumpserint demoliendis montibus ut immanem ipsi molem construerent. Tum et stultitiam patrum detestatus est, qui tantas perdendi temporis illecebras in urbe paterentur.

47   At Oenops, ludio ille philosophus de quo supra ridicula illa recensuimus, cum procul vidisset cumba opertum adventantem, ratus novos adesse histriones, secessit cum turma eorum qui aderant, ut si quid scaenae Charon commentaretur ex insidiis annotarent.

48   Medio in theatro illi cum advenissent, 'Enim[84] et quid tibi haec, o Charon?' inquit Gelastus. Negavit Charon videri sibi aut theatrum aut ornamenta istiusmodi talia ut ulla ex parte cum floribus

friends rejected them because of their ugliness. Consequently, realizing that they were all made from the same clay, they put on masks fashioned to look like other people's faces. This artificial method of looking like human beings became so commonly employed that you could scarcely distinguish the fake faces from the real ones, unless you happened to look closely at the eye holes of the masks that covered them. Only then would observers encounter the varied faces of the monsters. These masks, called 'fictions,' lasted until they reached the waters of the River Acheron[21] and no further, for when they entered the river they were dissolved in its steaming vapor. So nobody reached the other bank unless he was naked and stripped of his mask."[22] Then Gelastus said, "Charon, are you making this up as a game, or are you telling the truth?" — "No," said Charon. "In fact, I plaited this rope from the beards and eyebrows of the masks, and I caulked my boat using their clay."

While Charon had been telling this story, they arrived not 46
far from the theater. In his desire for knowledge, Charon asked Gelastus who had piled up such a massive structure, and what it was used for. When he understood that that theater was used for acting out stories, he laughed heartily at the folly of humans, who had exerted so much effort to demolish mountains just so they could build a vast pile like this. He cursed the folly of the city fathers for allowing in their city such great inducements to wasting time.

When Oenops, the actor-philosopher whose ludicrous exploits 47
we recounted above, saw someone approaching covered by a boat, he thought that new actors had arrived. He and the troop of actors already there withdrew from sight, to spy out whether Charon was rehearsing a scene.

When they reached the middle of the theater, Gelastus said, 48
"So, Charon, what do you think?" Charon answered that the theater and its decorations were nothing compared with the flowers

quos apud pratum excerpserat essent comparanda. Et mirari quidem professus est quod pluris faciant homines quae possint vilissi-
morum manu assequi quam ea quae ne cogitatione quidem satis
queant attingere. 'Et flores' inquit 'neglegitis: saxa admirabimur?
In flore ad venustatem, ad gratiam omnia conveniunt. In his hominum operibus nihil invenies dignum admiratione praeter id, ut vituperes tantorum laborum tam stultam profusionem. Dehinc tu, o'
inquit 'philosophe, principio ex te fieri certior volo, quandoquidem, ut praedicas, multa hoc loco quae ad vitam bene degendam
faciant in medium afferuntur, cuinam ea commodent. Maiori-
busne natu? Stultum si eos aggrediantur commonefacere qui didi-
cerint usu quae conferant! An adulescentibus? Ineptum eos velle
dictis regere qui non auscultent! Proxime item velim dicas ab poe-
tisne quam ab philosophis vitae degendae rationes expetant.'

49   Tum Gelastus: 'Sit quod ais, Charon. Quae tamen ab poeta
cum voluptate audias, ea capias facilius, imbues plenius, servabis
firmius. Quod si praeterea videris hosce gradus consessu tantorum
virorum oppletos, neque ineptum opus dicas neque una interesse
pigeat. Et profecto, uti aiunt, non sine deo tam multi coeunt,
quando usu invenias ut quos singulos flocci penderis, si coierint
venereris et prae reverentia obmutescas.' Tum Charon, ad unas
atque alteras deorum statuas versus, 'Dic, Gelaste,' inquit 'ne tu
hos singulos flocci pendis, aut si coirent venerabere?'[85] Tum Gelastus subridens: 'Solus si essem fortassis riderem, plures si adessent
alii venerarer.'

50   Interea, dum statuas spectant, Charon seposita ab fornice audire visus est submissa voce colloquentem ac dicentem: 'Trita haec
sunt quae Gelastus confabulatur, deque tota istorum re nihil est
quod probem quam personatum Gelastum hunc: nam ei[86] profecto nihil fieri potest similius.' Audit et alios Charon dicentes

he'd picked in the meadow. He professed himself amazed at how men placed more value on things that the vilest hands could accomplish, rather than on things that defied understanding. "You spurn flowers," he said; "shall I admire stones? Everything about a flower is beautiful and pleasing. In these man-made constructions, you won't find anything wondrous apart from the wondrous extravagance of misplaced labor. Now explain to me first, O philosopher — since you claim that in this place they perform publicly many things which contribute to the good life — who benefits from them? Adults? How foolish they must be if they try to teach people who have already learned from experience what they're talking about! Youngsters? What a stupid idea, trying to govern with words young people who don't listen! Second, I want you to tell me: who asks poets how to live rather than philosophers?"

"It may be as you say, Charon," replied Gelastus. "But what you hear with pleasure from the poets, you understand more readily, you internalize more deeply and you remember with greater tenacity. Moreover, when you see these tiers filled with vast numbers of men, you will not call the building foolish nor will you regret being here. As they say, only a divinity makes this many people gather together, and you'll learn from experience that, though as individuals you may think them worthless, when they form a crowd you'll esteem them and fall silent out of respect for them." Then Charon, turning first to one then to another of the gods' statues, said, "Tell me, Gelastus, do you think *these* are individually worthless; won't you respect them when they're gathered together?" Gelastus, smiling, said, "If I was alone perhaps I would laugh, but if there were many others present I would revere them."

Meanwhile, as they looked at the statues, Charon seemed to hear a low voice talking in a remote arch, saying, "Gelastus' lines are *so* commonplace! The only thing I like in this entire dialogue is the fellow wearing the Gelastus-mask: indeed, nothing could be more like him." Charon heard some voices saying that during his

49

50

fuisse bene doctum Gelastum in vita et prudentem, alios contra fuisse quidem stultum et procul dubio delirasse cum ceteras ob res, tum quod tantis iniuriarum offensionibus lacessitus seque dignitatemque suam neglexerit per animi pusillitatem. Neque probare illius vitae rationem, qui perseveravit omnibus aeternum prodesse cum se multi in dies lacesserent et laederent. Non illis quidem cum Oenope rem fuisse, qui se ad propulsandas vindicandasque[87] iniurias magis quam ad firmandam insolentium temeritatem fortem esse ostenderet nimis ferendo.

51   Quae Oenopis verba cum etiam Gelastus subaudisset vocemque loquentis cognovisset, 'Velim' inquit 'videas, o Charon, quam is quidem iactator sese perstrenuum praestet.' His dictis in obloquentes proripuit. Illi propius accedente mortuo et apertius perspecto et cognito obstupuere, et Oenops[88] nihil sibi antiquius duxit quam ut relicto captivo avolaret[89] extemplo. Ergo ad Charontem rediens Gelastus 'Et qualis' inquit 'tibi visus est noster athleta, qui meo primo pedis motu verterit terga? Et hominem demiror, cum mihi in vita apprime fuerit[90] familiaris, aut ea de me oblocutum aut me viso metu potius quam voluptate affectum. Sed nunc intellego fictum hominis ingenium et ex tuo illo personandorum artificio obductum;[91] fronti fictam, non veram benivolentiam exstitisse, qui profecto neque viventis patientiam totiens lacessivisset neque defuncti nomen impeteret, si amasset.'

52   Inter haec dicendum eccum saxum grave cumbam Charontis incutit sonitu maximo (illud enim ebrius ille barbarus multa vi[92] impulerat). Quo ictu Charon absterritus inclamavit ut pleno intonuerit theatro. Gelastus vero ira concitus in ebrium se conferebat. At Charon 'Desine,' inquit 'o desine, Gelaste! Tu illos umbra, illi nos saxis petunt. Sat peragrati sumus. Hic praeter ineptias et im-

lifetime, Gelastus had been learned and wise, while others argued that he was stupid and certainly mad, mainly because he had been injured and insulted but had neglected his own dignity out of meanness of spirit. They did not approve of his way of life, because he always continued to help everyone, even though people attacked and hurt him every day. This was not the case with Oenops, a man who showed his courage by fighting and avenging injuries rather than stimulating the recklessness of the insolent by excessive forebearance.

When Gelastus overheard these words — they were Oenops' 51 words — and recognized the speaker's voice, he said, "Charon, I want you to see how tough this boaster really is!" So saying, he charged at his detractors. As the dead man came near to them, and they saw clearly who he was, they were stunned. Oenops thought it best to abandon his prisoner and take to his heels immediately. So Gelastus returned to Charon and said, "What kind of a man do you think our athlete is, who turned tail as soon as I took to my feet? During my lifetime, this man was particularly friendly towards me. I am amazed that he would either disparage me or be struck with fear rather than pleasure at the sight of me. But now I know that the man's attitude was feigned and derived from that artificial habit of masking you mentioned. He projected a false front, not true good will, and if he had loved me he would surely not have tried my patience so often while I was alive, nor attacked my good name after my death."

While he was talking, boom! — a heavy stone struck Charon's 52 boat; it had been thrown hard by that uncouth drunk. Charon, startled by the blow, shouted so loudly that the entire theater echoed with the noise. Gelastus was roused to anger and set upon the drunk. "Stop!" cried Charon. "Stop, Gelastus! You're attacking them with your shade, but they're coming after us with rocks. We've travelled far enough. Here I have found nothing apart from folly and wickedness, nothing it has not made me unhappy to see;

probitatem comperio nihil quod vidisse non pigeat, et ineptias odisse et improbitatem[93] evitasse conferet.[94] Abeamus!' Charontem revocabat[95] Gelastus, ille saltitans una et tremens diffugiebat.

53   Hoc spectaculo theatrales illi dii multo risere, quo risu factum est ut maximam, inauditam insperatamque in calamitatem inciderint omnes dii. Id qui evenerit proxime recitabimus, si prius quae Charonti etiam obtigerint insperata et cognitu festivissima succincte rettulerimus. Audito igitur statuarum risu, Charon 'Ridete' inquit 'ut libet: ego rideri quam caedi malo.' Putabat enim proscaenicos illos turbatores risisse, tametsi admiraretur retinnire omnia deorum risu.[96] At Gelastus, non insuetus theatri, sese confestim in pedes conicit, atque 'Papae, o Charon, papae! Siste, adsum!' vociferabat.

54   In quem versus Charon expavefactum admiratus[97] 'Quid tibi est?' inquit. 'Saxone percusserunt?' Ille vero vix sui compos, titubans, haesitans 'Audistin' inquit 'statuas?' 'Quid tum?' 'Risere' inquit. 'Quid igitur?' inquit Charon. 'Malles plorasse? An pro metu reris statuas risisse?' Non se poplitibus sustentabat Gelastus metu exsanguis factus. Eaque de re Charontem sequens primo dato in trivio ab urbe reversam cumbae puppim arripit atque: 'Hic, quaeso, siste, o Charon!'

55   Ille vero 'Vestros' inquit 'mortalium personatos et fictos mores odi, quandoquidem tu qui saxa non metuebas risu te absterritum simulas, et qui tantopere negabas velle te huc ad mortalium sedes regredi, hinc invitus divelleris. Et habeo tibi nullas gratias si me[98] a colligendorum florum voluptate abstraxisti et ad iurgia rixasque adduxisti. Quod si non saxa modo, sed etiam risus hic statuarum pertimescendus est, quis hinc non aufugerit? Sed tu ut libet, ego

this world has taught me to hate folly and avoid wickedness. Let's leave!" Gelastus called Charon back, but he bounded away, all atremble.

At this spectacle the gods in the theater laughed mightily, and 53 because of this laugh, all of the gods fell into the greatest, strangest, and most surprising catastrophe. We shall tell how this happened shortly, once we've recounted briefly the unexpected and highly amusing things that happened to Charon. When he heard the statues' laughter, Charon said, "Laugh if you like! I'd rather be laughed at than killed." He thought that those thespian nuisances were the ones laughing, although he was surprised how the gods' laughter made the whole place ring. But Gelastus, who knew the theater well, immediately started to run, shouting, "Oh my god, Charon! Oh my god! Hold on, I'm behind you!"

Charon turned towards the terrified Gelastus in amazement. 54 "What's it to you?" he said. "Did they hit *you* with a rock?" Gelastus, barely in control of himself, stammering and faltering, said, "Did you hear the statues?" — "What of it?" — "They *laughed*," said Gelastus. — "So what?" said Charon. "Would you rather they wept? Or was it fear that made you think that the statues laughed?" Gelastus was white with fear and his knees shook. So he ran after Charon, and at the first crossroads they reached upon leaving the city, he seized the stern of the upsidedown ship and said, "*Please*, Charon, stop!"

"I hate you humans with your masks and your fake morality!" 55 said Charon. "Although you weren't afraid of stones, you pretend you're terrified by a laugh. Although you vehemently denied that you wanted to return here to the mortal realm, now you're reluctant to tear yourself away. I don't thank you for dragging me away from the pleasure of picking flowers and for drawing me into quarrels and brawls. If people here have to fear not only stones, but also laughing statues, who wouldn't run away? You can do what you like, but I'm leaving." Gelastus, upset by the bitterness of the

vero abeo.' Tum Gelastus duri decrepiti[99] acerbitate motus 'Ne[100] tu,' inquit 'o Charon, argutiis et verborum captiunculis quibus versari philosophos praedicabas nunc apud nos uteris!' 'Etenim tanti est' inquit Charon 'disertis congredi: namque apud doctos discimus.'

56   Tum Gelastus sibi consulens non quo Charontem levaret onere, sed quo illum, si se dimisso perseveraret citato gradu fugiens, abire interpellaret, 'Ego vero' inquit 'ex te quoque, ut par est, aliquid ediscam oportet. Cedo: remum tractare enim assuescam.' Tum Charon: 'Remumne in sicco?'[101] At ille rapto remo inter reptandum[102] scapulis gestiebat, 'Sic' inquiens 'clava se habebat Hercules! Quod si mihi in theatro adfuisset is remus, sceleste Oenops, quem tantis officiis et beneficiis prosecutus sum, luisses. Nam te quidem inter mortales monstrum petissem et cuius improbitatem atque nequitiam patientia pertuli perculissem.'

57   Tum Charon 'Gelaste' inquit 'huc velim animum adhibeas. Annos ego multos atque item multos[103] portorio adfui; cum innumeris sapientibus et usu doctis habui colloquium de his rebus. Hoc velim scias: stat omnium sententia prudentissimorum non semper oportere uti patientia, statuuntque ceteris in rebus apud mortales id observandum, ut nihil nimis, solam vero patientiam aut nullam penitus aut omnino in vita nimiam habendam. Et fortassis non pauciores reperias qui doleant quod patientes fuerint quam qui non fuerint.' Tum Gelastus 'O' inquit 'dictum prudens! Ex me id iudico: plus quidem molestiae ex patientia subivisse me possum asseverare quam ex intolerantia offendissem.'

58   His confabulationibus ad mare iam devenerant, quo loci cum circumspectans haesitansque Gelastus constitisset, subirritatus Charon 'Istic' inquit 'etiam haeres?' Tum Gelastus 'Nolim succenseas,' inquit 'o Charon, tuam enim rem aeque atque meam ago.

tough old fellow, said, "You, Charon, were just now claiming that philosophers were wrapped up in cleverness and verbal sophistry—now you're practising the same thing on me!"—"That's why it's so important to mix with articulate people," retorted Charon; "it's from clever people that we learn."

Gelastus ruminated inwardly, not on how to relieve Charon's 56 burden, but on how he could stop him leaving, if he persisted in abandoning him and running away. "It's only fair," Gelastus said, "that I should learn something from you, too. I give in: I'll take up rowing."—"What, are you going to row on dry land?" replied Charon. But Gelastus seized the oar and sauntered on, shrugging his shoulders. "Thus did Hercules wield his club!" he declared. "If I had had this oar in the theater, you would have paid the price, Oenops, you bastard—you whom I helped out with so many services and acts of kindness! I would have sought you out, you monster among humans, and I would have beaten you, the man whose wickedness and worthlessness I suffered so patiently."

"Gelastus," said Charon, "I want you to pay close attention. I 57 have spent many, many years on my ferry, and I have discussed such matters with countless sages and men of great experience. I want you to know this. All the wisest men think that one should not always be patient, and they claim that in other mortal affairs the following words should be observed: nothing in excess.[23] Only in the case of patience must one either have too much of it in life or too little. And perhaps you'll find that more people regret their patience than their impatience."—"Wise words!" replied Gelastus. "This is my experience: I can state that I suffered more trouble from being patient than I ever did from being intolerant."

Conversing thus, they arrived at the sea, where Gelastus 58 stopped, pausing to look around. Charon, annoyed, said, "Why are you stopping here?"—"Charon, I don't want you to get angry," answered Gelastus, "since I'm acting in your interests and mine. I make no claim that I shall be a suitable guide on this vast expanse

Ego me tam vasto in aequore, nullo se praebente calle nullisque re-
cognitis semitis,[104] ducem futurum commodum non profiteor.'
Tum Charon 'Pronam' inquit 'audivi esse ad inferos viam, modo
petas id ubi non videas neque audias quippiam. Eo igitur versus
cursum dirigemus, ingressi navim.'

59   Tranquillo mari navigans, Charon 'Vides' inquit 'minus cre-
dendo vobis philosophis ut mecum fiat commodius. Tu, si te au-
dissem, iam cum me suspicionibus obruisses. At non credidi: ergo
opportunissime navigamus. Sed mare hoc cur te simulasti metuere, qui Acheronta videras? Non inficior videri hoc vastius, sed
nego aut profundius esse aut turbulentius.

60   'Verum et quidnam illinc monstri ad nos perscindens[105] mare
illabitur? Ne non fortasse hoc illud est quod ad inferos tantas dedit tragoedias et fluctibus versari ferunt? Pro! et quam optato ad-
venit! Quod enim quale esset potui numquam intellegere; id nunc
aderit coram atque conspiciemus—et bene est! Nunc demum iuvat mortales adivisse. Atqui num vides? Eccam rempublicam na-
tantem!'

61   Tum Gelastus 'O' inquit 'Charon, et quid tibi in mentem venit
ut tam apte rempublicam appellares navim? Quod si eam cupiam
verbis admodum expingere, nihil afferam illustrius. Istic enim
aeque atque in republica imperant pauciores, parent plurimi, et hi
parendo condocefiunt imperium gerere. Tum et quae ad animi libidines student, quae ad spem parant, ad salutem curant, omnia
temporibus accommodant atque obsecundantur. Adde quod istic,
uti in republica, aut unus aut aliqui aut plures totam rem moderantur. Qui quidem si observant praeterita, cogitant futura, cir-
cumspectant praesentia et omnia ratione et modo aggrediuntur et
tractant, volentes nihil sibi rerum bonarum potius esse quam uni-
versis, reges ii sunt et bene agitur; sin contra ad se omnia referunt

of water, where no pathway offers itself and there are no recogniz-
able tracks." — "I have heard that the way to the underworld slopes
downward,"[24] said Charon, "so long as you look for it in places
where you can't see or hear anything. Let's get into the boat and
steer in that direction."

As he steered though the calm sea, Charon said, "You see how   59
it's better for me not to trust you philosophers. If I'd heeded you,
you would have overwhelmed me with worries, but I didn't believe
you, so we're steering along very nicely. Why did you pretend to be
afraid of the sea, when you've seen Acheron? I don't deny that this
seems a larger body of water, but I don't agree that it's deeper or
choppier.

"But what kind of monster is that, slicing through the sea in   60
our direction? Is it the same that inflicted so many tragedies on
the underworld and is said to dwell in the sea? Oh, how glad I am
to see it! I could never imagine what it was, but now it's here in
front of us where we can see it — wonderful! Now I'm finally glad
I came to see the mortals. Can't you see it? Look at it, it's a swimming state!"[25]

"O Charon, where ever did you get the idea to give it the apt   61
name 'ship of state'? If I had wanted to paint its picture in words,
I could not have done it more brilliantly. For there, just as in a
state, a few give the commands and the majority obey, the latter
being trained through obedience in the exercise of power. There,
too, they try to support and accommodate to circumstances all
their passions, their hopes, and their concerns for security. Moreover, just as in a state, either one person, several people or the
many can govern the whole thing.[26] If the rulers observe precedent, take thought for the future, behave with circumspection in
the present, and make all decisions with reason and measure, desiring only the common good and not their private goods, they are
truly kings and act well. But if on the contrary they judge everything in light of their private interests and neglect everything apart

et cuncta prae iis quae collibuerint neglegunt, tyranni sunt et pessime agitur. Tum si parent dictis, si praesto sunt, si adsunt volentes atque agunt unanimes quae imperantur, aequabilis tunc et firma est res; sin discrepant, si recusant et respuunt, perturbatur illico respublica atque in discrimine est. Sed quid agimus inconsultissimi? Imminenti ab calamitate non refugimus — incidimus in piratas!'

62   Piratarum audito nomine, Charon, quo nihil tactrius aut truculentius inveniri posse persaepius intellexerat, expavit. Verum etsi perterritus contremisceret dissimulavit, quo Gelastum mordere dictis prosequeretur. 'Et quantis,' inquit 'Gelaste, subterfugiis incohatum ad inferos reditum interpellabis? Nunc te incerta navigandi ratio detinet, nunc te praedonum cognita pericula detorquent. Quos quid est cur metuas, cui ne vitam quidem possint auferre? Sed abigenda est haec molestia: te in sicco relinquam.'

63   His dictis navim ad litus vertit et multa vi remo impulit. Sensit Gelastus Charontem expavisse. Idcirco arridens 'Tibi quidem,' inquit 'o Charon, recte fuga consulis. Nam si cepissent callosum navitam, inter[106] infelicissimos remiges mancipassent. Adde quod promissam istam tuam barbam et capillum, te imitati, ad rudentum opus convulsissent.'

64   Itaque Charon cum ad litus appulisset offendit incolas, qui propinquis balneis diversabantur, praevisis piratis fugam capessentes atque admonentes ut crudelissimos et consceleratissimos vitarent montesque conscenderent. Negavit Charon suam posse navim aut relinquere aut longius asportare: erat enim fessus et defatigatus, obnixius dum litus peteret navigando. Eam igitur subduxit in contiguam paludem lutoque immersit, se autem inter proximos palustres calamos abdidit.[107] Gelastus vero cryptam conscendit atque illic intra caespitem delituit.

65   Eccum e vestigio piratas, facta praeda, alacres e navi certatim proruentes! Sese in balneum committunt ibique ludi gratia crapu-

from what gives them pleasure, they are tyrants and act badly. If [the citizens] obey precepts, if they're responsible, if they are united and willing to follow commands, then the state is stable and strong. But if they quarrel, if they protest and reject authority, then the state is thrown into turmoil and endangered.[27] But what are we doing, thoughtless men that we are? We're not fleeing from imminent disaster — we've stumbled upon pirates!"

Charon was terrified to hear the word "pirates." He had often heard that there was nothing fouler or more fell. However, frightened as he was, he hid his trembling so that he could continue to carp at Gelastus. "Gelastus," he said, "how many devices will you throw in the way of our return to the underworld? At one moment you're prevented by your doubts about steering, at another you're discouraged by the well-known danger of brigands! Why should you fear them, since they can't take away your life? I've had enough of this hassle — I'm leaving you on dry land!" 62

With this, he turned towards the shore, plying his oar vigorously. Gelastus figured out that Charon was terrified. He smiled, and said, "Charon, you're right to advise escape. If they caught a horny old sea-dog like you, they'd chain you up with their wretched oarsmen. Then they'd tear out that long beard and hair of yours and make them into ropes, following your example." 63

After Charon had reached the shore, he ran into some of the inhabitants who had been staying at the nearby baths. Having been forewarned about the pirates, they were in flight and advised taking to the hills to evade those cruel and wicked men. Charon said that he could neither abandon his boat nor carry it very far; he was tired and exhausted by his struggle to reach shore. He pulled his boat up into a neighboring marsh, sank it in the mud, and hid himself among the nearby marsh reeds. Gelastus climbed into a grassy culvert to hide. 64

All of a sudden the pirates are here! They've seized their plunder and are now racing eagerly from their ship! They fling them- 65

Ionum regem miro et inaudito instituto inter se creant. In coronam enim circumsistuntur, mediis vero[108] aquis unus dimittitur mus et ad quem mus nando applicuerit, is habetur rex. Hoc sortis genere ex sociis navalibus quidam bene honestus factus exstitit rex. Ergo, dum animi omnium risu et ioco soluti lasciviunt, quaeque ad balneorum voluptates convenirent iucundissime exsequuntur.

66   Interea lixa, unus ex libertinis navalibus abiectissimus, per calonum et lixarum conspirationem sese quoque ludi gratia regem constituit. Hinc prior ille sorte[109] creatus rex, quod[110] a plurimis impeteretur, ultro cessit. Tota perinde res agitur ludo et miris iocis ridetur, factumque probant omnes, et inprimis archipirata, atque favet. Hinc novus rex sese firmare iuramento concrapulonum fidem ait cupere. Idcirco in medium iubet afferri atram fuligine patellam qua omnes, veluti in ara, etiam inviti iurent, quoad ipsum ad archipiratam deventum est. Is quod negasset iurare, raptus ante regem, de collegii sententia pro contumace damnatus est, atque erat in contumaces poena ut immergerentur.[111] Itaque is ut ceteri contumaces immergitur, verum enimvero ita immergitur ut inter manus suffocaretur.

67   Perterrefactis archipiratae familiaribus et enecati casu et coniuratorum audacia, vix sui erant compotes. At manus regia, successu exsultans, repente puppim clavumque occupant, salutem[112] libertatemque omnibus suo esse facinore partam proclamant. Et congratulantes, petito mari alto, qua venerant abeunt.

68   Hunc archipiratae casum Gelastus quasi ab specula confestim Charonti renuntiatum accurrit. Nihil umquam avidius accepit

selves into the baths and there, as a lark, make one of their number King of the Drunks—a wondrous innovation! They form a
circle, then let loose a mouse in the middle of the water. Whichever man the mouse swims towards is considered king. This selec-
tion process ensures, of course, that a truly sterling fellow gets to
be king over his shipmates. Thus they begin their carouse, relaxing
in laughter and good cheer, and enjoying to the full every pleasure
of the bath-house.[28]

Meanwhile a sutler, one of the lowest of all the freedman sail- 66
ors, became king of the revels owing to a cabal among the servants
and provisioners. So the man previously chosen king, at the urging
of the majority, willingly abdicated. The whole affair was conducted as a hilarious game, and all of them, particularly the pirate
leader, approved and supported the deed. The new king said that
he wanted to cement their sottish loyalties with an oath. He ordered a bowl, black with soot, to be brought out. They all had to
swear on it as though on an altar, even if they didn't want to. Then
it was the pirate leader's turn. He said that he wouldn't swear, and
so he was hauled before the king and condemned for contumacy
by sentence of the piratical college. As the punishment for contumacy was to be dunked in water, the pirate was dunked like others
guilty of this crime, but the gang held him under so long that he
drowned.

The pirate leader's friends were utterly terrified both by the 67
drowned man's misfortune and by the boldness of the conspirators, and nearly fainted. But the king's gang, rejoicing in their success, immediately took over the helm and issued a declaration that
their crime was a new birth of freedom for all. Congratulating
each other, they made for the high seas, returning whence they'd
come.

Gelastus, who had watched the fate of the pirate leader as 68
though from a lookout point, quickly ran back to Charon to tell
him about it. Charon had never welcomed any news more eagerly.

Charon. Ergo, ut erat a vertice ad vestigium usque obsitus et foe-
dissimus, in medium prae gaudio animi resultans, Gelastum amplexatus est eumque exosculando totum effecit lutulentum, 'Nunc'
inquiens 'resipisco. Potuitne commodius uspiam cecidisse res? Et
illud abrasum ulcerosumque caput quis putarit tantos fovere animos? Nunc illi ultro suam erga me omnem iniuriam remitto.
Quod si adfuisses, Gelaste, risisses.'

69   'Tua ego risissem' inquit Gelastus 'iniuria?' 'Quidni' inquit Charon 'cum et ipse, qui tum[113] periculi metu plorarim, nunc rideam?
Namque istic ad hunc salictae truncum unus et item alter conservi
in coniurationis consilium concesserant. Ego eorum adventu perculsus alter immobilis eram prope factus truncus. Prostratum
enim me habebam luto et solo sublato vultu auscultabam quid
tractarent. Eorum verba vix subaudiebam, sed audire visus sum dicentem: "Sat est. Hoc probo: submersum suffocabimus." Me illico
pavor occupat, oblitum mei. Compositis rebus, illi quae simulandi
gratia quasi exposituri attulerant mactatae pecudis intestina et
ventres in eos confertos (quibus delitescebam) calamos ad me con-
iciunt. Atque inprimis egregius ille rex raso capite caprae caput ita
iactat ut, ni declinassem, luissem. Optavi quidem mihi tum cumbam aeque atque in theatro adesse pro casside, atque "Hui" inquam "etiam demortuae hic arietant pecudes."'

70   Haec Charon, atque e vestigio rapta cumba sese undis commit-
tebat. Hortabatur Gelastus ut balneis ablueretur ne tantis sordibus illibutus apud inferos irrideretur. Negavit Charon id se factu-
rum affirmavitque apud inferos malle sordidissimus videri quam
apud mortales lautissimus, modo taeterrimas beluas, homines, fugiat. Tum Gelastus 'Novi' inquit 'quid consilii captes: vis enim tu
quoque hinc ad inferos personatus redire.'

Thus, though caked with mud and filthy from head to foot, he jumped for joy and hugged Gelastus. Kissing him, he completely covered Gelastus in mud. "Now I'm myself again," Charon said. "Could anyone have hoped for a better outcome? Who would have thought that that shaven and sore-covered head could have nurtured such fine ideas? Now I forgive all the injuries it did me! If you had been there, Gelastus, you would have laughed."

"Would I have laughed at your injury?" asked Gelastus. — 69 "Why not," said Charon, "when I'm laughing too, though earlier I was weeping with fear at my peril. A couple of slaves met near the trunk of that willow tree to devise their plot. Unnerved by their coming, I froze as though I were a second trunk. I lay face down in the mud, only raising my head to hear what they were talking about. I could barely overhear their words, but I seemed to hear someone saying, 'That's enough. I agree — let's drown him while he's under water.' I nearly fainted, I was so afraid. With the matter settled, they threw the intestines and stomach of a slaughtered goat (which they'd brought with them, pretending they were going to dispose of them) into the thick rushes near where I was hiding. That distinguished king with the shaven head threw the goat's head so forcefully that I would have done penance if I hadn't ducked. I wished I'd had my boat there to use as a helmet as I did in the theater, and I said, 'Whew, even dead goats butt hard in this place.'"

Charon finished speaking, and immediately seized his boat and 70 launched it in the water. Gelastus encouraged him to wash himself in the baths, so that he would not be ridiculed in the underworld for being so covered in filth. Charon refused to do this, maintaining that he preferred looking filthy in the underworld to being spotless on earth, so long as he could escape those filthy beasts, mankind. Gelastus replied, "I know what you have in mind: you want to return from here to the underworld wearing a mask."

71   Haec Charon atque Gelastus. Demum petentes altum et quae de piratis et rege recensuimus repetentes, incidit ut Charon Peniplusii[114] illius cum rege habitam disceptationem pulcherrimam et dignissimam recensere institueret, quam viso lupo se in reditu recitaturum foret pollicitus Charon. Sed ab historiis recitandis novum ortum periculum interturbavit.[115] Namque verticibus turbinibusque obvolvi mare atque atrocissime sese versans insurgere et scopulis illuctare incipiens omnem salutis spem navigantibus ademerat, praeterquam ut ad proximam cautem asperrimam et difficillimam applicarent.

72   Eo igitur confugientes obstrictum vinctumque Momum reperiunt, tantarum causam tempestatum quaeritantem[116] vel magis quam suas aerumnas dolentem. Tempestatem quidem fecerant rixantes inter se venti. Namque atrocissimi apud theatrum facinoris ab se admissi culpam quisque in alium quempiam reiciendo altercabantur, inde in tantos irarum impetus exarsere tantosque motus excivere ut mare caelo commiscuerint.

73   Exciderat enim ut Charonte ab theatro diffugiente tellus omnis risu deorum commota supploderet. Quo risu Aeolus excitus ex antro rem sciscitatum evolavit. Venti antro inclusi, animis auribusque suspensi atque solliciti, vocem audire visi sunt Famae deae quae quidem stridentibus alis aethera pervadebat, deorum Charontisque factum decantando. Ventos idcirco tanta illico invasit spectandorum deorum ludorumque cupiditas ut refractis claustris, repagulis deiectis obicibusque convulsis, temerario impetu una omnes in theatrum irruperint, tam multa immodestia ut super intensum theatri velum vinclis abruptis cum parte muri traherent in ruinam, sequentibus una statuis quas fastigiis murorum nonnulli caelicolarum deposuerant. Is[117] et veli et statuarum casus non sine maximo fuit deorum malo. Namque alii quassati, alii obruti ruina, nulli non aliqua ex parte collisi exstiterunt.

Such was Charon and Gelastus' exchange. While they were   71
making for the high seas, repeating the story about the pirates and
the king that we have just told, Charon decided to recount the delightful and apt dispute that Peniplusius had with the king; after
seeing the wolf, Charon had promised he would tell the story on
his return.[29] But a new danger arose which interrupted the telling
of stories. The sea began to envelop them in whirlpools, tornadoes
and dreadful waves, and began to beat against the rocks. The sailors' only hope of safety was to head for a nearby crag, one which
was extremely rugged and difficult of access.

Taking refuge there, they came upon Momus, bound and   72
chained, who was even more absorbed in investigating the cause of
the great storm than in grieving over his troubles. The winds,
fighting among themselves, had created the storm. They had quar-
reled, blaming each other for the terrible crime they had committed in the theater. They had burst into such a violent rage, their
passions were so roused, that they churned up sea and sky.

For when Charon had fled from the theater, the laughter of the   73
gods had caused the whole earth to tremble and shake. Aeolus,
awakened by the laughter, flew out of his cave to find out what
was going on. Though shut in their cave, the winds were on high
alert, and thought they heard the voice of the goddess Rumor, flying through the air on whirring wings, descanting upon the deeds
of the gods and of Charon. As a result, the winds were seized with
a great desire to watch the gods and the games. They broke out of
their prison, bent back the bars, tore out the bolts, and burst together into the theater in a heedless rush. They were so out of
control that they tore the fastenings from the veils stretched over
the theater and destroyed part of the wall. The statues some of the
gods had placed on top of the walls fell with it. The collapse of the
veils and the statues was a grave affliction for the gods. Some were
shaken, others buried in the wreckage, and all of them were battered to some extent.

74   Atqui, ut ceteros omittam, Iovem ipsum vinclis veli illaqueatum
ita deturbarunt ut resupinis pedibus, naso retunso rueret in caput.
Cupidinis vero statua superne decidens deam Spem paene oppressit, non tamen defuit quin absterso humero alam decusserit;
Speique item statua Cupidinis pectus, obliquo velo labans, vicis-
sim perculit. Dii attoniti quo se vertant[118] non habent.[119]

75   At Iuppiter, quod unum fuit principis prudentissimi, suo secum
ingenio praecurrit disquirens quidnam pro temporis necessitate sit
agendum caelicolis. Etenim occurrit animo ut metuat ne mortales
iudicent ingratos fuisse diis ludorum apparatus et bene de superis
merendi studium posthac intermittant, si forte vacuum statuis
theatrum offenderint. Alia ex parte ingrato ab tumultu suos revocare instituerat. Ergo, quod facto esse opus intellegit, imperat ut
quisque deorum illico suam in theatrum referat statuam atque
mox abeant, ne apud mortales comperta re irrideantur: convenire
quidem deos quidvis incommodorum pati potius quam auctoritatem suique opinionem amittant. Paruere Iovis dicto omnes praeter
Stuporem deum, qui quidem exsanguis factus obduruerat. Sed
cum caelo dii recenserentur,[120] non Stupor modo aut Spes, quae
mutilata apud mortales remanserat, verum et Pluto et Nox dea de-
siderabantur.

76   Illi quidem, maxime Pluto, qua de causa remanserint periucun-
dissimum erit intellexisse. Dea quidem Nox (ut de illa prius dicam) prout tulit casus iisdem sub theatri gradibus cum Apolline
iuxta suas obdiderant statuas in eamque, quod esset vacua, illam
sortibus plenam, quam supra recensuimus ab Apolline furto sub-
reptam, crumenam indiderat ne ex mortalium numero, apud quos
maximos versari fures senserat, quispiam conferta multitudine

Not to speak of other mishaps, the winds ensnared Jupiter himself in the fastenings of the veils. Thrown off balance, he was knocked off his feet and fell on his head, breaking his nose. The statue of Cupid, falling off the roof, almost crushed the goddess Hope; her shoulder was sheared off and she lost a wing. Then in turn the statue of Hope was pulled down by a fold of the veil and smashed into Cupid's chest. The startled gods did not know what to do. 74

But Jupiter did the one thing worthy of wise princes. He thought ahead and asked himself what the gods should do given the constraints of the situation. The fear came into his mind that humans would think the gods were displeased by the preparations for the games. If they came into a theater empty of statues, their enthusiasm to please the gods might be suspended. On the other hand, he had decided to get his gods out of that disagreeable chaos. So he gave the orders he thought were necessary: each god was to put his or her statue back in its place and leave immediately, so that the mortals wouldn't laugh when they discovered what had happened. It would be better for the gods to endure any inconvenience rather than lose their authority and reputation. Everyone obeyed Jupiter's orders apart from the god Stupor, who had become lifeless and petrified. But when the roll of the gods was called in heaven, not only Stupor and Hope, who remained behind among the mortals in a damaged condition, but also Pluto and the goddess Night were missing. 75

Why those gods, particularly Pluto, stayed behind is a particularly amusing story. I'll mention first the goddess Night, whose statue, as chance would have it, had been placed on the same step of the theater as Apollo's. She had placed inside her empty statue the purse full of fortunes that she had stolen from Apollo (as we have related above) lest any of the mortals — among whom, she knew, there were some peerless pickpockets — steal it in the press of the mob. When Apollo was desperately striving to obey Jupi- 76

subriperet. Cum igitur Iovis imperio ardenti opera pareretur, Apollo casu non suam sed Noctis statuam suum in pectus sustulit ita ut crumena inter ferendum intra pedes deflueret, sed crumenam, quod operi esset intentus, neglexit.

77   Nox vero dea aeque tumultuario illo in opere sese agitans, quam reliquam comperit[121] statuam comportavit. At errore animadverso, rata Apollinem non temere alienam obversasse statuam, oe in filiae gremium furti sui conscia[122] lugens commendavit. Noctis filia est Umbra, et eam quidem Apollo ita amat perdite ut nusquam esse nisi Umbra comite didicerit. At crumenam ipsam Ambago, dearum mendacissima, pede in eam offenso repperit. Hinc tanta in deum Apollinem indignatio adversus Noctem exarsit, cognita re, ut ex eo tempore nihil sibi antiquius deputarit quam ut exosam fugando persequeretur. Illa Umbrae gremio sese tutatur delitescendo.

78   Plutonem vero immania velorum involucra irretitum detinuere, quoad lenones, qui fornicibus cum suis scortorum sordibus accumbebant, fragore exciti adfuere. Ii quidem inventum Plutonem loro ad gulam obducto traxere. Post id alii saxo pedem contundere aggressi sunt ut viderent aurone solidus esset, uti suspicabantur; alii vitreos oculos, quod esse gemmas arbitrarentur, dum eruere innituntur ita contrectant ut altero pupillam extruserint, altero confregerint. Non tulit eum dolorem atque iniuriam Pluto animo forti, sed ingemuit atque plus uno ex maleficis lenonibus multavit. Nam, ut erat pondere vastus, sese in latus vertens quos potuit suppressit, huic pedem et huic manum conterens atque comminuens; exinde ab sordidissimis relictus foro dicitur aberrare luminibus captus.

ter's command, by chance he picked up Night's statue rather than his own. While carrying it against his chest, the purse fell down to his feet, but he was so preoccupied by his own efforts that he overlooked it.

But the goddess Night, who was equally flustered by the confused activity, picked up an abandoned statue she had found. Realizing her mistake, and believing that Apollo would not have casually exchanged statues, she regretted her theft and threw herself weeping into her daughter's embrace. Night's daughter was Shadow, and Apollo loved her so desperately that he declared he would have no one else besides Shadow as his companion. But Ambiguity, the most mendacious of goddesses, came across the purse by stubbing her toe on it. When Apollo discovered what had happened, he blazed up with so much indignation against Night that from that moment nothing was more important for him than harassing and putting to flight his hated enemy. She hid herself, taking shelter in Shadow's bosom. 77

As for Pluto, the vast folds of the theater's cover pinned him down until his shouts alerted a group of pimps, who were lolling around their brothel with some filthy whores. When they found Pluto, they wrapped a leather thong around his neck and pulled him out. Some tried to pound his feet to a pulp with a stone to see whether they were made of solid gold, as they suspected; while others, thinking his glittering eyes were jewels, strained to pluck them out. They manhandled Pluto's eyes so roughly that they pushed the pupil of one eye out and broke the other. Pluto did not suffer the pain and injury courageously, but groaning, exacted punishment from more than one of those vicious pimps. He was extremely heavy, so he turned onto his side and squashed as many as he could, crushing and shattering this one's foot, that one's hand. It's said that he was then deserted by those vile men and wandered around the forum, blinded. 78

79   Itaque istiusmodi in theatro gesta sunt. Ceterum venti, tantorum scelerum se fuisse auctores conspicati, alter alterum spectans commutuerant. Dehinc metu conscientiae intra se animis vexari, proxime mutuo alter alterum arguere temeritatis atque immodestiae coeperant; postremo conviciis excandescere et tumultuare perseverabant. Demum ardescente rixa luctationum perduellionumque campum sibi mare occupaverant, ex quo repens illa, quam supra commemoravimus, procella oborta est.

80   Hac igitur procella acti Charon et Gelastus ad eam cautem ubi obstrictus haerebat Momus devenere, quo loci miserias Momi advertentes sese recrearunt. Namque qui laboribus periculisque acti[123] pessime agi secum arbitrabantur, ut Momi vultus vix ab aestuante oceano respirantes una et lacrimas undantes videre, alieni mali misericordia suos mitigarunt animi dolores. Atqui et quis esset et quid illic tam graves perferret poenas sciscitati, si quid opis possent admodum praestituros polliciti sunt. At Momus 'O nos' inquit 'miseros, et quid est quod naufragus ad relegatum possit afferre opis, praeterquam ut sua mala collugeant?' His dictis multo illacrimavit, dehinc ut se fractum confectumque procellarum mole paululum ab aquis levarent exoravit.

81   Quo levato extemplo Momus atque Gelastus sese mutuo agnovere. Multas enim, cum apud mortales degeret, Momus cum Gelasto de rebus maximis et gravissimis habuerat disputationes. Idcirco nonnullis commemoratis utrimque tum[124] factis tum dictis, 'Ego vero' inquit Momus 'tum cum apud vos philosophabar, Fraudis deae ductu caelo proscriptus, aberrabam, sed pro gravissima accepta iniuria in vindicanda mei dignitate malui semper me inter mortales humillimum videri quam inter philosophos deum. Dedi tamen[125] aliquid gravissimo dolori et iustissimae indignationi meae; plura tamen dedi deorum nomini, quando ea perpeti potui

So incidents like this took place in the theater. The winds, real- 79
ising their responsibility for these acts of wickedness, looked at
one another and fell silent. Fear and remorse tormented their
minds, then they all began to berate each other for rashness
and undisciplined behavior. After that they blazed up, screaming
abuse, and continued to fight. In the end, as their quarrel raged,
they made the sea the battlefield of their internecine struggles.
That is why the sudden storm arose which we described earlier.

The storm drove Charon and Gelastus to the crag where 80
Momus was bound and fastened. They were comforted when they
heard Momus' woes. They thought they themselves had experienced the worst possible hardships and dangers, but when they
saw Momus' face, gasping in the boiling ocean and swimming with
tears, pity for another's trials softened their own woes. They
wanted to know who he was and why he had to endure such harsh
punishment. They promised that they would certainly provide
whatever help they could. But Momus said, "Oh, how wretched I
am! What help can a shipwrecked man offer to an exile, apart
from sympathy?" Momus wept violently, then begged them to lift
him a little way out of the water, for he was broken and nearly
consumed by the pounding of the waves.

When they had lifted him, Momus and Gelastus immediately 81
recognized one another. When he lived among humans, Momus
had often held disputations with Gelastus about important and
weighty matters. So after they had exchanged a few memories of
these debates, Momus said, "When I used to philosophize among
you, having been proscribed from heaven at the instigation of Mischief, I made many mistakes, but because of the serious injuries I
received while avenging my dignity, I always preferred to be the
lowest among mortals rather than a god among philosophers. Yes,
I made some concessions to my heavy grief and my righteous indignation. But I made still more concessions to the name of the
gods, for so as not to harm the divine order by revealing my iden-

ab homunculis, ne ordini superum officerem ipsum me propa-
lando, quae ne inimici quidem ut diutius ferrem potuere perpeti.

82 'Profuit aut ad misericordiam malorum nostrorum excitandam,
aut ad illorum qui nos oderant iracundiam exstinguendam, incre-
dibilis illa aerumnarum mearum tolerantia. Caelo idcirco restitutus sum, et quo videas Iovis optimi deorumque aequitatem, me
quidem, quod nulla re praeterquam bene agendo et recte consu-
lendo offendissem, proscripserant. Quod vero et deam et virginem
in templo oppresserim, omnes risere! Redii ad superos vetus Momus ille qui semper fueram, sed novo animi instituto imbutus. Et
qui in eam diem consueveram opinionem ad veritatem, studia ad
officium, verba frontemque ad pectoris intimas rectasque rationes
referre, idem post reditum didici suspicioni opinionem, libidini
studia, dolis confingendis frontem, verba pectusque accommodare.
Non plus dico, nisi me perversis istiusmodi artibus quamdiu apud
beatorum illud collegium exercui, tamdiu et principi carus et uni-
versis probatus et singulis commendatus et (audeo dicere) inimicis
quoque fui gratissimus.

83 'Illud ad rerum nostrarum exitium fecit, quod tantis honoribus
honestatus mea interesse arbitratus sum ut cederem iam malis
artibus et ad pristinam animi libertatem ipsum me restituerem,
spretis servilibus assentationum blanditiarumque delenimentis. Et
sum ipse mihi conscius quid egerim, quid studuerim prodesse diis.
Sino ceteras res: tanta me habuit deorum cura ut Iovi, cum de novandis rebus cogitaret, multis vigiliis veteres omnes illas de deorum regumque officio rationes collegerim quas eram solitus commentari tecum, mi Gelaste,[126] tabellisque conscriptas dederam.
Sed ille quanti eas fecerit hi casus edocent. Non id, quantum videre licet, honestum utileque consilium placuit Iovi, at placuit me
in has miserias relegare.

84 'Vos hic quid magis vituperabitis: an desidiam in neglegenda republica an iniustitiam in administranda? Sed institutum hoc prin-

tity, I allowed myself to endure from the homunculi things that my own enemies would not have wanted me to endure for long.

"My incredible tolerance for hardship proved helpful in that it 82 aroused pity for my woes and softened the anger of my enemies, and I was restored to heaven. Consider the fairness of great Jupiter and the gods. They proscribed me — me, whose only offense was acting well and providing good counsel! When I ravished the virgin goddess in the temple, they all laughed! I returned to the gods the same old Momus I had always been, though imbued with a new resolution. Up to that day, I was in the habit of matching my beliefs to the truth, my zeal to my true allegiances, my words and my expressions to the innermost, sincerest workings of my heart. After I returned, though, I learned to adapt my opinions to prejudice, my zeal to lust, and my expression, words and heart to devising tricks. I will say no more, apart from this: as long as I used these perverted arts in that college of the blessed, I was dear to my prince, universally approved, individually trusted, and, I daresay, liked even by my enemies.

"What caused my destruction was being loaded with great 83 honors. Thanks to this, I thought it would be better for me to set aside those wicked arts and reclaim my former freedom of spirit, casting off the servility of a yes-man and a flatterer. I'm fully aware of what I've done, how I've studied to benefit the gods. Passing over everything else, I was so concerned for the gods that when Jupiter was contemplating renovations to the world, I spent many sleepless nights gathering together those old systems of governing gods and men I used to discuss with you, my dear Gelastus. I wrote them down in notebooks and gave them to him, but events have shown how much value he set on them. As you can see, that honest and useful advice did not suit Jupiter, but it did suit him to drive me out into this wretched state.

"What would you criticize more in this case: his apathy in ne- 84 glecting the state or his injustice in governing it? He himself sees

cipis quam sit e republica ipse videat. Iustum vero esse nemo bonus asseret, nequedum scimus quam futurum sit ut bene vertat iis qui nostra laetentur calamitate. Neque is quidem, qui recta consulentes malo afficit, prava molientes bonis prosequitur, quamdiu sic se gerens futurus sit felix satis habet constitutum. Sed haec curent alii, quibus relictum est quod sperent: nos nostris miseriis ferendis vacemus.'

85   Cum haec dixisset Momus, tum contra 'Tui me' inquit Gelastus 'miseret, o noster Mome! Sed quid ego meas calamitates memorem quo te afflictum consolem? Ego, a patria exul, aetatis florem consumpsi continuis peregrinationibus, assiduis laboribus; diuturnam per egestatem, perpetua cum inimicorum tum et meorum iniuria vexatus, pertuli et amicorum perfidiam et affinium praedam et aemulorum calumnias et inimicorum crudelitatem. Fortunae adversos impetus fugiens, paratas in ruinas rerum mearum incidi. Temporum perturbationibus et tempestatibus exagitatus, aerumnis obrutus, necessitatibus oppressus, omnia tuli moderate ac modice, meliora a piissimis diis meoque fato sperans quam exceperim. Atqui o me beatum, modo mihi ab cultu et studiis bonarum artium, quibus semper fui deditus, feliciora rependerentur! Sed in litteris quid profecerim aliorum sit iudicii. Hoc de me profiteor, omni opera, cura, studio, diligentia elaborasse ut me quantum in dies proficerem non paeniteret. Praeter opinionem atque exspectationem successit. Nam unde gratia debebatur, inde invidia;[127] unde subsidia ad vitam exspectabantur, inde iniuria; unde boni bona pollicebantur, inde mali mala rettulerunt. Dices: "Ea fuere quidem eiusmodi ut hominibus evenire consueverint, et te meminisse hominem oportet."

how unstatesmanlike his princely conduct is. Indeed, no good man would claim that it was just, and I still don't know whether it will turn out well for those who rejoiced in my misfortune. Even he, who inflicts evil on those who give him upright counsel and rewards those who plot acts of corruption—even he can't be certain how long his happiness will last when he behaves like this. But let others who still have hope worry about this. My only task is to endure misery."

When Momus had spoken, Gelastus responded, "I am very 85 sorry for you indeed, my dear Momus! But how shall I recount my own misfortunes so as to console you in yours? I wasted the flower of my youth in continual wandering and constant hardship, an exile from my country. Battered by perennial poverty and by the continual injuries both my enemies and my own family inflicted on me, I endured the treachery of my friends, thefts by my relatives, the slander of my rivals and the cruelty of my enemies. Fleeing the hostile blows of fortune, I fell into the utter ruin of my affairs that was awaiting me. Harassed by upheavals and the storms of the times, overwhelmed by hardships, crushed by need, I bore everything calmly and moderately, hoping for better things than I had received from the holy gods and from my destiny. Oh, how blessed I would have been, if I had been repaid more happily for my cultivation and study of the liberal arts, to which I was always devoted! But it is up to others to judge my accomplishments in literature. I will say this for myself: I employed every effort and all my devotion and zeal so that I would never regret the expenditure of my time. I was completely unprepared for what happened. For where I was owed thanks, I was repaid with envy; where I expected subsidy, I received injury, where good men promised good things, evil men returned evil. You will say, 'These are the sorts of thing that usually happen to men; remember that you were a man.'

86 'Tum[128] vero, Mome, quid dices si audies quae Charonti huic deo acciderint? Dum res hominum non ignorare digno certe et prudenti instituto elaboravit, saxis fugatus palude collituit. Postremo terra marique extremis periculis perfunctus aegre huc ad te casu appulit. Qua abeat, quorsum tendat, ubi consistat, nil certi habet, ut congratulandum in tantis malis putem mihi vel quod deos malorum meorum comites habeam, vel quod deos meliores ad res natos tristiori paene videam in sorte quam ipse fuerim constitutus. Vobis item inter vos, o Mome tuque Charon, maeroris levandi argumenta sint quod alterum quisque alter videat casibus non immunem.'

87 His commiserationibus superaccessit Neptunus deus, qui quidem, cognita ventorum protervia, nubibus imperarat ut eos superne pressando coercerent, quoad ipse cursu[129] obambiens insolescentes commodius argueret. Eo pacto cum dictis tum tridente omnes toto mari delirantium immodestias castigarat, ac deinceps ad Momum consalutandum accesserat.

88 Quo loci inventis Charonte ac Gelasto, voluit fieri certior quid ita applicuissent; cognita eorum peregrinationis historia vehementer insaniam ventorum inculpavit, qui quidem una stultitia tam multorum flagitiorum causa fuerint: ludos interturbarint, maria perverterint, deos affecerint. Dehinc poscente Momo et Charonte ordine cum ceterorum deorum, tum et Stuporis et Iovis et Plutonis casus explicavit. Postremo 'Estne' inquit Neptunus 'quod me amplius velitis? Pacatis enim oceani rebus me ad Iovem superosque restituam.' Tum Gelastus: 'Si per te licet, o Neptune, pervelim optimo maximoque Iovi[130] et sua et hominum causa suadeas

"But what will you say, Momus, when you hear what happened   86
to Charon here, a god? When he took pains to learn something
about human affairs, a worthy and prudent undertaking, some
rocks forced him to flee and hide in a marsh. In the end, when extreme danger on land and sea had nearly finished him off, painful
chance brought him here to you. He is at a loss how he may leave,
where he might go, where he can find rest. Indeed, I think I am to
be congratulated in the midst of such evils that I have gods as
companions in my woes, and that I see gods, born for better
things, suffer a gloomier fate, almost, than I myself have faced. Between the two of you, Momus and Charon, you should have
grounds for relieving each other's grief, because each of you can
see that the other is not immune to misfortune."

The god Neptune joined them as they commiserated with   87
one another. Neptune had realized the violent recklessness of the
winds, and had commanded the clouds to press down on them
and restrain them, so that he might make a rapid circuit around
them, the more easily to condemn their insolence. In this way,
with words and with his trident, he had chastised their mad and
undisciplined behavior upon the seas. Then he had approached
Momus to greet him.

When he found Charon and Gelastus there too, he wanted to   88
be informed as to why they had landed there. On hearing the
story of their travels, he cursed the madness of the winds violently,
for it was their folly alone that had caused so much scandal. They
had thrown the games into confusion, churned up the seas and
harmed the gods. Then, at Momus' and Charon's request, he systematically recounted the misfortunes of the other gods as well as
those of Stupor, Jupiter, and Pluto. Finally Neptune said, "What
else can I do for you? Now that I've calmed the ocean I should return to Jupiter and the gods." — "With your permission, O Neptune," said Gelastus, "I would really like you to persuade Best and
Greatest Jupiter, both for his own sake and for that of mankind, to

ut tabellis[131] Momi in moderanda republica utatur. Illis enim plurimum adiumenti inveniet ad se levandum suasque res mirifice firmandas.'

89   Negavit Neptunus futurum ut Iovi quispiam rerum agendarum modum praescribat: ambitiosum enim principem quidvis prius[132] posse quam instrui, neque esse ut volentem admoneas aut nolentem excites; utraque illum in re semper sui fuisse consilii, dum mavult suum ostentare quam alterius favere ingenio. His dictis abiit. Abiit et Charon atque inter navigandum 'O' inquit 'Gelaste, esse quid hoc dicam in principe, praesertim Iove, quem sapientissimum praedicant? Mitto illa, voluptati plus satis inservire, potentatu ad insontium calamitatem abuti, imperare quam imperio dignum videri malle et imperio dignum videri cupere quam esse: haec toleranda sint. Illud profecto grave est, principem ita institutum esse ut neque bene consulentibus delectetur neque bonis consiliis moveatur.'

90   Tum Gelastus 'Et quid putas,' inquit 'o Charon, cum illo agi qui, assentatorum circumventus corona, in dies dediscat se eum esse qui possit errare, et ex licentia libidinis modum et ex libidine officii rationem metiatur, ut nondum satis apud me constitutum sit praestetne principem esse istiusmodi an servum?' Tum Charon 'Facis' inquit 'ut redeat in mentem quod narrare inceperam ante tempestatem de Peniplusio: res profecto digna, tametsi nequeo non ridere cum illius memini, qui se vilissimum hominem maximo regi praeferendum asserebat.' Tum Gelastus: 'Quid esse hoc et ipse dicam, o Charon, in quibusque animis ut metu offenso omnes voluptates animi abiciamus, et periculo transacto e vestigio voluptas

use Momus' notebooks to govern the state. He will find many helpful things in them that will lighten his burdens and wondrously strengthen his position."

Neptune said that no one would dictate due measure to Jove in   89
the conduct of his affairs. That prince was so conceited that he would do anything before he would take instruction. You couldn't restrain him when he wanted to do something and you couldn't stir him when he didn't. Faced with two possible courses of action, he always followed his own counsel, preferring as he did to show off his own genius rather than back someone else's. Having said this, he departed. Charon also left, and as he was sailing away, he said, "Gelastus, what is it about princes, especially Jupiter, who is supposed to be supremely wise? Let's put aside that he is a slave to pleasure; that he abuses his power, causing disaster for the innocent; that he prefers to rule rather than to seem worthy of ruling; and that he wants to *seem* worthy of rule rather than *to be* worthy of it: all this one can tolerate.[30] But it is certainly a serious matter if a prince is brought up neither to be glad of good advisors nor to be influenced by good ideas."

Gelastus replied, "Well, Charon, what do you think will hap-   90
pen to someone who, surrounded by an audience of flatterers, daily forgets that he is someone who can make a mistake, measures the limits of his lusts according to his license and the exercise of his duty according to his lusts? I haven't yet settled for myself whether it would be better to be a prince like this or a slave." — "You've reminded me that just before the storm, I had started to tell the story of Peniplusius," said Charon. "It's a really worthwhile story, although I can't help but laugh when I remember him, for he maintained that being the lowest of men was preferable to being the greatest of kings." — "Charon, what is it about people's minds that when we experience fear we cast off all desire for pleasure, and when we've surmounted the danger, that desire immediately returns? When you saw the storm, why were you so

redeat? Sed tu quid ita visa tempestate expavisti, ut non coeptam historiam modo neglexeris, verum et tui paene oblitus sis?' Tum Charon: 'An secus potui, tantos aquarum montes circum intumescentes et irruentes intuens?' Tum Gelastus: 'Esto montes ut libet! Enimvero tu, qui me increpabas quod piratas timerem, cum ne vitam quidem possent auferre, et mare invium neglegebas, quid metuisti? Marene ipsum, quando Acheronta non videris, sed consenueris? Aut quid demum? Veteranus navita periculumne timuisti, Charon, cum te immortalem habeas?'

91   Tum Charon contra: 'Navita et immortalis ut libet, hoc scio oportuerat si forte periclitassemus: aut totas illas perpotare aquas aut enecari.' Tum Gelastus: 'Places, Charon: verum sequere, narra disceptationem illam. Videre videor futuram non ignobilem.' Tum[133] Charon: 'Audies rem dignissimam, ac iuvat quidem eam recensere, posteaquam huius[134] fluvii fauces, si satis rem teneo, ingressi sumus. Novi aquarum suetum odorem et, ni fallor, spelunca istaec suppressa et humilis ea est qua ituri sumus. Haec ego adivi loca nonnumquam otiosus. Ergo, posteaquam remum linquere et prostratos secundis aquis dilabi opus est, iacentes iis de rebus recensendis delectabimur.

92   'Meam in navim Megalophos rex et Peniplusius praeco una ingressi,[135] de loco coeperant contendere dictis lepidissimis. Nam se ille principem et honore quovis dignum multa sua virtutis facinora referens asserebat. Contra Peniplusius sic disceptabat: "Te, o Charon, arbitrum statuo: vide quid inter nos intersit quidve conveniat. Homo fui ego, hic etiam homo, nam neque tu natus caelo neque ego stipite, o Megalophe. Publicus fuit servus is, ego item publicus. Hoc negato aut quid sit regnum dicito, Megalophe. Num id non est publicum quoddam negotium, in quo etiam invito id agere oporteat quod leges imperant?

93   "'Fuimus ergo pares,[136] nam legibus ambo astricti eramus, quibus si obtemperavimus tu atque ego fecimus ex officio: adeo ergo

afraid that you not only abandoned the story you'd started, but you almost lost consciousness?" — "What else could I do, seeing such mountains of water swelling and crashing around me?" — "Well, call them mountains if you like! You reproached me for being afraid of the pirates though they couldn't take my life, and you despised the dangers of a pathless sea, but what were *you* afraid of? Didn't you grow weak in the knees on that same sea when you couldn't see Acheron? What happened in the end? Did you — a veteran sailor — fear danger, Charon, despite being immortal?"

"A sailor and immortal if you like, but I know what we would   91
have to do if we were endangered — either swill down all that water, or be killed." — "Whatever you like, Charon. But go ahead, tell your story. I can see it's going to be a fine one." — "You'll hear something really worthwhile, and I'll be glad to tell it, once we've entered the mouth of this river, if I remember it right. I recognize the familiar smell of the waters, and if I'm not mistaken, this low and humble cave is the one we're heading for. I used to visit this place sometimes when I wasn't busy. We need to ship oars, lie back and let the current carry us along. While we recline, I'll be glad to tell the story.[31]

"King Megalophos[32] and the herald Peniplusius boarded my   92
boat at the same time, and in the wittiest possible way began to jockey for position. The former declared that he was a prince and worthy of every courtesy, and recounted his many virtuous deeds. Peniplusius took him up as follows: 'I nominate you as our arbiter, Charon. Consider the differences and similarities between us. I was a man, he was a man too, for you weren't born in heaven nor I in a tree-trunk, Megalophos. He was a public servant, and so was I. Deny this, Megalophos, or tell us what kingship is. Isn't it public business when one must do what the laws command, even if one is unwilling?'

"'We were equals, therefore, for laws bound us both. If we   93
obeyed them, you and I did so out of duty, and therefore we were

345

fuimus et servi ambo et pares, Sumus etiam aliis in rebus pares,
aut si impares ego superior in quibus te praestitisse arbitraris. Etenim[137] tu gradu te habitum feliciori putas: id videamus an ita sit.
Sino voluptates et studiorum atque institutorum progressus, quae
omnia et faciliora et commodiora et promptiora et habiliora nobis
fuere quam tibi. Tum et illa praetermittamus, quod te multi oderant, tu multos timebas, mihi omnes favebant, ego nullis non fide-
bam. Tibi ad tete ferendum, ad tuas libidines complendas multis
erat opus, multa cavebas, plura dubitabas, omnia erant in periculo;
mihi adversabatur istorum nihil, plura in rebus meis exsequendis
suppeditabant quam ut illis omnibus uterer. Tibi numquam[138] non
deerant quibus esset usus.

94   "'Sed haec, ut dixi, praetermittamus. Divitias tu ex regno si tibi
congregasti, pessime fuisti functus magistratu et gessisti non regem te, sed tyrannum. Si reipublicae eas parasti, fecisti quod de-
cuit, sed ne illa quidem tua est gloria: universorum ea est civium
laus, non tua, qui quidem aut partas bello aut auctas censu effecere. Dices: 'Mea cura et diligentia urbem resque imperii ornavi
atque servavi meis legibus pacem et quietem; meo ductu et auspi-
ciis laudem et amplitudinem civibus meis peperi.' Nos vero in his
omnibus quae soli fecimus, frustra fecimus; quae vero multitudinis
suffragio et manu fecimus, cur nobis ascribamus non reperio.

95   "'Sed quae tua fuerit opera et quae mea in istiusmodi rebus re-
censeamus. Tu integram noctem aut dormiebas vino madidus aut
per luxum ducebas; ego in specula vigilabam, urbem ab incendio,
cives ab hostibus teque ipsum ab tuorum insidiis custodiens. Tu
leges rogabas, ego promulgabam; te contionem habente saepius

both servants and equals. We are also equals in other matters, or if we are not equal then I am the superior in matters where you think you excelled. For example, you think you are happier in your rank: let's see whether that's true. I'll pass over pleasure and improvement in studies and principles, which were all easier, more useful and more achievable for me than for you. I will also leave out the fact that many people hated you and you feared many, while everyone wished me well and there was no one I couldn't trust. You needed many things to maintain your position and satisfy your desires; you were wary of many things and uncertain about most things; everything was a source of danger. Nothing like this stood in my way, and the resources I had for carrying out my affairs were greater than the uses to which I could put them. You always lacked things you might have used.

"'But as I said, I'll leave this out of account. If you amassed 94 wealth from your kingdom, then you were a corrupt magistrate and your conduct made you no king, but a tyrant. If you acquired riches on behalf of the state, you behaved appropriately, but even that was no glory of yours: the whole citizen body, not you, deserved the praise, since it was they who either won the war or paid more taxes. You will say, "My devotion and diligence embellished the city and the empire. I maintained peace and quiet through my laws, and procured honor and prosperity for my citizens thanks to my leadership and authority." Yet in all those situations where we act alone, we act in vain, but when we act with the approval and united force of a group, I don't see how one person can take the credit for himself.

"'Let's review what you did and what I did in the following sit- 95 uations. You used to spend the entire night either in wine-soaked sleep or in debauchery, while I stayed awake on watch, guarding the city from fire, the citizens from their enemies and you yourself from the plots of your own family. You authorized laws, I promulgated them. When you held a council, the people often objected

populus reclamavit, me publicum quid iubente omnes attentissime auscultabant. In expeditionibus militem hortabaris, ego signum dabam; te miles observabat, me classicum canente aut hostem invadebat aut revocabatur. Denique tibi universi assentabantur, nobis nemo non parebat.

96 "'Sed quid agimus? Tune otium civibus parasti, cuius causa tanti tam frequentes armorum discordiarumque motus in urbe fuerint? cuius artibus et studiis publica et privata, sacra et profana omnia sint referta invidia, simultate omnique[139] denique flagitiorum genere? Tum ceteras quidem stultas rerum administrandarum ostentationes quid est quod referas? Quid est quod te iactes quod templa et theatra non ad urbis ornamentum, sed ad gloriae cupiditatem et ineptam nominis posteritatem comparaveris? Et istas elegantes leges quanti putabimus, quibus improbi non pareant et probis indixisse non oportuit?

97 "'Ac[140] 'Poteram quidem' inquies 'multare et esse malo maximo refragantibus. In hoc maleficii genere quis me potentior, quis paratior?'[141] Tu quidem unos aut alteros cives non sine discrimine, non nisi tumultu et multorum manu affecisses; ego totam urbem, si voluissem, perdidissem tacendo atque dormiendo.

98 "'Restant duo quibus te longe superabam. Tui te dominum bonorum fortunarumque omnium praedicabant; ego re ipsa eram non id tantum, ut dixi, quod ea potuerim perdere, sed quo omnium bona et fortunae agebantur ita atque dispensabantur ad unguem uti volebam ipse. Namque fiebat ulla[142] in provincia, ullo aut publico aut privato in loco nihil me invito; tibine tuorum quidem bonorum et fortunarum ex arbitrio quippiam succedebat? Plura[143]

loudly, but they all listened to me most attentively when I made public proclamations. On military expeditions you harangued the soldiers; I gave them the signal to fight. The soldiery used to listen to you respectfully, but when I blew the trumpet they engaged with the enemy or retreated. In short, everyone flattered you, but there was no one who disobeyed me.

"'But why go on? You claim to have brought peace to your citizens, when on your account there were so many armed riots and so much strife in the city? When because of your machinations and partisanship all matters public and private, sacred and profane, were filled with mistrust, feuds and every kind of scandal? Why do you go on retailing the rest of the foolish parades of magnificence that marked your administration? How can you boast of temples and theaters built, not for the adornment of the city, but out of a desire for glory and for the foolish perpetuation of your name? Why should we rate so highly those fine laws of yours which criminals disobeyed and the upright had written in their hearts? 96

"'But you will say, "I was certainly able to punish opponents and do them harm. Who was more powerful and better armed than I when it came to this kind of havoc?" Certainly you could have harmed one citizen or another, but not without crisis, tumult and the combined force of many other people. If I'd wanted, I could have destroyed the whole city by keeping silent and sleeping. 97

"'There are two other ways in which I far surpass you. Your adherents claim that you were your own master and master of all goods and treasure. In reality, I not only could have destroyed everything, as I said, but I was also in charge of all goods and treasure, so that I could distribute them exactly as I pleased. Nothing happened in any province, in any public or private place, unless I wanted it to. Did any of your own goods and treasure prosper as you wished? You always wanted more than you could get, while I 98

volebas semper quam posses; ego rerum omnium nil plus volebam
quam quod esset; sic enim volebam omnia esse uti erant, et nihil
magis. Reliquum est quod si tua tu amisisses bona ipsum te sus-
pendisses, ego risissem.'"

99   Dum haec apud inferos agerentur, Iuppiter aula reclusus, in
solitudine secum ipse temporum suorum casus et institutorum
successus repetens, sese dictis huiusmodi castigabat: 'Quid tibi voluisti, hominum pater et deum rex? Quis te erat beatior? Pusilla-
rum ferendarumque rerum taedio quantos labores, quae pericula,
qualia incommoda subivisti! Tuis in capiendis consiliis quam tibi
fueris satis Kalendarum dies docuit. Bene consulentes respuisse,
inconsultorum libidini obtemperasse quid conferat argumento erit
aeterno imminutus nasus. Eorum vota supplicantium fastiditi[144]
reiciebamus, quorum foeditatem irridentium postea pertulimus.
Nos esse nimirum beatos paenitebat, quando novis voluptatibus
captandis veterem dignitatem intermisimus. Novum quaerebamus
exaedificare mundum, quasi pigeret diutini otii; et otio abundantes
otium quaerebamus, et otium quaerentes otium demerebamur.
Quid igitur assecuti sumus? Indignos caelo inter deos accepimus,
benemerentes aut exterminavimus aut amisimus. Sed quid agimus? An parum poenarum pro admissa stultitia accepimus, ni
etiam acerbis his curis animi ingratisque durissimorum temporum
recordationibus ultro excruciabimur?[145] Abite hinc tristes curae!
Verum aliquo me exercam opere necesse est, ne nos vacuos et desides occupent tristes memoriae. Ac novi quid faciam: hoc enim
conclave dissolute habitum coaptabimus.'

100   Positis idcirco stragula et vestibus omnem subselliorum ordinem commutare aggressus est librosque complures abiecte exposi-
tos et pulveribus obsitos digno loco astruxit. Dum haec compone-
ret, venere in manus tabellae Momi, quas superius Iovi datas

never wanted more from the world than there was, for I wanted everything to be just as it was, and no more. In the end, if you lost your goods you would have hanged yourself, whereas I would have laughed.'"

While this was happening in the underworld, Jupiter, hidden 99 away in his palace, thought over in solitude his ill fortune and the failure of his plans. He reproached himself in this wise: "What were you hoping for, father of men and king of the gods? Who was more blessed than you? What hardships, dangers and discomforts have I borne merely because I was fed up with minor annoyances! The Kalends taught you how little you can rely on your own counsel. Your broken nose will provide you with eternal evidence of how you rejected good advice and complied with the desires of the misguided. We spurned and turned up Our noses at the offerings of suppliants whose filthy mockery We later were obliged to endure. We regretted Our presumably blessed condition when We abandoned Our old dignity to grasp at new pleasures. We sought to build a new world, as though Our prolonged leisure was irksome to Us; rich in leisure, We sought leisure; and seeking leisure, We ceased to deserve it. So what did We accomplish? We welcomed unworthy gods into heaven and either banished or lost the deserving ones. But what are We doing? Have We paid so small a price for Our admitted foolishness that We should willingly let ourselves be tortured by these bitter anxieties and the unpleasant memories of cruel times? Be gone, grim cares! I must apply myself to some new task, lest grim memories besiege me in my idleness and inactivity. I know what I shall do, I shall tidy up this messy room!"

Jupiter threw off the bedclothes and started to put the furniture 100 in order. He put a number of dust-covered books that were strewn about negligently in their proper places. While he was arranging them, his hands fell upon the notebooks Momus had given him (as we recounted above). When he found them, Jupiter could not

recensuimus. Inventis non potuit facere Iuppiter quin iterum perturbaretur maerore seque suosque casus repetens. Tandem tabellas perlegit animi laetitia adeo maxima et dolore adeo maximo ut utrisque addi amplius nihil posset,[146] tanta erant in his grata una atque ingrata. Gratum erat quod in eis inveniret ab philosophorum disciplinis sumptas optimas et perquam necessarias admonitiones ad regem mirifice comparandum atque habendum. Ingratum erat quod tantis praeceptis tamque ad gloriam et gratiam accommodatis per suam neglegentiam diutius potuerit carere.

101 In tabellis ista continebantur: principem sic institutum esse oportere ut neque nihil agat neque omnia, et quae agat neque solus agat neque cum omnibus, et curet ne quis unus plurima neve qui plures nihil habeant rerum aut nihil possint. Bonis benefaciat etiam invitis, malos non afficiat malis nisi invitus. Magis notabit quosque per ea quae pauci videant quam per ea quae in promptu sunt. Rebus novandis abstinebit nisi multa necessitas ad servandam imperii dignitatem cogat aut certissima spes praestetur ad augendam gloriam. In publicis prae se feret magnificentiam, in privatis parsimoniam sequetur. Contra voluptates pugnabit non minus quam contra hostes. Otium suis, sibi vero[147] gloriam et gratiam artibus pacis quam armorum studiis parabit. Dignari se votis patietur et humiliorum indecentias ita feret moderate uti a minoribus suos pati fastus volet.

102 Huiusmodi erant in tabellis complurima, sed illud omnium fuit commodissimum inventum ad multas imperii molestias tollendas. Nam admonebat ut omnem rerum copiam tres in cumulos partire-

help but be overwhelmed once again with grief, reviewing his misfortunes. In the end, he read through the notebooks with such mingled joy and sorrow that nothing more could be added to either emotion, so many were the reflections in those books that were at once pleasant and unpleasant. It was pleasant to find in them the best and wondrously valuable advice, derived from the teachings of the philosophers, about how to acquire and maintain royal power. It was unpleasant that through his own negligence he had deprived himself for so long of such fine teachings, so suited to glory and to grace.

The following was written in the notebooks. The prince should   101 be instructed that he must neither do everything nor do nothing. What he does he should not do alone, nor with everyone else. He should make sure that no one individual has too many things, nor that the many have nothing and have no power. He should reward the good even when they don't want rewards, and he should visit evils upon the wicked only when he is unwilling.[33] He should take notice of people for their less obvious qualities rather than for their immediately apparent ones. He should refrain from making changes, unless compelled to do so for the sake of maintaining his authority, or unless he has some guarantee of increasing his glory. In public affairs, he will display extraordinary generosity, in his private affairs he will observe frugality. He will fight against pleasures no less than against enemies. For his subjects he will obtain security, for himself glory and grace, relying on the arts of peace as upon the practice of arms. He will permit himself to be thought worthy of prayers, and he will bear calmly the importunities of the humble, just as he wants his own pride to be tolerated by his inferiors.

Much advice of this kind was written in the notebooks, but the   102 most useful advice pertained to lightening the many tribulations of power. The notebook advised that all resources should be divided into three piles. The ruler should make one pile of good and desir-

tur: unum bonarum expetendarumque rerum, alterum malarum, tertium vero poneret cumulum earum rerum quae per se neque bonae sint neque malae. Has ita distribueret ut iuberet ex bonorum cumulo Industriam, Vigilantiam, Studium, Diligentiam, Assiduitatem reliquosque eius generis deos desumere plenos sinus et per trivia, porticus, theatra, templa, fora,[148] denique publica omnia per loca aperto sinu ultro obviis porrigerent et volentibus grate ac libens traderent. Mala itidem sinu pleno et aperto Invidia, Ambitio, Voluptas, Desidia, Ignavia ceteraeque iis similes deae circumferrent atque sponte erogarent non invitis. Quae autem neque bona neque mala sint, uti ea sunt quae bona bene utentibus et mala male utentibus sunt, quorum in numero putantur divitiae, honores et talia ab mortalibus expetita, omnia Fortunae arbitrio relinquerentur ut ex iis plenas manus desumeret, et quantum cuique videretur, atque in quos libido traheret, conferret.

FINIS

able things, another of evils, and a third pile consisting of things that are in themselves neither good nor evil. He should distribute these as follows. He should order Industry, Vigilance, Zeal, Diligence, Constancy and other gods like them to fill their pockets from the pile of good things, then empty their pockets freely at crossroads, in porticoes, theaters, temples, fora and all public places, offering the good things to whomever they met and handing them over graciously and gladly to whoever wanted them. At the same time, Envy, Ambition, Pleasure, Laziness and Cowardice and other gods like them should fill their pockets to the brim with evils, and should go about disbursing them spontaneously to whoever wanted them. The things that were neither good nor bad would be good for those who used them well and bad for those who used them badly; these included riches, honors and such things as mortals sought. These should all be left to Fortune's judgement. She should fill her hands with them, and decide who should receive them and how much to give each one, as the fancy took her.

THE END

Note on the Text

༄༅༅

The text of Alberti's *Momus* survives in at least four manuscripts of the fifteenth century and two early printed editions, and has been edited twice in modern times, by Giuseppe Martini in 1942 and Rino Consolo in 1986. (The bilingual Latin-German edition of Michaela Boenke published in 1993 reproduces the text of the Consolo edition.) The most important work on the text, however, was undertaken by Alessandro Perosa in preparation for a new critical edition which unfortunately was not completed before his death.[1] As Perosa's investigation showed, previous editors of Alberti's text had neglected the two oldest and most important witnesses, *F* (Venice, Biblioteca Nazionale Marciana, Marc. lat. VI 107 [2851]) and *P* (Paris, Bibliothèque Nationale de France, lat. 6702). *F* represents an earlier stage of the text and contains autograph corrections. Perosa believed these to have been made in an unsystematic way and without direct reference to the author's archetype. Perosa supposed *P* to represent a later stage in the textual evolution of the *Momus;* it too contains numerous autograph corrections and changes and was written by a more careful scribe. *B* (Oxford, Bodleian Library, Canon. Misc. 172) and *O* (Vatican City, Biblioteca Apostolica Vaticana, Ottob. lat. 1424), on the other hand, seem to be derived from *P.* A fifth manuscript (Wrocław, Biblioteka Uniwersytecka, Rehdiger MS 171), listed by P. O. Kristeller,[2] is no longer extant.

Of the two printed editions, both published at Rome in 1520, that of Etienne Guillery also follows *P,* whereas the edition of Giacomo Mazzocchi appears to be based on a composite witness or witnesses whose relationship to the various stages of Alberti's archetype is unclear. Perosa and Cecil Grayson (in a review of Consolo's edition)[3] are agreed in regarding its often superficially

357

attractive readings as the work of a later editor, presumably Mazzocchi himself.

For the present edition, F and P were collated in their entirety
from microfilm. Doubtful readings of F were confirmed through
personal inspection of the manuscript, and many readings in P
were checked *in situ* by Dr. Greti Dinkova-Bruun, to whom we are
much indebted. Our text is based primarily on P, presumably the
last copy made under the author's supervision. The critical apparatus records shared or individual variants of FP that illustrate in a
significant way Alberti's revision of the text (a complete listing of
Alberti's interventions merits a separate study). Also included in
the apparatus are omissions in FP and the more plausible variants
offered by F, along with occasional citation of readings from the
editions of Martini and Consolo. Orthography, punctuation and
capitalization have been modernized in accord with the require-
ments of this series.

The Notes to the Translation, while much indebted to the
notes that accompany the edition of Consolo, have been checked,
modified and expanded.

SIGLA

F	Venice, Biblioteca Nazionale Marciana, MS Marc. lat. VI 107 [2851]
P	Paris, Bibliothèque Nationale de France, MS lat. 6702
Consolo	The edition of Rino Consolo (1986)
Martini	The edition of Giuseppe Martini (1942)
Perosa	The study of FP by Alessandro Perosa (1988)

NOTES

1. Alessandro Perosa, "Considerazioni su testo e lingua del *Momus*
dell'Alberti," in *The Languages of Literature in Renaissance Italy*, ed. Peter
Hainsworth, Valerio Lucchesi, Christina Roaf, David Robey and J. R.
Woodhouse (Oxford, 1988), pp. 45–62.

2. *Iter Italicum*, vol. 4 (London and Leiden, 1989), p. 428.

3. See *Giornale storico della letteratura italiana* 164 (1987), pp. 458–63.

Notes to the Text

꙳ৡৼ꙳

PREFACE

1. coniuntusque *F*
2. profectos *P (with final* s *partially erased?)*
3. agamur *F*
4. morantur *corrected in P from* moderantur; moderantur *F*
5. et Pindarus *omitted in F*
6. Nos *F*
7. in *F*
8. Tum et a me *F*
9. meritas *corrected in P from* emeritas; emeritas *F*
10. qui in *Martini, Consolo;* qui *corrected in P from* quin; quin *F*
11. proscripta *F*
12. tu *added suprascript in P by Alberti; omitted in F*

BOOK I

1. *There is a small stain in P after* obversatorem
2. ab *corrected in P from* abs; abs *F*
3. quod *Martini, Consolo;* quo *FP*
4. scaraveonibus *Perosa, p. 62 n. 43;* scataveonibus *F, P (corrected from* scatauconibus); sca-canionibus *Martini;* statanio-nibus *Consolo*
5. dii *corrected in P by Alberti from* divi; divi *F*
6. posset trahi *Martini, Consolo;* possent trahi *P;* possent trahi *corrected in F by Alberti to* traheretur
7. apud se *added by Alberti in the outer margin of P, and he corrects* probari *from* admirari; se nullius admirari *F*
8. tempus *F*
9. obtrectare *corrected in P from* obtrectari; obtrectari *F*
10. irrumperent *F*
11. ut per varios . . . querimonie *added by Alberti in the outer margin of F*
12. ac *F*
13. magistratus *corrected in P from* magistratum; magistratum *F*

14. exagitentur dilabentur *Martini, Consolo*; -gitetur -betur *FP*

15. animal *corrected in P from* animans; animans *F*

16. socus *F*

17. perfidia *corrected in F from* perfidea; perfida *Consolo*

18. uerinnam *FP* (uerīnam *here and in section 23 [FP]*; uerīna *[P] and* uerina *[F] in section 24*)

19. integritate *F*

20. et *omitted in F*

21. rege *P*

22. illic *corrected in P from* illier; illuc *F*

23. quosve *F*; quos *P*

24. metusque *corrected in F to* metumque

25. quecumque *corrected in P by Alberti from* queque; queque *F*

26. auctore *omitted in F*

27. daturi *corrected in F from* -tura; datura *P*

28. quo *corrected in P from* quod; quod *F*

29. habiturum *corrected in P from* -tarum; habituram *F*

30. observandum *corrected in P by Alberti from* admirandum; admirandum *F*

31. quecumque *corrected in P by Alberti from* queque; queque *F*

32. per *corrected in FP from* pro

33. comminus *corrected in P from* quominus; quominus *F*

34. demonstrabat *P*

35. unde . . . accursitarant *omitted in F*

36. Enim *F*

37. ista ex pugna *after* ipsorum *is cancelled in P*; ipsorum ista ex pugna *F*

38. integrum statas veteres *F*; statas *omitted in P, with space left for a word of approximately six letters*

39. ope *corrected in P from* opere; opere *F*

40. profisciscens dea *expunctuated in F*

41. Eccam *corrected in P from* Ercam; Ercam *F*

42. reptantem *corrected in P from* rectantem; rectantem *F*

43. plausu laetitiaque *Martini, Consolo*; plausum letitiamque *FP*

44. exhilarati *corrected in P from* exhilarate, *and in F from* exhilaratem

45. modoque *corrected in P from* moduque; moduque *F* (*with suprascript correction apparently cancelled*)

46. composito et gradu *F*
47. lento ~~motu~~ gradu *F*
48. quod procul *corrected in FP from* procul quod
49. multo <magis> quidem *Consolo*
50. demissi *apparenctly corrected in P from* dimissi; dimissi *F*
51. simules . . . dissimules *corrected in P from* simulas . . . dissimulas; simulas . . . dissimulas *F*
52. dedignatur *corrected in P by Alberti from* demiratur; demiratur *F*
53. duas *F*
54. appeteret *P*
55. nuntiet esse (*corrected from* fore) *P*; renūptiet fore *F*
56. negligerent *corrected in P from* -gant; negligant *F*
57. quos *Consolo*
58. thindaridas *corrected in P by Alberti from* thindarides; thindarides *F*
59. detrectarique *FP*
60. proferemus *F*
61. *F's reading is uncertain; perhaps corrected to* pecuniarum
62. sumus *F*
63. coherenda *F*
64. Sicine . . . concitabas *omitted in P*

65. desperatus *Consolo;* desperatis *FV*
66. sint *F*
67. se *added suprascript by Alberti in P; omitted in F*
68. Admirantibus multoque *cancelled before* invidentibus *in P;* Admirantibus multoque invidentibus *F*
69. adeste *added suprascript by Alberti in P; omitted in F*
70. utilima *FP* (*corrected in P from* utillima)
71. voveto *corrected in P from* vovito; vovito *F*
72. prosecuta *P;* prosecuta est *F*
73. ne . . . tantas: viri *deleted in P before* tantas *and added suprascript by Alberti after* ne; ne quoque sibi una viri tantas *F*
74. resciscerent *F*
75. non *F*
76. recuperaturus sim *corrected in P by Alberti from* recuperarim; recuperarim *F*
77. atque admirationem *after* voluptatem *cancelled in P;* voluptatem atque admirationem *F*
78. circumsepto *corrected in P from* ?, *with* circunsesso *added by Alberti in the inner margin;* circumsepto *F*

79. vertat *corrected in F from* avertat
80. atque contremiscebat *omitted in P*
81. omnes animi motus (motus *added by Alberti in the outer margin*) F
82. metus *omitted in F*
83. allecta *Martini, Consolo*
84. Enim sese FP. *Perosa, pp. 57–58 suggests that the inversion marks above* Enim sese *in P are not those of Alberti; in several other instances Alberti corrected initial* Enim *to* Etenim *or* Enimvero, *and Perosa lists these interventions on p. 57, noting also four occurrences of non-Albertian inversion marks; for the other three examples of inversion marks placed above* Enim *and the following word, see below,* 1.85, 94 *and* 4.48; *in* 1.63 (Martini, p. 34.20), 75 (Martini, p. 40.10) *and* 2.36 (Martini, p. 68.11) enim *begins the sentence and there do not seem to be any interventions by Alberti or later corrections.*
85. diis *corrected in P by Alberti from* divis; divis *F*
86. strupranda *F*

87. consequi *corrected in P by Alberti from* interpellare; interpellare *F*
88. nove etiam (*corrected from* et *and the following* vindicandi *cancelled*) inimicitie *P;* nove etiam vindicandi inimicitie *F*
89. edere *F* (*corrected suprascript by Alberti from* edera), *Martini, Consolo*
90. nitebatur *F*
91. nonnunquam *corrected suprascript in P by Alberti from* nunquam; nunquam *F*
92. imiscens *F*
93. garriens *F*
94. versum *Martini, Consolo;* versus *FP*
95. multa *Martini, Consolo*
96. confulta *P*
97. unico cilii nutu (*corrected from* nutus) *F*
98. videndi *F*
99. venerari *corrected in P by Alberti from* mirari; mirari *F*
100. dirimere *corrected in P by Alberti from* irritare; irritare *F*
101. leta ad terras aplicuit *placed after* gratia (*end of the sentence*) *in F*
102. nixu (*corrected from* nuxu) *F*
103. interturbaret *corrected in P by Alberti from* interpellaret; interpellaret *F*

104. densso *corrected in P from* depresso; dempso *F*
105. praemeditaris *Martini, Consolo*
106. foco *corrected in P from* foci; foci *F*
107. *See n. 84 above.*
108. is horum ex numero eorum *F*
109. praebuerant *Martini, Consolo;* praebuerat *FP*
110. mei *corrected in P from* meo; meo *F*
111. luctante *F*
112. qua *F (corrected suprascript from* quo), *Martini, Consolo;* quo *P*
113. ex *Martini, Consolo*
114. consultaturi *F*

115. tum *(corrected from* cum*) has been expunctuated in P after* oratione; oratione cum *F*
116. veniendum *corrected in P by Alberti from* ruendum; ruendum *F*
117. ~~laudem deam~~ matrem *P;* deam matrem *F*
118. omissis *corrected in P from* obmissis; obmissis *F*
119. dee *corrected in P by Alberti from* dive; dive *F*
120. *See n. 84 above.*
121. unam *corrected in P;* nisi unam *added by Alberti in the outer margin of F*
122. diis *corrected in P by Alberti from* divis; divis *F*
123. malim *corrected in the inner margin of P by Alberti from* velim; velim *F*

BOOK II

1. desiderarent *corrected in F to* desideraretur
2. alii *after* et *expunctuated in F*
3. et *omitted in F*
4. novitatem ~~probantibus et mirifice~~ probantibus *P, with* cancelled probantibus *written by Alberti over erased* admirantibus; novitatem admirantibus et mirifice probantibus *F*
5. alia *corrected in F to* altera

6. quod *corrected in P from* quam; quam *F*
7. integre *P*
8. socia legata *expunctuated in P, with* collega *added in the outer margin by Alberti;* sotia legata *F*
9. compararet *F*
10. et *expunctuated in F*
11. superstitiosa quadam severitate *corrected in P from*

quod superstitiosam quandam severitatem; quod superstitiosam quandam severitatem F

12. occasionem *Martini, Consolo*
13. obsecundabunt F
14. confirmare F
15. commodetur *Martini, Consolo, but see Perosa, p. 62 n. 43*
16. detorqueat F
17. impediri *corrected in P by Alberti from* interpellari; interpellari F
18. consultatum P
19. quin *corrected in P from* quidni; quidni F
20. arrisisset *Martini, Consolo;* adrisissent FP
21. nimis *corrected in F from* minis
22. a matre *omitted in F*
23. quod valeret *added by Alberti in the inner margin of P; omitted in F*
24. gemmam F
25. intueor F
26. et *omitted in F*
27. et *omitted in F*
28. iumenta huius phebi ea subisse F
29. aspernatorem *corrected in P from* imperatorem
30. accumules *corrected in P from* accommodes

31. dum . . . deprecanti *omitted in P*
32. etiam *expunctuated in P (later correction by another hand?)*
33. plebes *Martini, Consolo;* phebes F; phebe *corrected in P from* phebes
34. tandem *added by Alberti in the outer margin of P; omitted in F*
35. usquam *added by Alberti in the inner margin of P; omitted in F*
36. his *omitted in F*
37. auderent *Martini, Consolo;* audebant FP
38. herent *corrected in P from* haberet; haberet F
39. cessent *Martini, Consolo;* cessant FP
40. intercluditur *corrected in P by Alberti from* interpelletur; interpelletur F
41. consternatur *apparently corrected in F from* consterne-; consternetur P
42. bene beateque F
43. nocteque P; dieque *added by Alberti in the inner margin of F after* noctuque
44. umbra et P; imbre ac *corrected in F from* umbro *(last letter uncertain)* a
45. est F
46. spectare F

47. te *expunctuated in* F

48. non *Martini, Consolo;* num
FP

49. posteaquam F

50. quibus *corrected in P from*
qua; qua F

51. ex usu vel taedium *omitted in*
F

52. fore tum ut F

53. afferunt F

54. errores F (error- *also occurs in*
sections 48, 49, 51, 95 of book 2)

55. geometra *corrected in P by*
Alberti from geometer, *with*
γεωμετρησ *added in the*
outer margin; geometer F

56. imprudentiam F

57. qui *Martini, Consolo*

58. arte F

59. fastidiis F

60. utimur F

61. κύκνοσ *added by Alberti in*
the outer margin of P

62. an *corrected suprascript in P by*
Alberti from ne; ne F

63. mediumque item (item
cancelled in P) intra F

64. enimvero *corrected in P by*
Alberti from enim; enim F

65. alucinabatur *Martini,*
Consolo; allucinabat FP

66. enimvero *corrected in P by*
Alberti from enim; enim F

67. fiet F

68. eam . . . statuam: statuam
after eam *in P was apparently*
written by Alberti, then
cancelled and placed by Alberti
at the end of the sentence after
anteponendam; eam
statuam F

69. scapularum *corrected in P*
from spatularum; spatularum
F

70. soccos F

71. pendebat F

72. diisque et F

73. videre ut factum F

74. sensere *added by Alberti in the*
inner margin of F after
gratam; *omitted in* P

75. idcirco *added by Alberti in the*
inner margin of P; omitted in F

76. et *added suprascript by Alberti*
in FP

77. Enimvero *corrected suprascript*
in P by Alberti from enim;
enim F

78. non augenda P; minuenda
(*corrected from* minuendi) F

79. sui *corrected in P from* tui

80. comi F

81. ducet *corrected in P by Alberti*
from ducere se (?); ducere se
F

82. accersurus *corrected in P from*
arcessurus; arcessurum F

83. reddat F

84. tamen F

85. culpa *corrected from* culparum (?) *in* P *and* culpam *in* F
86. fame *corrected in* FP *from* famem
87. corroborarent F
88. eiusquam F
89. nomen immortalitati affectent (*the last word added by Alberti in the outer margin*) P; nomen studeant immortalitati F
90. deducendo *Martini, Consolo*
91. pravum F; parvum P
92. constantique F
93. possint F
94. simus P
95. prospecta F
96. optanda homini ducerent FP; homines optanda ducerent *Martini, Consolo*
97. cornicibus *corrected suprascript in* P *by Alberti from* cornibus
98. prospicerem F
99. fuisset F
100. lampadas *corrected suprascript in* P *by Alberti from* lampades; -pades F
101. asportarunt F
102. delfinas *corrected in* P *by Alberti from* delfines; delphines F
103. cete *corrected in* P *by Alberti from* cetas (τα κύτ- *added by*

Alberti *in the inner margin*); cetas F
104. eos expunctuated *in* P *after* pessime; eos pexime F
105. participes facere non P; participes non facere F (non *added by Alberti in both instances*)
106. erogentur P
107. nostrum (-o- *corrected from* e ?) F
108. admisimus *corrected suprascript in* P *by Alberti from* amisimus; ammi- F
109. nos *cancelled and expunctuated in* P *after* ereptis; ereptis nos F
110. numerum *corrected in* P *by Alberti from* numen; numen F
111. medio *corrected in* P *by Alberti from* media; media F
112. γαννμηδησ *added by Alberti in the outer margin of* P
113. nullam *corrected suprascript in* P *by Alberti from* ullam; ullam F
114. infesti *corrected in* P *by Alberti from* irriti; irritati F
115. absumerent *Martini, Consolo*; assumerent FP
116. optavi FP (*cf. Perosa, p. 62 n. 43*); optari *Martini*; optasse *Consolo*

117. et *added suprascript in P;* atque *F*
118. idcirco *omitted in F*
119. ad *F*
120. cogitarent *corrected in F to* cogitent
121. a mente divina *corrected in P by Alberti from* divina a mente; divina ab mente *F*
122. quod *Consolo;* quid *FP*
123. atque *F*
124. qui *F, Martini, but see Perosa, p. 62 n. 43 and Cesarini Martinelli, ed., Philodoxeos fabula, p. 230*
125. deinde *F*
126. colamur *corrected in F from* colimur; colimur *P*
127. eum hic *corrected in F to* tum hos
128. eos *omitted in P*
129. qui *Martini, Consolo, but see Perosa and Cesarini Martinelli (cited in n. 124 above)*
130. erga mortalium *corrected in P from* immortalium; immortalium *F*
131. quem *F*
132. quidem *added in P by Alberti; omitted in F*
133. diliget *F*
134. negarent *F*
135. versis *Martini, Consolo*

136. tīnin *FP* (tinnim *or* timnin ?); Tinnim *Martini,* Tinim *Consolo*
137. spem *F*
138. secundare *corrected in P from* secumdare; secum dare *F*
139. principe *F*
140. aeolus *corrected in P apparently from* ealus, *and Alberti has added* αἰολοσ *in the outer margin;* eulus *F*
141. expilarent . . . decerperent . . . adigerent *Martini, Consolo;* expilaret . . . decerperet . . . adigeret *FP*
142. Ealum *P;* Eulum *F*
143. misceret *corrected in P from* miscere; miscere *F*
144. imperii *corrected in P from* imperiis; imperiis *F*
145. commoditate *corrected by Alberti in the outer margin of P from* admiratione; admiratione *F*
146. adrestituerem *F*
147. erinnybus *corrected suprascript in P from* erinis; erinis *F*
148. depromisisset *F*
149. querere *corrected in P by Alberti from* admirari; admirari *F*
150. videbis *F*
151. ab *F*
152. pestis mulier calamitas *F*

153. Enimvero *corrected in the
inner margin of P by Alberti
from* enim; enim F
154. felicitatem F
155. tu *expunctuated in P after*
forte; forte tu F
156. visuntur F
157. gestumque F
158. gnaviter *corrected in P from*
graviter; graviter F
159. ne tu F
160. sectare *corrected suprascript in
P by Alberti from* secta; secta
F
161. fraudi id liceat deae P
(fraudi *corrected from* deam

[*corrected to* dee, *then
expunctuated*] fraudem; dee
added suprascript by Alberti);
deam fraudem id liceat F
162. dedicare (?) F
163. sevire F
164. martis prudentiam requiro
qui *corrected in P by Alberti
from* martem ipsum demiror
quod; Martem ipsum
demiror quod F
165. at F
166. an *corrected suprascript in P by
Alberti from* ne; ne F
167. Lautus . . . te *omitted in P*

BOOK III

1. novitate *corrected in P by
Alberti from* admiratione;
admiratione F
2. et *omitted in F*
3. incommodum F
4. magis *added by Alberti in the
outer margin of P; omitted in F*
5. praeter *omitted in F*
6. accommodabat *Martini,
Consolo;* -bant FP
7. At . . . consulet (*end of
section 5) omitted in F; there is
an erasure after* aggrederetur
(*end of section 4), and a note of
at least three lines has been
erased in the outer margin*

8. ultro *added suprascript in P by
Alberti*
9. sic *added in P by Alberti*
10. inde *added suprascript in P by
Alberti*
11. Quid si *corrected in P by
Alberti from* eritque
(*cancelled*) ex (*erased*)
12. Itaque fecit tabellas
obsignatas: tradidit: atque
abiit *cancelled in P after*
consulet
13. cuipiam *Martini, Consolo;*
cupiam FP

14. cuivis P; aviris *cancelled in F, and Alberti has added* alicui *in the outer margin*
15. peritiorum F
16. grandissimis F
17. tum F
18. fortassis *omitted in* F
19. observari *corrected in P by Alberti from* admirari; admirari F
20. se *omitted in* F
21. ediceret *corrected suprascript in FP by Alberti from* diceret
22. erat *corrected in P by Alberti from* eram; quidem *added suprascript in F by Alberti before* erat
23. plaudendi F
24. iam *added suprascript in F by Alberti after* ut
25. et visendi *added by Alberti in the outer margin of* F
26. condisceret *corrected in P by Alberti from* discedet; disceret F
27. paratas *corrected in P by Alberti from* parvas; parvas F
28. intuens *corrected in P by Alberti from* admiratus; admiratus F
29. percontatum *corrected in P from* percunctatum; percunctatum F
30. simus P

31. congruerant *Martini, Consolo;* congruerat F *(corrected),* P
32. persecare F
33. mirabile *corrected in P by Alberti from* admirandum; ad mirandum F
34. secandorum *corrected suprascript in P from* secando; secando F
35. per F
36. tamen P; tum *cancelled in* F
37. percunctare *corrected in P by Alberti from* perconta; percuncta F
38. hinc *corrected in FP by Alberti from* huic
39. hinc *corrected in P by Alberti from* huic; huic F
40. eorum *corrected suprascript in F by Alberti to* deorum
41. esse F
42. motibus *added by Alberti in the outer margin of* F
43. atque *added suprascript in P by Alberti;* aditus atque *omitted in* F
44. esse *cancelled and expunctuated in P after* predicat; predicat esse F
45. demissum *Martini, Consolo;* dimissum FP
46. petiit *Consolo*
47. reliquis hominibus F, *with* esse *added by Alberti in the inner margin after* hominibus

48. ut *F*

49. advertens *corrected in P by Alberti from* admiratus; admiratus *F*

50. percunctatus *F*

51. ut *expunctuated in FP after* intelligere

52. omnium dictorum ~~deorum~~ contumelia *F*

53. ne tua *P*; tua *F, with* ne *added suprascript by Alberti after* tua

54. labores *corrected suprascript in F from* –rem; laborem *P*

55. suscitanti *F*

56. ipse *cancelled in F*

57. numquam *F*

58. esse *deleted in P after* ducebat; ducebat esse *F*

59. sua *cancelled in P after* quanti; quanti sua *F*

60. recensentes *F*

61. instaurantes *F*

62. quam *F*

63. tum suis *P; omitted in F, with* cum suis *added by Alberti in the inner margin*

64. retrahantur *F, with a marginal note by the original scribe:* alias retardentur

65. alacritate (*originally* –tem *in F*) *corrected by Alberti in FP to* alachri-

66. vix crederet *corrected in P by Alberti from* admiraretur; admiraretur *F*

67. cocercebant *corrected by Alberti in FP to* coher-

68. imbecille . . . senio: haberet *added suprascript in P by Alberti after* imbecille, *and* haberet *after* viribus *is expunctuated*; imbecille attritis consumptisque viribus haberet senio *F*

69. enimvero *corrected in P by Alberti from* enim

70. his *corrected in FP from* iis

71. neptuni *corrected in P from* neptumni; neptumni *F*

72. vulcanus *added by Alberti in P in a blank (?) space; erasure in F*

73. perplurimi *F*

74. sibi *added suprascript in F by Alberti after* optimum

75. Diana *corrected in P from* Dianam; Dianam *F*

76. intuens fraus dea *expunctuated in F after* quae

77. Hinc *F*

78. temere *omitted in P*

79. principem *F*

80. satagentem *expunctuated in P and* sese agitantem *added by Alberti in the outer margin*; satagentem *F*

81. capronosum *Martini,*
Consolo; capernosum *FP*
82. suum *cancelled in P after*
illud; illud suum *F*
83. tuto *omitted in F*
84. obtemperetur *Martini,*
Consolo
85. pacto *corrected in F from*
peracto
86. indignitate *F*
87. se *expunctuated in P after*
dolere; se *added in F by*
Alberti after dolere
88. cum *F, Martini, Consolo;* tum
P
89. excederet *F*
90. quam *omitted in F*
91. et *added suprascript in F by*
Alberti after sapis
92. quam *deleted in F and* hanc
added suprascript by Alberti
93. animadvertit *corrected*
suprascript in FP by Alberti
from animadvertens
94. diligentia studebam *F;*
Alberti has indicated the
inversion in P by placing b
above diligentia *and a above*
studebam
95. apud quos aliquid grave
cancelled in F after
sermonibus
96. tum *F*
97. inspectantem *corrected in P*
from admirantem;

admirantem *corrected in F to*
spectantem *(Alberti has added*
this word in the outer margin)
98. an *corrected suprascript in P by*
Alberti from ne; ne *F*
99. vix feras *corrected in P from*
admireris *(?);* admirere
corrected suprascript in F by
Alberti from admireris
100. mirer *corrected in P from*
admirer; admirer *F*
101. et moderari *added in the outer*
margin of F by Alberti after agi
102. idcirco *F*
103. Ea enim *P;* Etenim *F*
104. utilissima *corrected in P from*
utillima; utillima *F*
105. coqui *corrected in F by Alberti*
to concoqui
106. conmendetur *F*
107. fervere *corrected suprascript in*
F by Alberti to fervescere
108. incessendam *corrected in P*
from incessandam;
incessandam *F*
109. invenio *corrected in P by*
Alberti from inveniri admiror;
inveniri admiror *F*
110. solliciter *corrected in P by*
Alberti from mirer *(?);* mirer
F
111. hoc in animante comperio
. . . vetat *omitted in F and*
added by Alberti in the outer
margin

112. accessit *F*
113. Non *F*
114. corrupturum *F*
115. o piissime orbis *P*: o *omitted in F, and Alberti has added* orbis *in the outer margin*
116. esse *added suprascript in F by Alberti after* dicantur
117. discernas *corrected in P from* discernes; discernes *F*
118. novissime *P*
119. enimvero *corrected suprascript in P by Alberti from* enim; enim *F*
120. hunc *V (corrected from* hoc*)*, Martini, Consolo; hoc *P*
121. omnia *expunctuated in P after* diceret; diceret omnia *F*
122. percuntaturus *F*
123. Apollo *omitted in P*
124. philosophum *corrected in F from* philosophus; philosophos *P*
125. interpretandi *omitted in F*
126. templa *F*
127. theatrum *added by Alberti in the outer margin of P; omitted in F*
128. circusque *corrected suprascript in P by Alberti from* circus; circus *F*
129. vastum *P*; invisum *F, and the original scribe has noted in the outer margin* vastum alias

130. extrema *cancelled in P after* item; item extrema *F*
131. advertentes (animadver- *F) corrected in FP by Alberti from* demirantes
132. et *F*
133. qui *cancelled in P after* odio
134. incessendos *corrected suprascript in P from* incessandos; incessandos *F*
135. contumeliam possit (*added by Alberti in the outer margin*) non curasse (*corrected from* curarit) *F*
136. nefanda et non *F*
137. praemium *corrected by Alberti in the outer margin of F to* mercedem
138. peregerunt *F*
139. cum *expunctuated in P after* Iupiter; Iupiter cum *F*
140. tum *F*
141. votorum *P*; veterum *F, with* edificiorum *added by Alberti in the outer margin*
142. Quod . . . sint *P*; Quod (*corrected suprascript by Alberti from* Quid) . . . fuerit *F*
143. hic *F*
144. intermittat *Consolo*; -mittit *F* (-mict-), *P*
145. tam impudenter *omitted in F*

BOOK IV

1. cadebant *corrected in P from* canebant

2. crotala *Martini, Consolo;* crocale *FP*

3. ut *corrected in F by Alberti from* quod (*apparently corrected from* quid [?])

4. factitarant *F*

5. atque *F*

6. nape *FP*

7. prope *corrected in the outer margin of P by Alberti from* pene; pene *F*

8. aborta *P*

9. intellexisset *corrected in P from* intellexissent; intellexissent *F*

10. sese admiratus *deleted in FP after* Momus

11. contulit *F, with a note in the inner margin:* concivit alias

12. ut *corrected suprascript in F by Alberti from* et

13. tam *omitted in F*

14. innimicissimis *F;* in inimicissimis *P*

15. qui *F*

16. instituerunt. Itaque fecere mortalium ergo *F*

17. quidem *deleted in P after* Facile; Facile quidem *F*

18. cogitari fasne sit *cancelled in F after* multitudinem

19. quod ad arbitrium . . . occeperit: ad arbitrium *added by Alberti in the outer margin of P, with* velle *expunctuated after* possit, ac *added suprascript, and* que vero *corrected from* quidem queque; quod possit velle et que occeperit *F*

20. ea *omitted in F*

21. ferme *omitted in F*

22. frusta *Martini, Consolo, but see Cesarini Martinelli, ed., Philodoxeos fabula, p. 196.6 and her note on p. 233 ad loc.*

23. sapere *omitted in F*

24. reddimus *F*

25. conquiescerent *Martini, Consolo;* conquiesceret *FP*

26. immanis *Martini, Consolo;* immani *FP*

27. asportavit *corrected in F by Alberti to* asportat

28. vertit *corrected in FP by Alberti from* vertens

29. statueque *corrected in FP by Alberti from* statue

30. facundum *F*

31. obdidere *F*

32. se sic *P;* sese *F*

33. in silva quidam *Consolo:* silva quidem *FP*

34. Sed *cancelled in F*

35. et *omitted in* F

36. tum F

37. vincire *corrected suprascript in* FP *from* vincere

38. simulacra deos veneraberis F

39. hic P

40. adeo *expunctuated in* P *after* demum; demum adeo F

41. venerabimur *corrected in* F *from* venerabuntur

42. aere FP

43. feroces F

44. grassatus *corrected in* P *from* crassatus; crassatus F

45. quod *apparently corrected in* P; quo F

46. et admirantibus *cancelled in* P *after* rogantibus; rogantibus et admirantibus F

47. esse *corrected in* F *from* esset

48. cupere *corrected in* F *from* cuperet

49. eo dum *corrected in* F *by* Alberti *from* eodem

50. invocemus F

51. concretis temporibus *corrected in* P *from* con- et tem-; concretis et tymporibus F

52. vituperatores non *corrected in* F *by* Alberti *from* vituperatoribus

53. studiosos . . . reddere P; studiosos modestiores reddere pietatis et gratificandis diis deditos nequeo artiumque ad pietatem faciant de se ipso me bene F *(uncancelled), with a signe de renvoi after* studiosos *indicating a revision added by Alberti in the outer margin:* artium bonarum et que ad pietatem faciant et gratificandis diis deditos nequeo modestiores *mod*

54. asseruerant P; asseruerarat *corrected in* F *from* asseruerant

55. theatrum *corrected in* F *by* Alberti *to* theatro

56. explicabant F *(corrected ex* -bat ?*)*; -bat P

57. erumnas F

58. transvecturum *corrected in* FP

59. appellebat *apparently corrected in* P *from* appellabat; appellabat F

60. id *omitted in* P

61. *blank space in* P *after* rei; rei omnium F

62. pictum *added suprascript in* F *by* Alberti

63. an non *corrected in* P *from* ne non; ne vero F

64. degere *added in the inner margin of* F *by* Alberti *after* quam

65. quid *corrected suprascript in* F *from* quod; quod P

66. siderum . . . novimus *omitted in F*
67. abduci *F*
68. in *omitted in P*
69. couniret *corrected in F (from* conuniret) *and P*
70. an *corrected suprascript in P by Alberti from* ne; ne *F*
71. miror *corrected in P from* admiror; admiror *F*
72. miror *corrected in P from* admiror; *omitted in F*
73. mortale tamen *P*; mortale *(corrected from* mortales) nec *(cancelled) F*
74. animans *corrected suprascript in P from* animas; animas *F*
75. pleniplusius *P*
76. in reditu *added by Alberti in the outer margin of P and apparently intended as a correction of* redeuntes *(which has not been cancelled)*; redeuntes *(corrected from* reddeun-) *F*
77. deputasse *Martini, Consolo*
78. his *(corrected from* hiis) legisse *F*
79. ut *omitted in F*
80. cupiditatis errore *P*; cupiditate erroreve *F*
81. redisse illic *corrected in P by Alberti from* restitutos; restitutos *F*

82. fictos istorum *(added by Alberti in the inner margin)* vultus *F*
83. aut *F*
84. *See book 1, n. 84 above.*
85. venerabere *corrected in P from* –rarere; venerabere *corrected in F from* –rarer
86. ei *P*; rei *corrected by Alberti in the outer margin of F to* eius
87. vindicandasque *omitted in F*
88. obstupuere *(corrected suprascript by Alberti from* obstuere) et maxime oenops *F*
89. abvolaret *F*; obvo- *P*
90. fiunt *F*
91. obductum *corrected in P from* –tam; obductam *F*
92. vi *added suprascript in F by Alberti after* impulerat
93. et improbitatem *omitted in F*
94. conferat *F*
95. revocabat *corrected in F by Alberti from* referat vocabat
96. illos turbatores risisse tametsi admiraretur retinnire omnia deorum risu *P*; illos deorum risu *F, with* turbatores risisse tametsi non intelligeret unde tinnirent omnia deorum risu *supplied by Alberti in the outer margin*

97. intuens *corrected in the outer margin of F by Alberti from* admiratus

98. me *omitted in P*

99. decrepiti *corrected in P from* -tis; decrepitis *F*

100. ne *F; the reading in P is unclear*

101. remumine (-ne *corrected by Alberti from* non) in sicco (*corrected by Alberti from* siccum) *F*

102. rectandum *F*

103. atque item multos *omitted in F*

104. me *cancelled and expunctuated in P after* semitis; semitis me *F*

105. perscindens *corrected in F to* pro-

106. navitam suos inter *F*

107. obdidit *F*

108. vero *P;* in *corrected suprascript in F by Alberti from* non

109. forte *F*

110. quod *corrected in FP from* quid

111. immergeretur *P*

112. occupant *corrected in P from* occupantes, *and* salutem *added in the inner margin;* occupantes *F*

113. tum *F;* tum (?) *corrected in P from* eum (?)

114. Peniplusii Consolo (*and see* 4.42 *above*); polifagi *FP*

115. interturbavit *corrected in P from* interpellavit; interpellavit *F*

116. tempestatum queritantem (mirantem *corrected by Alberti to* querentem; *this was further corrected, by an addition in the inner margin, to* queritantem) *P;* tempestatum ~~causa fuerant atrocissima apud theatrum ab se facinore~~ demirantem (*corrected suprascript by Alberti from* mirantem) ~~causam~~ *F*

117. Is *P;* te *deleted in F*

118. vertant *F;* verterent *Martini, Consolo;* vertrent *corrected suprascript in P by Alberti from* vertant

119. habebant *Martini, Consolo*

120. recensentur *P*

121. comperit *corrected in P from* comperuit; comperuit *F*

122. conscia P, *with the following* admissi *expunctuated;* consciam admissi *F*

123. perfuncti *corrected in the outer margin of F by Alberti from* acti

124. tam *P*

125. tamen *P;* tum *F, with* quidem *added suprascript by Alberti*

126. Gelaste *Martini, Consolo;* oenops *FP*
127. invidia redundavit *F*
128. Tu *F*
129. cursu *apparently corrected in P from* curru; curru *F*
130. Iovi *omitted in P*
131. tabellis *corrected in P from* tabellas; tabellas *F*
132. prius *added suprascript in P by Alberti after* quidvis; prius *omitted in F*
133. Tum *Martini, Consolo;* Tu *FP*
134. posteaquam nostri huius *F*
135. praeco una ingressi *omitted in F*
136. Sumus ergo pares *(corrected from* paresi*) F*
137. etenim *corrected suprascript in P by Alberti from* Enim; Enim *F*

138. nusquam *F*
139. omniumque *F*
140. At *corrected in F from* et
141. quis paratior *omitted in F*
142. ulla *P;* illud *cancelled in F*
143. nam plura *F*
144. fastiditi *corrected in F from* -diri
145. excruciabimur *corrected suprascript in F by Alberti to* excruciemur
146. posset *corrected suprascript in F to* -sit
147. suis sibi vero *P;* sibi *(cancelled)* suis sibi non *(deleted) F*
148. fora *corrected in P from* foros; foros *F*

Notes to the Translation

꘍꘏꘍

PREFACE

1. Terence, *Eunuchus* 41.

2. In Latin philosophical writers *animus*, here translated "rational soul," refers to the higher part of the soul, comprising the faculties of reason and will, while *anima*, soul, is a broader term including as well the lower psychic functions of growth, reproduction, movement and sensation. The implication is that Alberti's first group of gods stand for the "lower" passions and appetites of the soul, while the second group stand for the higher rational and volitional powers.

3. Compare Seneca, *De clem.* 3, 5.

BOOK I

1. Mario Martelli, "Minima in *Momo* libello adnotanda," *Albertiana* 1 (1998), pp. 105–107, suggests that elements of the figure of Jupiter in the *Momus* are based upon maxims in Xenophon's *Hiero* (a work translated by Alberti's friend Leonardo Bruni before 1403).

2. Alberti adapts one of Aesop's fables, "Zeus, Prometheus, Athena and Momus," for this episode. In Aesop, Zeus makes a bull, Prometheus a man, and Athena a house, and Momus is summoned to judge them. Momus criticizes all of the creations, just as Alberti's Momus does, and Zeus chases him from Olympus. See *Fables d'Ésope*, ed. Émile Chambry (Paris, 1967), Fable 124, p. 56; *Fables of Aesop*, trans. S. A. Handford (Harmondsworth, 1954), Fable 155, p. 159. Consolo cites Lucian's *Vera Historia* 2.3 and *Nigrinus* 32, where the incident is also alluded to.

3. Throughout *Momus*, Alberti makes Pallas (or Athena) and Minerva two separate goddesses. Ancient mythology identified Pallas Athena with Minerva. The goddesses first appear as separate entities in Boccaccio's *Genealogia deorum gentilium* 2.3.23; 4.63–64.

4. Mischief is the daughter of Erebus, god of the underworld, and Night, according to Boccaccio in the *Gen.* 1.14 and 1.21.

5. Compare the somewhat different version in Lucian, *Hermotimus* 20. That the mind was located in the breast was a doctrine shared by ancient Epicureans (see Lucretius 3.140) and Stoics; Alberti could have found out about the Stoic doctrine (which he here, typically, disagrees with through the mouth of Momus) from Diogenes Laertius, book 7, or from Calcidius 220 (ed. Waszink, p. 232).

6. This passage perhaps owes something to the speech of Momus in a fragment from the *Hermetic Corpus* preserved in Stobaeus; see *Hermetica*, ed. W. Scott (Boulder, Colorado, 1982), I, pp. 481–85 [= *Stobaei Hermetica* Exc. XXIII, caps. 43–46]. That Alberti knew and used this passage in the *Momus* was first suggested by Eugenio Garin in "Fonti albertiane," *Rivista critica di storia della filosofia* 39 (1974), pp. 90–91; see also idem, *Rinascite e rivoluzioni: Movimenti culturali dal XIV al XVIII secolo* (Rome—Bari, 1975), pp. 149–150. However, in this passage it is the energetic explorations and scientific investigations of the mortals that makes Momus call upon God to keep mankind in its place through grief, frustration and misery. See also 3.50 below, and note 19.

7. Alberti refers ironically to the habit of Jupiter, in particular, of transforming himself when in amorous pursuit into various animals or natural phenomena. Jupiter visited Danaë as a shower of gold, and the result of their union, Perseus, went on to slay the Gorgon Medusa. Leda, who went on to give birth to the heroic twins Castor and Pollux and to Helen of Troy, was seduced by Jupiter disguised as a swan.

8. The myth of Prometheus parallels the fate of Alberti's Momus. In Greek mythology (e.g. Hesiod, *Theog.* 507 ff.) after Zeus hid fire from mankind, Prometheus stole it and took it to earth. Zeus punished Prometheus by chaining him to a rock and sending an eagle to devour his liver, which grew back every night so that the eagle could gnaw on it daily. In an alternative tradition followed here by Alberti, Prometheus first invented man, using either clay (Pausanias 10.4.4), or clay and animal parts (Horace, *Carm.* 1.16.13 ff.). See also Lucian's dialogue *Prometheus*, and Martelli, "Minima," pp. 107–110.

9. Probably a reference to the tag, *Veritas filia temporis* ("Truth, daughter of time") found in Aulus Gellius 12.11.7, Apuleius, *Met.* 8.7 and other sources. In the *Philodoxeos fabula* Alberti introduces the character Alithia, daughter of Chronos, a Greek version of the character. Perosa, "Considerazioni," p. 60, note 39, suggests that the name Verinna (as it appears in the oldest MSS., along with forms like "Neptunnus") is derived from *verro*, to sweep.

10. "Quid tum?" can be translated as "So what?" or "What next?" It was Alberti's motto, probably taken from Vergil's tenth *Eclogue*. On commemorative medals of the 1440s, struck at around the same time as *Momus* was written, this motto accompanies Alberti's personal emblem of a winged eye. In 1436, Alberti drew an eagle and wrote "Quid tum?" on his manuscript of *Della pittura* ("On Painting"). The winged eye and the eagle share iconographical similarities: both represent alertness and ambition, as described by Alberti in "Anuli" ("Rings"), one of the *Intercenales*. The phrase "quid tum?" occurs throughout *Momus* in the mouths of several characters, spoken here by Mischief but uttered most frequently by Jupiter and by Momus himself.

11. Hesiod first names the mythical river Eridanus in *Theog.* 338. According to earliest tradition, the Eridanus was situated in northernmost Europe, or in western Europe, flowing into the Northern Ocean. Later Greek writers, followed by Roman authors, identified the Eridanus with the River Po.

12. Tages was a god in Etruscan mythology, unearthed by a peasant in the fields of Etruria. He sprang from the plowed earth in the form of a boy. Tages was Jupiter's grandson, and he taught the art of divination, contained in the *libri Tagetici* ("books of Tages,") to the Etruscan elders. See Cicero, *Div.* 2.23.50; Ovid, *Met.* 15.558. See also Boccaccio, *Gen.* 1.12.

13. Possibly a reference to Plato, *Tim.* 28A.

14. Possibly a reference to the doctrine of Anaxagoras, preserved most fully in Simplicius' commentary on Aristotle's *Physics*; Alberti may have known the less informative account in Diogenes Laertius 2.6–15.

15. Compare Seneca, *Ep. mor.* 41.5.

16. Alberti is probably thinking of the planetary epicycles of Ptolemaic astronomy, traditionally considered the strongest empirical evidence for an intelligence behind celestial motions.

17. This brawl provoked the humanist Francesco Filelfo, who had been similarly attacked, to write to Alberti and ask him whether Momus represented him; see Filelfo's *Odes* 4.6.

18. The Cynics were a philosophical sect that flourished in the third century BCE. They followed the principles of Diogenes of Sinope, who earned the name "the Cynic" (from *kuon*, dog) because he rejected convention and advocated shamelessness in behavior. See Lucian's dialogue, *Cynicus*, for a satirical discussion of the Cynic manifesto. In book 4 of the *Intercenales*, Alberti's dialogue of the same name contains a Cynic's condemnation of other professions. Unlike most other humanists, Alberti shows considerable sympathy with the Cynics.

19. Virtue is also an interlocutor in "Virtus," the first book of the *Intercenales*.

20. A toga with a purple border worn by Roman magistrates and Roman boys up to the age of majority.

21. Consolo cites Apuleius, *Met.* 6.6.2–4, as a possible model for this passage.

22. Or "among whom he had dwelt," reading "divertisset" in an Italianate sense.

23. *Mediusfidius* was a Latin oath, meaning "by the god of truth!" or "as true as heaven!" Fidius is a surname of Jupiter. Alberti jokingly personifies the exclamation in this passage.

24. Castor and Polydeuces (or Pollux), the Dioscuri, were stellified as Gemini in the zodiac. Polydeuces was the son of Zeus, and Castor the son of Tyndareus of Sparta, their mother was Leda, and their sister Helen of Troy. Like Hercules, they participated in the voyage of the Argo, and they were famous for their heroism and devotion to each other.

25. Matuta was a Roman goddess of growth and a popular cult figure. Cadmus was the legendary founder of Thebes, whose sister, Europa, was

kidnapped by Jupiter in the guise of a bull. Matuta and Cadmus are not linked in classical mythology.

26. Carmenta or Carmentis was a prophetess, a goddess of birth, and a nymph. In myth, she was the mother of Evander, the first settler at Rome, whom Aeneas visits to ask for help in his war against Turnus and the Rutulians in book 8 of the *Aeneid*. Her legend is recounted by Boccaccio in *De mulieribus claris* 27; see *Famous Women*, ed. V. Brown (Cambridge, Mass.: Harvard University Press, 2001), pp. 105–113.

27. An ancient Italian corn-goddess, usually associated with the Greek goddess Demeter. See Boccaccio, *De mulieribus claris* 5; *Famous Women*, pp. 29–35.

28. Perhaps meant to recall the rabble-rousing speeches of Stefano Porcari, who organized a coup against the popes; Alberti wrote an account of the conspiracy in 1448–49 (see Introduction, p. xvii).

29. For Alberti's negative views on mob behavior, see also his descriptions in the *Theogenius* and in several *Intercenales* in book 10, such as "Bubo" ("The Owl"), and "Nebule" ("The Clouds").

30. Thersites appears in book 2 of the *Iliad*. He is an ugly, cantankerous and critical Greek who rails against Agamemnon in the council of war.

31. Similar to statements attributed to Heraclitus by Plato, *Crat.* 402A and Aristotle, *Phys.* 253B9

32. See "Hedera" [Ivy] in the *Intercenales*, where priests decorate their temple with ivy which will eventually ruin it, and "Suspitio," where Suspicion is transformed into a monstrous plant which invades a temple and tries to suffocate the virgin Reason. The transformation of Momus into ivy is reminiscent of a number of changes in Ovid's *Metamorphoses*, such as that of Daphne (book 1) or Dryope (book 9). In these tales, maidens turn themselves into plants in order to evade rape; Alberti reverses the Ovidian precedent so that Momus' change of shape becomes an instrument of rape.

33. For the Latin compare Terence, *Adel.* 475.

34. Alberti derives his description of Fama or Rumor principally from Vergil, *Aen.* 4.174–188, especially lines 181–3: "a dreadful monster, huge,

NOTES TO THE TRANSLATION ·

which has as many feathers on its body as watchful eyes underneath —
marvellous to relate! — as many tongues, as many mouths sounding
forth, as many pricked ears."

35. I.e., abandon her offspring in the wild, exposed to the elements, a
common form of infanticide in the ancient world.

36. All of these are sites of famous classical battles. At Marathon in 490
BCE, the Greeks had their first great victory over Persia. Leuctra was the
site of the Theban Epaminondas' defeat of the Spartans in 371 BCE. The
Persian fleet was defeated off the island of Salamis in 480 BCE, and in the
same year the Spartans defended the pass at Thermopylae against the
Persian army of Xerxes. Cannae and Trasimene saw victories of the
Carthaginian general Hannibal over the Roman army during the Second
Punic War, in 216 and 217 BCE respectively. In 321 BCE, the Romans were
defeated by the Samnites at the Caudine Forks.

37. In Homer's *Odyssey*, Scylla and the Cyclopes are among the monsters
Odysseus encounters on his voyage home from the Trojan War. Scylla
and her rival Charybdis were traditionally located in the straits of
Messina; the Cyclopes were supposed to dwell in Sicily. Idalium was a
mountain-city in Cyprus, sacred to Venus. Gades, modern Cadiz, is the
oldest urban settlement in Spain; there was a shrine to Hercules nearby.
Byrsa was the citadel of ancient Carthage. Thala was a city in Numidia.

38. In "Virtus" (*Intercenales*, book 1), Virtue and Fortune are also depicted as enemies: Fortune gets a mob to attack Virtue, who is abandoned on earth, just as in *Momus*.

39. Hercules' ascent to heaven recalls Lucian's dialogue "Icaromenippus
or the Sky-Man," in which the philosopher Menippus also flies to the
seat of the gods.

40. In Greek mythology, Apollo made Hercules a slave as punishment
for a murder he committed. Hercules was sold to Omphale, a Lydian
queen, who set him to spinning and weaving; see Ovid, *Her.* 9.53ff. A
more heroic depiction of Hercules is found in the *De laboribus Herculis*
(ca. 1400) of the Florentine humanist Coluccio Salutati (1331–1406).

41. Seneca, *Dial.* 2.9.3.

BOOK II

1. Alberti's implied polemic against votive offerings follows the model of Lucian's *Icaromenippus* and *De sacrificiis*; the latter work was translated into Latin by Lapo Castiglionchio the Younger and dedicated to Alberti. But the polemic appears frequently in Alberti's other writings, for example in the *Profugiorum ab aerumnis* and several of the *Intercenales* ("Somnium," "Oraculum," "Vaticinium," "Religio").

2. The need for hypocrisy to achieve success in ordinary life is one among several anti-Stoic themes in the *Momus*; compare Seneca's *De tranqu.* 17. For Alberti's hostility to Stoicism, see his *Profugiorum ab aerumnis*, in Leon Battista Alberti, *Opere volgari*, ed. Grayson, 3 vols. (Bari, 1960–73), II, p. 115.

3. In Alberti's dialogue "Virtus" (*Intercenales*, book 1) Virtue appeals to Mercury for help when Fortune and her followers attack her. Although he is sympathetic, he eventually rejects her pleas.

4. In *On Painting* 2.25, Alberti discusses the role of gold in painting. Gold incorporated into a work of art, he argues, is far more precious than gold on its own.

5. Alberti's text here has parallels to ancient critiques of votive offerings, e.g. Seneca, *Ep. mor.* 10.5.

6. Similar sentiments are found in Alberti's *De commodis litterarum atque incommodis* 3.14.

7. Alberti's ironical encomium of beggars is modelled on Lucian's *On the Parasite or The Craft of the Parasite*, which was translated by the humanist schoolmaster Guarino da Verona in 1418. The life of the beggar was celebrated by Cynic philosophers who regarded it as a form of the philosophical life.

8. Alberti follows the classical *topos* of monstrous events as portents of civic upheaval; see, e.g., Vergil, *Aen.* 2 (the destruction of Troy) and Lucan, *Civ.* 1 (the beginnings of civil war in Rome). The whole passage is a send-up of *apathia*, the state of rational detachment from passions sought by the Stoic philosopher; an example of the attitude Alberti is satirizing may be found in Horace, *Carm.* 3.3, 1–8.

9. Possibly an echo of the speech of Momus in the *Hermetica,* as suggested by Garin (see 1.11 and note 6, above).

10. An *ascripticius* was a slave who was assigned to a particular piece of land, and who was transferred with it from one owner to another, analogous to a medieval serf.

11. Themis was the Greek goddess of justice and prophecy. Alberti's use of "qui" and the masculine future participle in the Latin suggests that he thought of Themis as a male divinity.

12. Several Greek philosophers expounded a view of the universe as the creation of a random collision of atoms. Alberti alludes to doctrines of Democritean and Epicurean atomism, such as the notion that atoms constitute every concrete object, and that their movement is largely arbitrary. The Latin scientific poet Lucretius gives a poetic account of Epicurean ideas concerning the creation of the world in the *De rerum natura* ["On the Nature of Things"]. The Epicureans did not deny the existence of gods, but believed they lived apart from mankind, had no interest in mankind's fate, and had no role in creation. Alberti also could have learned about the ancient atomists from Diogenes Laertius' *Lives of the Philosophers,* which had been translated into Latin by Ambrogio Traversari in 1432.

13. That the atoms of which the world was made existed in a void is an Epicurean view; see Cicero, *Fin.* 1.17, *Fat.* 24 and Lucretius 1.330.

14. Compare Lucretius 5.218. The argument that the beasts are better off than man is later turned around by Marsilio Ficino, who argues that the soul must be immortal, since otherwise the life of the beasts would excel that of man. See Marsilio Ficino, *Platonic Theology,* ed. and trans. M. J. B. Allen and J. Hankins, vol. 1 (Cambridge, Mass. 2001), 1.1.

15. Momus is referring to the fact that the ancient gods were often associated with mythological animals and monsters, for example, Athena with the Gorgon; Juno with the Hydra and the Nemean lion; Diana with her hounds; Bacchus with leopards, etc.

16. See Cicero, *Nat. deor.* 2.63.158, cited by Garin, "Fonti albertiane," p. 91, and idem, *Rinascite e rivoluzioni,* p. 149.

17. As Garin points out, this constitutes a rejection of the Ciceronian position, cited in the previous note, which argues that all of nature was created to serve mankind. Alberti's position is similar to Lucretius 2.179f. and 5.195f.

18. A difficult sentence, here translated literally. Alberti seems to mean that a normal man who was raised to heaven and offered the adulation given to gods, if he had it to do over again, would become anything rather than a god.

19. Lit. "to roll between the tables." Roman banquets were held on couches arranged in an open square, with small tables brought in for each course by slaves.

20. Hercules here and elsewhere is represented as a divine advocate for the human race.

21. See Grafton, *Leon Battista Alberti*, p. 309: "When Alberti satirized the imaginary arch of Juno, he may have been poking fun at the real Torrione of Nicholas V—the vast circular structure, known as 'the new tower,' that Nicholas began in 1447–48, in order to protect and to enhance the dignity of the old papal palace and the new one that he was about to construct. On 31 August 1454, this tower collapsed, causing more than one death, and had to be rebuilt." See *De re aedificatoria* 8.6 for the decoration of arches.

22. Alberti delights in fanciful etymology in *Momus*. "Tinis" is probably derived from the Latin *tinnitus* ["ringing" or "jingle"]. In classical mythology, Iris is the goddess of the rainbow, whimsically linked here with Juno's doomed arch.

23. On Alberti's antifeminism, see Cecil Grayson, "Leon Battista Alberti traduttore di Walter Map," in Grayson's *Studi*, pp. 91–102.

24. Jupiter's speech on the miseries of rule may be another send-up of Stoicism, in this case its preference for the contemplative over the active life, exemplified by the emperor Augustus' yearning for leisure even at the height of power; see Seneca, *De brev.* 4.

25. Thetis was a Nereid or sea-nymph, and the mother of Achilles. She is a key character in the *Iliad*, especially in book 18, where she obtains Olympian armor for her son.

26. Aeolus was the ruler of the winds. In different traditions, he either keeps the winds in a sack or shuts them inside a cave on his floating island. He appears in book 10 of the *Odyssey* and book 1 of the *Aeneid*.

27. The west, south, and north winds, respectively.

28. In "Flores," in book 3 of the *Intercenales*, Apollo is responsible for seasonal growth.

29. I.e., the offerings will be "nowhere" since they will be in a liminal position between the elements of air, water and land.

30. See Lucian's *Parliament of the Gods*, 7 (speech of Momus).

BOOK III

1. Alberti here mimics the conventions of the dedicatory letter: the profession of loyalty, the promise of utility, the pose of deferring to the dedicatee's superior wisdom.

2. In Alberti's dialogue "Cynicus" (*Intercenales*, book 4), Phoebus decides that the sophists should be transformed into fireflies.

3. In Lucian's *Vera Historia* ("True Story"), 2.17, Plato is also nowhere to be found, for he has moved to his own imaginary republic and is living under the laws he himself devised. Alberti (and Lucian) may be alluding to the notorious fact that, after the third century BCE, the doctrine the Academy taught was a variety of skepticism rather than the doctrine of Plato himself.

4. The following incident is based on an anecdote told in Diogenes Laertius 6.38 and in Plutarch, *Alex.* 14. In the anecdote, Alexander the Great offers to grant the philosopher Diogenes anything in his empire, but Diogenes asks only that Alexander stop blocking the sun.

5. Democritus (ca. 460–ca. 370 BCE) was known in the ancient world as the laughing philosopher. Aristotle famously said that Democritus found "truth in sense-appearance" (see *De An.* 404A27; *Metaph.* 1009B12; *Gen. Corr.* 315B9), hence Alberti's depiction of him here as an empiricist.

For Alberti's view of Democritus, see Luca Boschetti, "Ricerche sul *Theogenius* e sul *Momus* di Leon Battista Alberti," *Rinascimento*, ser. 2, 33 (1993), pp. 3–52.

6. Probably a reference to the Epicurean school, often referred to as "the Garden," whose doctrine Alberti would know via Diogenes Laertius, Cicero, and other sources.

7. Here and elsewhere the debates on the existence of the gods recall those in Lucian's *Zeus Tragoedus* between Timocles the Stoic and Damis the Epicurean.

8. In republican Rome, the *populares* were a non-noble social group which challenged the power of the senatorial class. In medieval and early Renaissance Florence, the *popolo* was a political organization representing the middle ranks of society and was, broadly speaking, in rivalry with the "magnates" or knightly land-owing classes.

9. Generally in Rome, a *privatus* was a citizen, a man in private life, as opposed to a *magistratus* or public official. In imperial Rome, *privatus* meant "not imperial," someone who was not associated with the emperor or the imperial family.

10. *Kalendae*, the first day of the month. The Kalends were sacred to Juno.

11. An obscure passage. Diogenes seems to be saying that the rescuers wanted him, Diogenes, to display the same emotional passivity (a quality thought philosophical by the ancients) as Mercury was displaying, but they themselves were violating philosophical passivity by taking an interest in Mercury's fate.

12. See Juvenal, *Sat.* 7.103 and 7.81.

13. Persius 3.49–50. The *canicula*, or "dog throw," was the unluckiest throw in a game of dice.

14. In Lucian's dialogue *Zeus Tragoedus*, Momus ridicules the opaque utterances of Apollo's oracle.

15. Ancient precedents for comic assemblies of the gods include Seneca's *Apocolocynthosis* 9.1–3, Lucian's *Deorum concilium* and Apuleius' *Met.* 6.23.1.

16. The divine assembly follows the practice of the Roman senate in canvassing the views of the senators in order of seniority.

17. A mythological monster who had — according to various traditions — a third eye in the back of his neck, or four eyes, or many eyes.

18. Alberti here is playing on Democritus' reputation in antiquity as "the laughing philosopher." Seneca famously preferred Democritus' practice of laughing at human failings to Heraclitus' tendency to weep at the follies of mankind; see *De tranqu.* 15; *De ira* 2.10.5; Juvenal 10.28; Lucian, *De sacrificiis* 15. On the fortune of this pairing in the Renaissance see Edgar Wind, *Pagan Mysteries in the Renaissance* (New York, 1968), pp. 48–49, notes 50–51.

19. Cf. the speech of Momus in the *Hermetica* (cited above, 1.11 at note 6), where Momus predicts that humans will endanger the gods' position by, among other things, "dissect[ing] the lower animals — yes, and one another also — seeking to find out how they have come to be alive and what manner of thing is hidden within" (tr. Scott).

20. Democritus here seeks the biological source of *pneuma*, the life force circulating in the body's vessels, which also determines health. For Alberti's sources for this passage (of which the most important is ps.-Hippocrates, *Epistola ad Damogetum*) see Luca Boschetti, "Democrito e la fisiologia della follia: la parodia della filosofia e della medicina nel *Momus* di Leon Battista Alberti," *Rinascimento*, ser. 2, 35 (1995), pp. 3–29. Alberti would have known the pseudonymous letters of Hippocrates in the contemporary translation of Rinuccio Aretino.

21. Possibly an allusion to two works of Democritus, the *Greater* and *Lesser Diacosmos*; see Martelli, "Minima," p. III, n. 12, and Diogenes Laertius 9.46.

22. Democritus refers to the music of the spheres, a Pythagorean and Platonic concept. See Cicero, *Rep.* 6.18 (the *Somnium Scipionis* or "Dream of Scipio"), for a well-known description.

23. For parallels in literature to the idea of graphic messages in natural objects, see Martelli, "Minima," pp. III–II2.

24. Alberti parodies the Socratic conversations depicted in the early dialogues of Plato. Socrates does not usually debate with members of the artisan class, but his dialogues often make use of homely analogies drawn from the crafts.

25. Jupiter alludes to the Platonic theory of forms. In Plato's dialogues, the "form" of a thing is its perfect essence, invisible, and perceived by thought rather than by sense. The form is unchangeable and eternal, as opposed to the transient objects of the senses. But Jupiter's ignorance of philosophy is shown by the fact that he has cut off Apollo's account of the Socratic dialogue just as Socrates was about to define a Form of Leather.

26. Cf. Plato, *Tim.* 43B.

27. Pythagoras (fl. ca. 530 BCE) was a Greek philosopher who wrote nothing but whose doctrine was widely influential, especially in the fields of metaphysics, natural philosophy, mathematics and music. Pythagoras espoused metempsychosis or the transmigration of souls, and is reputed to have invented the musical scale. See Diogenes Laertius 8.1.

28. Parmenides (fl. ca. 450 BCE) was a member of the Eleatic school of philosophy, whose chief doctrine was monism. See Diogenes Laertius 9.3.

29. Melissus (fl. ca. 440 BCE) was a philosopher from the island of Samos. Melissus was the last member of the Eleatic school. See Diogenes Laertius 9.4.

30. Theophrastus (372/369–288/285 BCE) was a pupil of Aristotle, later the head of the Peripatetic school. Most of his numerous writings are lost. See Diogenes Laertius 5.2.

31. Alberti takes a dig at Plato's Utopian writings — specifically, the *Republic* — following Lucian, *Vera Historia*, book 2.

32. Alberti mocks the Pythagorean concept of metempsychosis and reincarnation. Cf. Lucian, *Somnium seu Gallus* ("The Dream or the Cockerel").

33. In Apuleius, *Met.* 10.33, Socrates is described as "an old man of divine wisdom, whom the Delphic god preferred to all other mortals for his wisdom."

393

34. The Circus Maximus was an arena for chariot-racing in Rome, located below the Palatine Hill.

35. In his dialogue *Deorum concilium* ("The Assembly of the Gods"), 14, Lucian has Momus recite a pompous and pedantically worded decree condemning alien gods, which was Alberti's model for Jupiter's speech sentencing Momus at the end of Book Three; another parodic decree is found in Apuleius, *Met.* 6.23.2.

36. Momus/*humus* is another instance of Alberti's taste for facetious etymology. *Humus*, a feminine noun, was commonly given in medieval and Renaissance etymological works (for example, Isidore, *Etymologiae* 7.6) as the derivation for *homo*, human being. Is Alberti trying to say that Momus is Everyman?

BOOK IV

1. Not found in the classical pantheon, Stupor is an invention of Alberti's, a personification of intellectual slowness. See Prologue (6), where Alberti discusses the symbolic or allegorical function of the gods; Stupor symbolises brute force and dull wits.

2. Not many of these *dii maritimi* actually have anything to do with the sea, apart from the *Phorceae* or "daughters of Phorcys." In mythology, Phorcys was the son of Earth and the sea-god Nereus (Hesiod, *Theog.* 237). The Gorgons and Sirens were among Phorcys' other children; in general, he is the father of sea deities (cf. Vergil, *Aen.* 5.824).

3. In Lucian's dialogue, *Zeus Tragoedus*, one of the models for the *Momus*, Zeus and Hermes debate the different materials from which statues of the gods should be made, ranking the gods according to the expense and rarity of the materials.

4. The name "Oenops" is derived from the Greek *oinops* or "wine-colored," a common Homeric epithet used to describe the sea, but here is probably an allusion to the bibulous habits of the actor/philosopher.

5. One model for Alberti's gang of thieves here is Apuleius' *Met.* 3 and 4, especially the description of the robber camp at *Met.* 4.6.

6. A saying attributed to the Presocratic philosopher Thales; see Plato, *Laws* 10.899B; Aristotle, *De anima* 1.5, 411A; Cicero, *Leg.* 2.11.26; Diogenes Laertius 1.27. Alberti also quotes the saying in "Religio," in book 1 of the *Intercenales*.

7. *Florilegium proverbiorum universae latinitatis*, ed. E. Margolits (Budapest, 1895), p. 61.

8. In Greek mythology, Charon is the ferryman who conveyed human souls across the River Styx to the underworld for the fare of an obol. See David Marsh, *Lucian and the Latins*, pp. 105–110, for a discussion of the relationship between Alberti and Lucian's dialogue "Charon," in which Charon similarly visits the world of the living.

9. Apparently an invention of Alberti; the Hispides (Hispiades in the Mazzocchi edition of 1520) are unattested in classical literature. Consolo, following Martini, suggests that Alberti may have meant the Hesperides, the daughters of the evening star. This is puzzling, as the Hesperides were peaceful minor deities who lived in a garden at the edge of the world, guarding their orchard of golden apples. There is no mythological tradition depicting them as hostile to humans. Alberti may be referring to the personifications of Heat, Hunger and Fever introduced above, 3.65.

10. In Greek, *gelastos* means "laughable." Alberti's Gelastus is both laughing-stock and wit. For a model of the philosopher in Hades, see Lucian's dialogue *Menippus*. Eugenio Garin in *Rinascite e rivoluzioni*, p. 162, assimilates Gelastus to Lepidus, the pseudonym Alberti used as author of the *Philodoxeos fabula*, and hence reads passages such as that at 3.85 as autobiographical.

11. In Greek mythology, the Argonauts were the band of heroes who sailed on the Argo with Jason to reclaim the Golden Fleece. Polyphagus ("Glutton"), a figure not attested in Greek history or mythology, may be an allegorical guise for a pope; thanks to Peter's original métier of fisherman, nautical metaphors were often used to indicate the papacy.

12. Penelope describes these gates in Homer, *Od.*, 19.562–9: "there are two gates of insubstantial dreams: one is made of horn, the other of ivory. The dreams that come through the ivory gate are vain, bringing

messages that are unfulfilled. But the dreams that come through the horn gate are fulfilled." Vergil also describes the two gates in *Aen.* 6.893–6: "There are two gates of Sleep: one is made of horn, and through this, true shadows can leave easily. The other shines with white ivory, but the ghosts send false dreams to heaven." The *anabasis*, or ascent from the underworld, is a stock feature in epic journeys, as in the voyages of Odysseus and Aeneas. The *anabasis* of Charon and Gelastus, bickering, bearing an upside-down boat, is obviously a parodic version.

13. See *De re aedificatoria*, book 6, where Alberti praises flowers as the highest artistic achievement of nature.

14. In other words, motion is equivalent to change in general, the genus of which local motion (motion in the modern sense) is the species. Alberti here uses the standard terminology of scholastic Aristotelian physics.

15. Gelastus' speech is a garbled account of Aristotelian metaphysics, using technical terms such as "substance," "accidents," and "form." Scholastic philosophy, the butt of many humanist jokes, relied heavily on such Aristotelian terminology.

16. Having given a broadly Aristotelian account of change in the previous paragraph, Alberti now gives an account of creation reminiscent of Plato's creation myth in the *Timaeus*.

17. In Greek mythology, with some variation, the underworld is usually divided into three zones: Elysium, the Asphodel plain, and Tartarus. Elysium resembles the Christian heaven, the Asphodel plain is gray, featureless and neutral, and Tartarus is the place of brutal punishment for the wicked.

18. In the *Intercenales*, the interlocutor of "Paupertas" ("Poverty") is also named Peniplusius. The name is an oxymoron from the Greek words *penes*, poor man, and *plousios*, rich man; it might be translated "a man rich in poverty."

19. "Know thyself" was one of the exhortations carved upon Apollo's temple at Delphi, a motto cited frequently in ancient and Renaissance philosophical texts. In Diogenes Laertius 1.40 the saying is attributed to Thales.

20. In his description of the steep mountain, Alberti follows a literary tradition where steep, direct roads rather than circuitous paths stand for the strenuous effort necessary to acquire moral virtue and salvation. The most famous examples in the early Renaissance would have been Dante, *Purg.*, and Petrarch's "Ascent of Mont Ventoux" (*Ep. Fam.* 4.1); for an ancient example see Seneca, *De prov.* 5.

21. The Acheron was a river in north-west Greece which ran through gorges and disappeared underground. It was believed to be one of the four rivers of the underworld, and an oracle of the dead was situated upon it. See Herodotus 5.92.7.

22. In the dialogue "Somnium" ("The Dream") in book 4 of the *Intercenales*, among several surreal and disturbing images, the interlocutor Libripeta imagines rivers full of human faces and meadows in which men's beards and hair grow.

23. "Nothing in excess" was the second exhortation carved upon Apollo's temple at Delphi, alongside "Know thyself." It is a dictum frequently quoted in Graeco-Latin literature. The issue of whether one should give in to anger in certain circumstances or always remain impassive was a common point of contention between Stoics and non-Stoics in antiquity (see Seneca's *De ira* for an example); in the Renaissance the issue was raised in Leonardo Bruni's popular *Isagogicon moralis disciplinae* ("Introduction to Moral Philosophy," 1424). Here Alberti follows Bruni's opinion, opposing Stoic *apatheia*.

24. A parodic echo of Vergil's "Facilis descensus Averni" in *Aen.* 6.126.

25. The "ship of state" metaphor goes back at least to Plato's *Republic*, but is widely found in Western literature; other well-known examples would have been Horace, *Carm.* 1.14 and Dante, *Purg.* 6.77. Alberti reverses the polarity of the metaphor by comparing ships to states, rather than the other way around. The metaphor is ironically deflated when it is discovered that the ship is in the hands of pirates.

26. Alberti refers to the traditional three forms of government as analyzed in Aristotle's *Politics*: monarchy, oligarchy and democracy.

27. The criteria for good and bad government are also taken from Aristotle's *Politics*, especially book 3.

28. Compare Apuleius, *Met.* 4.8. A famous Renaissance description of the license of bath-houses is found in Poggio Bracciolini's letters; see *Two Renaissance Book Hunters: The Letters of Poggius Bracciolini to Nicolaus de Niccolis*, tr. P. W. G. Gordan (New York, 1974), pp. 24–31 [Letter III].

29. See above, 4.33 The early manuscripts corrected by Alberti read "Polyphagus" but this must be a slip for Peniplusius.

30. Alluding to the common moralist's dichotomy of "esse, non videri" ("to be, not to seem"), most famously invoked in Latin literature by Sallust, *Cat.* 54.6. It is a dichotomy commonly used by Alberti; see for example above, 2.33.

31. Compare Lucian's dialogue *Cataplus, or the Tyrant*, a conversation between Charon, Hermes, a Cynic philosopher and Megapenthes the tyrant.

32. Lit. "Big Man" (*megalo* + *phôs*) or possibly "Big Light" (*megalo* + *phaos/phôs*).

33. I.e., only when he has no private interest (such as revenge) in seeing a wicked person punished.

Bibliography

❧❦❧

EDITIONS OF THE LATIN TEXT

Stephan Guillery, ed. *Leo Baptista de Albertis Florentinus: De principe.* Rome, 1520.

Jacopo Mazzocchi, ed. *Leonis Baptistae Alberti Florentini Momus.* Rome, 1520.

Giuseppe Martini, ed. *Momus o del Principe.* Bologna: Nicola Zanichelli Editore, 1942.

Rino Consolo, ed. *Momo o del principe.* Genoa: Costa e Nolan, 1986.

TRANSLATIONS

FRENCH

Claude Laurens, tr. *Momus ou le Prince: Fable politique.* Paris: Les Belles Lettres, 1993.

GERMAN

August Gottlieb Meissner, tr. *Momus.* Vienna: Kaiserer, 1790.

Michaela Boenke, tr. *Momus oder Vom Fürsten/Momus seu de principe.* Munich: Wilhelm Fink Verlag, 1993. With Consolo's Latin text.

ITALIAN

Cosimo Bartoli, ed. and tr. *Opuscoli morali di Leon Batista Alberti gentil' huomo fiorentino.* Venice, 1568. With Bartoli's translation of the *Momus overo del principe.*

Both Martini's and Consolo's editions of the Latin text (see above) contain Italian translations.

SPANISH

Agustín de Almaçan, tr. *El Momo; la moral y muy graciosa historia del Momo, compuesta en latin por Leon Baptista Alberto.* Madrid, 1553. Reprint Madrid, 1598.

SELECTED SECONDARY LITERATURE

Furlan, Francesco, ed. *Leon Battista Alberti: Actes du Congrès International de Paris . . . , 10–15 avril 1995*. Turin: Nino Aragno Editore, and Paris: J. Vrin, 2000. Collection of articles, several relating directly to the themes and reception of *Momus*.

Garin, Eugenio. "Studi su Leon Battista Alberti," in his *Rinascite e rivoluzioni: movimenti culturali dal XIV al XVIII secolo*, pp. 131–196. Rome and Bari: Laterza, 1975.

Grafton, Anthony. *Leon Battista Alberti: Master Builder of the Italian Renaissance*. Cambridge, Mass.: Harvard University Press, 2002. Panoramic, lively and authoritative biography.

Grayson, Cecil, *Studi su Leon Battista Alberti*, ed. Paola Claut. Florence: Leo S. Olschki, 1998. Collected essays by a major Alberti scholar, several relating to *Momus*.

Marsh, David. "Alberti's *Momus*: Sources and Contexts," in *Acta Conventus Neo-Latini Hafniensis: Proceedings of the Eighth International Congress of Neo-Latin Studies*, ed. Rhoda Schnur, pp. 619–632. Binghamton, N.Y.: Center for Medieval and Early Renaissance Studies, 1994. Survey of the classical sources, contemporary allusions and reception of *Momus*.

—— *Lucian and the Latins: Humor and Humanism in the Early Renaissance*. Ann Arbor: University of Michigan Press, 1998. Essential study of Lucianic satire in the Renaissance, containing several sections on *Momus*.

Martinelli, Lucia Cesarini. "Metafori teatrali in Leon Battista Alberti," in *Rinascimento*, ser. 2, 29 (1989), pp. 3–51. Careful study of Alberti's interest in theater as literary site and symbol.

Perosa, Alessandro. "Considerazioni su testo e lingua del *Momus* dell'Alberti," in *The Languages of Literature in Renaissance Italy*, ed. Peter Hainsworth, Valerio Lucchesi, Christina Roof, David Robey and J. R. Woodhouse, pp. 45–62. Oxford: Clarendon Press, 1988. Indispensable survey of the *Momus* manuscripts and *editiones principes*.

Robinson, Christopher. *Lucian and His Influence in Europe*. London: Duckworth, 1979. Pioneering study of Lucian as literary model for later writers of satire.

Tafuri, Manfredo. "'Cives esse non licere': The Rome of Nicholas V and Leon Battista Alberti: Elements toward a Historical Revision," *The Harvard Architecture Review* 6 (1989), pp. 60–75. Examination of the relationship between Alberti and the papacy in the urban planning of fifteenth-century Rome.

Index

References are by book and paragraph number. Pr = Preface.